The
Righteous
Rebel

Catherine Cloud Templeton

Adam Cloud and
the Natchez Intrigues,
1790-1795

The

Righteous

Rebel

Catherine Cloud
Templeton

Eakin Press • Austin, Texas

FIRST EDITION

Published in the United States of America
By Eakin Press
An Imprint of Sunbelt Media, Inc.
P.O. Drawer 90159 ★ Austin, Texas 78709-0159

2   3   4   5   6   7   8   9

ISBN 1-57168-163-9

Library of Congress Cataloging-in-Publication Data
Templeton, Catherine Cloud.
    Righteous rebel : Adam Cloud and the Natchez intrigues, 1790-1795,
a novel / Catherine Cloud Templeton.
      p.   cm.
    ISBN 1-57168-163-9. -- ISBN 1-57168-164-7 (alk. paper)
    1. Cloud, Adam -- Fiction.   I. Title.
PS3570.E587R54 1997
813' .54--dc21   97-16100
                                                         CIP

This book is dedicated to the
CLOUD families of America,
the descendants of
William Cloud
of Calne, Wiltshire, England —
the first Cloud settler in America,
who arrived in 1682.

GENEALOGICAL CHART
OF CLOUD FAMILY
(Branch Pertaining to Author's Line)

WILLIAM CLOUD (1621-1702) m. Susan James*

Robert Cloud m. Phoebe Neale

Joseph Cloud m. Sisley(?)

Robert Cloud m. Magdalene Peterson

REV. ADAM CLOUD
m. Mary Grandin

John Wurts Cloud, Sr. m. Rebecca Johnston

John Wurts Cloud, Jr. m. Virginia Catherine
Washington

Virginia Elizabeth Cloud m. Otis E. Carter

Catherine Cloud Carter m. Harry M. Templeton

*William Cloud came to America in 1682 from Calne, Wiltshire, England. He and Susan had six children: Robert, John, Joseph, Susanna, Jeremiah, and William.

Contents

Acknowledgments

Map: Courtesy of Perkins Library, Duke University, Durham, NC
Artwork: Jane McKinney, advance publicity
People who read, helped, and encouraged my manuscript:
    Joan Jones, professor and writer, UCLA and
        Pierce College, CA
    Jane McKinney, Ventura, CA
    Carolyn Cole, Natchez, MS
    Kenneth W. Wills, historian, Episcopal Diocese of
        Mississippi, Jackson, MS
    Nigey Lennon, Los Angeles, CA
    Lynn Cooksey, Austin, TX
    Kathleen Sublette, Port Hueneme, CA
    Donaleen Howitt, Ventura, CA
    Ruth Carlson, Camarillo, CA
    Terri Grando, Thousand Oaks, CA
    Ventura County Writers Club — Critique Group
    Thomas Templeton and Patti Gray Templeton, Maui, HI

Special thanks for their encouragement and interest to:
    Rt. Rev. Alfred C. Marble, Jr., bishop, Episcopal Diocese of
        Mississippi, Jackson, MS
    Rt. Rev. James B. Brown, bishop, Episcopal Diocese of
        Louisiana, New Orleans, LA
    Rt. Rev. Robert J. Hargrove, bishop, Episcopal Diocese of
        Western Louisiana, Alexandria, LA

Historical research resources:
    Carolyn Martin Cole, Nathez, MS — Historian; descendant
        of Joseph and Sarah Perkins
    Eualalie Bull, Natchez, MS — Descendant of Col. Ezekiel
        Forman; furnished author a copy of Maj. Samuel
        Forman's "Narrative of a Journey Down the Ohio and
        Mississippi Rivers, 1789-1790"

Ron and Mimi Miller — Historic Natchez Foundation, Natchez, MS

Adolph and Lougenia Wagner — Caretakers of Christ Church, Church Hill, MS (Adam's Church rebuilt in 1822)

Jefferson College, Washington, MS

Mississippi Department of Archives and Natural History, Jackson, MS

Center for American History, University of Texas at Austin

Huntington Library Archives, San Marino, CA

Preface

In the fall of 1789, Adam Cloud, his wife and baby daughter joined a small caravan of families from New Jersey for a long, arduous journey to "The Natchez," which was then part of Spanish West Florida. They were lured by the promise of free land and religious freedom under a strict Spanish-Catholic monarchy.

Adam Cloud was a young ordained deacon of the Episcopal church from the Brandywine Valley of Delaware. The caravan leader was Col. Ezekiel Forman, plantation owner of Freehold, New Jersey, and a practicing lawyer in Philadelphia.

The families loaded their Conestoga wagons to the brim and followed Colonel Forman's bright yellow coach-and-four. In the rear trailed a string of wagons filled with the colonel's sixty slaves. They traveled the uncertain Forbes Road across Pennsylvania to the "Forks-of-the-Ohio." At the tiny settlement of Pittsburgh the families built their crude keelboats and waited a month for the Ohio River to rise enough to float safely downriver. Adam Cloud's family, with twelve other passengers, traveled aboard the colonel's seventy-foot keelboat down the Ohio and Mississippi rivers, enduring the vicissitudes of crowded keelboat life, and experiencing the astonishing beauty and dangers of wild America.

When they reached Natchez, the families were sworn in as citizens and allotted the free land promised by the Spanish government. Adam Cloud lived in the Natchez District for five years, until he was expelled. He returned twenty years later to build the first Episcopal church in Mississippi, and helped establish the state's Episcopal Diocese.

The story following is the writer's version of the remarkable true story of her great-great-grandfather in the unique pioneer world of a Spanish-American monarchy.

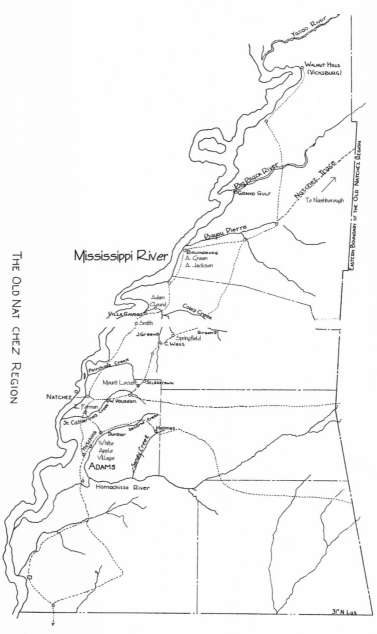

THE OLD NATCHEZ REGION

Yazoo River

WALNUT HILLS
(VICKSBURG)

Natchez Trace

EASTERN BOUNDARY OF THE OLD NATCHEZ REGION

Big Black River

GRAND GULF

To Nashborough

Bayou Pierre

Mississippi River

BRUINSBURG
A. Green
A. Jackson

Adam
Cloud

Coles Creek

VILLA GAYOSO

Smith

J.Green
Springfield
C. West
Green

Fairchilds Creek

Mount Locust
SELSERTOWN

NATCHEZ

E. Forman
W. Vousdan

St. Catherines Creek

Hutchins
Second Creek

Dunbar
Holmes

White
Apple
Village

Sandy Creek

ADAMS

Homochitto River

31° N Lat

Revised map from Charles Sydnor, A Gentleman of the Old Natchez Region:
Benjamin L.C. Wiles (Duke University Press, 1938)

BOOK I

1 Ohio River

January 1790.

The early dawn air was laden with light river fog, as the seventy-foot keelboat rounded a bend on the Ohio River. Two young men stood watch on the bow.

Adam Cloud rubbed his arms vigorously to ward off the chill he felt through his buckskin suit. In spite of a well-tied queue, his brown hair, misty with dew, fell about his face in careless disarray. Scanning through the mist, he watched for the dangerous Indian camp he knew was ahead. He prayed silently that he could spot the camp in time to warn the crew and the five boats following them. He turned to the stocky young man standing beside him.

"We should be near the area where tribes of the Miami Nation are at war with one another. Perhaps the Indian braves are off to war, and the camp will be empty," he said.

Maj. Sam Forman looked at Adam's tense jaws and the anxiety wrinkles which lined his forehead. He grinned and shook his head. "Wishful thinking, Adam, but maybe we'll be lucky. We're just fortunate that General Harmar warned us ahead of time at Fort Washington."

Adam cocked his head. "Do you hear rapid water? We must be nearing the Scioto River mouth," he said, his tanned lean face thrust forward anxiously. "Warn the colonel, Sam. We may not have much time."

Sam sprinted back to his uncle, who stood erect at the tiller. The colonel's shock of white hair was a glistening halo in the misty rain. His trim beard and abundant sideburns were accented by bushy dark eyebrows, which lowered into a frown upon digesting

3

Sam's news. The distinguished Col. Ezekiel Forman was patroon of the small fleet, and responsible for the welfare of the more than one hundred lives who peopled the five boats in the flotilla.

"The Scioto is a big river, and I'll give it a wide berth," the colonel said. "I can feel a slight pitch of rapid water now. Signal the boats following that I'm heading closer to the south shore. And alert Preece and Carter to man the oars. We should be able to slip past the Indian camp in this fog."

Sam ran to the bell fastened on the cabin roof and gave the appropriate signal understood by the crews. Jeb Carter and Lank Preece, the two husky mechanics, already had their long poles in the water. Sam ducked into the cabin and grabbed three muskets. David Forman, the colonel's adolescent son, and André Michaux, a young French passenger, followed him deckside, with powder bags and shot. They joined Adam at the bow.

Suddenly, a distress signal sounded from a distant keelboat.

"God help us! Someone's in trouble," Adam exclaimed.

"What a time for trouble!" David wailed.

"*Mon Dieu*! What do we do?" André said.

"Now, David. Don't panic," Adam spoke with far more calm than he felt. "We'll anchor on the south shore, far from the river-mouth. We can reconnoiter easily in this fog. Besides, we may not be near enough to the Indian camp to be heard or seen."

Adam looked at the Frenchman. "How is your marksmanship?" The question held a testy edge.

"Ah, no, *monsieur*. I am a swordsman, and nevair train with guns," André answered in halting English and a decidedly French accent.

Adam stared at him. "Can you load a musket?" André nodded his head. "Then help load the guns, and keep them loaded if we have to fight." Adam turned away in disgust and helped the crew moor the keelboat close to the shore.

By this time, the upper deck was swarming with women and children, curious of the alarm and activity.

"Go back inside, Mary, Eliza," Adam called. "It's one of the boats hung up on the river. Keep everyone inside, just for safety while we're moored." He never heard their replies, for the colonel was shouting.

"Adam, boys, launch the rowboat and see who's in trouble!" the colonel cried. "No, not you, David. You stay here with André and me. We must be ready if those Indians spot us and think we are vulnerable. You can be the lookout."

Adam and Jeb launched the rowboat while Lank went inside for guns, axes, and saws. He soon returned, and the three men rowed vigorously upstream to find the Grassley keelboat caught on a sawyer log. The three Grassley men were in the water, tugging and hacking at the log. Tied alongside in a skiff was Maj. Benajah Osmun, the colonel's overseer, and in the water were three black men from the slaveboat, hacking and sawing at the log to free the keelboat. The slave flatboat was anchored near the shore with some fifty slaves gesturing and hollering encouragement.

Adam looked up to see the Minor brothers' two arks approaching. They were latched together and heavily loaded with barrels of flour, bacon, cider and whiskey, five pair of millstones, and all their personal household goods.

"Theo, William," Adam called. "Throw out lines and hitch to the Grassley boat. You can pull downstream. We'll help Benajah at this end. There may be Indians at a camp ahead, so beware."

The Minors and their boatmen hurriedly secured lines to the stricken keelboat. Jeb and Lank joined the others in the water with axes and saws and hacked at a branch, while Adam kept his eye on the opposite shore. He noted, with dismay, that the fog was lifting.

On the keelboat the three Grassley families were in a state of pandemonium. The women and children leaned over the side, shouting advice to the cutters. One of the boys stood forward, watching for Indians.

"Jesus, Gran'ma. There's Indians on the shore. They've spotted us," Adam heard him call out. Adam turned his head and saw the outline of canoes on a north beach, which was now visible in the distance.

"Don't take your eyes off them," Samantha Grassley called back, "and holler if they launch canoes."

"Better get your guns ready," Adam called out.

The younger Grassley wives disappeared into the cabin and emerged with an arsenal of guns and ammunition.

Adam glanced at the two arks. The Minor brothers and their crew were furiously poling both boats to get a stronger pull on the keelboat. Their wives, Julia and Tullah Minor, were expertly loading guns.

Adam called to the Grassley boy, "Call loud and clear what you see, Jack," and he slipped into the water. "It doesn't look too good," he said quietly to Benajah. "We must do better. Time may be running out." He joined the men rocking the stubborn log.

Benajah reviewed the situation. "I'll take a position between the Grassleys' and my flatboat on shore, and pull with ropes," he said to Adam. "We can tug sideways while the men use the lever and axes. With the Minors pulling hard downstream, that just might get it loose." The two slaves climbed in the rowboat, lending weight. Benajah positioned the boat and they began pulling the lines.

The Grassley turmoil subsided, with everyone peering anxiously over the edge. Suddenly, the keelboat broke free with a heavy lurch. The shock sent shudders through all three boats. The Grassley children screamed, and the men in the water whooped as the boat began to drift.

"Jesus, Gran'ma! The Indians are launching canoes. How are we gonna get by them, Pa?" The Grassley boy was hysterical.

The men in the water quickly hoisted themselves onto their boats. Adam shouted, "Larboard, larboard! As close to the south shore as you dare, and push like the devil is after you."

The keelboat and two arks turned toward shore. Benajah Osmun's rowboat headed back to the moored flatboat, and Adam, Jeb and Lank rowed swiftly downstream toward shore. The flotilla was now strung out in a line, and every man with a free hand trained his gun on the Indian canoes. The Indians paddled upstream in both directions, toward the waiting fleet across the river, and one canoe toward the two rowboats heading downstream. Adam's rowboat had nearly reached Forman's keelboat when he heard one of the Grassley girls scream.

"Mama, Mama, Veralee is missing! She musta fell overboard when the boat jerked. She was right by me when the big bump came. Papa, look! Back there. Isn't that her thrashing in the water?"

Her father, Ed, shouted, "My God, yes!" He cupped his hands and called out, "Veralee, Veralee! Hang on, darlin'! We'll come get you."

Adam could barely see the little girl's head bobbing in the water. "I think she's holding on to something," he called to her father. "We'll go after her. Cover us, Ezekiel," he shouted. "We'll hug the shore on the way back."

Again Jeb and Lank turned back and rowed frantically against the current. Adam saw Veralee holding fast to a log branch that had snagged the keelboat. He prayed silently. *Dear God, save her. She mustn't drown. Give us strength to outpace those savages.* The next few minutes were agony.

"Hold on! We'll get you," he called to the struggling child.

As they approached, Veralee's head disappeared beneath the water, and Adam saw, to his horror, that the sawyer had submerged. He dove into the water and groped for the girl. The sawyer suddenly rose again, and he saw that Veralee's dress was caught on the sawyer branch. He tugged frantically at the dress. It came free, and he grabbed the girl, hoisted her into the rowboat, and climbed aboard.

Jeb and Lank turned again toward the shore and rowed swiftly downstream. Adam saw several Indian canoes advancing toward the five boats lined up on the south shore, and another canoe was headed directly toward their rowboat. As it drew closer, Adam made out distinctive scalplocks on the crowns of shaved heads. Several Indians held bows positioned to shoot within range. Shawnee warriors, he guessed; the fiercest fighters, according to General Harmar.

He felt a shudder of cold fear.

A volley of gunshots sounded from the fleet. The canoes halted midstream, as though uncertain. Adam lifted his musket.

"Stay down," he directed Veralee, and fired at the advancing canoe. He reloaded his gun.

"I kin load a gun," Veralee's voice piped from the floor.

Adam grinned at her. "The powder's right there. I'll keep you busy."

Another volley sounded from the fleet, and Adam fired again at the advancing canoe. He could see their scalplocks and hideous painted faces clearly now, as well as the close range of their bows. Suddenly, the Indians feathered their paddles.

"They're uncertain now," Adam said. "They've got our message that we'll put up a good fight."

Veralee handed Adam the powder pouch and he reloaded, pointed his gun, and blasted away, just as the approaching canoe turned back toward the Indian camp. Simultaneously, one of the Shawnees let fly an arrow as a parting shot. Adam felt a searing pain in his right shoulder.

"Whew!" Lank, rowing furiously, blew out suppressed anxiety. "That was a close call." He stole a look back at Adam as Veralee screamed out.

"Oh, help! Mister Adam's caught an arrow!" she announced.

"It's not fatal," Adam cried out. "Keep rowing, men. I think we won the skirmish."

"Hang on, Mister Adam," Jeb called reassuringly. "They've all turned back now, and we'll be ashore soon."

Adam felt dizzy and leaned forward. Everything went black and he fell at Veralee's feet. She took his head in her arms, sobbing desperately. "Don't die, Mister Adam. Oh, please, don't die," she wailed.

Cheers from the Forman boat were quickly replaced by outcries as the rowboat approached, and those on board saw Adam's plight. Mary Grandin shrieked as she saw Adam's inert form on the floor, and Eliza Forman wrapped her in her arms. The three Forman girls clung to them both.

"Adam's been hit," Jeb called out. "Take him aboard and we'll deliver Veralee to the Grassleys."

"Lift him gently. Lay him on his side," Ezekiel spoke to Dirk and Kudjo, the two male servants. "Let's see how much blood he has lost . . . Get back. He's alive," he snapped as everyone crowded over Adam's body.

André stooped to examine Adam's shoulder. "I saw the Cherokees remove an arrow from one of the braves once," he said in his heavily accented English. "It takes special cutting to remove one. Get him to his bunk and I will show you how." He turned to Mary, who stood looking down at Adam, her face drained from shock. "Do not despair, *mon cheri*. We will not lose him. Just you 'ave faith." He pressed her hands between his, but Mary scarcely heard him.

"Maamba, Sena! Heat some water and get out clean towels, quickly," Aunt Betsey called to the women slaves, wives of Dirk and Kudjo. Efficient and practical, the older woman was the Forman housekeeper, and nanny to their three young girls, Frances, thirteen, Margaret, eleven, and Augusta, nine.

Ezekiel and Eliza directed the slaves as they carried Adam to his bunk. There they found Aunt Betsey had already covered the bed with towels.

Mary gazed at Adam lying motionless on his bunk. Her young, delicate face was pale and distraught. "I feel so helpless," she murmured. "Can he die?" Her pleading eyes fastened on André. She shuddered at the sight of the ugly arrow dangling from Adam's bleeding shoulder.

"André, we are going to have to depend upon you," Ezekiel said calmly. "No one here has ever removed an arrow, and you have seen it done by experts. What do we do first?"

All eyes were on André as he rolled up his shirtsleeves. "*Mesdames*, everyone, wait outside, *si'l vous plait*. 'Tis not a pretty sight," he said. He looked at the knife on a towel beside Adam. "Heat it red hot in the kitchen fire," he demanded. "*Rapide!*"

The women and children withdrew outside, except for Aunt Betsey and Maamba, Adam's servant, who stood wringing her hands.

"I am an expert nurse, André," the housekeeper said. "I'll check his blood flow. Tell me what to do to help."

Mary Grandin paced the cabin floor for the next hour while she endured the shouts and cries from Adam's cubicle. Just hearing him cry out was reassuring; at least he regained consciousness now and then. But her cheeks were wet with tears, and she winced at every cry, feeling the horror of Adam's ordeal. The other passengers spoke fearfully, in subdued voices. Finally, Ezekiel entered the cabin, his shirt splattered with blood, and sweat pouring from his brow.

"He came through just fine," he said wearily, "but the next few days will be crucial. I guess we should be thankful André is a botanist. He says he must prepare and apply the proper healing herbs. Adam is still unconscious, thank God, but he will suffer great pain for some time."

Mary rushed to Adam's bedside and caught her breath as she saw his drawn face. She placed her ear to his mouth and heard his faint breath. André watched her touch Adam's forehead lightly with her lips, and he smiled as he wiped his bloody hands.

"Your hero, *mademoiselle*? There could be no one more brave. Would that I deserved such devotion."

Adam was removed to the cubicle occupied by Mary Grandin and the housekeeper, where he could receive intensive care. The next few hours were critical. André selected herbs from his botanical collection, and Mary helped pulverize and mix them into a paste.

Mary and Aunt Betsey tended Adam night and day in their cubicle, applying a paste poultice and changing the dressings. But Mary's alarm grew as his fever rose. She bathed his brow, taking soaked towels from Maamba's dark hands. Adam's comatose state soon changed to semiconscious agitation, and he thrashed about the cot, murmuring wildly. She finally directed that Maamba and Aunt Betsey restrain him gently with soft sheets, determined that he not reopen his wound in his unknowing frenzy.

Mary tried to catch the meaning of Adam's disconnected words in his delirium. She finally realized that he was reliving the agony of the last days of their wagon-train journey, in the desperate race to reach the Forks of the Ohio to save Anne from death. She saw it all again, in her mind's eye. In those final hours, as they raced on toward Fort Pitt, with Anne bedded down in the large Conestoga wagon, she had bathed her sister's forehead and heard her stertorous breathing. Once again she could see Adam's tortured face as he carried Anne inside the doctor's primitive refectory and learned of his wife's doubtful recovery . . . .

"Poor darling," she whispered, as she mopped Adam's face with a cool, damp towel. "I will help you forget. Just give me a chance."

Adam's recovery was more rapid than Mary expected, but the fever had taken its toll. His eyes had sunk deeply into his head, his cheekbones were more prominent, and his spare fat had melted away until his tall frame stood gaunt upon his bones. While Adam convalesced, his companions visited with him and thanked him for his bravery in saving Veralee.

"I felt helpless in the midst of the crisis," André had said. "Nevair 'ave I wish more than I owned a gun."

Adam looked at André with mixed emotions. "You'd better learn to shoot one," he responded. "A sword wouldn't do much against Indian warriors. You're in hostile land now."

Adam had thanked André for withdrawing the arrow, but he had to come to terms with himself. While the Frenchman had saved his life, he felt his own hostility deep down. André was considered an ineffectual nuisance by the men, and his attention to the ladies, and especially Mary, was galling. The matter of André's disclaimer of guns was puzzling. How could the gentleman be such a highly educated, polished man-of-the-world, and never have learned to use guns? Perhaps he never had the inclination as a scientist to learn the skill, Adam reasoned.

Adam was ashamed of his dislike for André. Love and understanding would overcome his doubts, and he must work harder to foster them.

2 Hopes and Dreams

During convalescence Adam's thoughts turned inward to past events. What had brought him to this place, at this time, drifting down the Ohio River toward Spanish lands; a man without a wife, a home, or even a country, with a year-old baby daughter depending on his care? Peace and contentment had seemed elusive since his youth. The vistas from his mystical experience invaded him again. Ah, that wondrous moment of ecstasy, spontaneous and unsolicited, that changed his life and began to direct him toward the ministry in earnest. He closed his eyes and relived it, as he often did in moments of repose.

He was eighteen, brooding over personal disaster, with a need to ride out his inner storm. That special day he had retreated to Naaman's Creek, on the family homestead in Brandywine Hundred, Delaware. British invasion of Philadelphia was expected hourly, Philadelphia College had just closed, and he was forced to leave for home. He deplored the disruption of his goal of eventual Episcopal priesthood, which required a college degree. The Anglican bishops had long since fled the colonies for England, leaving no one to ordain applicants for the priesthood. Now his education was abruptly cut off. He recalled the dismal feeling a youth can experience when the whole world crumbles around him. The future seemed bleak and he was torn with despair.

His favorite retreat was under an ancient oak tree, its branches reaching far out over the water, casting dappled shadows over the shimmering surface. It was spring, and he absently picked a wildflower nearby in the grass. Trying to shake out his emotions, empty his thoughts, he gazed into the flower, absorbing its essence as though to penetrate the mysteries of its form and substance. Gradually he had felt his consciousness expanding into a series of labyrinths, each revealing profound truths far beyond his youthful perceptions. The wisdom of the world seemed laid out before him. As the awesome, unspoken truths unfolded, he saw again, now in his mind's eye, the soft light which glowed with increasing intensity until his brain, encompassed by thought, vision and light, seemed encased in an ethereal cocoon. In the few seconds of rapture, he was filled with a sense that God had pierced his soul, communicating a wisdom of a higher order. The effect left a startling impression that he had penetrated a universal river of knowledge; he had experienced a spiritual and intellectual vision of fundamental truths of life.

What had happened to him? Was it real? He told no one for a long time, fearing people would suspect he was ill, or hallucinating, or, worse still, that he might be possessed by powers of sorcery. But the event awakened his spiritual outlook, and he felt compelled to learn more of this inner life, to satisfy his hunger for deeper spiritual understanding. Finally he had shared the event with Father Devereux Jarratt, his beloved mentor, an Episcopal priest who knew the secret places of his heart.

"Adam, you had a transcendental experience sought and realized by a few holy men of many faiths," Father Jarratt told him. "Search for this inner life and find it in your own way. It will not be easy, but don't give up your quest, for you have had an unusual gift of divine grace bestowed upon you. You must make yourself deserving of it by further enlightenment."

Father Jarratt had recommended literature that might give direction in Greek and Sanskrit, others in Latin and English. There hadn't been time to collect the books, for Adam had answered a sudden call to preach for the Methodists. It was a dynamic preacher, the Rev. William Hammett, who signed Adam on as junior preacher in the Methodist church. It didn't seem unreasonable then, for the priesthood was still a dream, and one could become an instant minister for the Methodists without a formal education.

Ah, but that was the rub! His memory skimmed over the six years as an itinerant Methodist preacher, riding hundred-mile circuits on annual assignments from Pennsylvania to North Carolina. He soon learned that Reverend Hammett's brilliant sermons were an exception, for the crude, unlettered elders, under whom he served, often filled him with dismay. Their main goal was recruitment for Christ, but their message offered a choice of hereafter salvation through redemption of sins, or the peril of hell. Their methods fostered feelings of guilt and fear among the good frontier folk, simple, earnest, hard-working farmers and their families. Most of the preachers were fiery zealots; their emotional delivery induced hysteria among the listeners, causing them to respond with loud shrieks, moans and laments, finally ending in falls or swoons. The "fallings" contributed to the record of effective preachers, whose ratings were determined by the number of religious collapses and conversions they could report.

Adam's own record had been marked by a significant lack of "fallings," and by a preaching style that one elder had described in stinging terms as "smart exhortations, above comprehension of the masses." He had found himself increasingly unable to accept the rigid Methodist doctrine of Original Sin, or justification and sanctification. Laced with commands of "thou shalt not," the negative messages seemed unfulfilling for the spiritually starved country people. In good conscience, he knew he could not contribute to the Methodist efforts any longer.

The day he rode home for Christmas from the East Pennsylvania circuit was a landmark turn in his life. Father Jarratt had poured balm on his troubled soul when he reached Philadelphia. As always, the venerable priest understood Adam's dilemma.

"My dear boy," he had said, his eyes tender with love, "you have made a contribution to the Methodist-Episcopal ministry against all odds. Your approach to imparting the truths of the spirit, as you see them, is more important than being a conformist in ways you cannot accept. Your outlook shows spiritual depth, your appreciation of man as a child of God. There is no greater ministry than that."

Adam had resigned from the Methodists, joined the Episcopal church, and finished his education, hoping again for the priesthood. The memory of his rejection for ordination still rankled.

"Your years of doubt and discredit by the Methodist hierarchy are not surprising in a man of your culture, with many years of scholarly pursuits," the newly appointed Bishop White had said. "But I have doubts as to your readiness for ordination as an Anglican priest. Your Methodist years place you in a somewhat ambiguous category, not thoroughly one of our Churchmen yet. I do not doubt your sincerity in your desire to become a priest, and I will place your application in abeyance for a time."

So there it was! he had thought. He was *too Methodist*, the verdict of his trial of ministry in the wrong sect. Aren't we all Christians — he wanted to say — hoping to open people's hearts to receive God's love? Shouldn't *love* be the test of discipleship?

The bishop had recommended that he study for the diocanate, and eventually he was ordained a deacon, serving under Father Jarratt for a few months at Christ Church, Philadelphia. He recalled Anne Grandin's loving look of approbation when she attended his ordainment.

Anne . . . he never doubted she loved him, but looking back on their brief life together, he realized she loved him more for his religious qualities than for his manhood.

They were married in Camden at the home of her sister Sarah and John Wurts, and honeymooned in Philadelphia at the Biddle's "Indian King" hostel. But no one had prepared Anne for consummation. It was an unsatisfying night, and over time he began to realize sex was distasteful to her. Only the utmost self-discipline had helped him through his sexual frustrations. The birth of their daughter, Rebecca, was his only solace.

A timid knock at the door interrupted his reverie.
"Enter," he called.

The door opened and Tizzi, a slight young slave girl, entered with Becky in her arms. Tizzi was fourteen, and the daughter of Maamba and Dirk.

Becky's baby face glowed with delight when she saw her father, and Adam's dark eyes brightened with sheer joy when he took her in his arms. Becky's tiny hand tousled his smooth forehead locks, and he tossed his head and laughed.

"Baby doll," he said, his eyes kindled with love, "I have missed you so much."

Adam played with his daughter until they heard the noon meal bell, and Tizzi came to take her away.

"We come tomorrow, Massah Adam," Tizzi said with a wide grin. "She shor' happy when she with you."

Maamba brought Adam's midday meal on a tray for two. A large, amiable, middle-aged Negress, she had come to Adam through Anne, formerly nanny to the Grandin children, just as her daughter, Tizzi, now served Rebecca. Her native wisdom engendered sage advice, and pervaded her concern for her master.

"Lawdy, Massah Adam, yo shor' don' eat enough to keep a sparrow alive. Efen you don' feed dem bones they'll go right through yo shirt." Maamba grinned at his brightened demeanor as he smiled. "Miz Mary say she gonna eat wid you!"

"Thanks, Maamba." Adam looked at the tray. "*Uhmm*, grits and chitlin's. I'll try to stuff myself today."

Mary entered and Maamba busied herself with arranging their dishes before she left.

As they ate, Mary chattered cheerily of daily events among their companions on board. Adam felt a warm glow as she talked. He appreciated her vitality, expressed in the sparkle of her bluest-blue eyes, and in her quick movements, as she shook away tendrils of her dark, curly hair. She spoke of André and the new activities in the cabin, where the children gathered about André's plant specimens learning to copy their distinguishing characteristics.

"He also draws exquisite maps, which help the children know where they are. I am finding out how the herbs are used for medicines," Mary said. "You know André learned from the Cherokees while he stayed with them."

"Yes. That's one of the few things we know about the man," Adam said grudgingly.

Mary looked at him keenly. "Why, Adam, you certainly remember his connections in Paris? He is a member of the French Societies of Natural History and Agriculture."

"Yes, he says he was sent by them to study the flora of our country. But what an odd time for a botanist to be wandering about America, when the French are in turmoil with a revolution. When he told us of the July bloody revolt by the masses, and the storming of the Bastille, I wondered why he wasn't there helping to get his country on its feet."

"Well, I don't presume to question his patriotism, for we don't know him that well." Mary saw need to change the subject. "By the way, Adam, our Spanish classes have been progressing, but we will do much better when you get back to help us. And André has offered to teach us what he learned of the Cherokee language and Indian signs. They may be useful among other Indian tribes where we are going."

André again, Adam thought peevishly, but he hid his feelings. "That's a fine idea. We will need it in our new world."

Mary smiled her brightest smile. "You do look so much better, Adam. You will be yourself in no time. Now, I'll let you rest. Perhaps tomorrow you may feel up to coming on deck a while."

She picked up the tray and dipped gracefully under the lindsey-woolsey curtain which separated his cubicle from the others along the narrow hall.

Adam pondered about how different Mary was from Anne. Her vivacious beauty, her impulsive, inquisitive nature added zest to any occasion. Looking back on their long, strenuous journey from the Grandin plantation, in New Jersey, Adam recognized Mary's maturity. On the journey she had provided loving support for his fragile, ailing wife, and his baby daughter. She often rode up front by his side, while he drove the wagon team, lending encouragement with a courageous, never-failing attitude, her undaunted spirit sparked with her Irish wit. He now saw her with different eyes. No longer was she just his wife's little sister. At eighteen, she showed herself to be a mature, caring woman, a true friend, ever since Fort Pitt.

His thoughts turned to Anne again. Where was he before the interruptions? Ah, yes. Their honeymoon . . . .

In addition to Anne's conception, he decided, the honeymoon proved propitious. He had browsed the Philadelphia bookshops and found some esoteric books in which he could further explore arcane knowledge of the spiritual world. It was during their honeymoon, also, that they met the Formans, through their nephew, Maj. Sam Forman. Ezekiel Forman had dazzled his brain with visions of rich Natchez plantation land, and a new, independent life among the Spanish in Louisiana Territory. Another turning point in his life, setting him on this new course to an unknown future.

After recovering from shock, his parents were supportive of his and Anne's decision to emigrate to Natchez. He was touched by his father's offer of help with income from his Wilmington shipbuilding industry.

"If you ever want to join the firm and help Robert run the business, you may," his father told him. "But, in any case, you and your brother, Abner, will share equally in the profits."

Not only did he now have a modest income to offer Anne, but he discovered he had married into a fortune when Anne's mother died and had willed her 500 pounds and three slaves. What a joyous feeling it was. He had lived in poverty on an annual Methodist preacher's stipend of fourteen pounds, often subsidized by his father, who furnished his horse and wardrobe. Dear parents, Robert and Magdalene Cloud. Would he ever see them again? His heart ached with homesickness for Brandywine Hundred and his family.

The grueling wagon-train journey of some 280 miles across the mountains of Pennsylvania had left no time for reading or study. Days and nights were consumed with closely following Ezekiel's coach-and-four, which led the caravan, watching for trail hazards, welfare of the horse teams, the comfort and safety of his ailing wife, her sister, Mary, and his baby daughter. Then Anne's tragic death from lung fever, and her burial in Pittsburgh had left him in turmoil.

It was at the little village of Pittsburgh, while building their boat, that André Michaux had asked to become a passenger, on his way to study botany among Indian tribes. There the two Minor couples had joined their flotilla. The Minors were on their way to Natchez, where their cousin, Stephen, was an important official for the new governor.

Thoughts of Pittsburgh always made him melancholy. He must dwell on other matters.

Perhaps now he could study seriously his books of religious mysteries, learn from the lives of saints and prophets, wise teachers of many faiths who had experienced moments of ecstasy similar to his own mystical event. Perhaps, at last, he would find inner peace. *Follow your own light*, Father Jarratt had told him. He would have to find that light again.

3 Indian Wars

Taking advantage of the bleak winter sunlight, Adam sat on the upper deck with Becky on his lap, Mary at his side. He was bundled in warm clothing over his buckskins, and a cap over his ears. He snuggled Becky inside his coat, her golden curls bobbing about, as her attention was divided between the scenery and a tiny doll in her grasp. Mary wore a blue hooded pelisse, muffled to the chin. The thin sunlight touched curly wisps of dark hair about her face, forming an aureole.

They surveyed the pristine beauty of the meandering river, with its placid six-mile-an-hour current. The surrounding Black Forest had high banks on each side, some with precipitous cliffs several hundred feet high.

"In spite of all this quiet beauty, the fear of Indians and bandits build up in the night, and it's hard not to feel uneasy," Adam said. "We can't forget that there are Miami Indian nations out there warring with each other."

"I try not to think of that. The scenery is calming, Adam. The river seems to laugh and sing in the sunshine. It's enchanting."

Adam looked keenly at her. "Are you glad you decided to make the journey with us, in spite of what has happened, Mary?"

"Of course I'm glad. I'm grateful I could be with Anne during her illness, and now I'm enjoying the adventure. All of life is ahead of us, and I will not bog down with sadness, much as I loved my sister."

"I've had time to think of my position in the past few days," Adam said. "I feel responsible for your return home, and perhaps I should return home too. I can still attain priesthood, and raise Becky near close relatives where she can receive proper education and the quality of life she deserves."

"Nonsense, Adam." Mary waved away the unacceptable thought. "Becky can be raised properly anywhere. You can carve out a future for her in Natchez, as you establish your own home. You said yourself, the soil is rich, and you can prosper."

Adam looked into Mary's large, trusting eyes, feeling his own uncertainty. She was related to the Formans only through an uncle's marriage, and the Formans should not have to become responsible for her.

"If you return with me, you could meet some nice young man in the civilized world to which you belong."

"Oh ho! Now he wants to determine my fate too! Stop that, Adam. I can take care of my own future. I want to go on, and I think you should too."

Becky squirmed and squealed irritably in her confinement on Adam's lap, and Adam swung her over to Mary.

"Poor little darling," Mary said, "she misses her mother terribly. Bunking her with Aunt Betsey and me gives me a chance to stay close to her. Is that good or bad, Adam? I want to do the right thing."

"Whatever you can do to fill the void is right," Adam said softly. "I only wish my own emptiness were not such an abyss. Sometimes it hurts almost more than I can bear."

Mary looked at him with mixed emotions, tenderness for his grief, and a deep desire to help ease the pain. "The journey should help put Anne's death behind us."

He smiled at her. "You're right, Mary. Thank you for being such a stout friend." He brushed aside her curly tendrils and kissed her lightly on the forehead. At that moment he observed André approach from the cabin, and fought back his annoyance.

"May I join you?" André asked. "I hope I am not intruding."

"Please do," Mary said. She thought André's looks added a special charm to his exquisite French mannerisms. A distinctive dimple in a cleft chin set off his strong face, nose and brows. His dark curls were neatly combed forward around his ears and temples.

"*Ah, oui . . . nos esquis mademoiselle,*" André bent to kiss Mary's hand. He gazed at her. "And the blue of her wrap matches her deep blue eyes."

Adam thought the man acted as if he might devour her.

Mary turned her head to hide her blush. "We were exchanging impressions of the beautiful river scenery," she said.

"*Oui,* the river is *magnifique,*" André Michaux said. "Did you know, *mademoiselle,* that the French named it *Le Belle Riviere*? I 'ave longed to travel its course since I read journals of the French explorers here."

Mary chatted with André about organizing his plants.

Adam noticed the Frenchman addressed only Mary, and that they seemed to have developed a bond. He decided it was time to intervene.

"Have you studied the *Pilot Guide and River Chart*, Mr. Michaux? Since we left Fort Washington, there are more islands in the river, and we all need to study what lies ahead."

"*Uhm . . .* no, *Monsieur* Adam." André was caught by surprise.

"The islands are becoming larger and heavily wooded. Islands form and dissolve over periods of time, so we can't even be sure there are not new ones uncharted on the map."

"Ah, this boat is *enorme,*" André answered, "but I had no trouble when I help pole the pirogue on my journey up the Monongahela."

"No one will object if you grab a pole and practice any time," Adam said testily. "There's quite a difference in poling a small boat and this behemoth, and none of us have been tested to our limits yet."

Ezekiel and Eliza Forman joined them on deck. Eliza was a young, attractive second wife to Ezekiel; her elegant beauty, and unusual auburn hair, were her husband's pride and delight. Always sensitive to the vicissitudes of their rough and untamed environs,

Eliza could be counted on to react with extravagance to events on the journey. Adam found them both good company.

Near the confluence of the Wabash and Ohio rivers, they passed a new French settlement that Governor St. Clair had told them about. Adam wondered if this tiny group of Frenchmen's cabins could be protected from Indian attack. Early in their river journey, they had stayed overnight at Fort Harmar, headquarters for General St. Clair, governor of the Western Territories. The governor had explained the difficulties of protecting frontier squatters and unplanned settlements. Some settlements had clustered spontaneously around scattered squatters, and others were promoted by land speculators who had received bounty warrants through military service. A few had purchased large tracts and formed companies of pooled shareholders. Communities which had established legal rights could expect better protection by the army, such as the community near the fort, called *Campus Martius*, which had established legal rights through the Ohio Company.

Soon after passing the settlement, the keelboat rounded a bend and met the rapid merging of swirling waters at the mouth of a river. Adam's spine tingled with the sight of dozens of Indian war canoes assembled on the distant beach; a few were already launched. Adam jumped to his feet.

"Egad! That must be a war party," he called out. "Let's ward them off before they can get close."

"Not yet!" Ezekiel responded sternly. "If they're assembling for war, they may not be interested in us." But he ordered everyone on the alert, and the men gathered their guns and ammunition.

David appeared on deck, alerted by the loud voices. "What'll I do?" he asked, his voice anxious.

"You can signal the boats following to arm for a fight," his father answered.

André Michaux stopped Adam at the cabin door. "How can I help?"

Adam stared at him. "Keep the guns loaded if we have to fight."

On the way out Adam took a brief look at the women and children in the cabin. Mary and Eliza were seated at the table cutting paper dolls with Liz Preece and Mazie Carter. Helping were the three Forman girls, Tizzi, and another small black child of Sena and Kudjo. Aunt Betsey supported Rebecca on her feet, while she tottered toward her father. Adam lifted his daughter and kissed her, setting her gently on her knees.

"Keep everyone inside," he said quietly to the women. "The walls are thickly reinforced so balls and bullets can't penetrate. You should be safe from gunfire."

Outside, the men watched the Indian activity in the distance and searched the nearby banks for danger signs. Dirk and Kudjo stood with the oars, awaiting orders. In the lull, Adam mused over André's lack of gun experience. Swordsmanship was admirable, but certainly useless on the frontier. Perhaps it was vital for survival in France. He was thankful the rest of the crew were good marksmen.

Ezekiel and Sam steered a sharp portside to the deep center of the river, while the men hunkered down behind the rails and set their gunsights as they passed the river mouth. More canoes were now launched and headed downstream.

"*Mon Dieu*, they 'ave guns," André exclaimed.

"Little good your sword would do you now." Adam could not resist the caustic comment. André glared back.

"By Jove, they're all headed downstream," Ezekiel called. "They don't want us. Sound the all-clear signal."

It was obvious that the Indians were in a hurry to get to their war, and the string of canoes disappeared downstream behind a large island which divided the river.

When Adam entered his cubicle, he found Sam with a dueling pistol in his hand.

"Is this yours?" Sam asked.

"No. It's not mine. Where did you find it?"

"It was on the floor; it had fallen out of its case."

The men looked at each other. It was certainly not David's.

"*Hmm* . . . How very strange. Michaux says he is only a swordsman, and doesn't own a gun," Adam said. "Well, thank God he could load my gun."

"And he's good at consoling the ladies too." Sam gave Adam a rueful look. "I'll be glad to reach Louisville. I must confess I felt a bit streaked after all that scare with the Indians on the warpath. We won't be safe until we get far south of the Indian wars."

That night Colonel Forman gathered the families together at their mooring, which he did frequently to review their progress. "You remember, Fort Washington was about halfway to the Mississippi? Be of good cheer, everyone. I figure we are nearly three-quarters there by now."

Everyone groaned. There were eleven hundred miles in all to travel on the Ohio, and Fort Washington had seemed an important milestone. Without towns and settlements to gauge their progress, it was difficult to know the distance.

Using the Cummings guidebook, the colonel outlined what lay ahead. They could expect more river obstacles, not only on the rest of the Ohio, but greater changes on the Mississippi. Concealed dangers were the most feared, he explained. Captain Osmun's flat-bottomed slaveboat could run aground as easily as the keelboats, on unsuspected islands of mud built up by river eddies. He warned them again to watch for river hazards; even those enjoying the scenery should be on the alert. They agreed upon new signals to indicate specific obstacles, such as floaters, planters, and sawyers. The crews thus assumed more responsibility for other boats than their own. They saw more Indians assembling their canoes for war, and sometimes, moored at night, the watchmen heard the dip of paddles bearing Indian war canoes stealthily downriver toward their destination.

In late January the weather grew severely cold. Ice began to block the river, adding new perils to the journey. Colonel Forman ordered the boats lashed together for safety.

When the fleet reached the mouth of the Kentucky River and tied up in late afternoon at Port William, Colonel Forman drew the fleet crews together and they studied the map. Louisville was only seventy miles downstream. The Falls-of-the-Ohio were known to be treacherous for untrained navigators, and were going to be a formidable challenge. The suck sides of the rapids could sweep an unwary boat out into its stream if they should miss the entrance to the small Louisville harbor. The fleet planned to reach there in broad daylight, following the guidelines of a string of islands which preceded the harbor entrance. By hugging the south shore, they should be able to pull into the harbor before they reached the dangerous suck of the falls.

Early next day Jeb and Lank jabbed their long poles into the ice floes, pushing away the heavy ice crust which impeded their drift downstream. When they finally passed the islands, the women and children assembled on deck in anticipation of the risky landing. Roar of the falls could be heard in the distance, growing louder as the crew inched the boat through the ice. They came upon the harbor suddenly. It was enclosed by river banks which rose to some fifty feet, forming a shelter for boats on the eastern border of the town. The awesome, crashing sound of the falls echoed against the cliff wall. There the river was wide, and it was easy to see how a boat might miss the little hidden harbor and be swept into a violent ride over the falls. Ezekiel deftly steered the boat to shelter, and the rest of the fleet followed his guidance.

"Let's hope we can find accommodations before dark," Adam said.

"Oh, heaven help us find rooms," Eliza said with a shiver. "I haven't thawed out since Fort Washington."

The men made their way to a tavern, fronting some sixty dwellings scattered about the town. To their dismay, the hosteler told them his rooms and the boarding houses were filled. The ice had blocked everyone else, and they would have to seek lodging at private residences. He gave them a list of the larger homes and directions for finding them. The men divided the list and agreed to meet back at the boat.

After several inquiries, Adam knocked on the door of a two-story house. A servant opened the door, invited Adam into the foyer, and left to call the mistress. A well-dressed lady in her early thirties greeted him.

"I am Mrs. Mason Downs," she said graciously. "How may I help you?" She studied Adam carefully as she listened to his plea for lodging. "Please come into the parlor, Mister Cloud." She spoke with a soft Southern accent. "Tell me a little about yourself, where you are from, how many there are with you, and where you are going."

Adam explained his journey and his situation. Mrs. Downs' eyes showed interest. "Oh, my dear man. What a bold adventure you have undertaken! And how sad with only servants to look after you."

"My wife's sister, Miss Mary Grandin, is with us, also, and needs a place to stay."

Mrs. Downs agreed to take them, and showed Adam the rooms available.

"We have another roomer, a friend of ours, Colonel James Wilkinson, of Frankfort," the woman mentioned. "Perhaps you know of him through his war record?"

"I know of his name. I'll make arrangements to bring our belongings right away. Now, Mrs. Downs, you have not given me a figure on lodging the three of us, and my servants. I would like to settle the fee with you in advance."

"Nonsense, sir. We wouldn't think of charging a fee for our Southern hospitality. It will be our pleasure to have you as our guests for as long as you need to stay. Your servants' help will be enough."

Eliza and Mary had glasses of wine ready for the weary men as they returned to the boat. Adam accepted his wine gratefully, and when he described his success, Mary could hardly believe their good fortune. Ezekiel and Sam reported finding an unoccupied home with a storehouse in the rear, where Sam could store his trade merchandise. André Michaux had secured a small room over the kitchen of the inn, by making a large gratuity to the *concierge*. The other men had no success in their search; their families would have to stay on their boat until spaces opened up for them. Major Osmun would stay aboard the slave boat.

4 Louisville

Mary and Adam exercised his horses daily. Adam rode Lancer, a chestnut gelding, and Mary rode Wendy-Bel, a strawberry roan filly. The first day they rode to the point overlooking the falls. They dismounted and walked as close as they dared, gazing down at the wild rapids churning the water into a deadly current. The sight was awesome. There the Ohio River was a mile wide, with all its water channeled into a drop of some four hundred feet. They tried to speak, but their voices could not surmount the roar of the falls.

Mary pulled Adam's head down and placed her lips to his ear. Except during his feverish unconsciousness, never had she been so close to him, and she felt a slight shiver of excitement.

"How do we get the boats over the falls?" she shouted.

Adam drew his face close to her. The scent of her warm flesh was spicy, wonderful, and he let his face touch her cheek. "We have two choices," he said. "We can stay on board and be steered through the rapids by a professional pilot, or can unload and have the goods portaged around the rapids. A skilled pilot takes the craft through. Goods are unloaded below the falls."

"Either way sounds terrifying," Mary replied. Her cheek felt his smooth jaw and her shoulders reflected a slight tremble. "I think I'd rather go with the portaged goods."

Adam replied in her ear with a short, easy laugh that Mary loved to hear. "We'll decide later which way we want to chance it."

They stood silent for a few minutes watching the mighty falls, each savoring the intimate effect of the other at the unfamiliar close range. They finally turned away and mounted their horses, heading toward home.

"What do you make of Colonel Wilkinson?" Mary asked. "I found him irresistibly charming, so genteel and handsome. He made me feel like a queen when we were introduced."

Adam had noticed the colonel's effusive responses last night. "He is personable enough," he answered grudgingly. "His large, tall frame makes him an imposing figure, and I had the feeling he could win anyone over with words. He certainly uses them with style. I'll tell you my impression when I know him better."

That evening Daisy Downs served them a new drink called eggnog, mildly laced with rum. Mary thought it delicious and asked for the recipe.

"Of course," Daisy replied. "It is only eggs and milk, but the secret is in the spices and proper mixing. Vanilla is hard to come by out here, but the drink has become the rage, and traders are catching on with the supply. The right amount of rum caps it off."

"Colonel Wilkinson always brings us rum when he comes to Louisville," Mason Downs said to Adam. "He has a store in Frankfort with a fine stock of liquors and imports."

Adam settled back in his chair, testing the flavors. "To change the subject," he said, "I have picked up a sense of dissatisfaction and unrest from talking to people here. In the *Pittsburgh Gazette*, we read the same theme of the West against the Union."

"There is deep resentment here over the inability to use the Mississippi River for free trade," Mason answered. "That right is considered indispensable to Western growth and prosperity, and is the crucial issue on the frontier. Colonel Wilkinson has done the most toward proclaiming the growers' right to send their goods downriver and trade with the Spanish."

Mr. and Mrs. Downs were ardent admirers of Colonel Wilkinson, and they extolled his many attributes and accomplishments without prompting. Adam and Mary learned that he was a member of the Kentucky Legislature, where he spoke with eloquence and force. His political leadership made him popular to the point of being a hero. He accused the Eastern establishment of proposing to sell the West's birthright for the benefit of the Atlantic States. Using the trade issue as a forceful political weapon, he had influenced the Assembly to petition the Virginia Legislature for Kentucky's independence from Virginia's jurisdiction.

"If denied statehood," Mason concluded, "Wilkinson reasons that severance from the Confederation would bring freedom to form an alliance with England, or with Spain, as one of their American colonies."

Adam silently acknowledged the Eastern Seaboard trade was well established, composing a powerful block with which to contend. He could see why established traders would resent competition from the West. Aloud, he said, "That seems a drastic move. It could play havoc with American frontier expansion. What was the outcome of the petition?"

"The stew is still in the kettle," Mason answered. "Wilkinson's strong advocacy received unanimous Assembly approval. State politicians are in a controversial uproar while we await the answer."

He added that Wilkinson was not only powerful politically, but in his successful private enterprises. His war service had brought him government-issued land warrants of 2,000 acres of prime land fronting the Ohio River, extending west from the Kentucky River to Louisville. He sold off lots and opened a store in Lexington, where he built his first mansion. Later he laid out the town of Frankfort, which gradually expanded around his trading enterprises, and there he built a second mansion. Wilkinson often came to Louisville to look after his vast tracts of local land, and to conduct his trading business with one of his partners, Michael LaCassagne.

"Mr. LaCassagne is a French gentleman and wealthy local merchant," Daisy said. "The colonel usually stays at his plantation, but the LaCassagnes are entertaining a distinguished visitor. Guess who, Mary? No less a personage than Martha Washington's nephew, Bartholomew Dandridge the Second! We have planned a ball in his honor, and you must come."

Daisy explained that the town had an established custom to honor notable guests with a special ball. Subscriptions among the residents and fort soldiers provided the expenses, and the garrison band played a repertoire of lively dance music. The excitement of a ball aroused Mary's interest, but she silently wondered how a wilderness society could handle such a social occasion.

"Just you wait," Daisy said, "the ball will leave nothing to be desired of your former elegant affairs. Mason has loaned a warehouse with a wooden floor for the occasion. A ball committee and the slaves will decorate."

Conversation between the ladies drifted to memorable balls they had attended. As Adam listened, a poignant image of Anne overwhelmed him, in her pink ball gown, kissing her friends goodbye at their farewell party. He felt a sudden sadness.

"I feel I must decline your invitation to the ball, Mrs. Downs. I'm really not up to anything like that just now," he said.

"Nonsense," Daisy Downs said. "A handsome, young gentleman like you should not stay home alone. You have had too many weeks of suffering and grief. It's time to shed the sad memories and just remember the best events of your marriage. It will do you good to have some gaiety."

"Do come, Adam," Mary pleaded. She pursed her lips in the fetching manner which told Adam she was serious. "If you don't feel like dancing, I'll understand."

Adam grinned. "With two such charming invitations, how can I resist?"

Alone that night in bed, he thought about what Daisy had said. *Just remember the best events of your marriage.*

Many he would always cherish. If only there had been more warmth between them. Adam sighed with regret and ran his hand over the cold sheet beside him. He suddenly thought of Mary, her face so close while she spoke into his ear. He wasn't sure he wanted to go to this ball. He would be so tantalized by Mary and other women. It didn't seem right just yet.

"You calls fo' me, Miz Mary?" Maamba entered Mary's room while she was dressing for the ball.

"Maamba, my hair is a disaster," Mary wailed. "See if you can make me more presentable. I would like it piled high, to keep it in bounds. But first, help me with my camisole stays." She tugged at laces as she spoke.

"Effen I brush it good, it allus straighten out, Miz Mary," Maamba said, as she tightened the strings of the soft cambric sheath. "But yo' haih's so curly, I allus tells you to jest let it curl. You looks prettiest that way."

"Well, I don't agree. It's too unruly. I like it smooth, if we can make it stay."

"You got plenty reasons to want to look yo' best," Maamba chuckled as she brushed Mary's curls. "Massah Adam some prize catch now."

"Now, Maamba, don't hint at such a thing. My sister has only just died, and I'm not trying to take her place."

"You don't fool ole Maamba, Miz Mary. I knowed you got, eyes for Massah Adam for all dem years, when I belong to yo' mama and watch you grow up. I'd welcome being yo' family again, and Massah Adam, he need a wife bad."

"Pish-tosh, Maamba. You jabber like a fool," Mary said. "There, that looks smooth. Now fold my hair over this ribbon and roll it high."

Mary's eyes shone as she and Adam stepped inside the hall with Mr. and Mrs. Downs. Adam looked at Mary with an appraising eye. He saw a vibrantly beautiful, bewitching nymph. Her satin gown matched her sparkling eyes. Had he really ever noticed before that they were such a deep violet-blue? Those dark, generous brows, which he remembered were once heavy for an adolescent, now added a special strength to her face and accented the magic of her eyes. Her pleasurable mood was catching, and Adam felt a wave of her happiness.

"You'll stand them on their toes tonight," he said with a grin.

Mary surveyed his dark-chocolate velvet suit. "That color becomes your brown eyes and hair. You look wonderful," she said.

He smiled at her compliment. "I must confess it's nice to dress for the occasion after spending weeks in buckskins." He reflected on how she somehow always made him feel good.

Mary's eyes roamed the room. She commented on Colonel Wilkinson's attire of green waistcoat accented by white ruffles at his throat, white breeches and hose, and silver-buckled shoes.

"The powdered hair becomes him," she said, "and makes his huge brown eyes even larger." Mary looked at Adam again. "But I'm glad you don't powder your hair. I like it soft and natural, just as it is."

The Formans joined them, and as Eliza swept in on her husband's arm, Mary thought she looked exquisitely beautiful. She wore an emerald taffeta gown, and her auburn hair was coifed with a feathered plume.

The ladies compared impressions of the crowd. They surveyed the guest of honor, dressed in silver-and-white satin brocade, with a touch of cobalt blue, his head crowned with an elaborate powdered coiffure.

"Mr. Dandridge-the-Second literally glitters," Eliza said. "'Tis not considered good taste to outshine your wife. Poor woman. She looks like a mouse beside him."

"His splendor outshines the Sun King at the Court of Versailles," Sam Forman said. "Let's hope some of the ladies have eyes for the rest of us poor, insignificant men."

"Ah, there you are, *Mademoiselle* Grandin." André Michaux appeared at Mary's side. "How ravishingly beautiful you are tonight." Mary blushed at his effusive compliment. He kissed her hand and held it, while gazing into her eyes. He bowed to the men and kissed each of the ladies' hands.

Daisy told them that the first dancing partners would be selected by numbers drawn from a hat. The ladies would draw first, and each would be claimed by the gentleman drawing a matching number. She introduced them to Captain Mahaffey, commander of the fort, who passed the hat among them. Adam's number matched with a pretty, middle-aged woman. Mary drew Captain Mahaffey, Sam was paired with a diminutive blonde, and so it went.

The first dance was a minuet. Afterward, Mary was besieged by surrounding gentlemen for a place on her dance card. The dances progressed with reels and round dances. The music became louder and the dancing livelier until the dancers collapsed on the benches to rest. Adam danced once with Mary, but was content to watch from the sidelines. He noticed that André stayed by her side between dances, acting as if he were her escort. He made his way toward Mary and her coterie of admirers, and Sam joined him.

"That Michaux fellow is insufferable, Adam. He's making a nuisance of himself. Shall I get rid of him?"

"Mary doesn't seem to mind," Adam answered. "She is enjoying the attention."

"That's just the problem. He tries to cut everyone else out, and has become too possessive. Perhaps I can insult him enough to back off."

"Be careful, Sam," Adam warned, "don't make any trouble."

"Mary," Sam said, as they approached the group, "there are some new friends I want you to meet. This Frenchman has had you long enough over here. Perhaps these good officers will excuse you for a few moments."

"Ah, but *Mademoiselle* Mary has so many admirers, she needs someone to look out for her interests," André said, his eyes caressing Mary.

"And what makes you so qualified as a protector among these valiant American officers?" Sam said in a derisive tone.

André stiffened. "*Monsieur*, what do you imply? That I am not their equal?"

"*Certainly not*, you, you . . . popinjay. How do you serve your country? While your French compatriots revolted, you ran away when you could have stayed to help build a new nation."

André's flashing eyes seethed with anger. He towered over Sam as he drew his slender, graceful form up to full height. "*Monsieur*, I am no coward. You insult me. I challenge you to apologize, or accept a duel."

A murmur arose from the officers as they moved toward Sam.

"Now that's enough!" Adam said firmly, and he stepped between them. "This is no time for animosity. We are here to enjoy the evening. I'm sure Sam will withdraw his remarks, Monsieur Michaux. There will be no duel." His eyes pleaded with Sam.

Sam pressed his lips together and stood hesitantly, suppressing a retort. "Sir," he finally said to Michaux, "no insult was intended. You'd better cool off outside."

André gave him a withering look, turned on his heel, and abruptly left the room.

"That was positively frightening, Sam. I didn't know you could be so ruthless," Mary scolded.

"I find him an obnoxious fellow," Sam answered.

The next day at breakfast, Adam addressed Mary as she slipped into her chair and picked up her coffee cup. "I noticed you and the colonel had a lively discussion while you danced. What was that all about?" he asked.

Mary gave him a sly look. "I hoped you would ask," she said.

She warmed up to her audience of Adam and the Downses, as she told him what she had learned from the colonel. He had confided that his wife was miserable living in Kentucky. The "make-do" life-style seemed rough and crude. Her maiden name was Ann Biddle, of Philadelphia, where she was raised in a cultivated, cultured Eastern home.

The Biddle name brought Adam a pang of nostalgia. Her father owned the hostel where he and his wife, Anne, had honeymooned. Her uncle, Nicholas Biddle, was the prominent banker who guarded Anne's inheritance funds. Wilkinson's important connections seemed to multiply, Adam thought, as information about him accumulated. He must get to know him.

Adam went to the wharf later that day to arrange for delivery of new goods to the boat, and chanced to meet Colonel Wilkinson.

"Mr. Cloud, sir," the colonel's greeting was warm, "how pleasant to see you. I had to miss breakfast at the Downses' for an early breakfast meeting. Last night, at the ball, I enjoyed a conversation with your lovely sister-in-law. She is a beautiful and vivacious lady. And, may I say, so devoted a fan of your attributes that I felt I must make it a point to know you better. And here the opportunity presents itself so soon. By the way," he added, "should I call you Reverend Cloud?"

"You may call me Mister," Adam answered. "I do not want to highlight my church connections. In Natchez, Protestants are restricted under the Catholic monarchy. I'll have to wait and see what role I will play as an Episcopal minister there. As for Miss Grandin," he smiled at his thought, "she is slightly prejudiced on my behalf as part of her family. I am sure she is just being kind. You know, of course, that I just lost my wife. Mary has been a consolation, for we share the same grief."

"Yes, she spoke of your loss," Colonel Wilkinson said. "Please accept my sympathy. But come now, a man so fortunate to have such a perceptive lady for a dear friend must be deserving. Miss Grandin says you also know of my wife, and her family in Philadelphia. I hope you have the opportunity to meet my Ann some day. I am sure the ladies will be most compatible, having come from similar family backgrounds."

Adam explained his slight knowledge of the Biddles. He wondered how much information he could glean from this chance encounter with the colonel, but before he could decide on an appropriate question, Wilkinson opened the way.

"I'm planning an extensive trading venture with the Spanish in New Orleans in June, and am trying to assemble a variety of goods which are sorely needed by the Spanish," Colonel Wilkinson told him. "I'm negotiating with my friend, Mr. LaCassagne, for the purchase or consignment of four thousand pounds of lead ore, which he has acquired."

Adam's interest was piqued. "Do you plan to make the journey yourself?"

"I hope to, but in case I cannot leave my other business, I have established agents in New Orleans to receive and dispose of my cargoes."

"What do the Spanish want in trade goods?"

"I can see you are interested in trade ventures, Mister Cloud. Let us sit here. I'll tell you more." Wilkinson indicated a crate and they sat. "Two years ago, I took two flatboats with cargoes of tobacco, beeswax, apples and butter from Kentucky down the Mississippi to New Orleans to try my luck at opening trade with the Spanish. The governor-general had just announced the river was conditionally open for American trade. My purpose was to get the best deal for future shipments."

"I'm acquainted with the problems of river navigation rights," Adam said. "You must have jumped at the chance to trade. Was your venture successful?"

"It was beyond my wildest dreams. I hoped to further my own fortunes, as well as those of eager growers and traders from the American frontier settlements. I met Don Esteven Miró, governor-general of Louisiana, in New Orleans. Despite all the rumors of Spanish hostility to Americans, it was easy to bargain with him. I sold my cargo to the Spanish state and received several thousand dollars credit, together with the privilege of bringing up to sixty thousand dollars worth of Kentucky produce to New Orleans, duty free. They asked for more tobacco next time."

"That was indeed a coup." Adam looked at Wilkinson with respectful admiration.

"My success was greeted at home with whoops and hollers, and I was promptly reelected to the Kentucky Legislature," the colonel continued. "I find the position lends prestige to further my future Spanish deals. The Cumberland Territory Legislature was so pleased they named all the settlements along the Cumberland River the Mero District, M-e-r-o, in honor of Governor Miró's generosity." His eyes twinkled with remembrance. "The governor was very flattered."

"You certainly found a soft spot in his armor," Adam remarked.

"Yes, it paid off. I took advantage of the deal with Governor Miró, and last year took down a big load of tobacco. But I had a surprise when I arrived. A fifteen-percent duty on merchandise had been mandated by the Spanish Council of the Indies, in Cuba. Also, contrary to the early agreement, the king of Spain decreed that the state would no longer purchase our tobacco."

"That must have been a blow." Adam's face reflected dismay.

"You needn't worry, Mister Cloud," Wilkinson's tone was conciliatory. "Those who pledge allegiance to Spain, like yourself, will be in the best position to grow and sell almost anything that will do well, even if the state is not the purchaser. There are a thousand ways to get around the trade barriers. If you ever need help, just contact me and I can provide, hopefully, some influence." Wilkinson stood. "But I have detained you long enough, and we both have business to conduct."

"I thank you for your information, sir," Adam replied. "I hope to see more of you at the Downses'. I would like to hear more about Natchez."

"It will be my pleasure," Wilkinson said. "By the way, sir, that Frenchman, Michaux, spoke to me at the tavern just now. Who is he, and what is he doing here?"

Adam explained the circumstances of their acquaintance.

"Well, if he's not a special friend of yours, I would be wary of him. Anyone living among Indians usually has doubtful intentions. I do not wish to alarm you, but something about him bothered me."

"I will take your observations under advisement," Adam answered. "Good day, sir."

He wondered about Michaux as he turned away. The dueling pistol came to mind. André seemed too benign to be suspected of subterfuge, yet he denied owning a gun. And Mary mentioned he drew "exquisite maps," but for what purpose? *Stop that,* he reprimanded himself. *You must not harbor any more ill thoughts about Michaux.*

That evening Colonel Wilkinson had supper at the Downses' home, and Daisy included Colonel Forman, Eliza, and Sam. They lingered at the dining table, reluctant to interrupt the convivial flow of conversation. Wilkinson proved to be a delightful raconteur. He described some of his military experiences under General Washington, as he fought with General "Mad" Anthony Wayne's troops, from Boston to Montreal. They were surprised to learn the colonel had a medical education which he chose to forgo in pursuit of the trading business and his role in the Kentucky Legislature.

"You promised to tell us more about Natchez," Adam reminded him.

"Ah, yes. On my last journey home from New Orleans, I decided to travel by land, up the Trace to Natchez." He looked at the ladies as he explained. "The Natchez Trace is a narrow foot trail about a hundred and fifty miles long from New Orleans to Natchez. Boatmen use it after they float their wares downriver. They sell their flatboats and walk, or ride, the entire trip all the way up to the Ohio River. Poor buggers . . . pardon me, ladies, for the expression, but the Trace is very demanding and dangerous."

"What miserable lives they must live," Mary exclaimed.

"Yes, they lead grueling lives. Anyway," the colonel continued, "the journey to Natchez took about ten days. By the time I arrived I was feeling quite ill. I sought the help of the physic at Fort Panmure, and there I met the newly appointed governor, Lieutenant Colonel Manuel Luis Gayoso. The governor took a personal interest in me and graciously took me to his home to recuperate. During the while we became friends."

"What is he like?" Eliza asked. "Is he a dark and foreboding Spaniard?"

"Not at all. You will like Gayoso. He is an *hidalgo*, which is what the Spanish call a don of important birth, and a delightful man of keen intellect. He was educated in England. He speaks fluent English, French, and Latin, along with his impeccable native tongue. He also stocks one of the finest wine cellars in Natchez."

"Now that speaks of a cultivated man," Ezekiel said.

Wilkinson turned to Adam. "I believe you will find mutual interests. You are close in years, and he appreciates an educated man. Furthermore, he also just lost his wife and baby daughter. The baby died at birth, and his wife died of fever a month after he arrived in Natchez."

"Your description of the man is reassuring," Adam said.

Mason Downs replenished the wine glasses and passed a box of cigars to the men. Colonel Forman took one and the host lighted it for him.

"What can you tell us about Natchez itself?" Ezekiel asked. He puffed the cigar to insure it was lighted, and the aroma of rich tobacco wafted around the table.

Wilkinson described Natchez as two towns. Upper Natchez was still an embryo town, situated on a high bluff overlooking the river, with only a few buildings. There was a Spanish garrison, Fort Panmure de Natchez, formerly called Fort Rosalie by the French, a few business structures, an administrative Government House. Governor Gayoso's home was nearby.

"You mean, it's not even a village yet?" Mary sounded incredulous.

"It has the beginnings of a village," he responded, "but the planters live out of town on their land. The primary town below the bluff is called Natchez-Under-the-Hill. There are several houses, taverns and warehouses, but most of the buildings are pubs, brothels, and gambling houses."

"Unfortunately," Wilkinson continued with a rueful expression, "this part of Natchez has a population of rowdy, brawling boatmen and traders. Among them are scoundrels and renegades. It can be rough and dangerous there. The military is sent to subdue any rioting." Turning to the ladies again, he added, "You wouldn't want to go in that section unless you had to."

"One would think the government would clean up such an awful place," Eliza said.

"Perhaps, in time," Wilkinson surmised, "but Natchez depends upon the river front as its lifeline, and the boatmen are the life-blood of survival."

Adam leaned forward, eager to learn as much as he could from Wilkinson. "The future control of the Mississippi River will affect us as residents of the Spanish province," he said. "What does it forebode if Kentucky pulls away from the Union? Wouldn't the frontier be cut adrift in an uncertain wilderness?"

Colonel Forman spoke up. "I have heard the petition to withdraw is more of a pressure device, an ultimatum of 'give us statehood and safe protections, or we will secede'."

"It is something like that," Wilkinson admitted, "but there are those who really are serious about alliances with Spain, or even England again. There are several ways to go, and I am swinging in the wind to catch the best advantages."

"Your friendship with Governor Miró must be a tremendous advantage for you," Ezekiel said. "May I ask you a personal favor? Would you write me a letter of introduction to him, in case I go to New Orleans?"

"Of course, sir. It never hurts to know the highest authority. I will be pleased to give you a letter."

The group rose from the table and the colonel went to a parlor desk. Daisy Downs supplied the stationery. After he wrote and handed the letter to Ezekiel, he took another sheet and wrote again, and, to Adam's surprise, handed him a letter addressed to Governor Gayoso.

"For you, Mister Cloud. I have commended you as a citizen of highest stature, with excellent connections in the states. You should make a good friend there."

"Thank you, sir, for the commendation, and for a most pleasant and instructive evening." Adam flashed a warm smile. "We wish you good fortune in your upcoming trade."

Adam retired that night reflecting on his good fortune in making such an influential new friend.

The travelers were anxious to be on their way. The ice was breaking up fast when Adam and Mary gathered with the Formans to discuss departure plans, and to say goodbye to Maj. Sam Forman. He would stay on to sell his merchandise, and join them in Natchez when he accumulated an ample tobacco supply.

It was late February when Col. Ezekial Forman's keelboat led the little flotilla off below the roaring Falls-of-the-Ohio.

5 Mississippi
River

André Michaux's presence became more visible each day. Everyone called him by his first name now, but Adam could not bring himself to feel a kinship with the Frenchman. Michaux was expected to fill in for Sam, after Louisville, but he was not good at his assignments. His attention wandered on the job. He spent every spare moment with the ladies, on deck especially whenever Mary was present, or in a corner of the cabin, poring over his collection. Adam's irritation mounted as he watched André capture Mary's attention.

"This is the only time I get to talk with you, Mary," Adam said one night as he was putting Becky to bed. He was in a peevish mood. Aunt Betsey sat on her bunk mending stockings. "That blasted Frenchman hovers around you all the time, and I hardly get in a word. Don't you find him a bit tiresome?"

"Not really." Mary suppressed a secret smile. "He is very attentive, and it's rather exciting to be admired." *Could Adam actually be jealous?* she wondered. She had to admit she enjoyed his discomfort.

Adam said nothing. He felt shame that the Frenchman irritated him. His own critical attitude disturbed him and it was difficult to ignore his inner rage. He stalked out of the cubicle abruptly without further comment.

"That was unusual behavior for Adam," Aunt Betsey remarked. "I wonder if he knows he is jealous?"

"Could it be? Oh, Aunt Betsey, I don't want to hurt his feelings, but I guess you know how I feel."

"If you feel so strongly about Adam, there is nothing wrong in putting his feelings to the test. It may be too soon to expect him to forget Anne, but one never knows. Let André swoon over you as much as he will. A little tension never hurts a budding romance."

The placid environment of the Ohio had changed. More islands kept the crews on continuous alert, and unusual Indian activities raised further apprehension. Ezekiel decided the boats should float all night under the full moon in order to get past hostile Indian country more quickly. Soon after they passed the mouth of the Cumberland River, they noticed the rocky cliffs and hills were giving way to more level, wooded shore, indicating they were nearing the Mississippi River.

They passed Fort Massac, an old French fort located on a point in the riverbend. Adam could see crumbling log barracks surrounded with overgrowth in what had once been clearing. The place looked abandoned, but they passed it midstream in case it might shelter bandits. Days later, the flat terrain provided the travelers with a better view of what lay ahead. The blue Ohio was turning murky, and everyone came on deck to watch for the Mississippi. Lank Preece stood at the tiller while Ezekiel, Adam, and David stood watch at the prow.

"There it is! The great river!" David cried out.

In the distance they saw the broad sweep of a tawny body of water, looking more like an ocean than a river. The Ohio turned brown as it caught the big river current, and the swirling turbulence stirred a muddy, sudsy flow between the two bodies of water. By the time the keelboat reached the mouth of the Ohio, the water carried a torrent of mud, branches, and uprooted trees.

"Where are we going to land?" David asked. There was anxiety in the boy's voice as he looked down into the bobbing morass of flotsam and jetsam.

"There's a landing point on the map called 'Bird's Point,' if we can find it, David. This is going to take some doing," Adam answered.

The boat entered the maelstrom, bobbing and swaying with the turbulence. Ezekiel and Lank used all their strength to hold a steady direction, while Adam, Jeb, David and André braked the long oars. The keelboat neared the point, and Ezekiel shouted, "If those buggers can make it, so can we." He indicated the thirty boats tied up at the landing.

All aboard cheered as the keelboat reached the bank.

"I feel like we are almost to Natchez, now that we're on the Mississippi," Mary said.

"Don't be fooled," Eliza Forman warned. "We have some seven hundred miles yet to go."

The point was a desolate place situated in a small clearing, banked with canebrakes, overlooking the two rivers. A crude building of combined store and tavern hugged the waterfront. Adam, Ezekiel, and David went ashore, leaving Lank, Jeb, and André to look after the ladies.

As Adam and the Formans waited for the fleet to moor, they surveyed the variety of cargo aboard the broadhorns and barges. Some carried pelts and dried meats, others were stacked with Monongahela rye whiskey from Western Pennsylvania, and tobacco from Kentucky and Tennessee planters. There were wares of manufactured and woven goods from the Ohio Valley and the Seaboard, and produce from rich Upper Mississippi farmlands. Several boats held swine and cattle.

When their companions joined them, the men entered the store amid a rowdy, milling crowd of boatmen. The stench of whiskey, cigar smoke, and sweat invaded the nostrils, and sounds of rank epithets, loud curses, and shouts filled the fetid air. They watched one group boisterously engaged in "shooting the cup." A tin cup was placed on a shoulder while a marksman took aim paces away. The wagers were bet with loud boasts and settled with gunfire, curses, and cries of foul play.

Adam looked the Kaintucks over. They struck him as men of doubtful reputation, possibly cutthroats and villains, or fugitives from justice. Their clothing looked as if they purchased their outfits from the same slopshop — red flannel shirts, and a loose jerkin, long to the hips, in fading shades of blue. Their dirty trousers of coarse brown linsey-woolsey were leather belted, and fastened on every belt, he noted, was a hunting knife or two, and usually a tobacco pouch. Untanned coonskin caps crowned their heads, most with the fur turned inside out. By the stench in the air, he surmised the men had not bathed during the course of their travels.

Adam and the others worked their way to the bar and listened to the conversation. Periodically, a ruffian would send a hearty squirt of "chaw'n t'baccy" toward a brass spittoon, followed by loud guffaws and challenges for the next round. Their colorful speech, generously laced with profanities, seemed to Adam like another language.

Moving in closer, Adam picked up on a remark about an Indian escapade.

"Should we fear any of the tribes down the Mississippi?" he broke in, to no one in particular.

Adam felt four sets of critical eyes, as the boatmen turned to him.

"Where ya goin'?"

"To Natchez. Will we have to fight Indians?"

"Nah. The're as fren'ly as a wagtail pup," one said.

"They're more civilized than them blasted yellow-dog cusses up the Mississippi," added another.

"That's good news," Adam said. "What about the water on the river? Is it potable? It looks so muddy."

"Aw' that's no problem. It clears up further downstream. If ya filter it, it's pure as dippin' from a rain-barr'l."

Adam liked the looks of the last speaker. He wore a pleasant expression, looked cleaner, and was more courteous. He addressed questions to him, but others chimed in with comments.

"I suppose you have had enough experience on the river to give navigational advice," Adam said.

"Sure 'nuf," another boatman spoke first. "Fer one thing, never hitch yer boat below a bend in the river. Like as not comes Hell's-a-snortin', and yu'll be buried with a cave-in like a mudfish come mornin'." He spat a deft parabola of tobacco juice, reaching the spittoon with a resounding thump. The others cheered.

"There's a lotta difference in navigatin' the Big River than the Ohio." The young man whom Adam had addressed spoke up. "It's wider and deeper, an' it's full of swirls, eddies, and heavy silting. By comparisin', its twists and turns are downright awesome sometimes."

"You speak like you know what you're talking about," Adam said. "What is your name?"

"Dusty, sir. Dusty Rhodes. I got me a couple a partners an' we've made the trip three times to Natchez, once on down to New Orleans."

"I'm Adam Cloud." He extended his hand and Dusty clasped it with a callused shake. "Would you come over to a spot where we can be alone, Dusty? Our boatmen need some advice before we start downriver, and I'd like for our flotilla patroon to hear what you have to say."

"Sure," Dusty answered. "You get 'em and bring 'em over there." He indicated a place in a less crowded corner. "You can meet my partners too."

Adam gathered his companions together, and for the next half hour Dusty described to them how to avoid river pitfalls.

"I am concerned over navigating the Mississippi," Ezekiel said. "We found a navigation map but it lacks details. Dusty, you sound like a clear-thinking young man of experience. I would like to hire you as our pilot. Do you think you can get our seventy-foot keelboat down to Natchez safely?"

Dusty grinned with pleasure. His smile was infectious, and his eyes beamed intelligent response.

"I'd like that, sir. I cud use the extra money. But I'd have to clear it with my partners. It leaves 'em one less to manage our flatboat. I see 'em across the room. If you wait, I'll ask 'em."

Dusty soon returned with his partners and introduced them. Mort, the team patroon, struck Adam as a serious, unsmiling young man. Jiggs was a thin, wiry man of about forty years, amiable and vivacious. They agreed to let Dusty pilot the Forman boat, and the three left to talk over their affairs. Soon Dusty returned and found Adam, Ezekiel, and the Minor brothers sipping glasses of *negus,* a spiced wine.

"I'm ready, sir," Dusty said to Colonel Forman. Grinning widely, he added, "and I've broughtcha some Kentucky rye for yer boat. My partners ask if they kin join yer outfit downriver. An' there's a couple others who want to join too."

"Of course," Ezekiel said. "The more boats the safer we will be. Just give me their names."

When the men returned to the boat they found Mazie and Liz in the cabin sniffling and dabbing away tears. Eliza, Aunt Betsey, and the girls were gathered around trying to console them, while Lank and Jeb stood by.

"What has happened? What's wrong?" Ezekiel asked.

"Ask Lank and Jeb. They just turned on André and beat him," Eliza answered in a distraught voice.

"We roughed him up a bit, that's all," Jeb said. He glanced about with a sheepish look.

"He had it comin'," Lank added. "God-damned French frog. Pardon me, Mister Adam, but I can't help the cussin'. He can't stay away from the ladies, and we found him flittin' around our wives."

Adam hurried to his cubicle, where he found Mary sitting on André's bunk, holding a wet pack to his swollen eye. Maamba stood by with a pail of water. Adam bent over the Frenchman for a good look at his wounds.

"Anything broken, Michaux?" he asked.

"No, Adam, just my pride," André winced with a painful grin. "I was unjustly accused because of my kindness to the ladies. I meant no harm. They are all so nice to me."

"I'm sure they are," Adam said tersely, with a scathing glare at Mary. "Mary, why don't you let Maamba take over with the cold packs and let André nurse his ego? He needs to consider his behavior."

Mary glowered at Adam. "How could you be so caustic to André after he saved your life?" she snapped, and quickly left the room without a further glance at him. Adam followed her out, his lips grim with reproach, and joined the men in helping get the boat under way.

Five more flatboats filed behind them as they pulled out, swelling the fleet to ten boats. The Forman crew bent their attention to the might of the river and its current. Dusty proved to be every bit his worth in pay. As they drifted, Dusty described the river and its course.

"If'n ya tries ta fight it, it'll heave ya liken a b'ar catchin' a trout," he said. "Its depth at the mouth of the Ohio is about eighty feet, but it increases to a hundert feet and narrows when it reaches the sea. This helps ya unnerstand th' currents and why th' river plays so many tricks on ya. It's plenty dangerous with shoals, sucks, snags and sawyers, an' I'm sure ya know all about those. But the most danger ya have ta watch for is runnin' aground them sandbars."

In the evenings, when the passengers gathered in the cabin to hear Dusty's plentiful travel tales, Adam felt the chill of Mary's censure. She would not look at him and avoided him during the daytime. He tried to ignore the hollow feeling inside him as he listened to Dusty.

Before teaming up with his partners, Dusty told them, he worked for hire with other traders, for which he was paid only forty or fifty dollars a trip. Now, with partners, his profits were better than the poor, hired boatmen who had to pay back their own expenses. He explained that some even made their way back upriver in a tedious process called "warping." A round trip took nearly nine months when they pulled their way upstream. Dusty shuddered at the thought.

"We allus buy us cheap hosses, and maybe a burro fer extra baggage. We kin make it back up the Trace to Nashborough in about three weeks. It's near five hundert miles from Natchez to Nashborough, an' takes six to eight weeks iffen ya walk."

"Are there no amenities on the trail?" Ezekiel asked. "Way stations, or ordinaries for food and lodging?"

"Nah. Just wilderness all the way 'til ya get close to Nashborough. An' it's mighty dangerous, too, not only from animals in the forest, but from Indians, or white men that travels the trail. They's a rough lot; I'd say some are the meanest kind of rapscallions. They kin jump ya and rob ya on the trail. Piles of dried bones have been found where some poor bastards got the'selves ambushed by a robber or a redskin."

"How absolutely dreadful," Mary said. "I don't want to hear any more of this." She arose and left for her cubicle.

"Ugh, nor do I," Eliza said, following. Mazie and Liz joined them.

"Excuse me, ma'am," Dusty spoke to the retreating women. "I didn't mean to scare ya. But that's jest the way it is out there."

"What happens to your flatboats if you don't take them back upriver?" Adam asked.

"We sell 'em on the spot. There's a good market for flatboat lumber, 'specially in Natchez, where they got no mills. But you gotta watch fer worm-eaten timber."

"I'd like to put in my bid for your flatboat when we get to Natchez," Adam said. "I'll need lumber for my house."

"Sure," Dusty said. "But I'll have to talk it over with my partners. I reckon they'll agree."

Adam considered his good fortune in the lumber deal, but he secretly hoped to build with stones, like the old family home in Brandywine Hundred.

The Forman keelboat approached the first sign of civilization one morning, a settlement called New Madrid, some sixty miles downriver on the western shore. A small fort stood at the water's edge. Pigs and chickens wandered between forty log cabins, several stores, and a mill. The fort looked newly built. Ezekiel decided to pay the commandant a visit, which was a peacetime tradition among army officers.

They landed at a newly built platform, and Adam signaled to the other boats that they would catch up with them by nightfall. He accompanied Ezekiel up a narrow path to a small guardhouse. They expected an identity challenge but, to their surprise, a congenial soldier greeted them with a wide grin and a casual salute. He launched into an excited torrent of Spanish.

"What is he saying, Adam? Your Spanish is better than mine," Ezekiel said.

"Here goes," Adam replied. "This is my first try on a native. Let's hope he can understand me." He turned to the soldier.

"Buenos dias, señor. Como se llama este lugar?"

The soldier understood well enough and answered in measured Spanish.

"He says the fort is called L'Anse la Graisse, and is newly established in the name of his majesty, the king of Spain. The commandant is a Lieutenant Foucher."

The soldier ducked into his guardhouse and brought out a tiny pet raccoon, rattling off rapid Spanish while he held it out to them.

"I think he wants to trade the raccoon for something from us," André said.

"No hay trato. No venimos a negociar," Adam said slowly. *"Por favor, llevenos a su commandante."*

The soldier's face fell. He stuffed the raccoon back inside and led them soberly through the gate to headquarters. There he announced them to Lt. Pierre Foucher, fort *commandante*. Colonel Forman introduced himself and Adam. The lieutenant shook hands warmly and invited them to sit.

"Excuse this incomplete fort," the young lieutenant said, in halting English. "We are only a few months old, and there is still much to do to get settled. It is a long time since I have seen anyone but my troops and the settlers here. I have only four officers and thirty men to defend the fort and the adjoining settlement from river expeditions, which might prove a threat to the territory of Louisiana." He paused, then added hastily, "The threat of Indians, of course."

"Have you no friends among the settlers?" Adam asked.

"Not really. Most are *campesino* families, a mixture of French, Spaniards, Canadians, and half-breed Indians. Now Americans are usurping land in the countryside, staking sections for plantations without government approval. They are of no concern to me unless the Indians anger over taking their lands. That would be a threat to my settlement." He shrugged as though to shake off any responsibility.

Ezekiel then rose politely to leave. The lieutenant looked disappointed.

"Ah, *amigos,* do not go. The village people are holding a *fiesta* beginning this afternoon. There will be music and dancing. You and your ladies may dine with me for midday dinner, and stay the night. You will enjoy the *fiesta.* It will be so lively."

"I'm afraid we cannot accept," Ezekiel said firmly. "The fleet will be looking for us, and we must not cause them worry."

No amount of pleading could change the colonel's mind. They thanked Lieutenant Foucher for his gracious invitation, and bade him farewell.

"You will see no other villages until you near Natchez. *Vaya con Dios!*" he called.

6 Chickasaw Bluffs

The crew began to adjust to the new life and demands of the Mississippi River, which presented an intricate maze of islands and shoals. The lookouts concentrated on the sandbars, and all hands were needed to avoid disaster.

The river had an air of amiability, coursing along its channel with a determined purpose. It would suddenly change with a new direction in a bold, sweeping curve, adding mystery in a promise of something new around the bend. But inevitably, in endless monotony, the scene repeated itself. On the east bank were forests, with long beards of gray moss shrouding the trees; its melancholy features evoked an ineffable sadness. On the west was unbroken flatland ending at river's edge in caving banks of clay, bordered with cane thickets.

The river teemed with wildlife attracted by its verdure. Mary helped the children identify the many species feeding at the water's edge. Long trains of pelicans and geese flew overhead in graceful formation, following their annual flyway to nesting habitats. Across the open land they could hear bobwhites call, and turkey buzzards always hovered somewhere.

The vast flocks of wild birds provided a bounty for the table. The men sortied off to hunt, felling as many as twenty ducks in one shot, and bringing back all they could eat. They caught a plentiful supply of fish, frying them in bear oil for breakfast. In his inimitable style, Dusty told them of a record six-foot catfish weighing 250 pounds. It became a favorite game to vie for the largest catfish caught among them.

At night, the deep stillness was broken by the lap of the river against the boats, or the rilling murmur of rapid water as it formed vortices against a nearby island. The *kwawk* of a night heron or the hoot of a forest owl were familiar sounds, and the howl of a panther added funereal echoes to the silent woods.

The little band of travelers no longer feared Indians, and laid firearms aside except for emergencies. To while away the time, they gathered each evening and sang ballads accompanied by the Grassley families' fiddles and harmonicas.

Soon the February sky became low and gray, and the weather grew disagreeable every afternoon with head winds, thunder, and lightning. The squalls made navigation difficult, and it took all hands to keep the boats from crashing as they approached shore. They were often forced to moor early in the day, seeking shelter on the banks where they could cook their meals out of the fierce wind.

Many miles downstream, the first in a series of high bluffs, on the east bank, presented a prominent change of scenery.

"That's the Chickasaw Bluffs," Dusty informed them. "The islands around 'em make navigatin' tricky. 'Specially the one called the Devil's Race Ground, and fer plenty reasons. The island's full of sawyers and dangerous snags, whippin' up a strong current."

The crew cautiously negotiated the dangerous island. They were getting more skillful over the river's challenges.

Some thirty miles farther, around a deep bend, a fourth bluff hove into view. Perched on top was a building that did not appear on the map. It overlooked the mouth of a river flowing into the mainstream, and a steep path led to the bluff. Always curious, and never wanting to pass up a visit to a military post, Ezekiel pulled ashore, and the flotilla moored on both sides of him. The ladies rejected the steep climb, but the Forman girls and most of the flotilla crews climbed to the top, where they reached the porch of a newly built trading post. The Kaintuck boatmen crowded the entry, pushing and shoving to enter.

The proprietor introduced himself as William Panton, partner in the British firm of Panton, Leslie and Company, of Pensacola. Colonel Forman explained that they were on their way to Natchez.

The Forman girls looked about, and Margaret suddenly grabbed her father's arm. Augusta squealed, and clung to Frances.

"Papa, there's an Indian over there," Margaret whispered.

"Don't be afraid, lassies," Mr. Panton smiled at them. "He'll not harm you. The Chickasaw tribe is friendly since travelers trade here."

The girls stayed close to their father, staring wide-eyed at the native. Adam studied him. He wore an intricately woven headband with several feathers, which trailed down his long hair in back. A breastplate of tooled and beaded leather and several necklaces dangled over a calico shirt. Adam moved behind the girls to reassure them of added protection.

"As a matter of fact," Panton continued, "Governor Miró granted us the license to build here and provide trade goods for the Indians. They are forbidden to trade with the British or French, but we have permission to establish duty-free trading posts at strategic points serving the various Indian tribes across Spanish Florida. This is our western post, built especially for trade with Chickasaws."

"Have the Indians accepted the post?" Adam inquired.

"They are using it more and more," Panton said. "The Chickasaw Bluffs have long been a stronghold of their nation, but the Spanish consider them strategic for their own use. The situation requires delicate diplomacy, for the Indians say the Spanish are encroaching on their land. Governor Miró saw the trading post as a way to placate the Indians and serve them at the same time."

"A diplomatic move," Adam observed.

"My plan is to win over their chief to let me train one of the tribesmen as a factor. If they prove efficient, I will let them run the store under supervision of our Natchez factor."

"*Pardonnez-moi,*" André spoke to Panton, "are the Chickasaws friendly enough to accept a visitor to their village? I am a botanist studying native plant life and hope to stay with a tribe long enough to learn from them."

Mr. Panton's eyebrows rose. "You are French, sir. Have you any knowledge of Indian life?"

"Ah, yes, I lived with Cherokees recently. They were most friendly."

"In that case, I suppose you could stay with the Chickasaws. Their village is just south of here. Their chief is called Piomingo. It won't do any harm to ask."

"*Merci,*" André said, beaming with pleasure. "I shall ask the colonel to stop there."

The boatmen browsed amid the shelves, purchased a few items, and drifted out to the boats again. Ezekiel wished Panton luck in his enterprise. Panton told them that the next settlement would be more than three hundred miles downriver.

To their dismay, the crew found a strong gale had risen outside, and it was difficult to walk against it down the path. Lightning flashed and thunder rolled through the atmosphere. Their concern mounted when the flotilla pushed off. The wind became more violent, whipping up high waves. The keelboat was tossed about like straw. Adam and André hung on to one oar together against the violent waves, and Adam wondered if they might have to combat such violent weather for the next three hundred miles.

"What do you think, Adam?" Ezekiel shouted against the tumult. "Should we chance this gale further?"

"The lead boat's already pulling in," Adam shouted back.

The forward boat pulled hard toward shore. The rest of the flotilla followed, the crews bending themselves at the tiller and oars, battling the wind's force. Adam was alarmed when he saw an Indian canoe heading for the lead boat.

"Who's in the lead?" he called out.

"It's Mort and Jiggs," Dusty shouted. "They could be in real trouble. Better git our guns ready fer a fight."

"Give the 'guns-ready' signal!" Ezekiel shouted to David. "I'll try to keep a safe distance."

David gave the signal and dashed inside the cabin for guns. Adam considered their predicament. He saw the boats behind them being buffeted about like toys. Reaching shore was imperative, but there might be an Indian ambush awaiting them. Adam searched his mind desperately for a way to escape and wondered if they could fight the storm long enough to land downstream, past any ambush. He glanced again at the flatboat ahead and, to his astonishment, saw that the Indians were helping the crew row to shore.

"If we can last it out, we might get help too," he said. "These oars are likely to snap like twigs." André's grim, white face told Adam he had heard.

"Gee whillikers," Dusty shouted, "those Indians are coming back for us!"

The Indians gestured to follow them through the sandbars. Adam was too busy in the next few minutes to feel relief at their sudden rescue. Following the canoe, they plied the oars fiercely, with all their strength, avoiding the sand ledges. The keelboat finally reached shore, and the canoe turned back for the next incoming boat. The Forman crew dropped anchor, and Adam waded ashore to moor.

He soon realized the task on shore was as formidable as that on the water. The ropes whipped about in the frenzied wind, and he had difficulty grabbing an end. Just as Adam caught a line, a strong arm reached out beside him. An Indian secured the rope to a tree and pointed to the second line. Adam tossed it, and he fastened it to another tree.

Reeling from tension and exhaustion, Adam faced the Chickasaw savage beside him. He held out his hands. Palms up, he remembered; that shows I'm not hostile. The Indian returned the gesture and they grinned at each other.

"Thanks," Adam said, not knowing what else to say.

"Big wind," the man answered.

They nodded, grinned again. Adam returned to the boat and the Chickasaws remained on shore, watching the activities aboard. While the servants prepared the midday meal, the passengers discussed the unusual event.

"That was one magnificent gesture I wouldn't expect from Indians," Adam said, his face glowing with admiration.

"I would like to make their acquaintance," André said. "It will help me gain admittance to their village."

"Why don't we invite them aboard to dine with us?" Ezekiel said. "We can show our thanks that way. Adam, would you ask them?"

Adam walked to the prow of the boat, leaned over the rail, and beckoned the Indians aboard. They scrambled up, showing eagerness to enter the cabin. Ezekiel gestured for them to sit, and they promptly sat on the floor. The crew members smiled awkwardly and took note of their strange visitors. Their clothes were an assortment of woven vests, calico print shirts, and leather breeches. Each wore moccasins and leggings sewn with deer sinews and decorated with wampum and porcupine quills. The Chickasaws smiled and stared back, nodding and shaking their heads.

"Do they understand English?" Mary asked.

"Probably a little. Be cautious," Adam said.

While Adam gave the pre-meal prayer, the Indians watched in astonishment at the bowed heads. Maamba and Sena offered them food, and to everyone's surprise, the first Indian declined. Mystified, they watched each Indian decline the food until one Indian accepted. It was obvious the Indians followed a specific protocol, showing deference to the man of highest rank. They seemed to enjoy the food, wolfing down large portions stuffed into their mouths with their fingers.

After dinner, Ezekiel mixed some whiskey with a little water and handed it to the leader. He stood, took the glass in a genteel manner, and shook Ezekiel's hand. With a gentleman's grace, he then shook hands with each of the men, not omitting his own people, whose hands he shook as politely as he had the rest. He raised his glass in a toast.

"Long life," he said with dignity.

Adam offered the other Indians a drink, and each, in turn, politely acknowledged the compliment with handshakes and a toast.

"That was as graceful a gesture as Lord Chesterfield could have made," Adam said. He raised his glass and toasted them.

André began a conversation with Indian signs. The natives responded with more signs, and André tried a few Cherokee words, which they understood. Groping further for communication, Adam discovered the Indians spoke a little English and Spanish. Gradually, they exchanged information. The Indians revealed that their chief was Payo-Mataha, Piomingo of the Chickasaw Bluffs tribe.

When the Indians rose to leave, André signaled to the leader. Using sign language and English, he asked if he could visit their village for a while. The leader answered and André interpreted.

"Colonel, they say the Great Chief Piomingo would like to return the courtesy you have shown them tonight. We are invited to their village tomorrow morning."

"Tell him we accept with pleasure, and thank him for their courageous assistance with our boats today," Ezekiel answered.

"Well, I never." Eliza was almost speechless when the visitors left. Everyone seemed stunned at the outcome of the incredible evening.

"Are you really going to visit the village?" Mary sounded dazed, as though it was hard to accept any of what had happened.

The Forman girls began to plead and wail at their father not to go.

"Certainly we are going," Ezekiel said. "There is no doubt in my mind they are friendly. Even savages have a lot of good in them, and they clearly showed it today."

"They will expect gifts," André reminded them.

"Of course," Adam said. "Will you ladies get together some trinkets they might like? Nothing expensive."

"Like what?" Mary asked.

"Oh, jewelry, coins, mirror, combs, some bright-colored calico," he answered. "We'll take them to the chief."

The wind was as strong as ever next morning, and the crews resigned themselves to another day of waiting out the storm. The women and children watched anxiously from the deck as Ezekiel, Adam, David, and André joined four Indian escorts waiting on shore. All but André carried guns. The Chickasaw leader stepped forward, scowling.

"We come friends no guns. Bring guns no make friends."

Ezekiel looked chagrined. "We will disarm," he said hastily. "Leave the guns behind," he said to the others. "It seems we have committed a breach of etiquette."

They returned to the cabin to leave their weapons. Seeing the men lay down their guns, the women tried to dissuade them from going. Suicide, pure folly, disregard for personal safety, they pleaded, but to no avail. The men assembled on the bank again. The Indian leader nodded and led them into the forest.

Breaking out of the forest they came to a clearing and saw before them a vast compound of mud-daubed structures and sheds. Indians were coming and going about their tasks amidst boisterous children and dogs. They showed no sign of apprehension as they stared at the visitors. Their guides led them for a long distance through the village to a large, open field, where a noisy crowd cheered and shouted at men and boys playing a game.

"See Chief Payo-Mataha," the leader said. He led them to a mature Indian watching the play. Their guide spoke to him in the Chickasaw tongue, showing respect appropriate to one of high rank. Adam examined the chief. His raiment reflected his royal personage. Attached to his headband were woven, beaded strips, strands of beads and tassels, and three large feathers which hung about his face and trailed down his long hair in back. He wore a colorful hip-length tunic, ornamental breastplate, soft leather breeches, anklets laced with thongs, and richly decorated moccasins.

The chief turned, smiled sedately, and extended his hand to Colonel Forman. Ezekiel shook hands and introduced himself and his companions.

"Ah, bring boy," the chief said, looking at David. He beckoned to a youth standing with the group. "My son, Yellowtail," he said, grinning widely at the two boys. "We watch *toli*. You like game?" He gestured toward the playing field.

Adam watched a few minutes and began to get the point of the game, noting that it was not unlike cricket. Each player held two sticks, fitted at one end with an oval hoop laced with thongs, with which the ball was caught, rolled, pushed, and tossed toward end goals. The players did not seem bothered by the wind, which was less severe than on the river, for the forest acted as a wind-brake. Adam was amused by their sparse, but striking costumes. A beaded horsehair breastplate adorned their naked, sweating chests. Only a small loincloth clothed their limbs, suspended from a wide belt woven of horsehair, beads, and dangling tassels. Over the breech trailed a mane of white horsehair fastened to a loop, which swayed about as they ran. The players were fiercely competitive, throwing themselves into action with grunts, shouts, and laughter. The cheering spectators added to the excitement.

When the game ended, Chief Payo-Mataha gestured to his visitors that they should leave with him. Ezekiel and David walked beside him. Adam and André followed, with an entourage of Chickasaw men in the rear.

"This village looks well organized," Adam said. "Can you make sense of its pattern?"

"Ah, yes, most interesting," André said. "Indian villages are well planned, I have found. This one stretches, I guess, about two leagues, or more. The structures are placed in clusters for each family. The Cherokee winter huts were well fortified for cold weather. They use different huts for summer."

Adam noted the construction as they passed the family compounds. Some were circular winter houses, built around thick posts, enclosed by interwoven saplings and poles. The roofs were daubed with a thick clay and grass mixture, some topped with hides for extra warmth. The open summer houses were framed of posts and saplings, covered with split boards and woven bark. Nearby, each family had an open granary with stores of corn.

They reached the center of the village, and the chief motioned them to enter the men's longhouse. Adam saw its outer mud-roof was overlaid with reed mats and bearskin hides. The inside was surprisingly spacious; the clean dirt floor showed signs of having recently been swept, the grooves of the broom's pattern still undisturbed. Handsome baskets, pottery, rugs and blankets were placed or hung about the lodge, lending a decorative touch to an otherwise unfurnished area.

The chief motioned his guests to join him and his braves on the floor. To their astonishment, the chief began to undress. He left only his breechcloth, his anklets, and his headband on his otherwise bare body. André Michaux saw Adam's bewildered look. He leaned toward him and whispered that each chief usually had some special ritual allowed only for himself.

A bevy of squaws and young maidens placed pottery vessels of food and drink before them. They drank bowls of porridge and ate morsels of fish and game with their fingers. Adam could not identify the meat; he hoped it wasn't dog. Telling himself it must be venison, he plucked a piece of meat from the central bowl.

The chief talked throughout the meal, with a fair smattering of English and Spanish. Piomingo's questions indicated that he was acquainted with the white man's culture. He was curious why his guests would live among Spaniards, who, he said, encroached on the Chickasaw hunting grounds. In contradiction, Adam noted, he bragged about the negotiations with Governor Gayoso over the new trading post at Chickasaw Bluffs. The chief was obviously pleased with the outcome, pointing out that the Chickasaws wanted friendship with the Spanish, and that the new treaty would be beneficial.

"Bring goods, much trade for our people," he said.

"We saw the new trading post," Adam said. "We congratulate you on your deal. It was a useful treaty." He thought the compliment sufficient. He did not want to tread the waters of Spanish policy.

Colonel Forman adroitly steered the conversation to the food and the fine hospitality afforded them. The chief smiled and selected a flat, fried bread cake, rolled it around a piece of meat, and suddenly placed the cake in the colonel's mouth, as a complimentary gesture. Without change of expression, Ezekiel accepted the morsel. What aplomb, thought Adam, just as if it happened every day.

After dinner, two braves handed Piomingo a large pipe, colorfully decorated with green horsehair and feathers, and ceremoniously lighted it. The chief drew puffs of smoke and passed the pipe to Colonel Forman, who took a draw and passed it to Adam.

Adam nearly choked. The tobacco was so strong he motioned to David not to try it.

The Indian women sat behind the men, quietly watching and listening during the meal. One of them spoke to André Michaux, who roughly interpreted for Adam.

"She wants us to know that the women were aware of our intent to bring guns this morning, and they appreciate our restraint. She says that last night some of the white traders came ashore and brought some *la tafia* which they shared with the Indian men. The rum made them drunk and rowdy, and the women feared for the white guests. They removed their men's knives and hid them, so there was no trouble."

Adam was touched by her concern and beamed his appreciation. He must remember to tell Mary, he reflected. She would appreciate the Indian women's ingenuity and humanity.

"With your permission, Colonel Forman, I will speak to Piomingo about my need to stay in his village," André said. He turned to Chief Piomingo and spoke at length. The chief sat quietly for a few moments, appraising the Frenchman as though he had just met him. Finally, he nodded and spoke.

"You good man. No bring gun. Your mission peace. You stay." He grinned his approval and shook André's hand.

Colonel Forman rose to leave, and Adam suddenly had an appalling thought. He pulled the colonel down beside him and whispered.

"We forgot the gifts!"

Ezekiel looked dazed. "Oh, my God! We forgot them in the mix-up over the guns." He barely moved his lips. "That's a terrible breach of custom. I'll have to fix it." Colonel Forman faced the chief. "Your Excellency," he said graciously, "we have enjoyed the fine meal and your kind hospitality. I must apologize. We left in haste this morning and must return to our boat for our gifts."

The chief nodded and began redressing himself. He led the way through the village, accompanied by his son, Yellowtail, and twenty braves.

André Michaux stepped in beside Adam. "Wait, I go with you," he said. "I must gather my collection and say farewell to our companions."

The gale was still whipping up a frothy sea when they reached the river. André went to his cubicle for his belongings.

"Quick, Liza," Ezekiel said. "We forgot to take our gifts."

Eliza brought out the gifts and Adam sent Dirk to fetch two hams. He returned to shore with Ezekiel and David, heaping the gifts upon the chief with appreciation for his hospitality. Chief Payo-Mataha thanked them with dignity.

"Mister Michaux will be with you shortly," Adam said, secretly relishing the thought of being rid of André. On board, he overheard Mary and the Frenchman saying goodbye like old friends.

"I have asked André to visit me in Natchez, Adam. He will acquaint me with his newest knowledge from the Chickasaws," Mary said.

"*Oui, Mademoiselle* Mary," Michaux purred as he kissed her hand. "You shall read my notes, which should be many volumes by then. I will slowly make my way downriver until I find you in Natchez. *Adieu* until then."

Adam managed a wan smile and nodded. *Can't be too soon for me,* he reflected. *His kind needs watching.*

André made the rounds of tender farewells to all on board, and thanked the colonel for his generous offer of passage. Adam watched him join the waiting Indians. Chief Payo-Mataha held up his hand in farewell, and the little band disappeared into the forest.

Monotony and boredom enveloped the passengers in the next three hundred miles. Adam seldom reminisced about past events now, but the thought of nearing their destination and a new life brought a sense of uneasiness.

As he faced an uncertain future, he saw a need for strong spiritual vigor. He must be free of any nagging religious doubts, and wondered if he could ever accept rigid dogma again. He wanted to reconcile all the religions and philosophies of the world, and synthesize them into the highest level of spirituality. He studied avidly his esoteric books on advancement of the soul. The life of saints and mystics opened new doors not available in his former studies. He practiced their prayer and mind control techniques when he could be alone. Gradually, he recognized a different, rapturous love of God through his worship. He began to awaken daily with a sense of joy and anticipation. An inner peace enveloped him.

One day Dusty called out, "Ya ho! Here's the Yazoo River!"

Everyone crowded the decks, and as the keelboat rounded the bend, a view of great beauty spread before them. The river flowed from a wide mouth on the left bank into the gentle Mississippi River. Flocks of wild geese and swans foraged its surface and willow-covered banks. High, steep, broken hills formed a backdrop, with a forest of lofty trees hung with moss and mistletoe. Further downstream they reached a small settlement astride a plateau, graced by a waterfall splashing into the river from the heights. Dusty informed them it was Walnut Hills, an illegal American settlement. Surprised and curious, Ezekiel elected to go ashore, and the flotilla moored with him.

"Oh, Ezekiel, must we stop again?" Eliza wailed. "We are getting so close to Natchez I can't bear another delay. Please, let's go on. This isn't even a military post."

"It probably is not, but whoever lives here may make a difference to us some day. Any settlement is important to the way the land develops."

"We'll make a quick visit and tell you about it," Adam said.

"The place is beautiful. Imagine trees blooming in February," Mary said. "Find out what kind they are, Adam."

Only the Minor brothers accompanied Ezekiel and Adam, and after an hour they returned full of information.

"We found a mixture of Spanish, Indian and a few American families in the settlement," Ezekiel told them. "It is rather a curious story. The Americans said they were enticed there by land speculators who purchased three million acres from the Choctaw Nation, south of the Yazoo River."

"Wait, it gets more complicated," Adam said. "The land is Spanish territory, and the settlers are considered squatters. The land company has petitioned the Spanish government for land grants, and rights to establish a colony there. By the way, Mary, the place is abundant with walnut trees and blooming peach."

"Eliza, you will be happy to hear that Natchez is only about a hundred miles south of here," Ezekiel said.

"Joy of joys, we are almost there," Eliza cried. "It deserves a good hurrah from everyone."

One hundred miles more! Adam mused on deck during night watch. Stories of land greed crowded his mind. Illegal land speculation on the Ohio River frontier, described by Governor St. Clair and General Harmar; the desperate push by frontier growers for use of the Mississippi River; the American squatters near New Madrid; the dispute over Chickasaw and Choctaw land by Spanish claimants, and an illegal colony at Walnut Hills . . . . Where would it all lead? The peace and security of a parish priest in Delaware began to look more tempting as he contemplated the potential upheavals in the new land.

7 Natchez

The next sign of civilization after Walnut Hills was a cluster of cabins on top of a high bluff overlooking the mouth of a bayou. Dusty told them it was Bruinsburg, and that they should reach Natchez before night. In a flurry of excitement, the passengers retired to their quarters to make themselves more presentable, and soon returned on deck to watch for their destination. Adam held Becky, and Mary stood beside them.

"Look on the left for a long stretch of high bluffs with a forest on top," Dusty told them. "When ya see a steep embankment slopin' down to a flat landing with buildings on it, that'll be Natchez-Under-the-Hill."

All aboard strained to see around each bend, lest they miss the landmarks. They had seen long stretches of high bluffs along the forest background for some time. Adam felt the tension of nervous excitement as he anticipated Natchez around every bend.

Natchez appeared so suddenly they were startled. The river made a wide, abrupt turn, and their destination loomed directly before them.

"There it is, Natchez!" The name resounded among the passengers. They clasped hands and embraced one another. Adam's throat swelled with emotion. Mary grabbed his hand and squeezed tightly.

Dusty took command and Ezekiel headed the boat toward shore.

Adam pointed excitedly, and cried out, "Look, Becky, way ahead. That's Natchez!"

"Natchy-natchy!" Becky mimicked, liking the sound.

The lower area first drew their eyes.

"From a first view, Natchez isn't much to look at," Mary said in a flat voice.

Adam saw her disappointment and wanted to placate her. "It's not spectacular," he answered, "but I can't say I'm surprised. It looks just like Colonel Wilkinson described."

The terrain consisted of three tiers of land each about two hundred yards deep, running parallel to the river. The landing area, Adam judged, was at least a mile long, and numerous flatboats lined the shore. As they drew nearer, Adam made out three parallel streets and one principal street leading vertically from the levee to the foot of a bluff, which he judged to be nearly two hundred feet high. A steep road hugged the cliff wall to its summit. Several buildings clung to the edge of the incline, their facades facing the cliff wall, as though to hide from view the perilous drop below. Adam counted some twenty crude buildings and, scattered along the riverfront, a few shacks and wharves.

Suddenly, their attention was interrupted by the sound of a drumbeat-to-arms coming from the riverfront. The nearer the boat drew, the louder and more furious the drumbeats became. To their astonishment, a cannon shot shattered the air, and Adam saw a puff of smoke spiraling from a hilltop battery above the fort.

"Dear God, what was that?"

"Stand back!"

"Take cover!"

"We're being fired upon!"

"I didn't see any splash in the water," Adam said. "It must have been a warning shot."

"Keep your heads, men, we haven't been fired upon. We are being challenged!" the colonel cried out. "Liza, quick, grab a white cloth of some kind."

Eliza darted into the cabin and rushed out with a tablecloth.

"There, Adam . . . someone, wave it," Ezekiel ordered.

Adam hastily tied the flag to an upended fishing rod and slowly waved it. "Come to think of it, Ezekiel, we must look rather formidable, with a flotilla of ten unidentified boats rounding the bend," he said.

"Well, sir," Dusty said, "we *are* a mite unusual with so many boats together. Most of us come down as loners, or in small groups of two or three."

They heard no more cannon shots, and the drumbeats stopped. By the time they reached the landing many people had gathered to watch the flotilla arrive. A line of soldiers stood at-the-ready in grim formation, surveying the approaching boats.

"We must have drawn the whole population," Adam said.

"I must say, we're arriving in unforgettable style," Mary quipped. "Are you sure we are welcome?"

"Oh, Ezekiel! It's so exciting. We're creating a sensation," Eliza said. She hugged her husband's shoulders as he worked the rudder. "I do hope they give us a welcome."

The boats spread out to tie up, showing deference to Colonel Forman by permitting his boat closest to the wharf. Led by Ezekiel and Eliza, the passengers disembarked slowly, one or two at a time. As Adam stepped ashore, Dusty caught his arm and promised to let him know next day if his partners would agree to sell him their boat.

Adam surveyed the crowd. They appeared the most unlikely assortment of people he could imagine. He noted a mixture of Kaintuck boatmen, now easily recognizable by their disheveled appearance and rowdy manners, aside trappers and hunters, distinguished by their shaggy leather costumes and coonskin caps. There was a black-robed priest, and a few Negroes of varying shades, from deepest ebony to the lightest mulatto. Among them were "ladies of the evening," obvious in gaudy attire. Several well-dressed white men stood by, curiously watching the arrival.

The platoon commander stepped forward, smartly saluted, and identified himself in accented English.

"Lieutenant Juan Pedro Garcia, His Majesty's Royal Army, Fort Panmure de Natchez. Identify yourself, *Señor*, and state under what orders you arrive in the territory. "

"Some welcome!" Mary said to Eliza.

"*Shhh.*" Eliza squeezed her arm.

Colonel Forman stepped forward, drew himself up in all his military majesty, and saluted. "I am Colonel Ezekiel Forman,

Army of the American Republic, and citizen of the United States of America. Take me to your commandant at once. I have papers from Colonel Grand-Pré accepting us as emigrants seeking citizenship under the Spanish government. We are tired and have come a long way to reach your country. I must say this is not the welcome your governor led me to expect."

The young lieutenant flushed with embarrassment, but before he could reply, everyone's attention was directed to a horse and rider clattering down the cliff road. When he reached the lieutenant, the rider, in officer's uniform, dismounted and spoke softly to him in Spanish. The young lieutenant saluted, issued an order to his platoon, and they marched off toward the cliff road.

The officer turned to the crowd of newcomers. He suddenly burst into a wide grin of recognition and extended his arms to the Minor brothers. "Cousins! Welcome," he exclaimed, and embraced the two couples.

Theo Minor introduced Colonel Forman as patroon of their flotilla. The major saluted, extended his hand, and said, "Sir, I am Major Stephen Minor, post adjutant of Fort Panmure."

Adam examined the major during introductions. He looked to be about Adam's age, and as American as cornbread and hamhocks, he decided. A genuine Virginia gentleman, his cousins had described him. His courteous diplomacy confirmed the title.

"Sir, it is my pleasure to welcome you to Natchez." the major was saying. "I apologize for the way you were received. We have looked forward to your arrival but, of course, had no way of knowing when your party would get here. Word reached us several days ago that there was an invasion plot afoot by an army of the Kentucky region. Quite naturally, when we were expecting to see only several boats, the unusual size of your fleet led us to suspect you might be the hostile group, and our *commandante* took the precaution of sounding the alarm. When we saw that the boats were laden with goods, and when you raised a white flag, we were relieved to see that it was a domestic invasion instead." His broad smile swept the group. "You are welcome to our shore."

Colonel Forman was mollified by the explanation, and relaxed. "I understand your precautions, sir, and please know we are as relieved as you are that we are welcome. For a few moments, there, we were getting ready to defend ourselves." He then introduced the senior members of his flotilla.

"*Commandante* Grand-Pré sent me to greet you. He will welcome an opportunity to meet with you as soon as you find it convenient," Major Minor said. "Ordinarily you would meet first with Governor Gayoso, but unfortunately, he left yesterday for Cole's Creek to oversee a community project, and will not return until this evening. He will be disappointed he was not here to welcome you."

"I, too, am disappointed," the colonel said disconsolently.

"Now, colonel, I would suggest that you and your party find a suitable mooring place where you can have some privacy. Arrangements have been made for temporary living accommodations until you receive your land allotment. There are no inns here suitable for ladies of your rank," he said, looking at Eliza and Mary. "In the meantime, if you can bear to linger on your boats a while longer, we will confirm your living quarters as quickly as possible."

"Are we staying with you, Stephen?" William Minor asked. "We don't want to crowd you and Kate out of your home, but you did write that you expected us."

"Of course, Will. You can move in right away." He turned to the others. "But first, you might like to stroll up the street to see what we have here below the hill, and up to the level of Natchez town. *Commandante* Grand-Pré will be expecting you. Our Government House is located straight ahead on Front Street, after you pass the fort."

The newcomers returned to their boats so that they could locate a place to tie up. Colonel Forman chose a site upstream by an embankment with sloping ground, hoping it would be more secure and private. As they approached the spot, an alligator slithered off the bank where it had been sunning.

"Alligators, Father! Do we have to stop here?" Frances cried out. Margaret and Augusta chimed in, and the three began to whimper.

"This is really a terrible welcome," Eliza said. "We were so careful to stay clear of alligators on the way down, and now this.

Must we bed with them under our boat, Ezekiel? We must consider the children's safety."

Mary looked over the rail and shuddered. "Ugh. There are alligators everywhere. Just look at the repulsive creatures! I thought we would be welcomed with marching bands. Instead we are greeted with the roar of alligators. We have had enough of that," Mary said, scowling with displeasure.

Adam looked upstream and saw that Mary was right. He tried to allay the ladies' fears and disappointment. "Ladies, stay calm. The alligators will settle down. We've taken their space and disturbed them. You mustn't let your alarms spread to the others. We will have to get used to the disadvantages of a wilderness settlement. With God's help, we have come this far, and we are fortunate it is a settlement as civilized as this one is."

Mary pursed her lips, an expression Adam recognized as a signal for a decisive comment. It amused him that her soft, full lips could pout with such strength. It revealed the strong side of her personality, he thought.

"That remains to be seen," she said. "Wild beasts under our very boat is hardly reassuring. And from the looks of the riff-raff under the hill, it would be hard to imagine any civilized activities taking place."

Adam smiled and turned to Colonel Forman, who had purposely ignored the complaints.

"Ezekiel, I would suggest that we assemble everyone on shore and give thanks to God that we have arrived, that we are all safe and well, and ask His blessing in our undertaking here in Natchez."

Ezekiel sent Kudjo with the message, and soon the families were kneeling together. Adam's voice choked with strain and emotion as he gave thanks for their safe journey, and prayed for the strength and vitality to meet their new experiences. He felt certain that this stalwart band of people would thrive in the new life before them. Everyone rose, and with handclasps, embraces, tears and smiles, they wished one another well in the days to come.

Adam suggested to Ezekiel that they have a quick look at Lower Natchez. It was not easy to convince the ladies to bypass their sortie, but the men stood firm. Colonel Forman ordered his coach-and-four made ready to drive them all up to Government House when they returned. The Minor brothers joined them, and they set out on the principal street leading to the bluffs. It was lined with dwellings, taverns, houses of ill fame, and stores with living quarters above. Groups of boisterous men dotted the streets which were cluttered with garbage and unsavory refuse, the stench rising with the dust of activity.

"We saw nothing this wretched on the American frontier," Adam observed.

William Minor spat. "Ugh, disgusting." The brothers held their noses, making wry faces.

They entered several taverns where ill-smelling boatmen and trappers lounged about, and a few gentlemen were seated at gaming tables. They hurried by houses of ill-repute, where women brazenly displayed their charms outside.

"Lots of intermarriage here," Adam observed. "Most of the women are light-skinned mulattos or even quadroons. Those brightly colored turbans on their heads must be the local style."

Theo Minor grinned. "Honest marriage has little to do with their color, Adam. Those headdresses are called *tignons*. Spanish law requires the women wear them to mark their occupation."

"Leave it to Theo to know about the whores," William joshed.

"They don't concern me. It's the rougher element," Ezekiel said. "This is really a hotbed of roughnecks and renegades. Our ladies must never have occasion to come to this vile place."

"Well, they won't have to walk through it to get to the town above," Adam said. "Let's get back and see if they are ready."

Returning for the ladies, they found the carriage ready and the ladies anxious to explore Upper Natchez.

"How pretty you all look," Theo said. His face broke into a boyish grin, and he swept low in a gallant bow. Tullah took his outstretched arm with mock dignity, William and Julia followed, and they formed a procession, as Ezekiel and Adam each proffered an arm for Eliza and Mary. They marched to the waiting coach, where Moses, the coachman, stood smartly at the stepping block and opened the door. Spectators surrounded the vehicle, staring in disbelief at the handsome carriage, hitched to four matching bays. The coach was bright yellow, with black trim, and resplendent with new red curtains. The carriage top had been fitted in Louisville with a delicate black railing, lending the rig a sporty, country effect.

The friends entered Ezekiel's coach in a happy mood. Theo Minor broke into song:

"The lady in red is quite ready, she said,
Just pour me some wine for a starter.
Don't sit on the bed, please help me instead
To take off my pretty red garter . . ."

"Oh, not that one, Theo," William said. "Remember the company. How's this one?" and he started the popular ballad "Rolling the Rye." The others joined in until they reached the summit.

Ezekiel stopped the carriage to survey Upper Natchez. Fort Panmure was directly on their right. A crude path extended from it across vacant ground until it disappeared in the distant forest. The principal streets directly ahead were thinned of trees and laid out in plots. A few buildings were scattered about at random. Dense forest formed a backdrop behind the village.

"Where's the town?" William Minor asked. Tullah and Julia giggled, and everyone broke into a laugh.

"It's even smaller than Pittsburgh," Eliza said.

"Louisville looked like Paradise compared to this," Mary said. "I count thirteen buildings which appear to be both residences and business establishments."

"Remember, Colonel Wilkinson told us the town is reserved for tradesmen and business. Planters live out of town," Adam reminded them.

After several blocks they passed a town square lined with stalls and benches under the trees. Several merchants were clearing tables of food and wares, with the noisy help of wives and children.

"Don't tell me we have to do our marketing at those miserable little stalls," Eliza wailed.

"Now, ladies," Ezekiel said, "let's not judge too hastily. What we see here is a good beginning, and we are invited to help make it grow."

To the left, along the town bluff, was a wide unbroken strip of land at least a mile long. It was dotted with budding shrubs, forming a park, or esplanade. Straight ahead was Government House. A graceful arch marked the entrance over a covered porch, the only embellishment on what was otherwise a stark, oblong building. They alighted the carriage and entered. The unusual interior held a pleasant surprise. The double walls allowed deep-set windows, and the plaster sparkled with a mixture of ground seashells.

Stephen Minor greeted them and gave an account of Colonel Grand-Pré. Commander of the Royal Armies, civil and military commandant of the post and District of Fort Panmure, the colonel had served as acting governor of the district prior to Governor Gayoso's appointment. He was noted for running a tight regime, and was highly respected by the men under his command.

The major led them through a large, vacant assembly room to an adjoining office. The room was divided with a counter and shelves on one side, piled with massive volumes and ledgers, such as those used for keeping documents and vital records. The other side was furnished sparsely with a floor rug and a few pieces of furniture carved with ornate Spanish designs. Light from the setting sun streamed through a bare window and across a massive walnut desk, highlighting the silver hair of a tall, distinguished-looking gentleman in uniform. He rose from his chair as the major introduced him. He shook hands with the visitors, repeating each name carefully in fluent, accented English. Adam was impressed with Grand-Pré's military dignity and his genteel manners.

"You must be very weary from your long and arduous journey. Please be seated." He gestured toward high-backed Spanish chairs, and waited until all were seated. "Let me first apologize for your reception. It must have been startling, and for this we are extremely sorry. My primary duties are to assure the safety of this district. Over the years, this territory has been a constant target for ambitious American groups who seem convinced that a takeover of this western province of Spanish Florida would require only a simple invasion. Consequently, we stay on the alert for filibusters from various military threats of which we are apprised."

Adam's doubts began to multiply. *Are we moving into a war zone?* he wondered. *It's not just Indians now; it's avaricious American renegades . . . .* He caught the end of Gran-Pré's explanation.

"Thankfully, your flotilla carried the new arrivals we have expected for several months. In the name of His Majesty, I extend you my warmest welcome." He smiled and nodded to the group.

Adam's pulses quickened at the commandant's next words.

"Now, if you are ready, I can administer the oath necessary to establish your citizenship in this country, under the largesse of His Majesty, your benefactor. By the way," he consulted a document in his hand, "I assume that all who applied for entry have come with you. I do not see evidence of all seven families who petitioned for land grants. May I ask where they are?"

Colonel Forman explained that the others were still on board their boats, ready to be summoned when their presence was required.

"No, *Señor,* that will not be necessary now. Let us proceed with those who are here. Colonel Forman, I see that you are the initiator of the requests for citizenship. Can you state in your knowledge of those who accompanied you that each and every applicant is an individual of good repute, of desirable fortitude and industry, and that he or she may contribute the best of those assets toward becoming a citizen of this Spanish colony? Of these persons I name, may you speak thusly in their behalf."

He then named the Carter, Cloud, Forman, Grassley, and Preece families, Betsey Church, and Benajah Osmun.

Colonel Forman spoke forcefully. He foreswore that the character and desirability of each person applying for citizenship was beyond reproach; that all had outstanding records of honesty, thrift, and industry; and that each would make a fine contribution to the province of Natchez.

"I would point out," he added, "that two members of our families did not arrive." He indicated Adam by a nod and continued. "Mister Cloud tragically lost his wife, Anne Grandin Cloud, on the journey. She was stricken with a respiratory disorder and died in Pittsburgh. The lady next to him is her sister, Miss Mary Grandin. She does not request permanent residence here, and will be returning to her home in New Jersey after a visit."

Colonel Grand-Pré made a note of the names and turned to Adam. "*Señor*, let me extend my deepest sympathies. That is a tragic circumstance with which to begin your new life here. I see by your record that you have a little daughter. She should be a consolation to help ease the void in your heart."

"Thank you, sir, for your concern," Adam replied. "Yes, my little daughter is my delight, and my sister-in-law, Miss Grandin, has also been a consolation, as we share our bereavement."

Colonel Forman continued his explanation. "My nephew, Major Samuel Forman, also made the journey with us as our companion and able assistant. He remained in Louisville on business, and will be arriving within the next several months. He will also return to New Jersey, after a visit."

"What business would that be?" the colonel inquired.

"The import-export trade. He will seek an audience with you and your governor to discuss trade possibilities when he arrives," Ezekiel explained.

Colonel Grand-Pré recorded the information and turned again to Adam. "*Señor* Cloud, I see on your application that you are a Protestant Christian minister. You are well aware, I assume, that full active ministry is not legally permissible here in Spanish West Florida, and that your admittance will rest on your oath and understanding to abide by the rules of our government. Our citizens are free to worship privately, but the Catholic faith is the only religious practice tolerated publicly within the province. Public preaching, communal church services, baptismal and marriage ceremonies may be performed only by our Roman Catholic priests. It is to be hoped that those of your faith in need of spiritual solace will feel free to attend our services and use the ministration of our faithful priests, who are available to all citizens at any time. You will be expected to agree to these conditions as part of your oath of allegiance to the state."

Adam felt his heart thumping wildly. This was the plunge he had dreaded, giving up his past to an obscure religious future. He swallowed hard, and answered in his most forthright tone of voice. "*Commandante,* sir, I do not intend to assume an active public role in ministering to those of my faith, either by preaching, or conducting the rites and ceremonies of our Protestant church that are unlawful in this land. I understood this thoroughly, and made my decision to accept your terms before I applied for admittance. I intend to become a successful planter, and to that end I have been preparing myself for all things relating to agricultural pursuits."

"Very good." Turning to the two Minor couples, the commandant said, "Your characters have been attested to by Major Minor, and you may take the oath with the others. Now, I shall administer the oath of allegiance to you, following which you may sign and attest the printed oath as spoken. Please stand and repeat after me your allegiance to His Most Catholic Majesty, Carlos, king of Spain, following which you may individually swear on the Bible."

Everyone rose except Mary. In unison they repeated the words of a lengthy oath, binding them as citizens of Spain, Province of Natchez, subject to Spanish laws, decrees, and edicts. As he spoke the words, Adam felt a tense knot in his throat. Was it elation, or apprehension? He did not know; the feeling just appeared. In his turn, he laid a hand on the Bible, and signed the oath, dated March first, Anno Domini, 1790.

"Now," the colonel said, "for the rest of the business at hand, we can do no more, for it is late." He then explained the procedure for assigning parcels of homestead land. Each family would be interviewed and allotted a portion of land. He would discuss a schedule with Governor Gayoso, who would see them, one family at a time, in the next several days.

"Major Minor is now reviewing our inventory of temporary housing shelters," he continued. "Let us see what he has found."

He directed his orderly to summon the major, who arrived in a few moments. He explained to them that King's Tavern was the only hotel in Upper Natchez. It was often filled with rough boatmen, and therefore was unsuitable for family use. Some local residents had agreed to lodge newcomers, but until location of land grants were decided, it would be premature to assign them temporary housing.

"Final decisions are made by our governor," Grand-Pré added. "Therefore, I would advise you to be patient until tomorrow. You will be advised of the appointed time. Until then, I wish you a pleasant rest for at least one more night on your boat."

Colonel Forman thanked them for their help, and with a tentative appointment arranged for a midmorning meeting with Governor Gayoso, they made their way back to the coach and set out for the landing.

"Well, I never!" Eliza said. "No place to sleep except on our boats again. One would think they could have been better prepared for us."

"Back to the alligators," Mary said with some bitterness. "They have given us our best reception."

"I guess we're fortunate to move into Cousin Steve's home tonight," Tullah Minor said. "I do feel sorry for you, on the river again."

"I must admit I was disappointed, but not surprised," Adam remarked. "No one expected Paradise here. It's comforting to know our hosts are being as helpful as possible, even if we have to stay on our boats a while longer."

"At least we have not been abandoned on our own to pitch our tents in the wilderness," Ezekiel said.

"When I took that oath," Eliza said, "I felt apprehensive. I kept saying over and over to myself, are we giving up more than we gain here?"

"That was a formidable oath," Mary said, "especially when it required you to obey 'with the same exactness and loyalty of His Catholic Majesty's other vassals.' I'm not sure I would want to be considered a vassal."

It was now dusk, and the population Under-the-Hill had come to life with noisy activity. Moses drove hurriedly through the unkempt street, but not fast enough to miss the ebullient atmosphere. Bawdy women and boisterous men loitered or careened on the street, and the sounds of ribald talk and laughter sifted from open doors. Mary and Eliza stared at the scenes and exchanged knowing looks. Theo Minor broke into song again: *"The lady in red . . ."* William joined him this time, singing until they arrived at the landing.

Adam informed the other boaters what had transpired, and of their appointment with the governor next day. He had not long returned aboard his own boat when he heard voices outside. Taking his lantern on deck, he saw men and horses on the embankment. Peering into the darkness, he distinguished a figure mounting the landing plank. A melodic voice, resonant with rich cultivation, called out in impeccable British diction.

"Is this the craft of Colonel Ezekiel Forman? I am Governor Gayoso. I have come to pay my respects."

Colonel Forman heard the voice and joined Adam. "Certainly, Your Excellency. I am Colonel Forman. Welcome aboard."

"May I welcome you, sir," said the governor, as he stepped aboard. "How can I express adequately my disappointment in being unable to receive you when you arrived in Natchez? Please forgive the cannon-shot greeting. May I persuade you to think of it more kindly, in a different aspect? Please perceive it rather as a salute to distinguished travelers, such as yourselves, which it would have been had we known who you were."

"You are indeed gracious," Ezekiel answered. "We have already accepted it as a precautionary measure, which any good commander would make in the same circumstances." He turned to Adam and added, "This, sir, is Mister Adam Cloud, one of our companions. The others are preparing to retire, but you will meet them tomorrow."

Adam tried to make out the governor's appearance in the dim lantern light. A touch of velvet, lace, and braid under his cape indicated he was handsomely attired. He was of medium height, and stood erect, not in stiff military style, but with an air of easy grace.

"Ah, yes. At midmorning tomorrow, I shall look forward to meeting you again, and all the families with you. Until then, *Señors,* a pleasant evening."

As they watched him mount and ride away with his military escort, Adam said, "What a superb gesture—the governor making the effort to greet us at the end of a probably grueling day of riding upcountry. It is one that only a true Christian gentleman would make."

"I agree," said Ezekiel. "It will give Eliza good cheer. She has been so disappointed over the day's events."

No one slept well that first night in Natchez. Minds raced over the events, and loud street noises and debauchery interrupted their rest.

8 The New Land

Don Manuel Gayoso opened his eyes slowly, blinded by the light in his bedchamber. Chico, his body-servant, had aroused him from deep sleep when he opened the shutters.

"*Buenos dias, Señor,*" Chico said, peering to see if the governor was really awake.

"*Buenos dias,* Chico," Don Manuel groaned softly, unable to rid himself of his dream.

Shaking his head slightly, his eyes filled with compassion, Chico turned from his master and left the room on silent feet.

Don Manuel lay quietly for a few minutes, feeling grief and guilt roll over him in waves. This dream . . . how many more times would it haunt his sleep and begin his day with melancholy? If only he had not allowed her to come with him, if only he had persuaded her to stay at home in Spain where she was safe.

He pulled himself to a sitting position and shook his head sharply to clear the fog of his dream. But, as he reached for the steaming cup of coffee Chico had left by his bedside, it seemed that he could still hear the roar of the frothing, grasping Atlantic, and the hiss of the ropes that lowered the tiny, canvas-wrapped body of his stillborn daughter into her watery grave.

With an effort, Don Manuel put these thoughts from his mind. There was work to be done. As his bare feet hit the planks of his bedroom floor, he recalled the arrival of the families from New Jersey and his brief welcome at the landing last night. He wondered what they were like. He had read their application histories sent by Gardoqui, the Spanish minister of affairs, in New York. They seemed a fairly prosperous group, especially Colonel

Forman, who had brought some sixty slaves with him. The dossiers of the other families seemed to indicate adequate stability.

Chico returned and laid out the governor's wardrobe. As Gayoso dressed, his mind inventoried sections of the Natchez districts he would allot the Americans. He wanted to spread the population around the district so that orderly growth would occur. Colonel Forman, a man responsible for so many slaves, and a group of more than thirty white immigrants, should have preferential treatment. He would be eligible for a sizable land grant, perhaps 1,400 arpents. The smaller grants, he decided, would be determined according to their needs and status after he assessed the families' qualifications.

His dressing completed, Don Manuel surveyed himself in the standing mirror. The citron braid on his black coat set off the mustard-colored breeches nicely, he thought, but as he turned sideways he viewed the slight paunch below his waist. He patted his stomach and sighed.

Catching Chico's grin he said, "Too much sitting at my desk, Chico. Not like the military life. I must find time to exercise more frequently, perhaps walk to my office."

After a hearty breakfast Don Manuel found his horse saddled and ready, and he rode to Government House, only a few minutes away. He surveyed with approval his sumptuous headquarters, some of its elegant furnishings recently borrowed from Governor-General Miró. A Persian carpet covered the seating area, where tall, exquisitely carved chairs, upholstered with green plush, were neatly arranged for visitors. He was particularly fond of the massive carved desk, appropriate for a governor's office, and of the wall tapestry, shipped from his home in Portugal.

He scanned the agenda placed on the desk by his efficient secretary, Capt. Jose Vidal. Don Manuel's new position as governor of the province demanded a strict routine. He was already finding its administration a formidable job, filled with a bewildering variety of tasks. Early morning duties began with details concerning the upkeep and growth of the district. Don Manuel's heart was not in the minutiae at hand today, but he got through them as best he could. He knew most of the day would be taken up with land grant consultations and swearing-in ceremonies for members of Forman's travel group. Establishing satisfied settlers was paramount to provincial success. The population he had inherited, and was to receive, was mainly Anglo-American, with previous experience in self-government and independence. Their attitudes toward governance, he knew, would be very different from the monarchial system which their country had so recently overthrown. He would have to tread carefully to accommodate their wishes and expectations within the limits of the Crown.

At promptly ten o'clock, Captain Vidal advised the governor that Colonel Forman's family had arrived. Don Manuel greeted them warmly and surveyed the group while they seated themselves. He thought the family attractive, and the colonel himself pure *hidalgo el grande*, with a firm grasp of his own identity and status. The colonel's presentation showed he was totally prepared to settle his family in the new community and to venture into extensive new agricultural pursuits. It was obvious, from descriptions of his holdings and farming enterprises in New Jersey, that he had prospered as a planter of fruit orchards and grains. His long and successful career as a Philadelphia lawyer was a point in his favor. Don Manuel liked this man and saw in him a substantial addition to his province, undoubtedly a future leader in the community.

Mrs. Forman was a surprise to the governor. Her youthful appearance suggested a second marriage by the colonel, and by the looks of her he would have a lively companion in his declining years. Miss Betsey Church, sitting straight and prim, reminded him of his own childhood governess. He gazed at the three Forman girls, his eyes resting on the youngest. He wondered if his baby Henrequitta would have been as appealing. It was hard to concentrate on the matters at hand; his morning dream seemed to have traumatized him for the day.

Back to business, he sternly commanded himself, and began by addressing young David. "What a great adventure your journey must have been," he said. "I am sure your youth and strength were a welcome support to your parents. Have you finished your education?"

"Only preparatory, sir," David answered. "I plan to enter Princeton College next year. That's in New Jersey," he added as an afterthought.

"Ah, yes. New Jersey, where you came from. I have never seen your great country, but I hope to visit there someday," the governor said wistfully.

Don Manuel then laid out the Natchez district map and, using a pointer, described its pattern which he defined as subdistricts. To the north were Big Black and Bayou Pierre, and in a southerly direction lay Cole's Creek, St. Catherine Creek, Second and Sandy Creeks, Homochitto River, and the combined settlements of Buffalo Creek, Bayou Sara, and Viejo Tunicas. The settlement grants began at the mouths of the bayous, tracing inland along the creeks. The soil was rich, water sufficient to grow plenty of crops, and timber plentiful to build a dwelling. All districts had good road access to Natchez town, which would serve as the center for crafts, merchandise, and business.

Colonel Forman requested time to see the terrain before choosing a location, but indicated he liked St. Catherine Creek area, not too far from town, where he could begin on a trial basis.

"One factor in my decision to locate near town is the need for roads wide enough to accommodate my coach-and-four," he added.

Don Manuel was impressed. He had heard of the yellow coach, the first to grace the district. He would have to widen the roads if more carriages arrived. The governor set aside 1,200 arpents for Colonel Forman, and pointed out the location of an empty house for lease that his family might use for temporary quarters.

As he accompanied the Formans to the door, the governor noted the small crowd in the reception room awaiting consultation. He requested introductions and Vidal introduced them by family groups. Don Manuel acknowledged them graciously, expressed regrets that they had to wait, and instructed Vidal to conduct those who had not yet taken the oath of allegiance to Colonel Grand-Pré's office. This left Adam and Mary, with Becky in her arms.

"Please enter my office and be seated," Don Manuel said. *A charming couple*, he thought to himself, *and what a beautiful child.*

Adam and Mary entered and seated themselves in the comfortable chairs, and Don Manuel sat informally in a chair near them.

"Mr. Cloud, and Mrs . . . ?" he said, looking at Mary. He had noticed a discrepancy in names.

"This is Miss Mary Grandin, Adam said. "She is my wife's sister. That is to say, my recent wife." He swallowed hard. "My dear wife, Anne, was taken ill on our journey, and the doctor could not save her from a deadly lung infection. The journey was too arduous for her. I had to bury her in Pittsburgh." He paused, regained his composure, and said, "This is my daughter, Becky."

"How very sad for all of you," Don Manuel said, feeling a special pang of sympathy. "How do you do, *Señorita* Grandin, and *Señorita* Becky." Becky squirmed on Mary's lap.

Mary answered, trying to ease the strain. "I came along for the adventure, and to be of help to my sister and the baby during the journey. I will return home when I have outworn my welcome." Don Manuel thought he saw a flash of regret in Mary's steady blue eyes, before she momentarily lowered her gaze.

"It is a pleasure to welcome you to our province. Perhaps you can be persuaded to remain." He smiled back at her. "May I extend my deepest sympathy in the loss of your sister," he turned to Adam, "and your wife. I, too, have suffered the loss of my wife and baby daughter a few months ago. My nights and days are often filled with feelings of guilt and melancholy since those events. The fatigue from the long, tiring voyage contributed to her contracting the terrible fever when we arrived in Natchez."

Don Manuel caught the look of dismay on their faces. "But that is enough of my troubles. Let us consider the new life ahead of us here . . . I have read your dossier; I know that you are a minister of a Protestant denomination, but I would like to know more. Tell me about yourself. Anything you like. I will be pleased to get better acquainted."

Adam was delighted with this polished, courteous man. He found him to be as cultivated as Wilkinson had described. He was thus reminded of the letter from Wilkinson, which he drew from his pocket and handed to the governor.

"This is by way of introduction from a mutual friend, Colonel James Wilkinson, whom we met in Louisville," Adam said. "For whatever it is worth, it was a kindly gesture on his part. The colonel spoke highly of you, and satisfied some of our curiosity about Natchez."

Don Manuel read the letter and said, "I would like to hear more of your meeting with him, but that can wait. Do go on with information about your own lives."

He sat back and watched them intently as Adam unfolded a brief story of his upbringing in Delaware, his schooling, and his father's shipyard in Wilmington. He touched lightly on his Methodist preaching experience.

"It's over now," he ended. "My decision to migrate to Natchez preempted my career toward the Anglican priesthood. I would have had to wait several years more, and prove myself before applying for higher ordination. Now I remain satisfied with being ordained a deacon."

"I am well acquainted with the Anglican service," Don Manuel said. "I attended Westminster College and went to student church services there. I thought the service very beautiful, much like our Catholic churches." He paused for reflection. "I found very little difference in the Christian doctrines, myself," he added, "other than some minor dogma and rituals."

Adam was astounded at this show of frankness and religious tolerance. He had expected a more rigid attitude, and could not help but add his own comment.

"Sir, I admire your liberal outlook on the depth and breadth of Christianity. I respect the fact that this is a Catholic nation, and I will always abide by the limits placed upon my own ministrations to Protestants who may request my services. I will be content to attend my land without the multiplicity of demands otherwise expected of a minister of the Gospel."

"I see we shall have to explore further our inner convictions," Don Manuel said. "But do go on. Is there anything else you wish to add to your history?"

"Only that I spent a year on the Grandin plantation learning how to be a planter. It was there I acquired my wife's three slaves. I'm looking forward to the new venture, and believe I will succeed here."

Don Manuel noted Mary's rapt attention to Adam's narrative. He felt a twinge of envy for Adam's good fortune to have such a delightful young sister-in-law and a baby to bring him solace. He thought the couple would make a perfect match. He liked them instinctively.

Wilkinson's letter could be taken with a grain of salt, but it did apprise him that here was a man of recognized gentility and education, and probably well worth knowing. In Gayoso's opinion, Adam Cloud qualified as a borderline applicant. His three slaves were hardly adequate for his venture as a planter; he would identify more as a yeoman, and he certainly had not been reared as a farmer. In all fairness, though, he thought Adam should get more land than a family with no slaves. He decided to wait and see what Adam could do with his land allotment. He could grant more land if he proved worthy.

"With such determination," Don Manuel said, "there is no reason that you should not succeed. Now, let us look into a land grant for you."

They then pored over the maps and statistics of the different locales. Adam selected a plot on St. Catherine Creek, about two miles from town. The governor told him it was close to the area Colonel Forman had selected.

"Please look over the location carefully before you submit your application," Don Manuel said. "If you change your mind, do not hesitate to let me know and we can consider another one. Our official surveyor is William Vousdan, whose property is across the trail from the property you have chosen. I will acquaint him with your choice. He will lay out the property for a modest fee, and Colonel Grand-Pré will record the plat. The property is allotted on a fee simple basis. There are no feudal rights, and no noblesse." He paused and smiled. "I am pleased to grant you two hundred and forty arpents; six arpents of fine frontage on Santa Catalina Creek, and forty arpents continuance back from the frontage."

"That seems very generous, sir." Adam was glowing inwardly over his good fortune.

The governor explained that there were regulations concerning land development. Owners were not permitted to sell a grant for at least three years, and only if the required improvements had been made. He could obtain printed copies of the regulations from Colonel Grand-Pré when he recorded the grant.

"Do you have any questions?" Don Manuel asked, as he concluded his instructions.

"Only one, just now. Do you know where I can locate my family so that we may leave the riverboat?"

"Of course, you need temporary lodging. There is a good family, named Perkins, who indicated willingness to house incoming settlers until they can provide a home of their own. They have very productive acreage not far from your chosen area. Their home is spacious and probably would accommodate the three of you."

"I will be living with the Formans," Mary said. "Colonel Forman is a distant cousin of my family, by marriage."

What a pity; they belong together, Don Manuel thought to himself, but aloud he said, "Of course, *Señor* Cloud, I will give you a message to the Perkinses and hope that you can make satisfactory arrangements for accommodations." He scribbled a brief note, handed it to Adam, and added, "One of my clerks can give you directions to their plantation."

Adam again expressed appreciation for the generous land grant, and for the property information. The governor rose, extended his hand to Adam, and smiled broadly.

"I wish you well, that you prosper and learn to love the land, and that you enjoy the beneficent life here as citizens of New Spain."

He bent over Mary's hand, lightly brushed it with his lips, and said, "*Señorita*, I hope you will extend your visit to permanent citizenship of this country. You are a most welcome guest."

Gayoso interviewed the remaining families in turn, parceling out land to the Grassleys in the Homochitto River area. He appraised them as a closely knit, congenial group, born and bred on farmland, with a growing brood of children. He believed they would do well in the more distant location, which needed more population. The Swayzes were there with some of their friends from New Jersey, and the Grassleys, he reasoned, should feel right at home in what was called "The Jersey Settlement."

The governor located Preece and Carter in communities which were crying out for mechanics and dressmakers. He placed the Preeces at St. Catherine Creek, close to Natchez. He could open shop on a town lot already designated for tradesmen. The Carters he placed at Cole's Creek, where there were already some fifty families.

Adam and Mary left the governor with light hearts. Not only had Adam received a large land grant, but they were favorably impressed with Gayoso. An orderly directed them to take the Natchez Trace, the only road east from town.

They mounted their horses and, with Becky tucked in front of Adam's saddle, rode toward the Perkins plantation. The narrow, powder-soft trail led them silently through the surrounding forest.

"I'm glad we have only several miles to go," Mary said. "I'm trying not to think of Dusty's horror tales of this notorious path."

"I wouldn't worry," Adam replied. "This trail is used daily by residents, judging by the plantation roads marked along the way. I wonder where my property begins. Ah, here is the gate."

Joseph and Sarah Perkins were an older couple, kind and unpretentious. They showed genuine pleasure in the opportunity to assist newcomers, and invited Adam and Mary to share their midday meal. Adam found Sarah Perkins' manner warm and motherly, and her husband's frank and friendly. Six of their children still lived at home. The family had migrated with a group of Baptist families from South Carolina, in 1780, before the Spanish had set up a workable government in Natchez.

Adam was pleased to accept temporary lodging for Becky and him. Becky would be in good hands, Sarah Perkins assured him, and would become part of the family while he built his own home. Adam thanked Mr. and Mrs. Perkins for their kindness, and asked directions to the surveyor's home.

"Just below here, and across the road from your property," Joseph Perkins said. "William Vousdan may not take kindly to your good fortune. He has been after your property for years."

"Why hasn't he obtained it if he wants it so badly?" Adam asked.

"He claims that Colonel Grand-Pré promised it to him for his survey services before Governor Gayoso came. I don't know why he didn't get it, but he has always proclaimed loudly that it should be his."

"Well, I hope I don't get into trouble with him," Adam said with a sigh. "I can't help it if he didn't obtain it. The property is free and clear, and the governor has set it aside for me."

In the next few days, with Mary's help, Adam moved his belongings into the Perkins home. Maamba, Dirk, and Tizzi moved in with the Perkinses' slaves, and the Clouds became part of the Perkins household.

Adam located William Vousdan's property on the Trace, with the gate marked "Cotton Fields." He discovered the surveyor's land also straddled both sides of St. Catherine Creek. The plantation looked prosperous, with slaves preparing the soil for the spring crop. Adam rode to the house and saw a tall, lean man, with thinning hair, watching him from the porch.

"Good afternoon, sir. Are you Mr. Vousdan?" The man uttered a noncommittal grunt, and Adam continued. "I am Adam Cloud, your new neighbor across the road. I understand you are an official surveyor, and I hope you can survey my land grant. As you can see, I will have two hundred and forty arpents nearby." He handed him the property description.

Adam looked the man over while he read the paper. Vousdan's face was long and pinched, his countenance reflecting a sour mood. He looked downright mean. Adam had a fleeting impression that he might have interrupted an unpleasant occurrence. When Vousdan returned the paper, Adam noted that an agitated pink suffused his unhealthy skin.

"I usually work by appointment," he said. "I haven't had word yet from Governor Gayoso that you were ready for a survey."

"I'm sorry to surprise you," Adam said graciously. "Most of my time has been taken up with my move into living quarters at the Perkins plantation. I am so anxious to see the property I guess I simply bypassed the proper arrangements. If you could take the time today, I would like to have, at least, a general idea of the terrain."

"I guess I can show you a rough layout of your property."

Adam thought the reply sounded begrudging.

Vousdan called to a servant in a curt and impatient manner, and ordered his horse brought around. His temperament did not improve until they rode out the gate, crossed the deeply rutted Trace, and reached the end of Vousdan's property line across from where Adam's began. They traced the creek frontage and rode south, then east into the forest in an imaginary rectangle covering approximately half the depth of forty arpents. They finally arrived back at the frontage point again.

Even though he did not see it all, Adam was pleased with the terrain. His property rose from the creek in a gentle slope to a large, pleasant meadow dotted sparsely with trees. A towering forest lay beyond the meadow. He would have to plan the removal of trees very carefully to accommodate his house somewhere on the hill.

Adam was overwhelmed with the abundance of wild growth which would have to be cleared. Thick cane grew along the creek bed and between trees and shrubs. A tangled curtain of vines ran along the ground and upward, entwining everything in their path. Vousdan pointed out wild begonia, grape and coloquintada vines. Heavy and tangled as the vegetation was, Adam thought the effect one of surprising beauty. White drifts of flowering dogwood trees brightened the forest, dotted here and there with redbud, resplendent in their prime. Surrounding trees stretched to dizzying heights, and profuse masses of long, gray moss hung from the boughs. Vousdan named maple, elm, locust, sycamore, oak, and magnolia. There were many more, and Adam was sure Mary could list them all.

"How does one get through this heavy cane?" Adam asked. "It's removal looks to be quite a formidable undertaking."

"That'll be the most difficult part of your clearance work," Vousdan answered. "We use edge tools, and it will take a lot of strong arms and backs to clear away as much as your six acres of frontage will require. We burn the cane when it's too thick and plentiful to cut. Yours is mild growth compared to some I've had to cut through."

Vousdan offered only as much information as Adam requested. They set the day and time for the survey, and Adam left with an uneasy feeling that Vousdan would be uncooperative. He hoped he was a good surveyor, for he himself could be easily fooled by markers laid out for his land grant.

Adam would have been even more uneasy if he could have observed Vousdan's reaction and read his thoughts. Vousdan rode back to his plantation in a silent rage. This young tenderfoot was getting the parcel of land he had wanted for the past two years. He had planned to clear it, hold it for the three-year waiting period, and sell if for a good profit.

He thought he had a tacit understanding with Grand-Pré that he would earn extra land as a perquisite for his services. He still felt Governor Gayoso's stinging reply when he had asked for the new land grant. "What would you do with more property, Vousdan? You haven't cultivated or used all you have now." The governor had left him seething with hatred and humiliation.

Vousdan rode out to the bare field where slaves were tilling the soil. The winter ground was still too hard to turn but, seeing the skimpy rows, Vousdan deliberately picked a quarrel with his overseer, venting his rage on the man for the shallow ruts. He added a number of unrelated peccadilloes invented on the spot to show his displeasure.

"Get those lazy bastards to turn up the soil!" he shouted. "Give 'em plenty of lashes to do the work right."

The overseer cracked his whip at the blacks, cursing right and left, until he thought Vousdan was satisfied.

. . .

Adam rode Lancer to the landing and found Dusty and several companions breaking up flatboats. He was surprised that Dusty had procured a second boat for him, and was pleased with the stacks of excellent lumber. He made arrangements to hire a guard to protect his lumber from night pilfering until he could arrange for its delivery. Dusty agreed not only to deliver the lumber, but offered to help Adam clear his land.

Adam stopped at the Formans' newly rented house on the cliff road above the landing. Eliza and Mary were engaged in getting the household settled, and Aunt Betsey supervised the laundering and mending of clothes. The family gathered eagerly around Adam while he gave them an enthusiastic report of his brief property survey. Adam left satisfied that Mary was in good hands.

He then rode to Government House, where he filed his land grant petition and a survey request. He received property instruction sheets with tips on finding laborers, specifications for land development, drainage methods, sources of materials available for construction of houses and levees. On his way out he met Governor Gayoso in the reception room.

"Ah, *Señor* Cloud," Gayoso's voice had a cheery ring. "How are things progressing for you and your daughter? Come in for a bit and tell me if you need any more information."

Adam entered the office while the governor gave his orderlies some commands. He then turned his full attention to Adam, who described what he had accomplished so far, and mentioned that his survey would begin in a few days.

Sensing a shade of harassment in Adam's voice, Don Manuel said soothingly, "You have done well with the kind of help you have assembled. Some of these boatmen can clear land in good time, but others are quite lazy and worthless when it comes to honest labor. I hope you have the best."

"I trust Dusty for choosing good workmen," Adam said, "and Colonel Forman offered to loan me some of his slaves if I need them."

"You'll probably need them. By the way, I'm planning an event at my home next Sunday for the newest settlers in town. You can meet your neighbors and other successful planters. I hope you will come for the afternoon and early supper. My secretary is just now writing the invitations, and I will see that he hands you yours." He smiled and added, "Miss Grandin is invited also."

Adam left the governor, elated at the pleasant turn of events. Turning Lancer toward home, he mused on his good fortune. Bless Anne's dear mother for her generosity, he thought. How would he have managed with only his stipend from home to fall back on? He recalled his former years of privation as an itinerant preacher, and smiled when he compared his relatively smooth life then with what he was trying to accomplish now. While Anne's inheritance was now his, he hoped fervently that he could soon get by without dipping into her funds, or needing more shipyard profits. What irony to lose his wife, he mused, yet gain more than he deserved in worldly goods.

He rendered a fervent prayer, accepting God's will and asking that he be worthy of whatever He would bestow on him. *But please, God,* he begged, *no more tragic deaths!*

9 Who's Who

O n the appointed Sunday, Adam arrived on horseback at Governor Gayoso's home just in time to witness the grand entrance of Colonel Forman's coach. An array of ladies and gentlemen were also arriving on horses, or in small, crude carriages, in a confusion of bustle and chatter. A line of smartly clad black grooms whisked away the horses and vehicles to the stables.

Drawing the four matched bays to a smooth halt, Moses stopped the Forman coach in front of the portico. A coachman swung down, placed the stepping block, and opened the coach door.

Adam was amused at the spectators' excited comments over the handsome carriage. With its heavy coach springs, yellow body and black trim, it made a lasting impression on the governor's elite guests. All eyes were on the occupants as Ezekiel, Eliza, David, and Mary emerged. Adam thought, with amusement, that the king and queen of England couldn't have made a more elegant entrance. He dismounted and proffered a hand to Mary. She stepped to the carriage block and looked about her, commenting on the ladies' simple gowns, colorful parasols and sun vizards.

Adam took stock of the gentlemen's attire and liked what he saw. Waistcoats and breeches were of serge or corduroy, worn in a careless, half sailor-like air. Coats were loosely buttoned, showing white cotton shirts and simple jabots. All wore low, broad-brimmed hats of white beaver, felt, or woven Havana fiber. Their dress style matched the planters' easy, careless horsemanship, with bridles thrown across the horse's neck, or over the high pommel of a handsome Spanish saddle.

Adam offered Mary his arm and accompanied the Formans to the wide gallery.

"Welcome, my friends," the governor greeted them graciously. Adam thought their host's taste well suited to his station — garments elegant but simply embellished with a bit of lace on jabot and cuffs, his coat studded with handsome buttons. He wore his hair in smooth side-rolls coifed at midear. Adam looked at Colonel Forman's unimaginative style, typical for a Northern lawyer, his plain black coat buttoned under his chin, straight trousers, and narrow hat. His costume was a total contrast to that of the easy, nonchalant Southern planters, and Adam expected Forman would order a new wardrobe first thing in the morning.

Their host introduced everyone in both English and Spanish equivalents of their surnames. "Natchez tends to be informal," he explained. "We use the title 'Don' before our given names. I am called Don Manuel on private social occasions. Please mingle and get acquainted here on the verandah or out under the trees."

After introductions, Adam tried to remember names, and during the evening singled out individual guests that impressed him. He already knew Maj. Stephen Minor, Colonel Grand-Pré and William Vousdan, and soon could identify their wives. He met an attractive couple, John and Virginia Bowles, who lived on property adjacent to his, and another nearby couple, Job and Lydia Corey. James and Beth Moore were especially friendly and said their Linden plantation was beyond the Perkins home. Adam welcomed reunion with Theo and Will Minor and their wives, and Lank and Liz Preece.

The local parish priest, Father William Savage, approached Adam, bowed slightly, and said, "With an active past in the ministry, I expect you will miss your church affairs, Reverend Cloud. Please know that you are genuinely welcome to participate in the Roman Catholic services as our guest, at any time."

"Thank you. I will look forward to attending one of your services," Adam said with as much tact as he could display. "Yes, I shall miss our church rituals, but mostly I shall miss the opportunity to provide full service to those who need me. I am not sure what my options are among your rules and edicts."

Father Savage continued as if Adam had not spoken. "We hope you will encourage all those in need of succor to turn to our parish church. They can receive special counseling services, and every attention to their spiritual needs. Our church is open to receive everyone."

"Thank you," Adam said with stiff politeness. He noticed that his query had been ignored.

At dusk, the guests enjoyed a light supper at tables placed along the gallery. Adam gleaned information from conversations around him, and quizzed himself on the names and faces he could identify.

After supper the ladies retired to a separate parlor, leaving the men at table. A servant offered the gentlemen Havana cigars from a richly tooled leather box. Ezekiel and Adam sat with Don Manuel between them.

"Most of the guests live within a few miles of Natchez," Don Manuel explained. "The one exception is Sir William Dunbar and his wife, who are my overnight guests. They traveled up yesterday from Thompson's Creek, some nine miles to the south."

Adam glanced at the distinguished elderly gentleman down the table length, while Don Manuel described him. He learned that Dunbar was one of the first settlers in the province, descended from Scottish nobility. He had begun with the manufacture of barrel staves for the West Indian market. His enormous acreage now under cultivation produced indigo, among other crops.

Adam listened intently as the planters discussed the problems of getting settled, and he stored as much knowledge of the environment as he could absorb. He learned that the best times to purchase new slaves were February and March, to be ready for planting, or August and September for harvesting. Dunbar said he had written a treatise on how to grow indigo. Others offered advice on growing tobacco and rice, and pointed out unique uses for native plants. The abundant gray moss could be dried and used for stuffing chair pads and mattresses; the sugar-tree pods were good fodder for swine.

"That cane may seem a nuisance," John Bowles offered, "but its uses are almost limitless. We use it as cattle feed, to make chairs, looms, stakes, torches, woven carriage seats . . ."

"Not to forget cane makes the best trout fishing rods," Don Manuel added. He smiled and cast an imaginary line.

"How about tobacco?" Ezekiel asked. "I heard that it is your most profitable crop."

"The tobacco news is good," Job Corey said. "The king issued a decree last year that the government would buy up all the tobacco we could grow. So this year everyone is expanding tobacco production. I'm doubling my crop."

Adam recalled Colonel Wilkinson's explanation, that the urgency of American frontier growers to sell tobacco to the Spanish was the bone of contention between them. He thought it paradoxical that he could benefit from dependency on a royal decree, when he had lived through a revolution to be free of such royal whims. It was also a paradox, he thought, that the new American freedoms do not include the benefits of trading on the Western frontier.

"How is the fishing and hunting?" Adam asked.

"There's just about every kind of game you could want for your table," Stephen Minor said. "The forests are full of squirrel, mink, 'possum, raccoons, small foxes, and deer."

"The bears are mild-tempered and easily routed," Job Corey offered. "They're not as dangerous as wolves and panthers."

"If you want waterfowl or shellfish you can find them at any of the bayous and streams," James Moore said. "There are also otters and several kinds of turtles."

To Adam's dismay, he learned that the Natchez district had no stones, not even a pebble. Those who could afford them had to import them from the Big Black River.

"You will have to wait awhile for good bricks too," Colonel Grand-Pré interjected, then paused to puff on his briar pipe. "We can't get the lime to mix with them. Of course, you can settle for mud bricks, which stand up pretty well. The early French built some houses here of *bousiage*, a brick made from ground shells and mud. They plastered them over with a smooth finish, and they still look quite good. You may have noticed the same finish inside Government House."

Most of the settlers said they started out with the crudest of cabins, but were gradually refining and adding to them. All agreed that a framed, raised cottage proved cooler, freer from ground moisture, and provided more protection from insects. Some men offered to rent their slaves for clearing and building.

"I look forward to starting my house," Adam said. "It's been a long while since I used building tools. My father owns a shipyard, and I grew up around craftsmen. They taught me how to use every kind of tool, and I enjoyed doing some of the finishing work with my hands. My older brother, Robert, is a ship architect. He's a master builder, and is always devising new ways to build better parts. He worked out an elegant precision method of securing ship joints that is used on all of our ships."

The others showed interest in his ship-building experience, and urged Adam to describe Robert's new joint precision method. When he finished, Richard King spoke up. Adam recalled he was a former ship's captain who owned the only tavern in Upper Natchez.

"I built my tavern entirely by shipwright methods. You must visit me and see my handiwork," King said.

Don Manuel announced that he had selected a site for his new home in the forest, about two miles east of the fort.

Stephen Watts, owner of Belmont Plantation, south of Natchez, announced that he had found a site for the proposed new racetrack. Another man mentioned that the Choctaws would soon peacefully invade Natchez to collect their annual presents granted by the Crown. Adam learned that dates of slave auctions and other public notices were posted outside Government House.

"Speaking of important events," Don Manuel said, "I'm planning a public ceremony on The Commons soon, to celebrate the planting of chinaberry trees now under way."

Adam left the gathering feeling fortunate to have so many solicitous, kind neighbors and potential friends. He thanked the host, said good night to Mary and the Formans, and headed home with Joseph and Sarah Perkins.

The next few weeks Adam's days were filled with frenzied hard labor — clearing the creek frontage and widening the meadow for spring planting. With the borrowed Perkins wagon, Adam and Dirk drove Dusty and three boatmen from King's Tavern to the clearing site. They pitched the tents Adam had saved from the journey, providing a camp where the boatmen would stay the next few weeks. Each morning, carrying food, guns, and an array of knives, machetes, and ropes, the men hacked through the dense cane, some of it thirty feet tall.

Toiling beside the workmen, Adam cut his share of cane, fiercely slashing and flailing the axe and machete at the stubborn, thick stalks. For the first time in his life he experienced the physical satisfaction of hurling his sheer brute force at natural obstacles. The days grew warmer and humid, and the men shed their shirts.

The work became a nightmare for Adam; perspiration poured into his eyes and down his bare chest. Their body sweat began to attract spring insects, and the men fought off swarms of gnats and white flies. As they advanced through the lower creek areas, the swampy ground squished underfoot where they trod on a multitude of toads and frogs.

But they were winning, Adam thought with satisfaction, as he surveyed their progress each day. The heaviest cane sections were burned on the spot. Cut cane was stacked into huge piles, and the men stood back to watch Dusty set them afire. In a ritual of primitive jubilance, like a warrior ravaging an enemy village, Dusty would hoist a flaming torch and touch it to a canestack.

"Start yer trotters!" he would shout. With a mighty roar the fire exploded and Dusty would yell, "Take cover! Hell's a snortin'!" Everyone ran for cover and lay flat as the explosions burst in rapid succession. Flames leaped to the highest tree tops, catching some on fire.

Adam's first weeks of toil were physical agony. Every muscle and bone in his body ached and throbbed at night. Maamba prepared hot soaking tubs, and gave him vigorous rub-downs with bear's oil. His little daughter rubbed him in sympathy, her tiny hands tickling his sensitive skin. Becky would kiss an arm or a finger and say, "Make Papa well." But gradually he became accustomed to the labor, and little by little the cane was subdued. He then turned the men to clearing trees.

The boatmen's vigor and fortitude were astounding, and Adam knew Dusty had selected the best among them. Two brothers, Calvin and Drake, and Shorty, an older man, had been reared in frontier woods where their families had confronted similar clearing problems. Years on the rivers had not erased their ability to adapt to hard labor. Adam made sure their wages doubled their meager river profits.

One day, working in the field, Adam heard the familiar sound of the Forman carriage on his road. He pulled on his shirt and ran to greet them. As they alighted from the coach, Eliza and Mary laughed at his grimy face. He grinned, drew out a handkerchief, and wiped his face and hands.

"My friend, you have too little help to get your fields in shape," Ezekiel said. "It will take you until Christmas at this pace. Let me send you some of my workers."

"I must admit things aren't going very fast. I knew I wouldn't get to plant this year's tobacco crop," Adam said. "But I do want to clear enough meadow to grow some quick cash crops, like Indian corn and melons, maybe pumpkins, squash over the summer. I'll accept your offer if I can pay for your slave labor."

"Not a chance," Ezekiel said emphatically. "Your success is important to me, now that I got you here. What do you think, ladies? Can he get a first crop in before summer?"

Mary watched two mules struggle at the ropes, as they uprooted a stump. "Adam can do almost anything he sets his mind to," she answered, "but there is a limit how much nature will cooperate. I'll pray for good weather, Adam. And, if you want me to, I'll ride out to see you once in a while. I miss Becky, too, and plan to visit her at the Perkinses'. "

"That will be good for Becky, Mary. I'm so tired when I get home at night that just lifting her feels like a ton of stones. She needs me, I know, and I feel badly about being away from her so much, but the harder and faster I work, the sooner we can be together in our own home." He smiled at Mary and made an exaggerated bow. "Your presence and your prayers will be my salvation, m'lady." He hoped she would return soon. Somehow he felt she might bring him luck.

Mary came often by horseback, accompanied by David for protection, and Adam looked forward to seeing them ride up to the clearing site. One day Mary helped Adam choose the site for his house. After examining the location of the trees on the hillside, Mary suggested placing the house at the top of the rise.

"The trees will act as a buffer, and the house will be a safe distance from the trail. Besides, if you build it up there, you can see both the creek and the back meadow, providing a double view."

"Now that's a splendid suggestion," Adam admired her judgment. "Let's pace it off up there and see how the house would fit."

They walked up to the site and Adam scratched his house measurements in the dirt. "The foundation should fit here by removing only two trees," he said.

"Don't let anything happen to that enormous, beautiful magnolia tree, Adam. It will stand right in front of the house, like a sentinel. Becky can learn to climb on it. The house will nestle up here between the tallest trees, surrounded by the dogwood and blooming vines. Oh, Adam, how lovely it will be." Mary's eyes shone with the vision.

The clearing went faster with the help of sixteen Forman slaves. Using axe and froe, they chopped and sawed through the meadow and surrounding forest, saving selected timber for building and fencing purposes, chopping some for fuel, and burning the rest with the uprooted stumps. A large section of land was finally ready for tilling.

Adam returned the boatmen to King's Tavern to rest before they began their long journey home. The Trace began at the tavern, trailing due east into the woods, and then northeast to Nashborough, the nearest habitation on the north Cumberland plateau.

Laying a hand on Dusty's broad shoulder, Adam smiled warmly. "I'm going to miss you, Dusty. Be sure to let me know when you are in Natchez again. God's blessing go with you." He shook hands with Calvin, Drake, and Shorty.

"It'll be a few months before we make another tradin' deal and git back," Dusty said, "but I'll come see yer new house, you kin be sure."

Adam felt respect and affectionate regard for these stout frontier men, and he was genuinely fond of Dusty. Their colorful language and ever-ready sense of humor eased them through any situation, no matter how difficult, and Adam thought their exaggerated tales of exploits were outrageously funny.

The Forman slaves leveled the site for Adam's house, cleared more land along the creek, and fenced the required frontage. On the chosen site, Adam and Dirk erected a cabin, with the help of his neighbors, John Bowles and Joseph Perkins. Mary followed every aspect of the construction, admiring Adam's handiwork.

Adam used carefully hewn logs for the lower half of the cabin. The upper half he framed with adz-hewn planks in clapboard fashion, adding a dressy finish. He used scrap lumber from the boats for floors and inner walls. The cabin design, called two-pens-and-a-passage, had been suggested at Gayoso's party. It consisted of two small cabins, connected by a breezeway and fronted with a covered gallery, or verandah. The simple design would provide cool areas in summer. The separated side-wing afforded space for temporary slave quarters. Adam expected to acquire more slaves soon. They would build their cabins, sheds for livestock, and pens and runways for pigs and fowl.

Becky was the center of attraction at the Perkins house. Not only did Maamba and Tizzi care for her, but the Perkins children adored her. For diversion, Mary often took Becky home to visit the Formans. One day, accompanied by David, she rode with Becky to Adam's house. They found Adam on his knees flooring the gallery.

"Come join us, Adam," Mary called out. "We're going to pick strawberries. Take a rest, and let's have a lark."

Becky shrieked with joy and clung to Adam's neck, as he took her in his arms. "I've missed you, Becky," her father said. "Did you have fun with Aunt Mary?"

"Betsee, Betsee," she chanted in sing-song.

"Aunt Betsey really tickles her fancy," Mary explained. "She amuses her with funny faces."

"Aunt Betsey has a way with children," David said. "She always made us laugh with her antics."

"Thanks for the invitation, but I want to finish this last few feet of flooring," Adam said. "You go on and pick strawberries. There are loads of them in the second meadow. I should be finished by the time you fill your baskets."

Mary hid her disappointment, but settled Becky on her saddle again. Adam watched them ride across the tilled fields toward a meadow beyond the first woods. "Be careful out there," he called. "Watch for bears and anything else that moves."

As Mary rode across the field at a careful, slow trot, he recalled the first time he saw her, a young girl in her teens, wildly racing her horse up the carriage drive at the Grandin plantation. She had teased him about his preacher's garb, and he had bandied some gay repartee. From that day on he had teased her when he stopped at Belview Manor, always certain of her good nature and her tinkling laugh. She still possessed a full-blown zest for everything in life, he decided, but she had learned to tone her zeal for the sake of others. She had become a mature and balanced lady.

Within an hour the three returned, greatly disturbed that their berry-picking had been interrupted by a mother bear and cub, intent upon sharing the berry crop. Mary and David collapsed on the verandah steps to calm down, while Adam gently rocked Becky in his arms to restore her confidence.

Mary gazed absently into the yard. Mixed fragrances from blooming, cascading vines invaded her senses. Her eyes traced their intricate winding paths upward through shiny new leaves feathering the trees. Silently, she saluted the magnificent magnolia tree in front as an old friend. Its dense branches lent an air of stability, and the large, white flowers filled the air with perfume. Mary visualized life there after Adam and Becky moved in, her mind ever churning out plans for Adam.

She turned to him, her eyes dancing with excitement. "I have a name for your home, Adam — 'Cloudcrest.' It's on the crest of the hill, and you can use your family crest on the gate sign."

Adam laughed. "That's a pretty fancy name for a cabin, Mary, but I like it. 'Cloudcrest' it shall be."

"Have you thought about a second fence up here, Adam? Becky will need a secure place to play when she is able to run about. A fenced-off area could enclose a flower garden and a play yard for Becky."

"She could swing from the magnolia tree," David said.

"I would suggest the tree be trimmed and a large table and benches be set beneath it," Mary offered.

"You think of everything, Mary. How did you learn to be so practical? David, I'll let you hang the swing."

"Every home needs a woman's touch," Mary said, "and if you would like, I'll help get you settled. I can put your home in convenient and attractive order for you and Becky."

Adam had a warm sense of happiness. His heart swelled with a tremendous love and appreciation for Mary and David. He felt them bound irrevocably to him forever.

"You are too good to me," he said. "You are spoiling me, you know. But, of course, I accept your help."

Riding back to the Forman home, David looked keenly at Mary, and surprised her with a question. "The way you're carrying on with Adam's new house, one would think you're planning to live there yourself. Are you just being bossy, or do you have designs on Adam? You can tell me. I'm your best friend."

"Best friends don't jump to conclusions," Mary retorted. "I'm just trying to help him forget the past by showing interest in his and Becky's future, that's all."

David saw her blush. He realized she was less indignant than she was embarrassed. She didn't fool him.

10 Andrew Jackson

Mary began listing household necessities for Adam's home and sent him in search of merchandise to fill the orders. Returning home from King's Tavern one day, Adam saw a large band of people emerging on foot from the distant forest. Curious, he dismounted and waited in front of the tavern. As they drew nearer he saw the first few were an assortment of white men and women, several on horseback. A large group of blacks brought up the rear. Adam stood transfixed, remembering Dusty's tales about groups traveling the Trace.

Those in the vanguard moved slowly at first, but seeing the distant tavern, they quickened the pace. Those on horseback trotted ahead. One was a gentleman, sitting tall in the saddle in military style. He was accompanied by a black slave on foot, who tried to keep up as his master galloped toward the tavern. A group of trappers and hunters walked together, their bundled belongings piled on a dray dragged by a horse. Two peddlers followed, their drays loaded with pots, kettles, knives, and assorted dry goods. They were a disheveled pair, their clothes askew, but each wore a small, stiff black hat, which added a semblance of dignity.

The blacks in the rear drew Adam's interest. He estimated there were about thirty, of various ages. They walked slowly, footsore and weary, their bare feet shuffling in funeral procession. Their somber garments were tattered, loosely hung pantaloons and shifts, barely covering parts of their otherwise naked bodies. Four small boys and two girls walked together, holding ragged blankets as if ready to place them down for a rest. One ebony woman leaned against a tall young mulatto man. A woman holding a tiny infant repeatedly glanced back at a narrow, canopied, horse-driven cart which followed behind. Adam could see several sickly looking Negroes resting inside.

Behind them rode a white man, his lean body held easily erect on a handsome pacer, his reins thrown over the pommel of a hand-tooled Spanish saddle. He wore the traditional soft buckskin jacket and breeches of a frontier hunter, and a wide-brimmed black felt hat, cocked jauntily to one side. Underneath shone a wealth of long, thick, sandy-red hair, and a short stubble of untended whiskers. His saddlebags bulged. His gun lay carelessly across the pommel. Adam saw the handles of a pistol and dirk tucked under his belt.

Some of the first arrivals entered the tavern. The others continued toward town and the Lower Natchez road. The first blacks reached the tavern and waited in a disorganized group. Adam was startled when several slaves approached him and asked for tobacco. He looked at their weary, sweaty faces and wished he could accommodate them. The young gentleman drew his horse beside Adam and gazed directly down with intense deep-blue eyes. Adam judged him to be in his early twenties.

With an engaging smile, the stranger said, "It's a fine bunch of 'swan skins' I have here. Don't let their condition deceive you. We've come a long way. Everyone's exhausted."

"It was quite a sight to see you emerge from the woods," Adam said. "I congratulate you for your fortitude in bringing so many blacks under your care. Have you made the journey before?"

"A number of times," the young man answered. "The last time I was here I set up a trading post on my land at Bruinsburg. I'm Andrew Jackson, from the Cumberland." He extended his hand.

Adam responded with a shake. "Adam Cloud, new immigrant from Delaware," he said, "just getting settled at St. Catherine Creek. Are your slaves to be sold individually, or are you fulfilling a large order?"

"These will be offered at auction day after next, Under-the-Hill," Jackson answered. He motioned the slaves to walk ahead, and Adam remounted Lancer. They rode slowly across town behind the blacks, as Jackson continued. "One slave is a runaway that I'm returning to Governor Gayoso, at the request of Colonel Robertson." Seeing a blank look on Adam's face, he explained. "Colonel Robertson is a builder of Fort Nash, and pioneer leader of the Cumberland. He has probably done more to fight Indians and carve a place for the settlers around the Cumberland River than anyone.

"Some of the blacks were ordered by the Greens. They are a family here — Colonel Thomas Green, a widower with several sons and a daughter, each with a plantation. I stay at the home of Abner Green, a few miles up the Trace near Bruinsburg, where I plan to build a cabin near my trading post. The colonel is an old-time settler who tangled with the Spanish government."

"Why was that?" Adam asked.

"A few years back, he supported an American attempt to take over Spanish land. He was named commissioner of a proposed new American county on the Yazoo River, on land claimed by Georgia. They were going to call it Bourbon County, but the Spanish were not amused. He was actually incarcerated at New Orleans for disloyalty. I guess he was since forgiven, for he holds a place of high esteem here."

Adam recalled that letters from a Col. Thomas Green had tempted Ezekiel Forman to come to Natchez. "The arms of the land-hungry are indeed long," he said. "We saw the American colony at Walnut Hills that is trying to get Spanish land."

Jackson gave a wry smile. "That's a different claim, but I'll explain. I have studied law, and the Georgia case is one that interested me."

Georgia's claim to the land, he explained, began with its English charter which gave Georgia title to all the land from the Seaboard to the Mississippi, below the Yazoo River, which rises in Georgia. The river was named for the Yazous Indians, and it would be the subject of a long controversy, aptly called the "Yazooz Speculation," over the lands bordering its banks. Georgia gave up its claim to the settlement, but not to the original land title.

"The case is under study in the courts, and it will probably be a long time before it's cleared one way or another," Jackson continued. "To complicate matters further, Georgia sold the settlement rights to South Carolina speculators in 1789, and the settlement had new sponsors."

"I hope the land squabble doesn't reverberate down here and cause trouble in Natchez. I'm beginning to wonder how stable this place is," Adam said. They had reached the plaza, and Adam added, "I'll leave you here, Mister Jackson, and will plan to attend your slave auction. Good day, sir."

Jackson tipped his hat brim and headed his charges toward the cliff road to Lower Natchez.

Adam turned back toward the Trace again and rode home in deep thought. He recognized his need for slaves, yet he felt guilty at using other human beings to do his bidding without remuneration or reward. If they were free, he wondered, what future could slaves have in a strange land without survival knowledge? And yet, his man Dirk was unusually intelligent, learned quickly, and certainly showed he could think for himself. Maamba and Tizzi were devoted servants, competent and loyal, first to the Grandin family, and now to him. He trusted them with his most precious treasures, his daughter and his home; he hoped they might someday be ready for freedom.

Lower Natchez stirred with a crowd of men when Adam and Joseph Perkins arrived at the slave auction in Perkins' wagon. Held under a covered warehouse, the auction attracted settlers from miles around. Adam met most of the plantation gentry of Natchez that day. Perkins threaded through the crowd, introducing him to the men as he stopped to talk.

The auctioneer described, in crude terms, each slave brought before him. Scrubbed and river-cleaned, their polished skin gave them a healthy glow. The tall, lanky Andrew Jackson, now clean-shaven and freshly clothed, his sandy-red hair tied neatly in a queue under his jaunty black hat, moved in and out of the crowd, extolling the slaves' good points and joining the auctioneer as he began his pitch. Adam's stomach felt queasy as he watched the Negroes, all sizes and shades, and both sexes, being offered one by one. Wrestling with his conscience, Adam thought of his new farming plans. He spoke to Joseph Perkins and John Bowles standing beside him.

"This is my first slave auction, and I'm not sure I can bring myself to purchase another human being," he said.

"You'll get used to it," John Bowles said. "Just look at it this way — owning slaves is the free man's right to prosper on the land. Everyone justifies his conscience with that truism."

In the end, Adam purchased four slaves, three male fieldhands, and one female, salving his conscience "for the sake of building our future," he reasoned. He would treat them well, and vowed they would thrive under his care. At the completion of the sales, he was careful to record officially a designated limit to the years of servitude for each, and a manumission date.

The settlers lingered in the warehouse in convivial conversation long after the auction was over. Andrew Jackson joined Adam and a group of planters.

"Congratulations on your fine selection of slaves, Mister Cloud," he said. "I hope they prove the best of workers. Come with me," he added, "I want you to meet some of the settlers from up-country. You might as well get acquainted as widely as possible."

Adam followed Jackson across the room to a lively group of men roaring with laughter. "Mister Cloud is a new settler, gentlemen," Jackson said. "Meet Mr. Pedro Bruin, Cato West, and the Green brothers, Abner, from Bruinsburg, and the younger Thomas Green from the Cole's Creek area." Adam shook their hands. Jackson grinned broadly with amusement. "You would think they would have heard one another's jokes many times by now, Mister Cloud, but this bunch never runs out of extravagant tales and mischief."

Thomas Green politely acknowledged the introduction. "My plantation is twenty miles up the Trace. We call it Springfield Manor, and you are welcome to stop over any time you might come north to Cole's Creek. Anyone can tell you where it is."

"If you're in the market for horses, Mister Cloud," Abner Green said, "we can tout you on to some of Philip Nolan's imported horses. His Tejas brand is very sturdy."

Conversation about Philip Nolan ensued, and Adam's curiosity was piqued by the controversial figure. He learned Nolan was a wrangler and trader who ventured deep into Tejas and captured wild horses, selling them to the Spanish cavalry. Adam noticed that everyone described the man differently.

"He doesn't auction the horses off, Mister Cloud," Thomas Green explained. "Anyone can purchase one of his horses on the sly for about fifty dollars. The animals are very tough and wiry, and popular for long, hard rides. Opelousas, they're called, after the region where they are caught."

"They're as wild and ungoverned as young Nolan himself," one man said.

"Well, now, I'd simply call him adventurous," said another. "Don't discount the fact that he arrived with credentials from Colonel James Wilkinson. He appears to be his protégé here, and acts as his New Orleans agent sometimes."

"Not to mention his other ambitious connections," said still another, with a sly wink. The men frowned on the remark and began to disperse without comment.

Adam and Joseph gathered their slaves into the wagon and started home.

"What did he mean by that remark about Nolan — the one nobody answered?" Adam asked Joseph.

"Only that he's courting one of the Lintot sisters in hopes of becoming Stephen Minor's brother-in-law. The gentlemen here don't cotton to gossip and insinuating remarks, especially when they refer to ladies."

The Natchez planters were now tilling and planting in earnest, and Adam made the best use of his slave labor to sow his modest fields. Dirk proved a trustworthy overseer, toiling alongside the new fieldhands, gaining their trust and fostering gradual acceptance of their new home. With a plowshare hitched to a mule, the blacks followed with hoes, tilling the soil and planting seeds of Indian corn, pumpkins, squash, and melons. The slaves built their living quarters, and Adam designated a generous portion of adjacent land to grow their own corn and vegetables. He purchased a modest start of cattle, swine, chickens and geese, and gave the slaves a few chickens and two pigs for breeding.

During one of her visits, Mary turned a critical eye toward Adam's new slaves. "That new female fieldhand looks sullen to me," she said. "One must be very careful in selecting female blacks, for they tend to be more resentful than males over their fate."

"And how do I discern that?" Adam asked. "One can't read their minds. She looked healthy enough to breed, and that's what the men at the auction said to look for."

"You look at their expressions. I believe you will have trouble with that one. A female can be a troublemaker, especially around males to fight over her."

Adam gave her a withering look; she had wounded his pride. *Bossy women*, he thought to himself.

To everyone's delight, Sam Forman arrived early in June, creating a stir in the Forman household. The family now lived in a large newly built house on the St. Catherine land grant, just south of town. Ezekiel named the plantation "Canterbridge" for the handsome bridge the slaves built across the creek. He could now ride easily to both sides of his property fronting the creek, unhampered by flooding. His slaves were busy cultivating a large section for next year's tobacco crop.

Gathered for a midday meal, the family anxiously awaited Sam's tales about his stay in Louisville, and his journey downriver. Mary was arranging flowers for the dinner table when Sam joined her.

"My little Princess," Sam said affectionately, "you are a feast for starved eyes. There wasn't a lady in Louisville who could match your looks and your style. I'll wager the local swains are climbing all over each other for your attention."

"I wouldn't know," Mary answered. "I haven't met any of them. We've only been here such a short time, and the family has been so busy getting settled — Adam too. You should see his new house. It's just finished and I'm helping him with the interior arrangements. And Becky has needed me, too, poor darling, without her mother, and with Adam doing his building and planting, trying to get started here."

David overheard them as he entered the room. "Aha, Sam," he taunted, "you haven't seen what's going on. Mary is so wrapped up in Adam and Becky that she practically smothers them with attention. She spends every waking moment over there."

"Stop discussing me. It's none of your business," Mary flared out. She pressed her lips together and turned away.

"Sorry, Princess. Didn't mean to pry."

Aunt Betsey entered the room as the young men withdrew.

"What was that all about, Mary? I heard you reprimanding the boys."

"They are just being nosy, Aunt Betsey. My private life is my own, and they are teasing me because I'm helping Adam get settled."

"I don't wonder they're concerned. You haven't given attention to much else since our arrival. Perhaps it's time you faced up to your own intentions, Mary. It's no secret that you adore Adam."

Mary stood silent a moment, then blurted out unexpectedly, even to herself, "Well, it's pretty hard to hide when you love someone. I have loved Adam since the first day I ever saw him, and wanted him for myself even when Sister had him securely harnessed. I always respected their marriage and stayed at arm's length, but I kept on loving him just the same. So, what's wrong with wanting him now? I don't have to pay allegiance to Anne anymore, and I want to help him build a new life here. Oh, Aunt Betsey, I want that more than anything else in the world, even if I can't have him." Tears streamed down her cheeks. The motherly housekeeper put her arms around Mary. "There, there, child, there is nothing wrong in loving someone you can't have. Do you think he loves you?"

"I do know he cares for me. I thought if he finds he can't do without me, he might love me in time."

"That's no way to look at it, my dear. You shouldn't have to coax him to love you; you are too desirable in yourself. If he cares for you, you can fan the flame in many ways. Always being on hand when he needs you can make him take you for granted. Let him feel frustrated by not being so available, and try making him jealous. You can stir things up, and I'll wager he will discover his own love."

Mary recognized this wisdom, and silently pledged to herself to behave more distant toward Adam. She would not be on hand so readily. She would begin a different relationship this very day, when he arrived for dinner.

Attention was riveted on Sam at the dinner table. He related his experiences of the past several months in the intense, lively narration that endeared Sam to all who knew him. The girls were agog over a bear cub he brought for a pet.

His personal adventures finally exhausted, Sam shared a spicy rumor about Colonel Wilkinson. "It's not a pretty story," he said, "and it's based on hearsay. John Brown, a Kentucky representative in the United States Congress, was in Louisville for a few days. He passed on a story, being told in the East among other statesmen, that an influential American has been engaged in trading at New Orleans, and now acts as a secret agent for Spain in Kentucky. He is suspected of being employed by Governor Miró to induce the Kentucky legislators to separate from the union and ally with Spain. There was no doubt in anyone's mind that it was Wilkinson. One wonders how far he is willing to go."

Adam recalled facts he heard in Louisville, of Wilkinson trying to persuade the Kentucky Legislature to vote unanimously for separation, while, at the same time, Kentucky was pushing for statehood. "Is there any proof of this conspiracy?" he asked.

"Brown said there are other rumors which he put together to lend credibility," Sam replied. "One tale he heard firsthand in Frankfort. It seems a hard-riding traveler put up at a local Frankfort inn after traveling the Trace from New Orleans. He asked the colonel's whereabouts, and made no secret of the fact that his saddlebags were packed with $6,000 of clinking silver, all Spanish doubloons and dollars. The man claimed the silver was payment for tobacco Wilkinson delivered to New Orleans. But the payment didn't jibe with the amount Wilkinson said he got for his tobacco. It fed suspicion among those who had reason to believe he either lied or else exaggerated about how 'modest' his trading profits were."

"That's a convincing episode, but not exactly proof that he's engaged in a Spanish conspiracy," Ezekiel said.

"This is very difficult to believe," Mary said. "I can't imagine that charming, distinguished man engaged in any conduct unbecoming of an officer and a gentleman."

Adam tended to side with Mary's assessment.

A week later, Adam was nearing Melling Wooley's trading center with one of Mary's shopping lists. Suddenly, the boom of the battery cannon rent the air. The customers rushed out the door, mounted their horses, and galloped down toward the landing. Adam followed, curious about what kind of contingent was arriving. He mingled with spectators at the waterfront, and watched a large fleet of some sixty flatboats approach the landing and spread out along the shore. The boats were laden with goods, and Adam waited to see the leader of this unusually large trading fleet. To his astonishment, Col. James Wilkinson emerged from the lead boat. The colonel strode up and exchanged salutes with the guard captain. As they conversed, Adam stepped forward and Wilkinson greeted him with a wide smile.

"What a pleasure, Mister Cloud. I hoped I would see you again. I have thought of you often and wondered how you liked your new country."

"Thank you, Colonel," Adam clasped his extended hand. "I'm still shaping my life here and have a long way to go before I am fully acclimated. You have a sizable fleet there. Quite an undertaking to gather so much produce."

"Ah, yes, and it's a long story. But wait, sir. Let me take care of some details with the patroons. My horse is being saddled, and we can ride uptown together, that is, if you are mounted. I would like to hear more about your venture here."

Adam waited until Wilkinson's horse was brought ashore, and they conversed as they rode up the steep road. Wilkinson explained that his cargo included produce from Kentucky, Ohio,

Pennsylvania, Virginia, and the Cumberland district of Mero. He had brought a thousand hogsheads of tobacco to sell on commission, but the beginning was full of disaster. Three boats were grounded on the Kentucky River and unable to start with the rest. One boat leaked and sank on the Ohio.

"Only the good Lord knows what else can happen. I simply can't afford any more mishaps. But that's enough of my problems. How are you adjusting to your new life here? How is that lovely Miss Grandin?"

"Miss Grandin is well. She has proven a remarkable friend, and I don't know how I could have managed with Becky without her help."

"And why should you try? Have you not asked the big question yet, sir? You should know by now that she dotes on you. Don't let some local Romeo woo her away."

Adam felt his face flush with embarrassment, and Wilkinson laughed.

"Come now, Mr. Cloud, I don't mean to upset you. But the picture is just as plain as the nose on your face. I apologize if I have been indiscreet."

Adam forced a wan smile. "Of course not. I'll put my mind to it." He described his land and his crops, trying to concentrate on his words while his mind was on Mary. "Next year I'll have my acreage ready for tobacco. The king has offered to purchase all of our tobacco crops with a general government subsidy, and I'm disappointed I didn't arrive early enough to plant tobacco this year."

"Your good fortune is more assured than mine, sir, for we have no hope of subsidies, and I can't be sure my former privileges still stand. The duty-free offer has changed to a fifteen percent duty for Americans, as you probably know, and the Spanish are unpredictable. Rumors abound that new shipments will be discouraged at the whim of the Crown."

Adam seized the opportunity to sound the colonel out. "I thought you had been granted credit up to several thousand dollars, and special trade privileges," he said. "That could prove as good as the subsidy afforded to us. I pray that your privileges have not been rescinded."

Wilkinson answered lightly. "Oh, no, but I hope to do better this time. Governor Miró has written that everything is open for discussion when I arrive, and I look forward to continuing our close rapport. I always deal with the special interests of our Kentucky settlers at heart."

Adam was too flustered and confused over the hint about Mary to sort out any hidden meaning in Wilkinson's rapport with Miró, or in his "special interests of Kentucky." He would have to think about it later. They were approaching Government House, and he pulled rein to bid Wilkinson farewell.

"If you have no plans, it would be my pleasure to have you stay with me when you return. You won't know Becky. She is toddling all over the place now."

"I thank you, sir, for your kind offer," Wilkinson said. "I would be pleased to accept your kind invitation. I look forward to seeing you again, and Miss Grandin also."

As he returned to Wooley's store, Adam's mind still reeled from Wilkinson's remarks about Mary. To his surprise, Andrew Jackson stood at the counter stuffing merchandise into huge leather boxes. They exchanged cordial greetings, and Adam leaned against the counter as Jackson chattered.

"I have been building my new cabin, with help from my good Bruinsburg neighbors. I'm back again because my store is out of liquor, and the Bayou Pierre settlers are a thirsty bunch for the grape and the grain." Jackson laughed as he spoke. His face suddenly sobered, and his intense eyes looked directly into Adam's. "I meant no offense, sir. I learned from Governor Gayoso that you are a Protestant preacher. I suppose you frown on imbibing the hard stuff."

"What? Oh no, that's nonsense," Adam replied. "The Anglicans have never frowned on spirits, or believe it sinful to partake of it, as do some denominations. The only sin is to overindulge and bring harm to oneself or others. Excess in any activity can become a liability. Moderation assures us peace of mind and a better disposition."

Jackson smiled wryly and issued a mock sigh. "How well I know. I learned that the hard way when I tried to drink it all up.

You are a man after my own heart. I would favor you as my pastor, if I were to choose a church." He refitted items in one of the boxes to make more room.

"Well, don't count on it," Adam said. "I have put that part of my life behind me. His Catholic Majesty clamps a tight lid on non-Catholic activities, and my worship is confined to home and hearth. Here, let me give you a hand." He handed Jackson items for the box.

"That seems a pity. But you appear to be at ease accepting it," Jackson said. He crammed the goods down into the box.

"Not entirely," Adam said. "I have always had an inner call to preach, to bring hope and spiritual strength to my fellow men. I was confident, when I opted for my new life here, that I could forgo preaching and settle for a limited ministry. But the demands of my secular life, and the strict limitations placed on Protestants, create a nagging conflict with an underlying need to fulfill my spiritual goals, and my ecclesiastical mission."

Jackson stopped his packing and looked up at Adam, sympathy in his eyes. "I know how you feel. I have always sought a career in the law, but a beginning practice is not very lucrative on the frontier. The Tennessee Legislature pays me nothing for my time. I find myself engaged in money-making side ventures, like my store and the slave trade, which demand my attention when I'd rather concentrate on my legal practice."

"Here," Adam said, offering Jackson the last two items on the counter. Jackson tucked them in, fastened the lids, and they moved the boxes near the door.

Jackson smoothed disordered locks from his high forehead and clapped his hat on his head. "By the way, I saw you riding up with the Fancy Colonel just now. Has he charmed you into his intrigues? A word of warning, if I may. Don't get too close to the spider, or he will draw you into his web and nibble your reputation and your standing here."

"I know very little about him, and mostly from hearsay." Adam was all attention. "We met in Louisville on my journey down here. Is there something I should know to protect my reputation? That seems a serious charge."

"It's difficult to put your finger on any one thing, there are so many stories and rumors about his activities in behalf of Kentucky's independence. Many suspect he would sell out the frontier to Spain. But there is one report I had firsthand. Remember the little colony of Americans at Walnut Hills?"

"Yes, I do, and I have been puzzled over your explanation of the American claims to the land. You said Georgia sold the settlement to South Carolina speculators. The settlers told us the land company bought the land from the Choctaws."

"That's true, also, and probably for a string of beads. The South Carolina Yazoo Land Company has sold widespread subscription among frontier settlers."

"You mean they sell off parcels to Americans for speculation, even before the Spanish have granted permission?"

"Exactly. They claim they can persuade the Spanish to give up this land, but there is more afoot than that." Jackson beckoned Adam closer and lowered his voice. "Their land agent is a Dr. James O'Fallon, of Charleston, who has been soliciting subscriptions for land on the promise of a forceful takeover, if the Spanish government rejects their request."

Jackson looked around the store, and seeing they could not be heard, continued in his lowered tone. O'Fallon, he explained, had assigned Gen. George Rogers Clark to enlist Kentucky and Cumberland people to pledge support for an invasion army. Their aim was to organize a Western Conference, independent of the United States, with allegiance to Spain. Walnut Hills would be a center for Indian and slave trade.

An invasion army! Would they try to capture Natchez too? Adam felt a disturbing unease creep over him. "This is startling news. Where does Wilkinson fit into this?"

"General Clark told me personally that Colonel Wilkinson was invited to subscribe to the project, and that he accepted, provided that he be appointed the lead agent. He was insulted when O'Fallon was selected instead."

"Is Wilkinson still involved? How do you know these facts?"

"My source is Michael LaCassagne, a Louisville merchant who was recently in Nashborough. LaCassagne said that Wilkinson never withdrew his subscription to the venture, even though he now rejects the whole idea. LaCassagne himself is suspect as an agent for Wilkinson's interest. So where do they stand, and what do they really want? No one knows for sure, but there is intrigue here, I would bet my finest Kentucky horse on it."

How much was truth, how much hearsay? As upsetting as this news was, Adam did not like to make judgments based on hearsay, especially on Jackson's third-hand knowledge. "I'll keep that in mind when I see the colonel again. Thank you for the information." Adam paused with a new thought. "Speaking of horses, I admire that fine steed of yours. I assume she is Kentucky bred?"

"Yes. I got her from a Frankfort breeder."

"I would like to purchase some good Kentucky breeding stock. If it's not too much to ask, would you consider bringing me a select pair when you come down next time?"

"You would have to trust my judgment, and I might not please you," Jackson replied.

"From the looks of the handsome filly you ride, I would trust your judgment any time."

"I'll keep your request in mind. I must get back to attend the Tennessee Legislature next month, and I have some pending legal cases, so it will be a good while before I return again. I hope to see you then, Mister Cloud. Godspeed and good fortune in your first harvest."

As he watched Jackson secure his boxes to a waiting burro, Adam remembered his shopping list. He turned to trader Wooley for the kitchen items Mary and Maamba had requested.

On the ride home, his mind raced between thoughts of dangerous intrigue and Wilkinson's remarks about Mary. Was she really more than fond of him, or was it just her innate kindness that she gave all her attention to Becky and him? She had scarcely had time for suitors, or any romances yet. Was it fair to draw her into his domestic life, leaving her no opportunity to meet other suitors? How did he feel about marriage again, and with Mary? He could hardly imagine life without her now. Was it love?

It was a thought that began to haunt him.

11 Rocky Romance

Sam's presence in Natchez sparked a round of social events. Ezekiel's former acquaintance with Col. Thomas Green opened many doors, due to the Green families' popularity for their wealth and lifestyle. The summer social life included dances, parties, picnics, and exchange visits between homes. Sam was popular among the young settlers and mixed easily with the unmarried Spanish officers. Mary was invited everywhere with Sam, and Adam was often included.

One evening they attended an eighteenth birthday ball for Elizabeth Watts, at Belmont Plantation. Adam and Sam watched Mary from the sidelines, admiring her grace as she danced the cotillion with a young Spanish officer.

"Better wake up, Adam, or some swain will sweep her out of your life," Sam remarked.

"Mind your own affairs, Sam," Adam retorted. "Besides, it's for her to choose."

He turned away so Sam could not see his discomfort. Sam could be right, he thought, but the remark cut him. He had only two dances on her dance card, and now, watching her gave him jealous pangs, something he had never felt before.

He strode across the room to Mary's side, not sure what he would say. Mary greeted him with a dazzling smile.

"Ah, Adam, you know these gentlemen, I believe?" She turned to the group surrounding her. "Mr. Cloud is my dear friend and brother-in-law."

Adam nodded, and said, "May I have a minute, Mary? I need to talk with you."

Mary's eyes widened with innocent surprise. "Now, really, Adam, what could be so serious? Excuse me, gentlemen, I will be but a moment."

Adam took her aside. "Sorry to pull you away from the admiring mob, but I haven't seen you much this evening, and I hope your dance card is not filled."

"Oh, but it is, Adam. You only asked for two dances, and there are so many new acquaintances here tonight."

"I don't want to sit and wait between dances."

"Of course not, Adam, you needn't sit around at all. You can dance with any of the ladies here. Isn't this a glorious ball? Let's see." She glanced at her dance card. "I have the next dance with Captain Sariego. Have you met him, Adam? He does everything with such—um, gallant Spanish flair. So charming. Here he comes."

Adam acknowledged the introduction, and Mary tapped him lightly on the cheek with her fan. "Here, Adam. Would you be a dear and keep these for me?"

She handed him her fan and tiny reticule as the captain whisked her to the dance floor. A lively schottische began, and Adam seethed as he watched them. He turned away and walked outside. *I'm acting like a schoolboy,* he thought. *Get hold of yourself and take charge of the situation.* He returned inside and roamed the room, inspecting the single ladies. He approached Elizabeth Watts, who was among young friends. He kissed her hand, congratulated her on her birthday occasion, and requested a dance. Flattered by the attention of an older man, she found a place on her card for him. Elizabeth's young friends tittered among themselves; the girls were impressed with Elizabeth's handsome older partner.

Adam returned to Mary and found her surrounded by another group of gentlemen. "Here are your purse and fan, Mary," he said with unusual abruptness. "You'll have to find another keeper." He turned without waiting for an answer, and Mary's eyes followed him as he melted into the other guests.

A round dance began, and Adam claimed his partner. He put his best foot forward, hoping Mary would see his smiles for his dancing partner. When the dance ended, he returned Elizabeth to her friends, lingering only as long as politeness required. He strolled casually toward Sam, who was conversing with several ladies. He selected a partner among the ladies and placed his name on her dance card.

"Where is Mary?" Sam asked. "I have a dance coming up with her. How about you, Adam?"

"There she is, with that Captain Sariego. He's getting to be a permanent fixture," Adam said, and they strolled toward them. "Are you free for a moment, Mary?"

"Well, now, dear friends." she said, "I have missed you. I hope you are having as much fun as I am."

"This is our dance, Mary," Sam said. "Do you think you can break away from your admirers long enough to dance with your cousin? Excuse us, Captain. Keep the sidelines burning, Adam. This is a gavotte, and here we go."

They swept on to the dance floor, and Adam raged as he watched them. *She hardly glanced at me*, he fumed. *Well, I can fix that.* As they swung near, he tapped Sam lightly on the shoulder. Sam gave way with a grin, and Adam stepped in his place. Mary did not lose a beat as she laughed and took his arm. They swung into the sprightly dance and Adam felt an instant thrill as he held her on the turn. *That slender waist,* he thought, *owes little to whalebone.* His eyes feasted on her face, on the dimple that always appeared when she gave that light, tinkling laugh; on the dark, generous brows, her violet-blue eyes that sparkled and tantalized. Each time they faced, he held her closer until the blood pounded in his veins.

"This is your kind of dance," he said into her ear. "You are so light on your feet. I'll try to keep up with you," and he pressed her even closer at every turn.

The delicious scent of her, the sweet warmth of her flesh stirred his prurient nature and created a current between them. The rapid dance pace accelerated his body responses, until he felt a sweet ache and tightening in his groin. It had been so long since he had been aroused that he enjoyed the ecstasy. The music ended with a crash, and Mary stood before him, her expression bewilderment.

"*Uhmmm,*" Adam murmured, taking a deep breath. "Would you excuse me for a moment while I cool off outside?"

He left her with Sam and strode quickly to the door. Adam walked in the cool garden until his passion subsided. He realized he was obsessed with Mary; he knew he was deeply in love. He resolved to find a way to win her for himself.

After fulfilling the dance he had promised Sam's acquaintance, he waited impatiently to claim the last dance with Mary. It was a stately pavane, a befitting end to a romantic evening. Its measures of slow, swaying grace afforded dancers opportunity to flirt, respond to silent messages, and seal an understanding of intent.

Adam did not waste the opportunity. He began with a traditional bow and locked gazes with Mary as they followed the graceful patterns of the ancient, courtly dance. Each was silently conscious of the moments of passion experienced so unexpectedly in the gavotte. Neither broke the spell between them until the dance ended.

Caught in the bustle of thanks and farewells to the Watts family, they finally made their way to the door and found Sam waiting with the carriage.

"Will we be seeing you next Saturday at the governor's tree planting ceremony?" Sam asked. "Eliza will pack you a picnic basket if you will join us."

Adam's eyes were on Mary. "I wouldn't miss it. Maamba will pack me a basket, and I'll see you there. Good night, Mary," he said, holding her hand with a lingering kiss. He wondered if Mary had felt that special current, that magic thrill he felt between them.

"Good night, Adam. It was a lovely evening," she said softly.

Adam watched the carriage drive away, reluctant for the event to end. Frustrating as Mary was, he thought, it was a new beginning for him. A warm flood of joy swept over him as he mounted his horse for the ride home.

"Lancer," he said jubilantly, as he patted his mane, "we'll see her again on Saturday."

. . .

The week dragged by. Work supervision kept Adam busy at home, but his mind dwelt on Mary.

"Maamba," he said, as she served his breakfast, "what can I take in my picnic basket to share with others? I always look forward to treats other people share with me."

"Well, Massah Adam, it depends on who you wants to share with. If it's a certain young miss I know, I can think of a special kine of cake is her favorite. An' mos' anyone love a strawberry cake. That be pleasin' you?"

"Of course, Maamba. If you say everyone likes strawberry cake, then let's have one. I shall be leaving by ten o'clock tomorrow, so have my picnic basket ready."

When Adam entered town he joined the crowd of families and servants tethering their horses and carts near the central plaza. The Forman carriage was already there. He tethered Lancer and gave a small black boy a coin to watch over him. In his eagerness to see Mary again, he hurried toward The Commons, threading his way through the crowd until he found the Formans. They were seated on blankets spread on the ground.

"Good morning, everyone," Adam swept a bow. "Good morning, Mary." Her greeting was so matter-of-fact that he felt disappointed. Was she deliberately hiding her emotions?

"Hello, Adam. See who has joined us for the event." Mary indicated Colonel Green and his son, Everard, seated next to her. Colonel Green introduced his young son, and added that he would be leaving soon for school on the Seaboard.

Eliza added that the Thomas Greens would join them, with their children, and would spend the night at Canterbridge. Aunt Betsey took Adam's picnic basket and placed it under cover with the others, and Adam sat beside Mary on the blanket. That special thrill of her nearness swept over him. He felt awkward, not knowing what to say. He looked into her eyes, trying to read them, hoping for a sign that she held cherished memories of their recent rapport. She remained silent, and he could not guess her mood.

Sam joined them and announced, in his breezy style, that the rooms at King's Tavern were booked solid. All the undesirables had been shut out to make room for residents as far away as

Homochitto and Bayou Pierre. Almost everyone had a family staying with them.

The arrival of the Thomas Green family diverted the group's
attention, and they made room for them on the blankets. The
Green children mingled with the Forman girls, David and Everard
paired off, and everyone settled down, chatting among themselves.
Adam barely heard the conversation around him, concentrating on
how he might penetrate Mary's mood.

"You look ravishingly beautiful this morning, Mary," he ventured. "That yellow bonnet becomes you. Is that a new gown?"

"Thank you, Adam. Liz Preece made it for me," Mary said,
smoothing her skirt. "But speaking of yellow, did you ever see such
a dazzling sight as that?" She indicated Katherine Minor, who was
escorted to the band platform by her adjutant husband. "She's
dressed from head to toe in bright yellow, even her parasol. That's
enough yellow to knock out the eyeballs."

Katherine Minor raised a gold-handled lorgnette to her long,
sallow face and surveyed the crowd.

"She always wears yellow, haven't you noticed? That's why
she's called 'The Yellow Duchess'," Eliza replied.

"She doesn't outshine you, Mary," Adam said. Mary smiled
back, and her eyes sparkled from the compliment.

They watched the governor arrive on the platform where he
directed the seating for the Minors and Father Savage.

The festivities began with a marching band leading the parade,
and everyone arose, stirred by the music. Next came a foot soldier
carrying a huge Spanish flag, followed by Colonel Grand-Pré on
horseback, leading a cadre of officers and troops. The officers wore
dark blue coats with red collars and cuffs. Patterns of gold lace
adorned their chests, and a red stripe accented their white
breeches.

Adam moved closer to Mary and groped for her hand. She let
him keep it, and a pulse began to throb from his hand to hers. He
pressed her hand and their pulses grew stronger, triggering
resounding throbs throughout his body.

"Why are all the lace decorations different?" Mary asked, feeling Adam's closeness.

"The patterns denote rank." His voice was husky. He cleared his throat.

"The cavalry looks smart with their yellow coats and red collars," she commented, shyly groping for conversation.

The band settled on the platform and the troops stood at attention until Colonel Grand-Pré saluted the governor and commanded "at ease." The audience clapped and cheered at the impressive entry and sat again. Adam sat so close to Mary their hips touched. He could feel her breathing, and closed his eyes as he tried to match her rhythm.

Governor Gayoso mounted the dais and welcomed the crowd. "I am pleased to address the citizens of Natchez at this first special event. The past fourteen months since I came to Natchez have been most pleasant for me, and I hope for you also." He spoke of the current prosperity among the planters and craftsmen, under the beneficent rule of their Catholic Majesty, king and protector. He praised especially the Crown's generous purchase of their local tobacco crops, which assured a stable crop for the growers. The crowd applauded. He spoke of the order and good will among them under his new laws and regulations, and of his plans to build two churches, one in Natchez town, and another at Cole's Creek.

"We are now building new roads and adequate bridges for better travel conditions and shorter distances between destination points." The crowd applauded again. "I shall soon petition His Majesty for the establishment of a good school, to properly educate our children."

The roar of the crowd drowned out his next words, and the governor paused as an aide stepped upon the platform and handed him a note. He raised his eyes beyond the crowd, and his countenance registered complete astonishment. There was a hushed silence as the spectators turned to see a host of Indians emerging from the distant north woods toward the town's open spaces.

"That's the Choctaw Nation coming to collect their annual gifts," Colonel Green explained to the Formans.

"Did the governor invite them to this event?" Ezekiel asked.

"Probably not. They are early this year."

"Well, what happens now?" Ezekiel asked. "This is going to take some skillful handling."

"Protocol demands that they be made welcome," Colonel Green replied. "They always camp, some in the woods, and some on the palisades. But that was before Gayoso's time. Let's see what the governor does."

Adam's quizzical eyebrow peaked as he looked at Mary. "Are you afraid?" he asked.

"Heavens, no. This is better entertainment than the governor planned," she said. "I wouldn't have missed it for the world."

The Indians spread out on the empty town lots. Adam thought the scene so colorful he wished he could capture it on canvas. He took in every detail, etching it on his memory. Most of the men rode white, piebald prairie horses, each decorated with a wide collar from which hung tufts of horsehair dyed in bright colors. Some rode ponies laden with saddle bags and baskets strapped on their sides. The baskets were painted rich shades of deep purple, yellow and white, in bird designs and smartly stylized patterns. Some of the men were bare-waisted, wearing only loincloths; others wore calico shirts. Feathers dangled in their long hair.

Behind the men came women on foot, each carrying a colorful basket strapped to her forehead or her chest, some carrying a papoose on their backs. A few led ponies drawing sleds loaded with blankets and goods. The women wore gay blouses with leather skirts, or deerskin dresses, and moccasins decorated with wampum, porcupine quills, and beads.

"Their heads!" exclaimed Mary. "The children have flat heads, shaved on the crown. What odd course of nature could turn out a tribe with flat heads?"

"Nature had nothing to do with it, my dear," Colonel Green said with an amused grin. "They create the flat heads by placing bags of sand on their infants. The children wear the bowl haircuts to show them off."

Two riders approached the platform. One was an elderly Indian in black deerskin, sitting high and dignified on his mount. The other was a white man. His bleached mustache contrasted a face as tanned and weathered as leather.

"The Indian is a chief," Colonel Green explained, "and the other is Juan Baptiste, a half-breed who lives among them. He helps manage the tribe when they visit the district."

When the riders reached the platform, Adjutant Stephen Minor greeted them and presented them to the governor. Finally, the two riders turned, faced the crowd, and Don Manuel addressed the residents again.

"Our friend, Chief Franchimastabé, Grand Chief of the Choctaw Nation, is welcome to our village. He has come with his people in the annual ritual to renew Choctaw friendship and receive gifts from the Crown. Our Choctaw friends will camp further back toward the woods, so our ceremony and festivities may continue. They are invited to watch the ceremony and participate in the community celebration."

The riders returned to the Indians in the rear. Don Manuel then completed his address, dedicated the trees, and announced that the park was provided for the daily use and enjoyment of the residents. The official ceremony ended with a park blessing from Father Savage. The band music continued, while the crowd mingled.

The Forman group opened picnic baskets and laid out the food so everyone could share. Adam opened his basket and sat next to Mary.

"I always include you in any plans for the family, Adam," Eliza said. "I worry that you have no one to look after you but Maamba."

"You needn't worry about Adam," Mary said. "Maamba spoils him just like she did all of us when we were growing up. What did she think up for you today, Adam?" She peered into his basket. "Oh, Adam, a strawberry cake!" She drew it out and held it high. "Of all the things she knows I love, she made one for you. Was it especially to share with me? I can't wait for dessert."

Adam smiled. "You said she likes to please the ones she loves. It's a gift of love, from us both."

Their repartee escaped no one within hearing distance, and the
Formans exchanged knowing glances. The group finished their
repast with lively chatter, then put away the leftovers.

"People are strolling on The Commons," Colonel Forman
said. "We should join them and support the dedication. Come,
pretty lady." He rose and stretched out his hand to Eliza. Adam
offered Mary his hand, and they joined in a promenade stroll.

"I hoped we could have a quiet word together," Adam said.
"What have you been doing?"

"Nothing special," she said. "I went with Sam to visit the
Harper sisters. He likes one of them a lot. And several nice gentlemen I met at the dance have called upon me. I helped Eliza pack
some late strawberries, and we stitched a little."

"I missed your visit this week. The house is crying for your
attention. I haven't placed a single household article until I get
your approval."

She laughed. "Well, Adam, sooner or later you will have to be
on your own. I might just run out of things to do for you."

"Never," he said. "I don't believe anything will be right unless
you make it so. You have spoiled me, you know."

"Until Sam came, I hadn't met many people. Now it's different. I'm getting invitations and meeting everyone. My time for
home advice may be more limited now." She noted his downcast
face. "Oh, don't worry, Adam. I won't abandon you, or Rebecca.
You two are close to my heart."

Noises distracted them, and Adam noticed that the Indians
had become rowdy. Some had made their way to the taverns
Under-the-Hill and returned with liquor. They swilled and shared
their bottles, capering about until they became noisy and boisterous. Fights broke out among them, and a few had drifted into the
crowd.

"Look, some of the families are leaving. This can get dangerous," Adam said.

"We'd better get back to the carriage," Ezekiel called out.
"One never knows how far this can go."

The Indian men brawled and scuffled while some of the gentlemen escorted their families to the horses and carts. Indians

obstructed their passage, angering some of the settlers, who pushed and shoved their way through. Suddenly, a loud crack sounded in the crowd, and Adam saw Juan Baptiste lash a long whip among the Choctaws. The sound seemed to terrify them. Some shrank back to their camping area.

"Come, quickly," Ezekiel said. With the help of Adam and Sam he steered the family to the Forman carriage, parked some yards behind the large arena of horses and carts. A brief lull followed the whip cracks and they hurried through the melee. They found several Indians near the carriage who had become defiant, and two brown-skinned warriors, naked to the waist, faced the whites with knives drawn in menacing gestures.

Adam swiftly hoisted Mary into the carriage with the Forman women. Then Adam and Sam confronted the two warriors. Neither had a weapon, but Adam towered over the Indians, hoping the advantage of size, and display of bravado, would intimidate them. Adam looked for Baptiste and his whip, but they were not in sight. He locked eyes with one of the glowering faces before him.

"I'm not sure we can get a purchase if we have to grapple with those bare, sweaty torsos," he said to Sam.

"You take the one on the right, I'll take the other, and we'll see," Sam said.

Suddenly, a young gentleman stepped forward, confronted the warriors, and snapped a loud command in their language, immediately diverting their attention. His voice then changed to a soft, placating tone. The effect was magical. The Indians looked chagrined, their tension relaxed, and they slowly sheathed their knives. With more words from the young man, they turned and left.

Adam was astounded at this performance, and turned to the stranger. "Sir, I admire your bravery and skill with the savages. What did you tell them, to work such magic on their ugly mood?"

"I reminded them that their Chief Franchimastabé had come in peace. Think nothing of it," the man said. "I have need to subdue young hotheads often. Drink really crazes them, but their instincts are quite decent, and they can befriend you and display good manners when they are sober. It's against the law for the taverns to sell them whiskey, and you can see how dangerous it is. I'm Philip Nolan," he added. "And you are . . . ?"

"Adam Cloud, and this is my friend, Sam Forman. I am pleased to meet you. I have heard about you from other settlers." He turned to the carriage and introduced Nolan to those inside.

"Ah, *Doña* Mary Grandin," Nolan said. He held her hand with a lingering kiss; his gaze was a steadily confronting one. "I heard of your arrival with this distinguished family. It is my pleasure to make your acquaintance."

"Thank, you, and I yours." Mary darted him a flirtatious glance.

As the others acknowledged introductions and thanked him for his intervention, Adam took stock of the legendary man he had heard so much about. Nolan was uncommonly handsome, with black hair and brows crowning a deeply tanned face of exquisitely proportioned features. His eyes were almost black, and glistened with a fire of energy and alertness. His tall, muscular body well suited his reputation of a dashing adventurer, and his refined manner and modulated baritone voice bespoke a gentle breeding.

"We are exceedingly grateful for your help and intervention," Adam said. "I hope I may have the opportunity to act in your behalf someday."

As Nolan turned away, Eliza said, "What a gorgeous man. Mary, he certainly had eyes for you."

"He has a way with him, I'll admit," Mary answered. "He is almost too handsome."

Adam felt jealousy again erode his good mood. "Well, don't feel too flattered. He has a reputation for pleasing the ladies," he said.

"What's wrong with that?" Mary retorted. "He simply has courtly manners."

Feeling soured and unsure, Adam made his farewells and rode away. He considered the man a real threat. He must make sure Philip Nolan made no inroads with Mary.

. . .

A few days later, the soft whir of carriage wheels on the drive sent Adam flying to the entry of his house, and he was delighted to see Mary, Sam, and David alight.

"We haven't seen you for days, Adam, and we had to see how you are," Sam said.

"I've been confined with work here. It's good to see you," Adam replied, eyes feasting on Mary. "Come in."

Becky toddled toward Mary with outstretched arms, and Mary knelt for a hug.

"She has missed you," Adam said.

"We can't stay long," Sam said. "We promised to call on the Davises."

"Don't go, Mary," Adam said. "Stay and visit with Becky and me."

"I'll stay. I've missed her too." She turned to Sam and David. "You can stop by for me on your way home," she said, and they sped away.

Mary and Adam spent a playful hour with Rebecca until time for her afternoon nap. Adam seized the chance to be alone with Mary. He had agonized over where he stood with her, and now was a chance to find out. He had a sudden impulse.

"How would you like to take a nature ride?" he offered. "Wendy hasn't been exercised properly for some time. I think she misses you too."

"I would like that," Mary said. "It's been a while since I have ridden."

She accompanied Adam to the barn and he saddled the horses. Mary raised her skirt, showing Adam a bit of her ankle, as he helped her mount Wendy's sidesaddle. She gave him a tantalizing grin, and called out, "I'll race you."

They galloped across the field, slowing as they came to the first woods.

"Wait there," Adam called after her. "I want to show you something."

"Something, like what?"

"It is a special place I have found. Follow me."

Adam wound through the woods, Mary followed, until he stopped and dismounted. Mary gazed about her in wonderment at a small clearing in the forest, its centerpiece a stream bubbling over fallen logs softly coated with lichen. The sun filtered through the wild luxuriance of ferns, tangled vines, and moss-hung branches of pecan and oak trees, casting light and shadows in a cool and private bower.

"I come here sometimes, just to be alone and think," Adam said. He quickly dismounted and grasped Mary's waist. His pulses quickened as he swung her lightly to the ground. "Do you like it?" He waited anxiously as she absorbed the scene.

"It's beautiful," Mary said softly. "I feel as though I should whisper."

Mary's heart pounded as they sat upon a fallen log and watched the miniature waterfall ripple over the mossy logs.

She stole a glance at her beloved, in a moment of anticipation. His face was rapturous.

Adam felt a warm glow within, conscious of her nearness. "I've dreamed of sharing this place with you." His voice was low and husky. He was uncertain of what he wanted to say. "This is my sanctuary, my chapel. I call it my 'bliss station'." He groped for the right words. "Here, I wrestle with my soul, look for meaning . . . for my inner beliefs. That's why I brought you here. I want you to know the real me." He searched her face for approval.

Mary remained silent while she pondered his intent. This was not about her at all! It concerned him only. Her expectations collapsed, and she trembled within as she tried to suppress her disappointment before she spoke.

"Why, Adam, I am surprised that you must wrestle with your soul. Do you feel guilty of something? You always seem so secure and confident."

"Sometimes I do feel guilty, and I need to resolve my dilemma. I never told anyone except Father Jarratt, but I had a remarkable experience when I was only eighteen. It changed my outlook on life, but left me bewildered."

"What kind of experience?" Mary was alarmed. What terrible thing could make him feel guilty? She searched his face for a clue.

"It was a spiritual experience. A silent extension of the soul to a higher level of consciousness." He then described his youthful transcendental experience to Mary, while she listened in silence. "Father Jarratt encouraged me to explore the lives of the mystics. I have spent hours dwelling on the profound thoughts which surround their experiences."

"Perhaps you received God's Grace," Mary said. "But why do you feel guilty?"

"Because it is difficult to reconcile what happened to me with what is taught by Christian theologians. I know in my heart that I had a Christian experience, but if I made known my interest in the mystical life, I feel sure the Episcopal church would censure me. The Methodists never understood why I couldn't preach their dogma."

Mary struggled with feelings of emptiness and exasperation over Adam's self concerns before she answered. "I'm glad you shared this with me, Adam. But honestly, I think you are over-reacting to your inner problem. Just be yourself, and stop worrying about your soul. Stop looking inward so much, and use your talents out in the real world. You have so much to offer."

Adam sprang to his feet and stepped away a few paces. He was crushed. He had expected understanding, empathy, and instead she offered criticism. In his anger, he snapped off a twig from a nearby branch. He turned and faced her, holding the twig in a clenched fist.

"I bare my soul to you, and all you can say is 'get out into the real world'."

"I didn't mean it that way. Of course I understand, but you can't solve your dilemmas by brooding."

"I don't brood. I meditate, I pray for guidance." In exasperation, he snapped the twig into small bits.

"Oh, Adam, you make me feel like a wicked witch. I just meant you should get out more. I'm having such a good time that I want you to also."

"Good time, like flirting with all the young men? Like that Nolan fellow. I suppose you are seeing him."

Mary's anger mounted over the accusation. "Yes, he has called on me, and what's wrong with that?"

"I should think you would be more discriminating. The man has a dubious reputation, and he's making a play for Fannie Lintot."

"Oh, pother. I give up, Adam. Just take me home."

Mary jumped up in frustration and strode toward Wendy.

Adam threw the twigs on the ground and held the stirrup for her foot. Mary mounted her sidesaddle, grabbed Wendy's reins, and galloped off toward the meadow.

Adam followed slowly, seething with anger and disappointment. Why had he broached the subject of his dilemma anyway? It was a bad move. The event had soured when he meant it to be endearing. Maybe Mary was not as deep as he imagined, and she was really just flirtatious, shallow. What could he have been thinking to allow himself to get all stirred up over a young flibbertigibbet?

That night he agonized over his future. Perhaps he should reconsider his motives. He turned to his books of mystical theology. They taught that to reach the goal, the elusive spiritual illumination, that sweet Nirvana, the soul must be free. The distractions of a wife could impede such a spiritual growth, he decided. He must make choices.

12 Fulfillment

Adam nursed his hurt feelings for the rest of September. His love for Mary, his passion, his needs conflicted with his reasoning. He was not ready for a reconciliation, and Mary's unfeeling regard for his deepest concerns disturbed him.

He would repeat his first mistake if he married a woman who did not understand him. She might be disappointed in him, as Anne was, but for different reasons. Anne was too pious. Was Mary not religious enough? He had never probed her religious depth beyond that she was a member of the Episcopal church. He amended his regard for her. She was not really shallow. She was decent, kind, caring, thoughtful. The more he recalled her qualities the greater became his ache for her. Perhaps he had let too much time elapse since they parted in such a huff.

Sitting on his verandah one day watching Becky at play, and reflecting on Mary, Adam was surprised to see Colonel Wilkinson ride up the path.

"Welcome, Colonel," he called. He picked up Becky and walked toward his guest.

The colonel slowly dismounted. "Ah, my friend, you can't imagine how welcome your home looks after the weary ride from New Orleans. I hope your offer still stands for a haven."

Adam extended his hand and smiled with pleasure. "Indeed it does, and I'm pleased that you accept my hospitality, humble as it is. A widower and child have not much excitement to offer, but we have a warm place in our hearts for a friend, don't we Becky? Do come in."

Wilkinson tousled Becky's curls as they made their way inside. "My, how you have grown, young lady," he said. He dropped his travel bags on the floor and looked about. "Humble, nothing. You have a fine home here. It looks as though it has a woman's touch . . . but you said you are a widower. Have you finally . . .?"

"Now don't jump to conclusions," Adam laughed. "Mary helped me put it together, but we are still single."

"A pity. But I remember you are sensitive to the subject, and it's none of my affair."

Adam placed the colonel in Becky's room fronting the verandah. He gave Becky to Tizzi's care, and arranged for a hot bath to refresh the weary traveler.

"It will be ready soon, Colonel. Meanwhile you can relax." They returned to the parlor and Adam sat near his guest. "Now, how was your trade venture in New Orleans?"

"The outcome was deplorable," Wilkinson answered. "I was disappointed in the prices I received from the large quantity of goods we sold the government. The thousand hogshead of Kentucky tobacco brought only eight dollars per hundredweight. My other sales to merchants didn't even make up the difference." He shook his head in despair. "The entire shipment was on consignment, and I have suffered a drastic commission loss."

"Perhaps your losses may be recovered with another trade venture," Adam said sympathetically.

"Unfortunately, one can't put together such a large volume of goods in a short time. I shall have to look for other sources of income before I bring down another cargo. I stayed longer than I expected in order to form friendships with some important leaders of New Orleans. One never knows when one will need influential friends down there."

Adam wondered if the colonel would face bankruptcy. But if the rumor was true that he received six thousand silver dollars as extra emolument from the Spanish government, there must be plenty more where that came from. Yet, if he faced impoverishment from this venture, he could scarcely be accepting a pension from the Crown, as rumored.

After supper they settled down with a good wine and conversation. Adam opened discussion of the Walnut Hills settlement, anxious to clear up rumors about Wilkinson.

"When we stopped at the American settlement on our river journey, we were surprised to learn that the colony was illegal, and that its sponsors had petitioned Spain for legitimacy."

"That section around the Yazoo River has been a thorn in the sides of the Spanish for years," Wilkinson answered. "The South Carolina Yazoo Land Company is trying to take advantage of the settlement's existence. Meanwhile, the settlers are caught like pawns in the middle as the company sells more land and the Spanish deny their rights."

"It seems unlikely to me that the Spanish will give in and permit an illegal American settlement in its territory," Adam said. "The tradition of squatters' rights is nearly impossible to curb on the American frontier, but encroachment of Spanish lands is another matter. What do you think?"

Wilkinson sipped his wine for a while before answering. "Conquest of another country's land is an age-old pastime. Hegemony has been a tradition of ambitious rulers since Hammurabai. But acquisition through diplomacy is far better than aggression. Perhaps the Spanish will accede to the request. After all, they have accepted so many Americans here Natchez might as well be an American colony."

"Ah, but that's far different from an independent colony at Walnut Hills," Adam observed. "It would be a wedge of democracy in a monarchial land. Unless the American settlers give up, as I see it, the outcome could go either of two ways. The Spanish could eject them forcibly, or the Americans could try to take the area by force. Do you see either of those results from the controversy?" Adam hoped the question was specific enough to get a straight answer.

"It's hard to believe the Spanish would try to eject them without the United States coming to their defense. And it's hard to imagine the U.S. government foolish enough to start a war with Spain over such a remote and insignificant settlement. Perhaps, if no one does anything, the matter will rest until everyone gets used to the squatters."

If Wilkinson had meant to obfuscate the matter, he could not have been more skillful. Adam felt he had not learned a thing to prove a conspiracy on either side.

While Adam brooded that night over his rift with Mary, he had a sudden inspiration. Why not give a dinner for Wilkinson, and invite Mary? She admired the colonel, and a pleasant evening together might heal the breach between them.

At breakfast he broached the subject. "Just a small group, Mary and the Formans. They often speak of you."

"I had hoped to meet Miss Grandin again while I am here. Plan away. Except for tonight, I am available at your discretion. I'll spend today and evening in town."

Adam sent invitations for the next evening.

Wilkinson arrived from town next day in time to bathe and change his attire. As Adam finished dressing, he heard a horse trot up to the verandah. He looked out to see Philip Nolan dismount. Adam's thoughts exploded. *Blast his nerve! How could Nolan arrive at dinner time? Wilkinson invite him?* Adam opened the door.

"Please forgive this awkward intrusion, Mister Cloud," Nolan said. "I would not have come had it not been an emergency matter. May I see the colonel? It will take but a moment."

"Of course." Adam felt like punching his handsome nose. "You will find him in the front room across the verandah."

As Nolan and Wilkinson discussed whatever urgent matter had prompted such discourtesy, an unreasoning rage boiled Adam's brain. Courtly manner, balderdash, he thought. Nolan was either a rude oaf or a brazen scoundrel if he knew Mary would be here tonight.

The Forman carriage arrived and Adam greeted the guests outside. Sam and David were not with them. The greetings were effusive, and Adam felt their love and affection, especially Mary's.

He wondered if she had spent sleepless nights regretting her insensitive words.

The guests reached the entrance just as Nolan and the colonel emerged from the outside door of Wilkinson's bedroom. Mary's face showed her astonishment when she saw Philip Nolan.

"Sweet ladies," Colonel Wilkinson greeted Mary and Eliza as he crossed the porch. He kissed their extended hands and greeted Colonel Forman with personal warmth. "May I present my friend and protégé, Philip Nolan? He has made a brief, unexpected visit to conclude our business plans."

"We know Mr. Nolan," Ezekiel said. "He has been a recent visitor in our home."

"It is a pleasure to see you again," Nolan said, his eyes riveted on Mary. "But I'll be leaving at once."

Mary recovered her poise. "Nonsense, Mr. Nolan. You shouldn't leave now. Adam, is there room for one more place at the table? Mr. Nolan is Colonel Wilkinson's guest too."

Adam was stunned, but he managed a reply. "Of course you are welcome, Mr. Nolan. I'll tell Maamba to make a place." He hoped his disgust did not show.

"No, no, Mr. Cloud. I thank you, but I came for only a moment because I do not expect to see the colonel again. I leave early in the morning. Good night, ladies," he bowed to Mary and Eliza, nodded to Ezekiel and mounted his horse.

When Nolan had left, and his guests settled in the parlor, Adam walked to the kitchen. His stomach churned from the encounter, and he stood a few moments suppressing his rage.

Wilkinson dominated the evening conversation. He recounted little anecdotes of his life and travels, and tales of the Kentucky frontier. Adam tried not to dwell on the fact that Nolan had called on Mary. He tried not to think of Nolan at all, but Wilkinson continued to mention him.

"I am pleased that you know Philip. He is like a son to me, and since he lives here, I miss him. We helped raise Philip almost as one of our own because of unfortunate circumstances which befell his parents. We offered him an advanced education, but he declined to suffer through the courses. Philip is a lively and interesting chap, and quite courageous."

Mary described the incident when Adam and Sam had bravely confronted the drunken Choctaws at the dedication of The Commons, and Nolan had turned them back with a few well-chosen words. Wilkinson spoke highly of Nolan's diplomatic skills, and of his ability to serve as his New Orleans agent in trading deals. He recounted several of Nolan's daring escapades in his adventurous capture of wild horses on the plains of Tejas.

By this time, Adam was weary of the topic of Philip Nolan and his adventures, and was glad when Ezekiel changed the subject.

"It is thought that the Opelousas breed are descendants of horses turned loose by early Spanish explorers," Ezekiel said.

"I have been told they are rather capricious, and never seem to forget their wild independence," Adam said. "I would prefer some good Kentucky stock, and have asked Andrew Jackson to bring me back a pair when he comes to Natchez."

"That will be the day," Wilkinson remarked sarcastically. "When he changes trading profits from Negroes for the sale of horses will be the day hell freezes over."

Adam detected animosity between Jackson and Wilkinson, and he changed the subject.

Mary lingered with Adam while the others exchanged farewells. "I wish you would call upon me, Adam. It has been too long a silence between us, and we need to talk."

"Why don't you ride back tomorrow? Colonel Wilkinson will be in town. We can be alone, and can really talk."

"I'll be here by noon, I promise." She kissed him lightly on the cheek as he placed her in the carriage. "Good night, Adam. It was a lovely dinner."

That night Adam could not sleep. Nolan courting Mary presented a real threat. He must act now or possibly lose her, if not to Nolan to another young swain. Would she consider him a potential lover? He was now thirty years old, and Mary only twenty. She was receptive to other men; perhaps he should give her more time to look over the options. No. He might lose her, and he could not bear the thought of life without Mary.

He thought of his brief life with Anne. Their lack of a normal sex life almost cheated him out of his manhood. He was virile, healthy. Mary was spontaneous, strong, with inner vitality. Surely she would not share her sister's attitude toward sex. She was warm, more hot-blooded, different. His thoughts of connubial intimacy made his body ache. He got out of bed and paced the floor. Before he slept, he made a final resolve. He would declare himself tomorrow and discover if she could love him.

Mary's arrival erupted in confusion. Maamba had prepared a picnic for them, but Rebecca clung to them both, begging to go.

"Not this time, darlin'," Adam said. "Aunt Mary and I are going alone. We will take you next time."

He helped Mary remount her horse, and felt sudden panic as he mounted Lancer. Would this ride be more propitious than their last ride together?

"I thought we would picnic in my private bower, if you would like it."

"Of course," she said. "It's a very special place."

Neither spoke as they rode, each sensing an eventful moment between them. Mary started her horse in a trot, then to a full gallop. She turned and laughed, and Adam felt himself relax. *It's going to be all right,* he told himself, and he galloped after her.

Fall colors of brilliant gold, rust and brown tinted the bower, and shafts of sunlight through the trees lent a mystical, vibrant quality.

Mary gasped at its beauty. "Oh, Adam, it's enchanting! The autumn colors lend a glorious magic to the place."

Adam grasped Mary's waist, swinging her down from the horse. He felt the excitement of her warm body as he held on to her tiny waist.

"You bring the magic, Mary. Without you it's just another space in the forest."

His magnetic eyes caught and held her as he drew her close. She studied his face.

"You are not angry with me anymore?" she asked.

"Of course not. Mary, you have become so dear to me that I haven't been able to think of anything but you for weeks. Do you know how much I love you? May I speak about it now?"

"Oh, Adam, if you don't I shall positively burst." Mary's heart was thumping. "I have been waiting forever to hear you say that."

"That's hard to believe. You went away so angry with me that I almost decided I had lost you. Are you really seeing that Nolan fellow, and other callers? I can't bear to think of you with anyone else."

"They mean nothing to me, Adam. I think of you only."

Adam's heart raced with her sweet declaration. He looked deep into her eyes. He brushed the curls on her forehead. He touched her face, her lips. His arms enveloped her and they kissed passionately.

"My darling, I've been longing to do this," he murmured in her ear. "Why did we wait so long? When did it really happen?" He loosened his hold and held her face in front of him, his eyes penetrating hers.

"It happened to me the first time I laid eyes on you," Mary said. She saw Adam's look of disbelief. "Honestly, Adam, I have loved you since that very first day you rode onto Belview Manor."

"But you were only fifteen!"

"I adored you all through Sister's conquest of you, and I cried the whole night of your wedding. I watched your marriage carefully, and felt in my heart that I could make you a better wife. Does this shock you? Do I sound covetous?"

Adam digested this surprising revelation. "No, not at all. You behaved as a loving little sister, and that's why I always looked upon you that way. Yes, I am surprised, and I suppose it is a good thing neither of us guessed. It would have hurt Anne. Dear, precious Mary. You are no longer the little sister." He hugged her again. "Will you be mine? You can fill my life with happiness, and Becky's too. Not only do I love you deeply, but I can't imagine life without you."

They kissed and embraced with passion until Adam finally broke away and held her with his eyes.

"We came for a picnic, and we found heaven," he said.

"You said this place was special. Heaven was here all the time. We just had to find it."

Her mind in a whirl, Mary sat on a log and emptied the picnic basket to stop her trembling. Adam helped her remove the food and drink, and their excitement mounted as they began to talk about wedding plans.

"I'm really not hungry, Adam. Are you? I'm too excited to eat."

"Not really. Maamba will scold us if we don't finish. Let's get back and tell everyone. Leave the food for the bears."

Riding to the Formans' home, Adam reflected on Mary's surprising revelation of her long-standing love. He recalled the prodding hints that Sam and Colonel Wilkinson had offered him, and wondered that he could be so dense.

The Forman family was delighted by the news, but not surprised. They revealed there had been wagers among them on when Adam would declare himself and ask for Mary's hand.

Eliza offered her home for the wedding, and excitedly suggested plans for the event. That night Colonel Wilkinson expressed his gratification and pleasure at the good news, and regretted he could not stay long enough to attend the wedding.

The next day Adam rode to Government House to post his wedding banns and to tell Don Manuel of his wedding plans. "It will be soon," he said, "right after the October harvest."

"How happy I am for you, *Señor* Cloud," the governor said. "The day you first sat before me I was surprised that *Señorita* Grandin was not your wife. I thought you would be an ideal couple."

Adam grinned. "It took me a little longer to discover that. But, Your Excellency, would it be possible to be married by one of the Protestant ministers here?"

"Ah, no, I am sorry, that is not possible. It is forbidden that anyone but a Catholic priest may conduct a marriage ceremony."

"Aren't there any exceptions?" Adam felt exasperated. The answer was too quick, too final. "Has there never been a Protestant wedding here?"

Don Manuel hesitated a moment, as if considering. "Well, yes, I did hear of a Protestant marriage before I came. As I recall, it was permitted because the couple did not intend to live in Natchez. But that would not be possible now. The church rules are firmly established."

Adam looked so crestfallen that the governor tried to soften the blow. He smiled and said, kindly, "I understand your wish, but you know, the Lord looks favorably on Catholic weddings too. You will be just as much married as if you wed in your own church. Unfortunately, we do not have a real church for the marriage, but I gladly offer you my home, if that would please you."

"Very kind of you, sir, and I thank you, but the Formans are planning the ceremony in their home. It will seem strange being married in a Roman Catholic ritual. Needless to say, I'm disappointed."

"Well, you will find very little difference from your own rituals. Father William holds a fine ceremony, with Friar Brady assisting. The friar is always fun at weddings. He has a lively wit and lends his lovable nature to the occasion. When you give me the exact date, I will inform Father William and you can make further arrangements." Don Manuel paused, noting Adam's glum expression.

"I would like to assuage your disappointment and show my good will. Your marriage, and the possibility of new progeny for your family, God willing, deserves a larger land allotment. I note you are also acquiring more slaves to help work your property. I will grant you another 500 arpents of land to expand your estate. When you have time, we can look over the map of unsettled land for your future use."

Adam was overwhelmed, and it took a few seconds before he could answer. "I am honored by your generous offer, Your Excellency, but right now I think I have all I can handle. I feel somehow I should earn the right to more land. This is a new world for me, and I must take one step at a time."

"What an honest, practical man you are, *Señor* Cloud. Most men would have jumped at the chance for more property, regardless of their worthiness. You are a rare breed, indeed, and I like your spirit. The offer can simmer for a while, but I shall not forget it. In the meantime, I extend you and your bride-to-be my heartiest congratulations for your coming nuptials, and may your life and plantation prosper."

Adam stopped at the Formans' and expressed his disappointment to Mary. "Having performed so many marriages myself, I felt demeaned that we must submit to a Roman ceremony. Do you mind terribly, my darling? At least we won't have to marry inside a Catholic church."

Mary smiled at his disappointment. "Oh, what's the difference, Adam? I would marry you even with an Indian ceremony. I agree with the governor. A proper marriage is sanctified in God's eyes, no matter where or who conducts it. Let's just not wait too long."

The wedding was held in the Forman parlor on the first of November. Guests included their new friends, the Perkinses, Moores, Bowleses and Coreys, and traveling companions, the Preeces from the St. Catherine district, and the two young Minor couples. The parlor had been lavishly decorated with vines, flowers, and pink satin bows. Eliza and her three daughters served as maid-of-honor and bridesmaids. But the setting barely penetrated Adam's euphoria. His eyes and thoughts were only on his bride.

His heart pounded like a schoolboy's when the lovely Mary Grandin approached him on Ezekiel's arm. There was never a bride more desirable, he thought. Her white bridal gown, designed and made by Liz Preece, set off her dark hair and rich skin tone. She carried red roses. Father William had agreed to shorten the rituals and use only candles, eliminating the Eucharist, the censer and incense. But Adam hardly noticed the Catholic ceremony.

"In the name of our Holy Mother Church, I pronounce you husband and wife . . ." Adam did not even hear the blessing. Mary was his now, and he kissed her in a joyous haze. The guests stirred with emotion. Becky clapped her hands, her eyes filled with mischievous glee, not sure what the excitement was all about.

A lively wedding feast followed, the wine flowed, and guests recounted stories of their own marriages. Friar Brady's Irish brogue and quick wit kept everyone roaring with laughter at his amusing tales. Leaving Becky with the Formans, the newlyweds drove home in the carriage with Moses.

As they crossed the porch, the door swung open and Maamba, Dirk and Tizzi stepped outside, greeting them with grinning faces. Adam carried his bride across the threshold, and Mary found herself entering the familiar home she had learned to love, now as her very own. The servants clapped hands, their eyes shining with genuine happiness. Moses grinned as he watched them from the carriage. Adam set Mary down and they looked about. The house had been decorated with boughs of berries and honeysuckle.

"Everything looks beautiful," he said, smiling at his servants with newfound approval. He poured them each a small glass of wine. "We are touched by your thoughtfulness and genuine affection." He raised his glass. "Thank you," he toasted, "and may we all share a long and happy life."

Then they were alone. Maamba had folded the bedcovers neatly back, and sprinkled bits of lavender on the pillows.

Adam watched Mary struggle with her bridal veil. He gently pulled the pins from the veil and from her hair, letting it cascade around her shoulders. He drew her in his arms and they swayed in a locked embrace. Adam gradually unfastened her neckline and moved on down the waist, until she could slip out of her gown. She undid his cravat, loosened his vest, and unbuttoned his shirt.

They stood facing each other. Adam's desire and passion swept through his mind and body. Neither spoke. Mary let the rest of her garments fall, and Adam drew aside the thin cambric sheath of her undervest. She stood before him nude. Only in his wildest dreams had he envisioned a woman willing to love him naked. Her body gleamed like warm ivory in the candlelight. Her breasts were firm and saucy, her thighs velvety smooth.

He quickly dropped his remaining garments and blew out the candles. They embraced until they stood trembling, and he carried her to the bed.

Adam had no idea of the intensity of his emotions as his passions unfolded, but he was gentle. He took his time with her, tenderly stroking and kissing, wrapping her in his arms, his body, feeling the ultimate thrill of her responses. To his delight, Mary was not shy. She was ready for marriage, and gave herself with such passion that Adam had no hesitancy in showing her every expression of physical ardor that would add to her pleasure. They consummated their marriage with ultimate trust and desire. He was so overwhelmed with emotion and happiness that he was certain there could be no ecstasy in heaven greater than his love.

The days and nights that followed were filled with unabated love and passion. They were immersed in a lover's world of sexual fulfillment and bliss, and Mary's responses matched his own.

Adam was glad he had supervised the harvesting before the marriage. He had little inclination to turn his mind to the farm, but he had to assess his crops.

"We have to face details sometime," he said to Mary. "The harvest is excellent for a first crop on the limited acreage, but we can triple the results from more acreage planted next year."

"The good harvest calls for a slave celebration; they worked so hard," Mary said. "Jenny Bowles and I thought our blacks should celebrate together, since many of theirs were loaned to us."

"That's a fine idea. We need a joyous occasion to initiate our plantation."

On feast day, Mary, Maamba, and Tizzi turned out dozens of corn cakes, the Bowleses provided meat, and the blacks roasted deer, cooked field corn, turnips, and greens. The slave celebration continued raucously into the night. As Mary and Adam prepared for bed the music, laughter, and shouting became louder and wilder with African drum beats, chants, songs and dances.

"What to you think, Adam? Should we curb this African frenzy?" Mary held still while Adam helped with her unfastenings.

"The poor souls miss their own culture. I think they should have a chance to revive it once in a while, but I worry that they may never be ready for Christianity." Adam sat on the bed, loosening a boot.

"Not only that," Mary said, as she leaned over him and pulled off his boot, "but the neighbors might be critical if we let them carry on this way. Word gets around through the slaves." She tugged at the other boot and tossed it over the bed. Adam slipped off her camisole, grabbed her waist, and pulled her on the bed. They snuggled under the blankets.

"Egad but you have it to give. How did one sweet little virgin learn so much?"

"My sister Sarah taught me everything I needed to know for marriage, when I lived with them that year. I liked to imagine it would be you that I gave myself to." Adam fondled her tenderly and she tingled with pleasure. "Do I please you?" she whispered in his ear.

"You do, oh, you do," Adam groaned as he caressed her soft, supple body.

Mary arched her neck for his kisses. "Do I please you as much as, well . . . you expected?" she murmured.

"More, even more, my precious," he whispered. "You are astounding. More than I ever dreamed of."

Mary raised slightly and leaned on her elbow, gazing closely into his face. "You mean, Anne wasn't . . . she didn't . . .?" Her voice trailed off in shocked disbelief.

Adam nodded, and Mary saw the painful memories in his eyes.

"You poor darling," Mary said softly. "You can wager I'll make up for every pleasure that you missed over the years."

"I don't need to wager. You're a lifetime guarantee of fulfillment in the exquisite demands of mating." He pulled her closer, but Mary put him off with another question.

"Adam, does our marriage and intimacy affect the possibility of your ordination as a priest?"

"Of course not, my darling. What ever gave you such an idea?"

"Well, since you told me of your unusual spiritual experience when you were eighteen, I have wondered why your studies were so important."

Adam remained silent for a few moments, considering how to explain. "The event was so miraculous that it has motivated my religious life from that day on. I feel compelled to find the path to spiritual evolution."

"I have been reading some of your esoteric literature, but I find most of it very obscure. What have you learned?"

"I found I had entered a higher state of consciousness, and that even higher levels, reached by saints and holy men of many faiths, are attainable. There are two paths whereby one can reach the highest state. One way is through a life of celibacy and spiritual contemplation, and the other through a life of active service for humanity. Both demand rigorous purification of the mind, body, and soul."

"And you had to choose between them?" Mary was beginning to see his dilemma.

"Yes, my precious." He drew her close again, and spoke softly in her ear. "My love and desire for you were so great that I realized I could never become a celibate recluse on the contemplative path. Instead, I could choose the active path of human service toward spiritual advancement, and still have you."

Mary's eyes welled with tears as she thought of Adam's commitment to her. His love fulfilled her life, and she must make sure he never regretted his choice. Love itself was a mystical force, its divine source revealed in fragments, like a many-faceted crystal casting tiny reflections on every loving act.

"I love you, Adam," she said from her depths, "and I thank God for your decision."

Adam felt for the candle by the bedside, snuffed it, and said, "I feel too wicked with you to be a priest."

"Let's be wicked. I'll never tell on you!"

Their aroused sexuality and passion mounted. The drifting sounds of drums and chants outside were exotic and sensuous, merging with their own body rhythms and throbbing heartbeats.

BOOK II

13 The Spanish Conspiracy

Adam looked down upon his sleeping bride, her dark hair in a tumble of curls around her pillow, her sweeping black brows and lashes framing her delicate oval face. So tender, yet so passionate was she. A kaleidoscope of memories of their first few weeks of marriage filled his mind. Never could he have imagined a wife so filled with love and desire. He counted his good fortune that she had been so persistent in her resolve to make him hers. He had fought off Mary's solace as though acceptance of her intent would somehow bring him guilt that he could capitulate to her wily charms.

He walked to the window and opened the shutters. The brilliant December sunshine flooded the room.

"Dear God," he prayed fervently, "keep this little cantle of the world as peaceful and quiet as it is now; and help me prosper for the sake of my little family."

He looked out upon the meadow which had yielded his first crops. It was empty now, except for the ragged stubble of harvested corn, and a few pumpkins and squash. They sparkled bright orange and yellow, as their blanket of morning dew drops caught the sunlight. He looked beyond to the two slave cabins, his new stable, and empty barn. His crops had long since floated downriver to New Orleans on a flatboat.

He felt a glow of pride. All of this had been accomplished in just ten months, since March — the beginning of his new life in Natchez. What could possibly intrude on this serene, peaceful place? True, the *commandante* had told them that rumors of a military invasion, a "filibuster" he had called it, had made them suspicious of any large fleets. But such threats from the American frontier had been made for a long time, and nothing ever came of them. He refused to worry over unlikely possibilities.

As he shaved, he glanced occasionally in the mirror at Mary to see if she was still asleep. She stirred, pulled the covers over her ears and slept on. He combed his shoulder-length brown hair, tied it in a queue with a leather thong, and turned to the wardrobe. He must dress well this morning, for he would be riding up the Natchez Trace with the governor and would be gone several days. He selected cinnamon twill breeches and a brown wool jacket. As he put them on, he relished his fortuitous good luck to receive an invitation from Governor Gayoso to accompany him to Cole's Creek. It had come as a surprise, and he was anxious to discover why he had been chosen for this honor.

He pulled on his boots and tiptoed out the door, closing it quietly so as not awaken Mary. Entering the adjoining bedroom, he grinned at Becky, playing quietly in her roughly hewn bed. Tizzi was asleep on her cot nearby. Becky let out a whoop when she saw her father, and jumped up and down with glee.

"Papa, I wake up," she called.

"Good morning, baby-doll," he said. He lifted her gently in his arms and kissed her while she clung to his neck. "Tizzi! Wake up, girl. Becky needs you," he called.

Tizzi rubbed the sleep from her eyes and sprang out of bed. "Yes, Massah Adam, we's prac'ly dress already."

Becky fondled a brass button on his coat. "You look pretty, Papa. Dress-up?" she queried.

"Yes, little darling, I'm riding away this morning. But I'll be back very soon, and Mama will be here with you."

He gently handed her over to Tizzi and tiptoed into his bedroom again. Again he glanced at his sleeping wife and then crossed the breezeway to the adjoining wing, where he heard pans rattling. Entering the kitchen, he saw Maamba assembling breakfast.

"Good mornin', Massah Adam." Maamba beamed her black round face in a good-natured grin. "You sleeps well? You up so early, even fo' I kin waken Tizzi."

"Yes, I'm up especially early, Maamba. I'm riding off for several days with the governor, and will need you to pack me some fresh clothing after breakfast."

"The governor! Lawdy, Massah Adam, you sho' in good company," Maamba exclaimed.

"That's a fact." Adam grinned with secret pleasure. "Miss Mary is still asleep, but I am sure she will want to join us for breakfast," he called out as he left the room.

He looked through the parlor, out across the long verandah to the huge magnolia tree; its dark leaves shone as if they had been polished. Becky's swing hung inert from one of its branches. Down the three hundred yard slope, and outside the gate, was a newly hewn signpost bearing the catchy name "Cloudcrest" to mark their plantation. He went back to their bedroom and found Mary awake, but still in bed.

"Good morning, my love," Mary said. She gazed approvingly at her handsome husband as he entered, so fully dressed and well-groomed. "You look nice for your journey, but I shall miss you. I can hardly bear for you to be away."

She held her arms wide for an embrace. Adam sat on the edge of the bed and kissed her.

"It will be only several nights, my precious. And you gave me enough love last night to hold me over until I return." He grinned at her as he savored the memory.

Mary ran her fingers down Adam's strong, lean face, and looked up at the pine knots in the ceiling.

"Adam, can't you call it off? Tell Governor Gayoso you can't go with him. Find an excuse. One of us is ill, or you have a sick child."

Adam absently poked a finger into the slight dimple on her cheek. "Not go with Governor Gayoso?" He raised one eyebrow in the quizzical gesture she had come to love. "We both agreed that it was a great honor for him to ask me to accompany him to Cole's Creek."

Mary sat up in bed and said slowly and deliberately, "*You* agreed, and I went along with it as I always do. But that's not my real feeling."

"Then tell me your real feeling. How else will I know unless you do? Help me." Adam bent over her, secretly appreciating the way her full breasts quivered under the delicate lace of her gown as she spoke.

"I'm concerned that the governor will capture your attention with the local politics. I have heard that he draws people to his bosom with his charm, then uses them to his political advantage. Perhaps Colonel Wilkinson's letter of introduction was a signal that you had political interests."

"His letter might have contributed in my favor, but I don't believe it had any underlying message."

"You're not taking me seriously, Adam." The dark wings of Mary's strong brows came together in a not unbecoming frown, and her lips pursed into the little pout that Adam had come to recognize as displeasure. "I need your undivided attention as I nurture Becky and tend to our home. You have enough to do here on the plantation with the crops and management of the slaves."

"You and the household will have my undivided attention."

"Then tell me, honestly, Adam, why do you think the governor wants you to accompany him today?"

Mary's serious question brought Adam to his feet, and he walked to the window.

"Perhaps he is going to give me some land up there. He offered me more when he saw my disappointment that we had to be married by a Catholic priest. He really seemed to feel badly about it, Mary."

"More land? Besides what you have now? There, what did I tell you! Why didn't you tell me this before? Was it a secret?"

"Not really, my dear. I could hardly believe it myself, and I declined the offer. I felt I had enough land as a beginner, and should earn the right to more."

Mary was silent a few moments as she got out of bed and groped toward her dressing gown. Adam helped her put it on and took the brush from her hand, as she sat at the dresser. He gazed at her reflection in the mirror with new eyes, and absently stroked her long, brown locks.

"Just you wait," she said finally. "Gayoso will want something for his generosity. And he's very close to Colonel Wilkinson. Even you have suspicions of their connections. Why should we care about what Wilkinson does up there in Kentucky? When he stayed with you last month, I suspected that underneath all of his handsome charm and courtly manners, he was an ambitious, driving politician. We're out of all that now. And you should be too."

Adam laid down the brush and stood quietly looking out the window for some minutes, for these were hard questions his lovely young wife was asking. Political involvement could be dangerous, and he hardly knew how to assuage her fears and unwarranted suspicions. He was beginning to suspect that beneath those charming curls lay a fearsome intelligence. He wasn't sure he could handle such beauty and passion in combination with a stubbornly questioning intellect. It was a side of Mary he hadn't really seen before. But he must say something. Mary's grave eyes were unwavering, and she was not to be put off. He turned and faced her squarely.

"I couldn't feign an excuse to Don Manuel now, Mary," he said firmly. "He will be here within the hour, and it would be an insult to him. Besides, he would see right through any excuse. He is extending the arm of friendship to me, and I'm grateful for his interest."

Mary closed her lips tightly at the unaccustomed rebuke. Sometimes her passionate husband bent over backward too far to defend others. She debated calling this to his attention, but decided she had better not.

Adam continued. "Don't forget that Gayoso is a public servant charged with the responsibility of seeing that all the different elements under his domain get along amicably. And he is our friend, too, Mary. You would recognize that if you were not being so unreasonable."

But Mary was not ready to be reasonable. "Some friend," she snorted in a most unladylike way. "Snatching you away for two days and nights from your family." She turned away from Adam, her shoulders squared in defiance, and brushed her hair vigorously, with short, swift strokes.

Adam erupted in anger. "I cannot talk with you when you're like this. I really don't want to continue the discussion, but let's get one thing straight. I must do some things, and relinquish others in order to live in harmony here in Natchez. Harmony, hah! I am going with Don Manuel, and *that's it.* Now get dressed; you should be ready to greet him."

He strode out of the room and sat moodily at the table, glum and silent as Maamba poured his coffee. Breakfast was a strained affair, formal and overly polite, unlike their usual laughter-filled meals. Each of them spoke only to Becky, who talked unabashedly, and giggled as she ate. Maamba had moved back and forth between the kitchen and dining table, offering grits, bacon, and apple fritters, refilling the coffee cups. Her usual smiling countenance and nonstop chatter could not change Mary's downcast eyes, or Adam's preoccupation with the month-old *Louisville Gazette* beside his plate.

Adam felt miserable and sick inside.This was their first quarrel, and he did not know how to overcome it. He kissed his daughter and prepared to leave.

Mary did not follow him outside where Dirk awaited him with his horse, saddled and packed with his overnight satchel. Adam lingered a few moments, hoping Mary would come rushing out to say goodbye. With one last look to see if Mary was on the porch — she wasn't — he walked his horse down the path toward the gate. He would meet the governor on the Trace so as to avoid embarrassment.

Adam waited nervously at the gate, feeling the crisp December air. He rubbed the soft suede of his big roan gelding's nose.

"Lucky Lancer," he muttered. "Mares don't interest you any more so they can't cause you much trouble."

Soon he heard a contingent of horses on the trail. Adam mounted and rode out on the Trace to meet Don Manuel and his escort of two officers, two soldiers and his manservant, Chico. The horses stomped and blew hazy puffs of steam from their nostrils as they halted.

Governor Gayoso greeted Adam with a genial warmth that exceeded his customary exquisite manners. He was attired casually in soft buff-colored breeches and jacket, and shiny black boots. His graying hair was carefully coifed in horizontal rolls at his ears. His hazel eyes were friendly, but penetrating, and Adam felt the sense of personal power which exuded from his trim body. His mellifluous voice had a cheery ring, and Adam absorbed his English with pleasure. Tinted with a polished British accent, his words flowed in beautiful cadence with perfect syntax. Adam recalled his strict boyhood tutors who demanded impeccable English, as well as Latin and Greek. His adherence to their high standards had served him well in his preaching days, and he always appreciated beautifully spoken English.

"*Buenos dias, Señor* Cloud. Thank you for your company. I trust you left your bride not too grievous at your parting?" He did not see Adam wince at this luckless remark. "As you remember, I promised you another land grant before your marriage, and the Cole's Creek area I have in mind should be to your liking. In order to get better acquainted, we can maintain a slow pace as we ride. We will be gone two nights, possibly three. We can depend on the hospitality of one of the local families, who always bid me welcome."

"Your Excellency, your generosity is indeed overwhelming. Of course I would like to see the area. This is more than I expected."

"Every time I pass by I have been impressed with the progress of your property improvements since your acquisition in March. You have wrought a miracle in such a short time, and with so few hands to bring it about."

Gayoso studied Adam's face as the young man received his praise. Adam's dark eyes reflected pleasure, but remained unflustered; they were expressive, warm, tender. His handsome features reflected a natural charm, suggesting undaunted wisdom and strength.

"It was no miracle, sir," Adam replied with an easy laugh. "Just a lot of hard, sweaty labor. I bought four new slaves and borrowed blacks from Colonel Forman's and other plantations. Friends and neighbors also lent a hand in building my home. My reward was a modest summer harvest."

Adam felt the silence of the deep forest around them. The extended ride up the Trace was his first, and there would be nearly sixteen miles to travel. The path was just wide enough for two horses to walk side by side. One officer and a soldier rode ahead, while the rest fell behind Adam and the governor. As the horses' hooves trod the soft, dry earth, crunching a carpet of fallen twigs and leaves, Adam found that the quiet scene of woods and shady trail produced a subdued mood. They rode slowly in silence for a while.

Don Manuel looked at Adam's pensive face and sensed they shared the same emotion. "Nice, is it not?" he said. "The Spanish call this trail *El Camino de Norte a Cumberland*. I feel refreshed every time I ride it. The ride affords time for reflection and creative thought."

"Your fearlessness is reassuring after all the lurid tales of encounters with wild beasts, bandits, and Indians I have heard about traveling the Trace."

"I suppose the trail has seen much violence since ancient days when it was blazed by buffaloes and wild animals. We are more likely to meet straggling travelers from Nashborough," Gayoso said with a smile. "We can ride leisurely. An overnight stay at Mount Locust will take us about halfway. With a long ride ahead, I believe we would be more comfortable on a less formal basis. Please call me Don Manuel. And may I call you Don Adam, or do you prefer your church title?"

"My Episcopal title is Deacon, or merely Reverend. I have not yet been ordained a priest, and I prefer the plain title of Mister. But just call me Adam, or Don Adam, according to your custom."

"So, Don Adam, I am somewhat relieved to know you are not fully frocked." Don Manuel observed Adam's look of amusement and laughed. "By that I mean I find it sometimes intimidating to be around one with holy orders. I mean no disrespect, but super-holiness disturbs me. Perhaps it is my own inadequacy in such matters which puts me at a disadvantage."

Adam studied his distinguished companion as they talked. Probably in his forties, he surmised. Urbane, sophisticated, polished, an *hidalgo* in the Spanish class structure. "I can't imagine you being disadvantaged for any reason," he replied. "You seem well-versed in many subjects, and speak many languages, I hear."

"Perhaps it reflects my English education," Don Manuel said. "During my adolescence I enjoyed an extracurricular education in the affairs of the Court of London, where my father was appointed to serve. My studies at Westminister College provided knowledge that I do not believe I could have received in Madrid. I found an openness to world affairs that I did not see reflected in the Spanish Catholic view."

Adam was astounded at this remark, and he wondered if he could pursue the train of thought further without offending the governor. He must be careful, but yet, the man seemed to invite serious discussion. Something, however, told him to hold back.

"Religious wisdom serves us best when it is tempered with worldly knowledge and experience," he offered.

"Speaking of the ministry," Don Manuel said, "that path ahead leads to a settlement called Selser Town, where another Protestant minister holds together a Baptist community. He is the Reverend Ricardo Curtis. Have you met him?"

"No, but I heard about the Baptist settlers from my friend Joseph Perkins, who emigrated with them from South Carolina."

"I'm not sure how much religious activity prevails here, but I understand the Reverend Curtis is a zealous evangelical preacher. No one monitors the community, and they seem to handle their own affairs without help."

Don Manuel pointed out an Indian mound, used for religious rites, and their topic turned to ancient religious myths. Before dusk, they reached Mount Locust, a stand for travelers which served as a way-station on the Trace. After supper, which was cooked and served by the Ferguson family, Adam and Don Manuel sat on the covered porch while the soldiers played cards at the dining table. Polly Ferguson brought them mugs of *negus*, and placed a lampwick on the rail. Don Manuel opened a small cigar box.

"Do you smoke?" he asked.

"Occasionally, thank you, I will," Adam said as he took one. Don Manuel offered the lampwick and they lighted up. He then opened the conversation.

"I was impressed with the letter of introduction Colonel James Wilkinson wrote for you in Louisville. He writes me that he will be coming downriver again soon with another trade fleet, and that he will get in touch with you. He seemed to like you very much. Had you become friends?"

"Casual friends, one might say, during our stay in Louisville, and again when he visited me last month. I found his activities intriguing," Adam replied. "Especially his trade ventures in New Orleans, and his dealings with Governor-General Miró. He had some kind things to say about you, and seemed to cherish your friendship."

"That's nice to hear. He was quite ill when he returned from New Orleans last year, and stayed with me for almost a week. We had long discussions about ourselves and our plans for the future."

Adam seized the remark as an opportunity to discuss Colonel Wilkinson, hoping he would not tread on sensitive ground. "Don Manuel, may I ask you something that puzzles me?"

"Ask away."

"Colonel Wilkinson's account of his trading ventures showed me why the use of the Mississippi River is the most important issue at stake with the frontier settlers. He said his first experiences were surprisingly successful, and that he made satisfying arrangements for his own trade missions with Louisiana's Governor-General Miró. I gather his aim is to open up the river trade for the western frontier, but that Spanish restrictions stand in the way."

"And for good reason," Don Manuel said. "The encroaching American frontier poses a threat to our government. Ever since Georgia laid claim to territory between the Yazoo River and the Thirty-first Parallel, in 1785, and established the settlement of Walnut Hills in Spanish territory, we have lived under constant threats of an armed filibuster to take over our territory. The fear of an irregular military invasion has forced us to restrict river trade. Before I arrived, it became necessary to seize illegal American cargoes on the river. The Americans retaliated by seizing Spanish cargoes at Vincennes, and the battle created a friction that has grown since."

"I didn't know the problem was so acute," Adam said. "But I am puzzled why Spain has invited so many Americans to live in Natchez."

"Alas, Don Adam, efforts to establish a solid Spanish colony here have not been successful. Spanish citizens are reluctant to immigrate to this wilderness. It seemed advantageous, therefore, that the government populate the region with desirable foreign settlers anxious for land grants, freedom of worship, navigation of the Mississippi, and an outlet for their goods."

"With due respect, Your Excellency, your interpretation of the phrase 'freedom of worship' differs from its meaning in my vocabulary." Adam's silent regulator bade him be careful, but the phrase stuck in his craw. He thought of that other preacher, Curtis, who must be struggling in his Baptist community. Gayoso's startled look told him he had blundered.

"The meaning differs only slightly," Don Manuel said defensively. "Many accommodations have been made by our Catholic leaders to allow all religious faiths to worship here."

Adam ignored his inner signal to accept this justification graciously. The subject was too precious to his heart and mind. "The difference is hardly slight to Protestants who have no churches. America was founded on the need for freedom of worship, and communal worship is the bulwark of Christian life. To deny that right is highly discouraging to individual faith; it either withers away or causes inner rebellion."

Don Manuel glowered. "If this is a prophetic warning, Don Adam, it falls on deaf ears," he said testily. "My role is to keep the peace, and I have no influence in our Catholic hierarchy. You are in our country now, and your faith need not wither." He rose and tamped out his cigar. In a conciliatory tone he added, "But we must get some rest. We should be up at dawn to reach Cole's Creek by early morning."

Adam regretted his outburst and wished he had bitten his tongue. It was no time to antagonize his host, and he vowed to make peace with Don Manuel.

In the morning, Don Manuel showed no sign of their disagreement the night before. They rode with more urgency, and conversation was suspended until they reached a change of terrain near Cole's Creek. Adam noted the rich groves of cypress on a high, flat plateau.

"I have selected the fifty-four families located on this plateau around the creek and two other bayous nearby," Don Manuel explained, "and I have permission from the governor-general to build an official auxiliary residence here. It will be essentially an administrative center for local affairs with a guardhouse and a new parish church. Roman Catholic, of course." He flashed Adam a grin.

"The sacred next to the profane," Adam said lightly.

"What?" Gayoso asked, not comprehending at first. "Oh, yes," he laughed. "Indeed, the Lord's house and the guardhouse."

Adam drew in his reins and paused to take in the view. They had emerged from the cypress forest to the edge of a broad meadow, a curving belt of timber surrounding it like a great protecting arm. The long, slender, upright cypress branches of gray-green foliage formed tall, stately pyramids, providing a dense screening and protection for the rich meadow grasses. Adam's spirits soared as he surveyed the profuse growth which covered the fields, indicating rich soil and an abundant crop yield.

Adam shook his head in wonderment. "The surroundings are beautiful, and it looks so peaceful," he said.

"I am very fond of this place. I always look forward to coming here where I can retreat, recoup my energies, and rethink administrative decisions without the usual daily pressures." Don Manuel spoke wistfully.

"Your responsibilities must be overwhelming in administering the affairs of more than one thousand people in the widespread Natchez district."

"The pressures are considerable," Don Manuel admitted, "but my well-informed staff are an immeasurable help to me. Still, one needs a respite from routine sometimes to get a better perspective. But come, let me show you my new homesite, and then see if I have selected one to your liking."

They reached a pleasant location on the plateau overlooking Cole's Creek, where Don Manuel said he had selected his homesite. They traversed the grounds, weaving back and forth from the creek bed. Adam was impressed with the variety of trees, interspersed with a few cypresses rising some sixty feet like sentinels among them.

"Here," said Don Manuel finally, "is the focal point for a section of five hundred arpents for you, if it pleases you. As you can see, it is on the creek and close to the spring which we would share as neighbors. *Señor* Jorge Matthews owns a large section next to it. He is a gentleman of fine standing whom, I am sure, you will find most agreeable."

Adam surveyed the scene — the level terrain, the surrounding forest, glimpses of the creek through the trees. He saw himself as the landlord of a second great plantation. Instantly his silent regulator flashed a signal. Surely this was not all for him, gratis and unsolicited? What had he done to deserve such largesse? Mary's words nagged at him. *Just you wait; he'll want something for his generosity*. He felt uneasy, tempted, but with unknown implications. He answered with as much aplomb as he could muster.

"Don Manuel, what can I say? I'm overwhelmed with your generous offer, and I am more than pleased with the land you have selected for me. I find it extremely flattering that you have chosen me for a future neighbor. What a spot! I can already envision my new home here."

"You will make the most of it, I am sure," Don Manuel said graciously. "Now, I have business to conduct with Juan Smith, who is a surveyor. He will help me select a site for the church. We will also study a new road layout which I am planning for better access to Natchez. Would you like to accompany me? Or perhaps you had rather look around your new property and determine its best use."

"I'll stay here a while and then look up the Carters. They came with us to Natchez, you remember, and you granted them land up here," Adam answered.

The governor took his leave with directions for Adam to find him later. Adam rode his acreage again, lingering and marveling at its features. He then traced his creek frontage to the river, gazing for a long time at the wide spread of the bayou mouth, giving easy access to river use.

He took a deep breath of satisfaction and congratulated himself. All this was certainly worth coming to Natchez for, he told himself. He then turned Lancer toward the settlement center.

The surprised Carters welcomed their former traveling companion with genuine warmth. Jeb's large muscular stature seemed to Adam even more formidable than when they had traveled together. He recalled the many incidents in which Jeb's prodigious strength had made the difference in getting the caravan through rough predicaments on land and across rivers. Mazie, he noted, was with child, her face reposed and radiant with content. The young couple said that Jeb's building skills and Mazie's dressmaking were in great demand at Cole's Creek.

They shared their midday meal with Adam and eagerly exchanged news of travel companions and mutual happenings since getting settled in Natchez. The Carters rejoiced with Adam on receiving his Cole's Creek land grant, and Jeb offered to help him build when he was ready.

Upon leaving his friends, Adam found the governor at "The Bluffs" plantation owned by John Smith. Smith was not only a surveyor but also a talented builder. The road survey had been completed, and the governor was ready to leave. Trailed by the governor's military contingency, they headed toward the plantation of Thomas Marsten Green. As they rode, Don Manuel spoke of the father, Col. Thomas Abner Green, who had emigrated from New Jersey, in 1782. He had received hundreds of arpents of Spanish land and had become prosperous.

"Yes, I have met Colonel Green and his sons," Adam said. "Andrew Jackson told me of his incarceration by the Spanish for treason."

"Yes, he nearly lost his lands because of his disloyalty, but since his pardon he has become a model citizen. Of course, his title of magistrate, bestowed by the Americans, evaporated with their land claim. The government purchased this area from him that is now the Cole's Creek district. He was generous to his children, granting them large portions of his estate. His daughter married Cato West, one of the largest ranchers in this vicinity. Abner Green's home is further upriver, at Bayou Pierre."

"One wonders why the colonel, with his vast land grant, should have risked so much in hopes of gaining more from the Americans," Adam mused.

"Disloyal citizens are not tolerated here," Don Manuel replied solemnly, "and it was highly fitting that he be incarcerated for his misdeeds."

Adam sensed a foreboding at this ominous remark, but he shrugged it off. It seemed so inconsistent with Don Manuel's genial character.

They reached Springfield plantation across a wide plain, close to Cole's Creek and the Trace. A dense forest surrounded the estate, hiding the house from view. Adam was impressed as soon as they entered the gate. A bridle path led through a border of cypress and red oak trees. A magnificent two-story mansion, painted dark red with white trim, presented an imposing and serene picture. Six white colonnades supported generous galleries across the width of the facade. The upper gallery was enclosed with a French-style wrought iron guard rail. Two magnificent spreading oaks stood like welcoming sentinels in front of the house.

The Green family, with their children, warmly greeted them on the lower gallery as they arrived. Thomas and Martha Green, an attractive couple in their forties, showed them inside. The children were sent upstairs for their evening meal.

Adam thought the Springfield interior as impressive as the outside. He studied every detail in order to be able to describe it accurately to Mary. A high ceiling and huge corner fireplace dominated the large front parlor. The recessed walls were decorated with elegantly paneled wainscoting, and narrow bands of hand-carved cornices in rococo designs. A spacious center hall led to a huge dining room designed for lavish entertaining.

After supper the group settled before the parlor fireplace, with steaming demitasse cups of *cafe au lait*. Don Manuel and the

Greens discussed affairs of Cole's Creek and Bayou Pierre, giving Adam an overview of the area and its settlers. The group discussed road upkeep and expansion, and Adam asked if there were plans to accommodate traditional carriages.

"What carriages?" Thomas laughed. "There's only one, Colonel Forman's, and I doubt if many others will be coming down the river on a keelboat."

"The time may come when everyone wants to order a conveyance," Adam said. "Ezekiel finds using his coach is not easy. Every time they plan to visit someone he has to send notification ahead so the bridle paths can be cleared of cane in order for him to pass through."

"This place is still so primitive," Martha lamented with a sigh.

Don Manuel acknowledged the need for wider roads and turned to Martha. "I understand your despair, *Señora,* but little by little this district will become more civilized," he said kindly. "Just you wait. We will soon have a new racetrack and other amenities that will further enrich our lives. New residents, like Don Adam and many others, bring fresh ideas and ingenuity to our way of life, and I have many more plans to make the terrain more livable."

Don Manuel's entourage set out at dawn next morning for a nonstop return to Natchez. The ride would be long and grueling for one day, he told Adam, but could be done if the horses kept a steady pace. The fast pace precluded any conversation.

As they rode, Don Manuel mused over a dilemma. Ever since Adam Cloud had presented him with the letter of recommendation from Col. James Wilkinson, he had wanted to query him about the man who had made such an impression on Governor-General Miró. Their discussion the day before had opened the door, but he had to sort out just how much he could tell Adam, for the nature of his own relationship to Wilkinson was highly secret. Miró's governance covered all of Louisiana Territory, and answered only to the hierarchy in Cuba and Spain. Gayoso received his orders from the governor-general. Miró had handed him the somewhat dubious role of carrying on a conspiracy with Wilkinson that had begun before his arrival in Natchez.

On his first trade venture to New Orleans, Wilkinson was openly direct with Governor Miró about the need for western frontier planters to obtain free navigation on the Mississippi. The governor, in turn, stated that they would never grant the concession while the area remained part of the United States. Wilkinson had then proposed he be permitted to begin a settlement in the Spanish river territory, which Governor Miró flatly rejected. Wilkinson then proposed that Spain maintain its denial of free navigation while he attempted to persuade the frontier leaders to break ties with the Union, thus making it more imperative that they secede. The final outcome of their understanding proved most favorable to Wilkinson. He was granted special credit and trading privileges and, for his continued cooperation, he was granted an annual pension. Since his assignment to work with Wilkinson, Governor Gayoso had been unsure of how much influence Wilkinson had with his own countrymen, and he needed verification of the colonel's political power.

Don Adam was the first person the governor felt he could trust to learn more concerning Colonel Wilkinson, but he knew he must be careful not to divulge very much lest he be implicated against his will.

By the time they reached Mount Locust for a short rest, he had made up his mind. He was drawn to this young American, and he would learn what he could from Adam. They had settled on the porch with a pitcher of cool cider.

"I have been thinking of your question about a better trade agreement with American growers," Don Manuel said. "When Colonel Wilkinson brought his trade goods here, he tried his best to open up trade relations for his countrymen. Did he seem optimistic when he discussed his trade ventures with you?"

"I couldn't say what he had in mind for the future. He told me that he had a successful trade venture into New Orleans, in 1787," Adam replied. "I found him irresistibly charming and convincing."

"He does have a captivating personality. He seems determined to find a way to open the Mississippi for trade with frontier farmers and trappers. But before we can determine any future trade agreements, we must be sure of his motives." Don Manuel paused to consider his next words and studied Adam's face, which was noncommittal. "I wonder how much influence he really has in the Kentucky Legislature. Do you know if is it strong, and does it extend into Tennessee? Do you know his standing with the army? If we are to consider his trade proposals, I would feel more comfortable knowing he can speak for the prominent territorial leaders."

Adam puckered his lips while he thought a minute. "I have very little firsthand knowledge of the colonel," he replied. "Most of what I learned in Louisville was hearsay. We both stayed at the boarding house of a couple named Downs, who know him well. The colonel was there on business, looking after his extensive property holdings. He has a business partner there named Michael LaCassagne. I learned that Wilkinson's war record was mixed with bravery and rumors of uncertain command. He quarreled and dueled with prominent officers and lived a rather racy social life. He smeared his reputation while he made and spent an early fortune on lavish living, but he married into a prominent Philadelphia family, and appears to be happily mated."

"That is quite a mixed record for a young man's early career. What of his present situation as a legislator?"

"The Downses praised him highly for his vigorous battle to persuade the Kentucky Legislature to secede from American ties. As you may know, frontier settlers are unhappy over neglect under the jurisdictions of Virginia and North Carolina. Wilkinson lost the first legislative round for Kentucky secession, but he is reported to have a sympathetic following." Adam paused and sipped his drink, carefully weighing his next statement.

"I hesitate to say this, but Colonel Forman's nephew, Sam Forman, gathered some information when he lingered in Louisville." He looked intently at Don Manuel. "There is suspicion among the Kentucky legislators that he may be working for his own self-interests by accepting bribes from Spain." He paused again and drank slowly, watching for the governor's reaction. Don Manuel swallowed hard to hide his astonishment. Was this information common knowledge? His face remained reposed.

"That is sheer nonsense," he scoffed. "We have maintained a friendly relationship with him, of course, and he has kept us apprised of his efforts to wean the frontier territories from the Union. Such an outcome would have enormous benefits to us. We need to learn as much as we can about American events which may affect us here."

"I can understand that," Adam said.

Don Manuel leaned forward and set his mug on the rail. Don Adam already knew enough that he needn't be so discreet. "You might as well know Wilkinson has written us lately that the land company, which sponsors the Walnut Hills settlement, is stirring up frontier growers to take the land by force. He is against such a move, for it runs counter to his legislative efforts toward Kentucky and Tennessee independence. We responded that a permanent American settlement would be a hostile act to Spain. He then offered to prevent further settlement, suggesting we could help by inciting the Choctaws to rise up against the settlers. He requested $10,000 to employ spies to infiltrate the plotters and create mischief and misrepresentation. He has warned us since of an imminent attack by an American volunteer army."

There it was! Verification of Andrew Jackson's information. Adam felt the jolt of alarm at this news. To hide his uneasiness, he rose, poured another mug of cider, and leaned against the porch rail, mug in hand.

"Sir," he asked, "what credence should be given to the threats of this controversial land group? Are you worried that there may be a filibuster against Natchez and New Orleans?"

Don Manuel's reaction was emphatic. "We can handle any invasion for a takeover, if it comes to that, and we will *never* give up the land at Walnut Hills. This land is ours, ever since Don Hernandez de Soto explored it, in 1540. Did you know that he was the first white man ever to reach the Mississippi River? And we should never have let it slip out of our hands to the French, or the British, who had no rights from us." Don Manuel paused, conscious of his heated fervor. He continued in a more subdued tone. "But my worry now is over the colonel's intentions."

"His posture is outrageous, and seems ambiguous, at best," Adam voiced his indignance. "It substantiates the rumors that he may be double-dealing with your government and the Americans. I wouldn't trust a man like that for five minutes, for the knife could be at my own throat for fear of disclosure. His loyalties seem so divided as to be a man without allegiance. As for his influence with the army, I know very little of what has happened since he left it. I do know that his leadership in the Kentucky Legislature, and in the militia, has won him distinction in his own state."

Don Manuel rose to cover his own inner turmoil. Adam's suspicions of Wilkinson substantiated his own misgivings. "We'll let the matter rest," he said, "but your rumors warn me I must, from now on, read between the lines of what he tells us in his letters. Governor Miró appreciates the contact with a distinguished American, but we need to assess his goals against our own, lest we are hoist by our own petard." He approached Adam and laid a hand on his shoulder. "What we have said here is strictly confidential, Don Adam. I trust you will keep this information to yourself, even from your bride. It is too sensitive for other ears."

"I keep no secrets from my wife, Don Manuel, but you have my word this will go no further. I appreciate your confidence, and I shall not breathe any of it, you may be assured."

During the remaining ride, Adam thought about Mary's premonition and marveled at her intuition. He determined he would have nothing further to do with this Wilkinson intrigue lest he find himself in a Faustian web of deception.

It was late evening when Adam returned home and noisily dropped his travel bag on the bedroom floor. He lit a candle and looked over at Mary where she lay in bed. She raised herself on an elbow and watched him as he began to undress.

"Silent stares aren't much of a greeting, Mary," he said. "Aren't you even curious about my journey?"

"I lay here for two nights just thinking of what you might be getting into, and I worried miserably over your safety," she answered.

She still sounds testy, Adam thought. "Dwelling on the improbable brings only anguish and grief. My adventure was more one of pleasure and surprise." Adam approached the bed and looked down on her bare shoulders. The sight of her breasts inside her gown aroused a twinge in his groin.

"That sounds nice," she said with little interest.

"Well, Mary, let me surprise you with a few things. First of all, may I say you are one remarkable woman. Your intuition was faultless, although somewhat overblown. There was some intrigue mixed in with the pleasure, but you needn't fear. I'm not implicated, nor do I intend to be."

Mary's eyes began to sparkle with questions, and she reached for her dressing gown at the foot of the bed.

"Oh, my precious, I have so much to tell you," he said. Mary stood and Adam helped her pull on the robe. They sat on the edge of the bed while his words rushed out in a torrent. "The governor granted me five hundred arpents right on Cole's Creek. The property is a paradise. It has a spring and is next to the governor's land. Don Manuel and I had long discussions and found we share many ideas. He seems to like me, and we have become friends." He searched Mary's eyes for hostile signs, but they were soft and inviting. "A nice couple named Matthews has a nearby plantation and I think we will find them compatible. We stayed at the beautiful home of the Thomas Greens, called Springfield Manor."

"That all sounds agreeable, Adam. But what about the intrigue? Did Don Manuel try to lure you into his political web?"

"You were right, Mary, he did want something for his generosity. Not that I didn't deserve it, mind you," he grinned, "but he pumped me about Colonel Wilkinson and told me the most incredible story of a cozy arrangement the Spanish have made with him . . ." He stopped abruptly. "Oh, my precious, it will take all night to tell it all to you, and I can't wait that long for you." He stood and pulled her to him. He encircled her waist and raised her off her feet.

"My darling, how I have missed you." Mary clasped her arms about his neck as his passion engulfed her.

"And I you, my precious," he groaned in her ear. He held her close and found her lips.

"Tonight we'll make up for two nights," she said. "I want you always to remember me every waking moment we are apart."

14 Mary's Nemesis

Between bites and sips at breakfast next morning, Adam related the events of the past two days. His voice ringing with enthusiasm, he described features of the property Don Manuel had given him, and the Cole's Creek district. Mary was scornful of his narrative about Colonel Wilkinson's deal with the Spanish.

"I don't care a fig about all that," she said. "Let's talk about the important part."

"Mary, I feel sure you'll like it there, and we can plan the perfect new house." He suddenly stopped. "Think of what I'm attempting to do with two plantations! I'll need more slaves, and of course an overseer." Adam stirred his coffee, his brows knit with concern. "It's a big undertaking and will be very costly. I can afford to do only a little at a time."

"The place sounds wonderful, Adam, and I can hardly wait to see it." Mary smiled at his dilemma. "You don't have to build a kingdom, as Ezekiel is doing with his hundred slaves and the vast acreage he has acquired. And don't forget, my darling, that you didn't marry a pauper. Mother left me the same inheritance as Anne's — five hundred pounds — and you now have mine to add to hers. My brothers reminded me that I must make permanent financial arrangements. I have had very little concern over finances because there was no need until now."

Adam laid down his fork, then leaned back and stared at her. "You're full of surprises. We never discussed finances, and I didn't expect any help from you." He paused to digest this sudden news. "Ezekiel has settled my inheritance from Anne with Biddle's Bank, in Philadelphia. In the meantime, drafts for my share of profits in father's Wilmington shipyard have provided enough to make-do here. This year I have realized my first modest income on my own, and that's a good feeling. I don't want to use your inheritance to get ahead."

"That's all very commendable, Adam, but it's nonsense. What I have is yours, and any money you spend for your success as a planter will insure my future as well. Let's just be thankful we have funds to count on and to use wisely. You can forget your poverty as a preacher. You will never be poor again."

Adam took her hand across the table. "My precious, I am overwhelmed with your generosity. I'll confer with Ezekiel about your inheritance, and I want the record to show the funds are your own. If I ever need any of it, it will be only by your consent."

"I had a caller yesterday," Mary suddenly remembered. "William Vousdan's wife, Hannah."

"Oh? What is she like? I recall her as being rather mousy," Adam remarked.

"She is very shy, and not easy to talk with. She came from South Carolina, and converted to Catholicism when she married. I had a feeling she needs friends. Poor little thing. She looks so unhappy."

"No wonder. I have heard that Vousdan beats her. Don't encourage her, Mary. It is best not to have anything more to do with them. Thank goodness I can have my new property surveyed by John Smith, who surveys for Don Manuel. I'll record the property tomorrow with Colonel Grand-Pré, and ride back up to Cole's Creek with the papers so John Smith can begin the survey."

"So soon? Oh, Adam, can I go with you?" Mary pled.

"Not this time, darlin'. It is too dangerous without an escort. I'll arrange to take you next time."

Watching Adam enter the Trace at early dawn, Mary tried not to think of the dangers. She concentrated on Adam's common sense and courage to get him through any trouble he might meet on the trail. Putting her worries aside, she turned her attention to the house and garden. Care of crops and domestic animals demanded intimate understanding and constant scrutiny. The vegetable garden had to be maintained during mild weather, and produce preserved for the coming months.

Some tasks required the servants to learn new skills. Many home essentials had to be made from scratch—homespun cloth, dyed with indigo and other dyes from plants found in the forest; shoe strings made from homegrown leather tanned in troughs dug from large tree trunks; laundering soaps, lye for cotton and linen, and for woolens and chintz a soap of mashed pulp from roots of the horse-chestnut tree; bonnets made from cotton, plaited and carded into plush.

Mary reviewed the slave performance and decided they were exceptional workers, all except Meg, the new young female worker Adam had bought in July. She was a tall and supple Negress, with strong, ebony-black handsome features. Mary thought her suitable for household work, but Meg showed marked defiance to orders. Mary puzzled over how she could get her to become more tractable.

Maamba, Dirk, and Tizzi were always dependable. They were trained by her mother and by Anne, who acquired them after she had married Adam. Dirk was huge and powerful and could do almost any kind of work. Adam gave Maamba and Dirk much latitude in using their authority with the other blacks, and allowed them special household perquisites.

Mary worked side by side with Maamba in the kitchen preserving vegetables. Maamba's jolly self was enveloped in billows of fat. Her rotund body moved slowly and deliberately, but her sound wisdom made up for lack of agility. She was comfortable and secure in her household status, and talked freely with her mistress.

"Miz Mary, you know our Tizzi ain't a chile no more. She goin' on fifteen. I don't want her to jes' th'ow herself away to any ole fiel' niggah."

"She should marry. If none of the three men here are suitable, I'll speak to Master Adam to keep her in mind when he takes in some new workers."

"Those three ain't for Tizzi. Besides, Meg got one of 'em fo' herself." Maamba's face expressed disgust. "Dat Meg is jes' no good. She rather sit on her arse than work. An' she mumbles that strange mumbo-jumbo. I think she a voodoo witch. I's scared of her."

Before she could digest this curious news, Mary heard the soft whir of carriage wheels on the drive. "The Formans!" she cried out, and reached the front door just as the bright yellow coach glided to a stop. She watched with emotion as the Formans emerged. Ezekiel alighted first and extended a hand to his wife. He had long substituted his dark wardrobe for the lighter, casual clothing of the Southern planters. He looked especially dazzling, his white hair coifed and curled, his beard and sideburns immaculately trimmed. Eliza, always smartly clad and elegant, hesitated on the carriage block. Her auburn hair glistened in the sun, as she bent her head and gingerly held her gown from sweeping the ground. Frances, Margaret, and Augusta, now fourteen, twelve and ten, bounded after her.

Mary smoothed down her kitchen smock and tried to tuck up the stubborn ringlets that had escaped from under her lace cap. "Welcome, dearest friends," she said as she embraced Eliza and the girls.

"We are simply bursting with curiosity, Mary," Eliza said. "We want to hear all about Adam's journey with the governor."

"Adam is gone again, surveying his Cole's Creek property," Mary explained. "Come inside and I'll tell you all about it. Becky is having her nap, girls, but you can wake her and help her get dressed. You can play outside."

The girls ran to Becky's room across the verandah, while the friends settled down in the parlor. Maamba brought them tea and cakes.

Mary excitedly described the new Cole's Creek property, and spoke proudly of the friendship Adam had established with Don Manuel on their journey up the Trace. She then shifted the subject to her difficulty with Meg.

"When Adam purchased four slaves before our marriage," she explained, "one of them was an ornery female whom I named Meg, short for 'megrim.' I knew right away she was going to be a real headache."

"What is the problem?" Ezekiel asked.

"I took Meg out of the field and am trying to train her for household duties, but she is proving difficult. She resents the work, and shows hostility at the slightest correction. Maamba tells me Meg spooks the other slaves with some sort of voodoo practices. I can't let her recalcitrance and superstitions affect the other blacks. I've just about lost patience with her." Mary looked at her guests for an answer.

"Some blacks can't adjust to their new culture," Eliza answered. "They cling stubbornly to primitive traditions for safety and comfort."

"Our Benajah Osmun is a skilled overseer," Ezekiel said. "He doesn't approve of punitive corrections but had rather convince slaves that safety and comfort lies in conformance. He uses rewards and praise."

"Do you think that teaching them Christianity helps?" Mary asked.

"I do, Mary," Eliza offered. "Our blacks have accepted Christianity very well."

"I could plan weekly lessons . . ."

Distant shrieks from the children interrupted Mary. She stood frozen, then bolted outside, with the Formans following. The girls ran crying toward them from the slavequarters. Tizzi, with Becky in her arms, ran wide-eyed with fear, as if running for her life. Mary and Ezekiel cried out as one.

"What is it?"

"What happened? Are you all right?"

Mary bent down to the children to understand their hysterical gibberish, which sounded like "chicken" and "awful blood." Eliza took the children inside while Mary and Ezekiel made their way toward the slave yard. To Mary's horror, she saw Maamba and Meg holding on to a headless white chicken, both tugging and shrieking as they pulled. Blood dripped on their hands as the women fought over the carcass.

"Here, stop that!" Ezekiel ordered. "What's this all about?"

Not loosening her hold on the chicken, Maamba cried out, "Dis slut kill my bes' layin' hen, and sprinkle blood all 'round. She put a hex on me, and I make her take it off."

With a wicked look at Mary, Meg let go of the chicken. Grinning defiantly at Maamba, she stalked off to her quarters.

In the center of the yard stood a brazier stuck with chicken feathers and blood. On the ground encircling the brazier Mary saw a ring of corn flour and fresh blood. She felt queasy from the grisly sight.

"She fixin' a conjure, Miz Mary. Ise gonna tear her eyes out," Maamba wailed.

"Now, now, Maamba, what's done is done, and tearing Meg's eyes out won't bring back your chicken," Mary said as calmly as she could. "That was a wicked thing to do, and I won't have any more of it. I'll speak to Meg, and have Master Adam deal with her when he returns. Take your chicken up to the house and I'll see you get another live hen to replace it."

Maamba dabbed her eyes with her apron as they walked back to the house, and Mary seethed with anger. Meg must be punished, she decided, but how? She would have to think on it. She bade farewell to her disturbed guests, with kisses and apologies for the children's fright.

Mary sat alone at her spinning wheel. The only sounds in the room were the soft whir of the thread and the rhythm of the treadle. Adam had been away two nights, and Mary ached for his nearness. But she found being alone was important, too, for she had time for inner reflection. Adam had his special bower in the woods where he often went to sort out his thoughts, to meditate and pray. Mary understood. She had her private thoughts, too, and found her own inner sanctuary during Adam's absence.

Her thoughts turned to her passion for Adam, the thrill of his love-making. She had only to think of it to feel the surge of passion she enjoyed from his caresses. *Could I be a wanton woman for such desires?* she wondered. She recalled sister Sarah's advice when she lived with her in Camden.

"The way to learn the joys of love-making," Sarah told her, "is to throw caution to the wind. There's no greater joy than the act of giving totally of one's self during sexual love. The bond between you will be greater for it."

She accepted Sarah's advice. And now she believed she was pregnant. She vowed to herself she would not deny Adam's sexual fulfillment, or romantic love, as Anne had done.

Most of all, Mary wanted to be a perfect wife and mother, but she had yet to prove herself as keeper of the household. She considered her responsibilities as Adam's wife. She must manage her household slaves firmly to assure her own domestic tranquility. Meg's defiance and strong will posed a threat. If marriage and sexual fulfillment worked for her own happiness, why not for Meg's?

Next morning Mary confronted Meg in the kitchen. Meg held herself proudly, her head high, shoulders straight. Her handsome ebony features were set in the blank look Mary knew slaves often used to hide their discomfort or animosity. Mary spoke bluntly.

"What you did to Maamba was wrong, Meg. Why should you want to bring her harm? She is patient with you, even while you defy her orders, and mine too."

Meg looked sullenly at the floor and said nothing.

Seeing she could not budge her, Mary repressed her exasperation and said firmly, "You must find other satisfactions than doing unkind things to people. I understand you and Ramos have paired. If so, the master will marry you two. Making a family of your own will fill your life with happiness and take your mind off of harming others."

Meg's eyes locked on hers, her face in a defiant grimace, like an evil sneer. Mary felt a slight shudder but did not divert her gaze.

"You should be grateful that you are not whipped, instead of receiving a husband, with our blessing. We expect good behavior from you. Love can work wonders in your life if you let it."

Late that night Meg slipped out of her bunk, crossed the Trace, and made her way down the Vousdan fence to a stile. She climbed over and crept across the yard to the slave quarters. She tapped on a cabin door and waited a few minutes. A young black man emerged. They embraced briefly, then silently stole to the barn, where they climbed to the loft and flung themselves on the hay. They conversed in between kisses.

"Ise in trouble, Kofi. I needs to get away fum there. Missus say dey gonna marry me to Ramos."

"You been foolin' 'round with dat no good niggah again? I tole you he get you in trouble."

"I cain't hep it. He's jes there, and you heah."

"You's my woman, N'leeta, and no one gonna take you away."

"If'n only that slaver not sold us to different white folks . . ." Meg let the thought dangle.

Kofi considered a bit. "Maybe I kin get dat whippin' man, Clem, to fine a way to git you ovah heah. Maybe yo 'massah would trade you fo' someone heah."

Meg tittered. "I got ways to make 'em sorry I works for 'em. Dey should want to get rid of me soon."

Kofi laughed with her. "You ole *tsunga* witch. Yo' voodoo kin fine a way." He pulled her close.

"*Shhh.* Did you heah somethin'?" Meg lay still.

They heard the unmistakable sound of someone climbing the ladder and saw dancing light beams glance the corner of the loft. To their horror, Vousdan's head of scraggly, oily hair appeared over the floorboards, and the lantern fastened on them. Frozen with terror, Meg and Kofi clung to each other.

"Come down from there," Vousdan leered. "Who do you think you are that you can use my barn for your fornicating? Come down at once! Now!"

The lovers crept slowly down the ladder and Vousdan held the lantern high, peering into their faces. He examined Meg's comely face under her knotted kerchief, her tall, full-measured figure, and her long legs. "Who are you?" he said gruffly. "Where do you belong?"

"My name N'leeta. Ise called Meg. I belongs to Massah Cloud." She did not flinch.

"Clem told me this was going on and I had to see for myself. I heard you talking, and I gathered you two were separated at auction. What have you to say for yourself, Kofi?"

"Massah Vousdan, suh, this my woman since we come on slave ship. We wants be together again."

Vousdan turned the lantern on Meg. "What did you mean by you 'got ways to make them sorry'? Did you mean the Clouds? What could you do to make them want to be rid of you? Are you a troublemaker?"

Meg drew herself up proudly. "Ise *Obeahwoman.* Ise power of *Obayifo.* I kin bring bad things by magic."

Vousdan considered her words. She looked convincingly powerful. He had seen few black women hold themselves with such proud dignity. He wondered how she would behave in bed. She could be useful to him in many ways, and especially bring trouble on that fatuous preacher, Adam Cloud. He looked at the nervous couple before him and made a decision.

"Kofi, you deserve a whipping and I'll deal with you tomorrow. Get on back to your quarters. I'll deal with Meg now."

Kofi gave a lingering look at Meg and ran out the barn door. Vousdan turned to Meg.

"Now, you *Obeah* witch, if you are what you say you are, I think we can help each other. I want to get rid of your master, Adam Cloud. You want to be my slave so you can join Kofi. If you do my bidding, we can both have what we want. Get back in the loft and we can talk."

Meg looked at his leering grimace and hesitantly climbed the ladder. Vousdan pushed her down on the hay, turned her on her stomach, spread her long legs wide, and mounted her. Her sexual prowess astounded him. When he was finished with her he was not sure whose rape had taken place, hers or his.

"Now what you want I do?" Meg asked, and Vousdan outlined carefully that her role was to harass the Clouds, at his direction, and give him sexual satisfaction when he demanded it. In the meantime, she and Kofi could meet as before, and they could be together permanently when the Clouds were run out of Natchez.

Before dawn, Meg crept back, exhausted, to her own quarters.

. . .

Mary hummed to herself as she bathed Becky in the kitchen in a portable tin tub. She thought of the new life within her and the baby to come. Christmas would be here in a few days. She would wait until then to tell Adam. They could combine Christmas and celebrate the coming event with a birthday party for Becky, who would be two years old, and for Adam, who would be thirty-one! She lovingly teased and tickled Becky, and they laughed together as Becky splashed water in the tub.

It was on this joyous scene that Adam entered the kitchen. They squealed with delight as he swept them in his arms, ignoring the bath water dripping from Becky's slippery limbs.

"I feel as though I have been to Cathay," Adam said. "I missed you terribly."

"And I you," Mary said. She gave him a long kiss, feeling his nearness again. "Here, Becky, get into this towel. Adam, she'll catch cold," she scolded.

Adam wrapped his daughter in the warm towel and carried her to the dining table, placed her on his lap, and rubbed her dry as they talked. He described his experiences with enthusiasm. John Smith had surveyed the land, and he had stayed overnight with them. The Clouds were invited to stay there any time. Smith grew and produced indigo, a very difficult and expensive process, and he suggested that Adam might find it profitable to grow indigo for seed to supply the growers. Adam also described his visit to the Matthewses', at Cedar Grove, the plantation nearest their own property. He found George Matthews to be a cultivated and highly educated man who spoke five languages, including Choctaw.

"His library is filled with excellent books, and he is an avid reader. He should prove as stimulating a conversationalist as Governor Gayoso," Adam said. "His wife, Grace, is charming, and, to make things perfect," he tousled Becky's curls and hugged her, "their little daughter is about Becky's age. You will have a play-mate, Becky."

"How delightful, Adam. I can hardly wait to meet them all," Mary said. "Don't forget, I go with you next time."

. . .

The new year brought heavy storms, leaving the terrain too soggy to attempt a trip up the Trace. Adam enjoyed time at home with his family. To Mary's delight, he built her a small carriage with a two-seat frame. Mary chose a cane pattern and the blacks wove the body. They had become adept at cane weaving, and Mary discovered that Meg enjoyed the work. Mary thought Meg appeared more adaptable. Perhaps marrying her to Ramos was helping to subdue the girl after all. She took the opportunity to praise the servant.

"That's beautiful work, Meg," she told her one day. "You are the best weaver here."

Meg stood silent by the weaving frame, her eyes on the ground. In a way she did not understand, weaving brought a satisfaction and release from her inner turmoil and hatred. Since her recent wedding to Ramos, she had felt triumphant in her cleverness. She had outwitted those demanding white folks with a private voodoo ritual. She had sewn small bundles of mistletoe in patches on her dress, and worn a mistletoe necklace about her neck at the marriage ceremony. There was one last ritual to perform. She would use the fire pit to throw in the chicken head she had saved. It would nullify any Christian marriage and insure her future with Kofi on the Vousdan farm.

Anxious to try out her new two-seat carriage, Mary decided to call upon Hannah Vousdan. In spite of Adam's caution to stay away from the Vousdans, it was only the polite thing to do to return a call as soon as possible, she explained to him.

She opened her armoire to select suitable wear. Groping to find a lost shoe in the far corner, her hand landed on something soft. She pulled it out and examined a black stocking doll stuffed with dry moss. The neck was tied with string, and numerous pins crisscrossed the body. *How odd*, she thought, . . . *must be a pincushion*. She decided to talk with Maamba about it later, and flung the doll on the bed.

Dirk had hitched Wendy to her little carriage. Mary settled Becky on the seat with her and drove to the Vousdan gate. She hoped that Vousdan would not be home, but when she dismounted at their front steps, Vousdan's voice roared out from inside, words of viscious abuse. A woman's scream followed. Mary hesitated, looked at Becky, and grasped her hand to retreat to the cart. The front door suddenly flew open and Hannah Vousdan stumbled over the threshold, Vousdan behind her. He pushed her roughly, and Hannah tumbled across the porch to the top of the steps. To Mary's horror, she saw he was about to strike her again.

"Stop that! You're hurting her!" Mary cried out.

Vousdan's face was livid with rage, but Mary's intervention startled him, and he held back his fist.

"How dare you treat your wife so! You are a *bully*." Mary shouted her words in anger.

Vousdan gave her a look so hateful that Mary shuddered. Without a word, he stalked off the porch, heading toward his fields.

Mary rushed to the stricken woman and helped her to her feet. "I am so sorry, Mrs. Vousdan. Are you all right?" she asked.

A young woman servant emerged from the open door. Hannah Vousdan looked at them both and said, weakly, "Yes, I will be all right. Binah, you can help me inside."

Mary and the servant helped her to the parlor, where Hannah lowered herself carefully into a chair with her back to the window. Mary knelt before her, and a wide-eyed Becky stood by her side.

"See poor hurt?" Becky's tiny voice piped in innocent sympathy.

"Do you hurt badly anywhere?" Mary asked. "Let's check for anything broken."

"No, it's really nothing," Hannah said. "Just a family argument." She looked at Becky's anxious little face peering into her own. "I am really all right, little one," she said softly. "My poor hurt will get well."

Some argument, Mary thought. But she realized Mrs. Vousdan did not intend to discuss the altercation. Badly shaken herself, she selected a nearby chair, respecting Hannah's need to regain her composure. The two women awkwardly attempted light conversation.

Mary scanned Hannah's face. Against the backlight, she could see no details, but she noted a swelling on one side. Hannah seemed frightened; her eyes darted to the door as though she feared Vousdan would reappear. She spoke aimlessly until Binah brought refreshments. Her mood was so distant that Mary wondered if they could ever share confidences. She groped for a way to reach her.

"It seems a shame we should live so close and not see one another," Mary said. "One never knows when a neighbor might need help. Sometimes I worry that our house may be invaded by evil travelers from the Trace. No one would ever know what happened to us until it was too late."

The cup rattled in Hannah's trembling hand as she poured tea. "I miss neighbors, like it was when I grew up in Charleston. We could always count on someone dropping in without notice almost daily. Out here, in the country, I have few friends. Mr. Vousdan is not very sociable." She handed Becky a glass of milk and passed the cookies.

The women struggled with conversation, settling on Becky's interests. Mary wiped the crumbs from Becky's face.

"We must go," she said, as soon as she felt it was polite. "I agree that friendly neighbors are important. With my little Becky to care for, I am at home most of the time. Please call upon me whenever you can."

As Mary rose to leave, she noticed Hannah's face was now a shiny vivid pink. Becky reached a tiny hand to her face. "Poor hurt," she said, and the ladies exchanged smiles at her tender concern.

In late January, the Natchez settlers received a serious blow. The governor called a town meeting at Government House and announced that the Crown would purchase no more than 40,000 pounds of their 1790 tobacco crop. The growers had assumed that the purchase of two and a half million pounds the previous year assured them full purchase of the current crop now in storage. Many planters would realize dire circumstances, for they had been encouraged to plant as much tobacco as they wanted. Some had borrowed money in order to purchase more acreage, tools, seed, and slaves to work their expanded fields.

Dismay and bitterness swept the highly agitated planters as they gathered in the plaza after the meeting to talk of their plight. Some blamed the Crown's decision on the purchase of Colonel Wilkinson's rich tobacco cargoes he had brought downriver from American growers. Others felt betrayed by the government for having encouraged them to enlarge their crops. Adam felt the shock, even though he had not planted tobacco. He pictured the many acres he had expected would bring him a fortune. At least he was not in trouble yet, he thought, as he listened to his friends and neighbors compute their losses. Jeb Corey said he would be ruined, and Ezekiel sputtered his disappointment.

"That blows my hopes," he fumed to anyone who would listen. "One of the main reasons we came here was for the rich tobacco yield. I haven't planned to plant much else, and I can't believe this is happening."

The heated complaints poured into Don Manual's lap, and he vowed to appeal to the Crown for a reversal of the decree.

15 Hannah's Plight

Afortnight after Mary's visit to Hannah, Adam and Mary had retired for the night when a horse galloped into the entry, followed by a loud pounding on the door. Adam opened the door cautiously, and Hannah Vousdan stumbled into his arms.

"Mary! Quick!" he cried out.

Mary threw on her dressing gown and rushed to the parlor. She was horror-stricken with the sight. Hannah Vousdan lay collapsed in Adam's arms, disheveled, her hair unbound, clad only in a nightdress covered with a loose cape.

"Hannah! What has happened? He beat her, Adam. I know he did!" Mary cried out.

Adam carried the inert woman to a chair, knelt beside her and gently took her hand.

"Tell us what happened, Mrs. Vousdan," Adam said. She wept uncontrollably, unable to speak.

Mary bent over her. "You need something soothing, my dear. I'll make some hot tea, and bring you a compress." She hurried to the kitchen.

Adam stayed by Hannah's side, trying to calm her hysteria until Mary arrived with the tea. Sobbing and gasping intermittently, Hannah sipped the drink and finally calmed enough to tell her story in halting phrases.

"Mr. Vousdan is a . . . beast," she said, "and I can't bear it . . . any longer. He's gone through all of my money, and now . . . is attempting to get rid of me. He's been hounding me for weeks. He's trying to get me to leave his house . . . as though I don't belong there!" she wailed.

"How can he do such things?" Adam said. "You are his lawful wife and he owes you protection, not violence."

"That's just the point," Hannah began to sob again. "He claims we're not legally wed because we married under a magistrate before we arrived here. He is Catholic and would not marry me in a Protestant church. I joined the Catholic church to please him after we came."

"That's incredible." Mary was shocked. "After all these years he wants to question your marriage?"

"Yes. He also berates me because I have borne him no children," Hannah began sobbing uncontrollably again, until her shoulders shook.

"Are you certain that he has used all of your assets that you brought to your marriage?" Adam sought the basic facts.

Hannah looked at their sympathetic faces. The effect calmed her and she was better able to talk. "Yes, it is true. Over the years he has acquired more and more property with my funds, and has sold some to his advantage. He claims the profit is his own, and now all my funds are gone. Every time he bought or sold something he has forced me to testify that I signed the deed of my own free will. I took the oath that states that I signed *fully and voluntarily without any fear of threat, or compulsion of my husband, or fear of his displeasure.* I know it by heart, I've had to swear to it so many times over the years. If I went against him he threatened me with divorce, and with exposing our secular marriage. I did not dare speak up because I knew he would only beat me."

"And now he wants to cast you out like an old shoe." Mary was incensed. "What can she do, Adam?"

"I believe she should take sanctuary with the Catholic church and appeal to the governor for justice. I have read that church sanctuary is a Spanish tradition, and if there is no physical structure to provide refuge, the presbytère is sufficient," Adam said. "Is that correct, Mrs. Vousdan?"

Hannah verified it was so, and after more discussion finally consented to place her fate in the hands of the church and the government.

"Perhaps exposing your husband's deeds against you will prove sufficient to bring his retribution," Adam reasoned.

"I fear what he might do to you," Hannah said. "He really hates you both. You, Mrs. Cloud, because you happened on our domestic scene and stopped him from striking me. And Mr. Cloud, he feels that you have stolen his property. He expected the exact parcels from the governor that you received, even though he had no claims on them. Colonel Grand-Pré led him to believe his work as surveyor earned him more land. When you also got the Cole's Creek property he was furious."

"Well, don't you worry about me," Adam said. "He can't harm me, but it is important that he not be able to hurt you again. If you feel up to riding now, I think we should go to Father William and not wait until morning. It is best that no one see where you have gone lest your husband makes more trouble for you." Adam looked at Hannah's sagging shoulders. "I will prepare Mary's carriage for us."

When Adam drove the carriage to the steps, Mary helped Mrs. Vousdan be seated, and covered her with a warm quilt. She watched them drive off into the night, with Hannah's horse trailing the two-seater. *What else can happen to such a fine woman*, she wondered, *so undeserving of her husband's abuse?*

Father William opened the door of the presbytère and stared curiously at Adam, then at Hannah in her nightdress and cape. "Come in," he said quietly. "Tell me what troubles you."

Adam guided Hannah to a seat and stood by while she told her story. Father William listened quietly until Hannah had finished.

"Now, now, my child, you may count on my help. You have come to the right place." He turned to Adam. "This unfortunate woman has had unusually rough treatment, and we shall help her through her ordeal. Thank you for bringing her to me."

Adam rode home confident that justice would prevail, especially under the protection of Governor Gayoso.

. . .

The story of Hannah Vousdan's flight to the Clouds spread across the community, and Protestant families began turning to Adam for counseling and spiritual advice. Taking his Bible and Book of Common Prayer to any home that summoned him, Adam read appropriate texts, and prayed with the family for divine guidance and comfort. He received deep satisfaction in reviving faith once again in families who had lost touch with their past convictions. People urged him to hold regular Sunday services, and some offered their homes. He was tempted, but he was bound to a government oath not to preach in public, and was fearful of arousing Catholic resentment. He decided to seek advice from Ezekiel.

During the next Forman visit, Adam brought up the subject. "How many people are considered a 'public'?" he asked. "I reasoned that, to be on the safe side, any religious activity beyond consultation and a simple ceremony within one family would be a breach of my oath."

To his surprise, Ezekiel imparted startling news. The Formans had stayed overnight at the home of Col. Anthony Hutchins, of White Apple Creek, where they heard a sermon by the Baptist preacher, Richard Curtis. Governor Gayoso had given permission for the event, at which others in the community were present. They learned, also, that the Rev. Samuel Swayze, a Congregational minister, conducted regular Sunday services for the residents of the New Jersey settlement at Homochitto River.

Adam knitted his eyebrows over this puzzling news. Could the strict rules against public preaching have been relaxed, or even rescinded, without his knowledge?

Consumed with curiosity, Adam sought the governor at Government House. Don Manuel listened to his account of the Curtis sermon, and smiled.

"I have no objection to a family, or even several families, wanting to hear the Word from members of their own faith. The lack of religious participation among Protestants is a blot on our Catholic tolerance. Not only do the residents stay away from our church, but they are deprived of the only spiritual guidance they prefer."

"I find myself more and more in demand, since Mary and I have been tending the sick. As you know, Don Manuel, ministering is the work I love to do best. I have missed serving others, and have had to restrain my compulsion to preach."

Don Manuel offered Adam a cigar. When Adam declined, he lit one for himself and rose from his desk. "Let's sit over here and have a talk, Don Adam." He sat in a comfortable chair and Adam chose one nearby. "I have heard of your visits to the sick, and that Mary is considered an archangel by the community. By the way," Don Manuel leaned forward and lowered his voice, "I have found an angel whose light has shone upon me recently. I have felt stirred for the first time since my bereavement."

Adam cocked his eyebrow with this unexpected news. "And who is the lucky lady?"

"You and Mary must keep this to yourselves, for it is a bit too early for the light of day. The lady is *Señorita* Elizabeth Watts, the daughter of my friends Stephen and Frances Watts, of Belmont Plantation. I have reason to believe she looks upon me with favor."

Adam grinned to hide his surprise. He recalled attending the young lady's eighteenth birthday ball last summer. "You'll be fortunate to win her. I hope the buds of romance reach full blossom and we can expect wedding bells soon. You have been alone too long." Adam smiled affectionately at his friend.

"Thank you." Don Manuel smoked in quiet, savoring his thoughts. He continued, "I heard of your kindness to Hannah Vousdan. You did the right thing to take her to Father Savage. We will take care of her needs and try to resolve the difficulty in the Vousdan marriage problem."

"She was in a piteous state, and we were glad to help her. I could give Vousdan a few lessons he has forgotten about Christianity," Adam said. "I'm trying to teach Christianity to our slaves too. There is so much superstition, and one of our slaves disrupts them with the practice of voodoo."

"Ah, poor devils," Don Manuel said. "Their native faiths are as ingrained in them as our Christianity in us. It will take a long time to convert them."

"The Bible tells us, in Hebrews 11, that *Faith is the substance of things hoped for, the evidence of things not seen,*" Adam mused. "Our slave is guided by her fervent faith that voodoo will make things right. Sometimes I wonder . . . who are we to try to replace belief in simple faiths that sustain primitive people in their need? Christians have enough trouble in maintaining their own faith during stressful times."

"Our Catholic faith is very secure." Don Manuel spoke with pride. "The church says that faith rests on a First Truth revealed in Holy Writ, a gift of God. Aquinus tells us that human nature has no power toward this end, and that it must come from Divine power only. That is why priests can distinguish the spiritual from earthly matters. That is why the Roman Pontiff, successor to St. Peter, Vicar of Christ, is supreme over state. The state is a subsidiary dominion: the king is subordinate."

"While your Catholic faith is very secure, and serves you well, I have trouble with that," Adam said. "The concept of faith springs from many wells. Man has a choice of accepting evil temptations, or following the instincts of virtue, decency, compassion for others. So, then, what *something* forces us to observe the desirable elements? Is it innate power from within, or is it outside enforcement, such as menace from the state?"

"I would say both. Many people accept the view that we carry the biological curse of being born with sin inherently within us," Don Manuel posed. "How do you feel about that?"

"Absolutely awful!" Adam grimaced as he spoke. "That would defeat faith by enlightenment, and would take the heart out of preaching. But, Don Manuel, I am challenged by your theory of modifying errant behavior through the church and state concept. Should the state become man's conscience? Freedom and liberty through self-restraint is man's test of himself in a world which teases the passions. I believe man does not need the state to speak for him."

Don Manuel rose from his chair and tapped his cigar ashes at his desk. He was disturbed by Adam's boldness. "Human passions provide difficult ground for any government rule. The sovereign state in which we live *is our protector.*" As he emphasized the words he faced Adam defiantly. "And our monarchical system assures us that our spiritual needs will be met by obedience to king and Christ."

Adam contemplated Don Manuel's vehemence with indecision. He rose slowly and faced him. Throwing caution to the wind, he responded to the governor's declaration with a sweeping gesture.

"Ah, my friend, if only you could have read the *Publius Papers.* They define man's noblest aspiration written into our American Constitution." Adam spoke with passion. He was warming to the subject which had nagged him since he left the Union. "I recognize the need for protection by the sovereign state, but I believe the state must provide opportunity for society to develop its own moral conscience. The French recognized this need and have turned the tide for individual growth in their recent 'Declaration of the Rights of Man and the Citizen.' The moral conscience of a society is stronger than any force that tries to repress it."

"I believe in promoting individual responsibility, of course," the governor conceded, somewhat testily. "That is why I make an effort to include Natchez residents in government participation. I am always open to ways in which I can improve my goals, or initiate new ones without impinging upon the Crown's sovereignty." In a defiant tone, he added, "I'll read your *Publius Papers,* Don Adam. We can discuss them after I have had an opportunity to study them."

"It will be my pleasure." Adam detected Don Manuel's defensive tone in the highly charged atmosphere, and saw need to lighten the subject. "I once served with a preacher who so undermined people's self-confidence that they lived in perpetual fear of their sins. I would hate to think my religious belief is based on an innate fear of myself, even though I realize it is possible there could be a beast within."

"We all carry a beast of burden, don't we?" Don Manuel commented lightly.

"My beast is the slip of the lip." Adam grinned, and meant the quip as an oblique apology for his boldness.

Don Manuel smiled with him. But when Adam left, the governor felt rankled over the confrontation on the subject of Spanish church and state government. Does this resentment prevail among the citizens, he wondered, or was Adam simply being devil's advocate?

Adam joined a group of planters in the plaza one day discussing the tobacco fiasco, when Philip Nolan rode up. Adam had thrown off his former dislike of this controversial man. Nolan's attention to Mary during Adam's courtship had threatened their marriage, but with Mary now his wife, he began to admire the young man's audacity. Adam had decided Nolan's close ties to Colonel Wilkinson could be an asset.

Reining his agitated horse to a whirling stop, Nolan did not dismount but blurted out his news in an excited voice. "I have just delivered a letter to Governor Gayoso. It concerns the latest facts about a possible invasion."

Adam felt a shock at this ominous news The listeners shouted anxious questions to Nolan.

"It's from Colonel James Wilkinson, commander of the Kentucky Militia," Nolan went on.

Wilkinson's name brought a few boos and acid remarks of his Louisiana tobacco trade.

"Wait," Adam called out. "Let Nolan tell us the news. Everyone can judge for himself after we hear it."

As the group quieted down, Nolan gave Adam a nod of thanks, and continued. "Colonel Wilkinson is in a military position to know, and he has an honored place in the Kentucky Legislature. We can believe him. He says that the South Carolina Yazoo Land Company plans to establish two thousand families in Walnut Hills. They want to secure an independent state, and have appointed a leader, Dr. James O'Fallon, to organize an armed filibuster. O'Fallon has appointed as deputies General George Rogers Clark, agent for Kentucky, and Governor John Sevier, agent for the state of Franklin."

General Clark's name brought more comments. Some remembered his failed threat to capture Natchez some years previously. Sevier's implication was impressive. He was brigadier general for the Eastern North Carolina District, and was remembered for his longtime efforts to gain official status for the state of Franklin.

Nolan raised his hand for quiet, and continued. "This time they hope to recruit one thousand well-armed men from the frontier infantry and cavalry to descend the Mississippi and take Natchez and New Orleans by spring." Nolan looked at the alarmed faces surrounding him, obviously enjoying the excitement generated by his startling news. Everyone clamored for more military information.

"That's all there is, so far," Nolan said. "Wilkinson doesn't want to see an invasion by Kentucky. He thinks it's important that they maintain a 'good neighbor' policy, and has set an example by being a friendly ambassador to the Spanish governors through his trading ventures."

Adam had his own private thoughts on the matter. Philip Nolan's whitewash of Wilkinson was amusing. Loyalty to his mentor was understandable, but he must surely know of Wilkinson's involvement as an early supporter of O'Fallon's mission. Well, perhaps not. Wilkinson was a devious fellow, and undoubtedly kept some things from Nolan.

Nevertheless, Wilkinson's new facts were alarming. Added to Andrew Jackson's early disclosure of the O'Fallon involvement, invasion was a reality — possibly within a few months!

Soon after the plaza announcement, Adam sought the governor again to verify Philip Nolan's news. Don Manuel confirmed Nolan's account, and added that Governor Miró had word from an authoritative source that the South Carolina Yazoo Land Company was fully determined to complete the settlement of Walnut Hills. Not only was there a threat from the frontier, but the Choctaws were suddenly on a rampage against the Walnut Hills settlement, and had attacked the settlers. The reports had caused concern for defenses. Governor Miró had ordered him to build a new fort near Walnut Hills, and to reevaluate current sites. Don Manuel told Adam he would be away much of the time in the coming months, occupied with these tasks.

"By the way," he added, "the trips north will take me often through Cole's Creek. Perhaps we could get in some good fishing there this spring while we are building our new homes. When I find a few spare hours, I will let you know."

The threatening events on the horizon filled Adam with apprehension. He recognized the pitiful inadequacy of the small New Madrid and Natchez garrisons against an invasion. The marauding Indians added to the growing list of alarms threatening the district: the tobacco controversy, military invasion threats, and now a possible Choctaw uprising. The peace and contentment Adam had sought now seemed elusive again.

Mary and Adam spent many hours drawing and redrawing plans for their new home. They agreed on a simple design, more spacious than Adam's first house, but disagreed on details. Heated discussions became frequent, neither wishing to give up a cherished vision, and they revised plans many times for the extra rooms they would need. One day they finally settled on providing a family keeping-room, a sewing room for Mary, and a chapel for Adam. They decided to name it "Evenstar," based on Becky's pronouncement of 'evening star'."

"I'll take more time to finish the interior walls for this house. They will do justice to the home of an elegant lady," Adam said

"Not to mention the home of a gentleman planter. Oh, Adam, it will be perfect." Mary glanced outside at the sound of an approaching horse. "It's Dusty Rhodes, our riverboat pilot!"

They rushed outside to watch their visitor ride up the path. Adam greeted him with beaming enthusiasm. He had a warm spot in his heart for this Kaintuck friend. Dusty dismounted, removed his coonskin cap, and wiped his hands on his breeches before he clasped Adam's hand.

"Welcome to Cloudcrest, Dusty," Mary said. "Now you can see how it looks since you helped prepare the grounds last year."

Dusty stayed the night, and at supper he surprised them with the news that he was tired of his riverboat trade and would like to settle down at a land job. Adam mulled over Dusty's qualifications. He might make a good overseer. He was smart, and a prodigious worker. His years of river trade taught him how to bargain, and he could act as Adam's factor in New Orleans.

The next day Adam broached the offer to Dusty, explaining that he would be ready for an overseer by the time he finished his Cole's Creek outbuildings. That would give Dusty time to complete another trading trip, when he would then be hired as overseer.

Dusty left Natchez overjoyed with the prospect of working for the Clouds.

16 Superstition

In February a large fleet of flatboats arrived at the landing under the sponsorship of Col. John Stark, an elderly Natchez merchant. The flotilla, collected at Nashborough, brought new settlers, slaves and large cargoes of produce and goods. Notice was posted that the slaves would be auctioned by Daniel Clark. On auction day, Adam and James Moore rode to the landing together, and Adam purchased four male slaves. Daniel Clark recorded their sale, and added a bit of news.

"By the way," he gave a sly wink, "our friend, Andrew Jackson, arrived on Colonel Stark's boat, and has brought a lady with him."

"A *lady!*" Adam exclaimed. "Is she his bride?"

"No, but they were mighty close." Clark winked again. "She came under Colonel Stark's protection, but anyone could see Jackson was her real protector. They disembarked with their servants at Bayou Pierre."

A few days later Adam was spending several nights with Jeb and Mazie Carter while working on the Cole's Creek plantation. Mazie had cleared the breakfast table when Jackson rode into the yard. Mazie bade him step inside, and his tall, lank frame filled the doorway. He removed his hat, uncovering his thick crop of sandy-red hair.

"I've come, ma'am, to ask your husband if he can do some work for me in the next several days up at Bayou Pierre." Jackson stared at Adam with surprise, and his face crinkled with a broad smile. "Mister Cloud, this is an unlikely place to see you. By Jove, I thought of you when I was on the river, for I recalled you wanted me to bring you a pair of Kentucky thoroughbreds. I'm sorry to disappoint you, but circumstances prevented me from bringing your horses this time."

"I can live without them," Adam answered. "In the meantime I have just purchased slaves from Daniel Clark's cargo, a financial outlay I shall have to stretch to meet. By the way, your arrival and secret landing with a guest at Bayou Pierre has created quite a mystery in town. Who is the lady? Will I get to meet her?"

Jackson gave a rueful smile as he sat at table with Adam. "I suppose everyone is buzzing about our arrival, but it's no mystery. The lady is a dear friend who was in deep trouble," he explained. "Her name is Rachel Donelson Robards, and I have known her for several years. In fact, I boarded at her mother's, the widow Donelson's home, some ten miles out from town, when I first came to Nashborough." Mazie handed him a cup of coffee, and he paused to sip the hot brew.

"Rachel's father, Colonel John Donelson, was well known in the Cumberland area. He brought the first flotilla of settlers to Fort Nash and started the colony of Nashborough with his partner, Colonel Robertson. He was killed while surveying the frontier, and his widow welcomed the protection of males on the plantation. There were other bachelors living there, and we received mighty fine care and courtesy as her boarders. Rachel visited her mother and sister occasionally from her husband's home in Kentucky. That's how I met her."

"You said the lady was in trouble," Adam said. "Go on."

"Yes, deep trouble, but it was not of her own making. As a clergyman, sir, you can understand the vicissitudes of a violent and unhappy marriage, which she endured for several years, until their separation. Out of spite, Lewis Robards filed for divorce on imaginary grounds of her infidelity. The man persisted in harassing her, and finally her family turned to me to take her away from the dangers and threats of a violent and excessively jealous ex-husband. Colonel Stark, as an obliging friend, arranged her passage, and my good friends, Abner and Charlotte Green, are delighted to have her visit them at Bayou Pierre. That's the plain story."

"The lady has indeed had an unhappy past," Adam said, thinking of the reprobate, Vousdan, and Hannah's painful bruises. "I know too well the bitterness and unreasonable demands of violent husbands. It is not uncommon, especially on the frontier where men often lack respect for the fair sex. How long does Mrs. Robards expect to stay? May we count her among our newest settlers?"

"I'm not sure," Jackson replied, "but I hope she will get to know the gentry of Natchez. The Greens expect to present her as soon as she has rested from the journey."

"I shall look forward to meeting her." Adam smiled and nodded as Mazie offered to pour him more coffee.

"By the way," Jackson continued, "I recall our last conversation concerned the fancy Colonel Wilkinson. You might be interested to know that his fortunes have taken a turn for the worse since his last New Orleans trading venture. His life style is not so fancy anymore. The news is firsthand from Peyton Short, my Kentucky friend who boarded a while with the Robards. He was Wilkinson's partner in his Frankfort store, and acts as his lawyer. The store has failed financially, and he has liquidated everything — the store, warehouses, horses, oxen, mules, even his phaeton carriage. He is selling off his Frankfort land as well. Peyton says he is six thousand dollars in debt. That's a mighty burden for any man to shoulder."

Adam recalled that Wilkinson had lost an earlier fortune in Philadelphia before they went to Kentucky. What a demeaning outcome for an energetic man, he mused, with so many irons in the fire, endless ideas and personal drive. He felt genuine pity for the colonel's misfortune.

"Do you suppose it was the New Orleans trading deal that broke him, or could it be that he was simply living too high on the hog for his income?" Adam posed. "From what he told us, they lived a lavish social life in Frankfort."

"Probably both causes," Jackson replied, "but it certainly won't be the end of him. Peyton told me Wilkinson rejoined the Kentucky Militia and will probably pursue an army career. He can ride on his records of former service, and with his drive and ambition will probably go far up the military ladder. That should keep him out of mischief."

Several weeks later the Clouds received an invitation from the Thomas Greens to a ball at Springfield Manor, honoring the mysterious Mrs. Robards. They were invited to go in the Formans' coach and spend the night at the home of Mr. and Mrs. Matthews. Mary was so excited over the coming event that Adam was reluctant to speak of his concern.

"I hate to be a spoilsport, Mary, but you are supposed to be in confinement," he pointed out. "Wouldn't you be embarrassed to go out in public?"

"Now, Adam, four months really doesn't show. No one would be the wiser if one of my gowns can be fitted to camouflage my *enciente*."

Adam shook his head in doubt, but her dancing eyes told him he could not stand in the way of her joy.

The two couples were in a festive mood as the Forman coach set out for Springfield Manor. Moses drove the carriage across town to the new road, christened El Camino Real, the King's Highway, which the settlers now called Bluff's Road. The roadway was wide enough to accommodate the carriage, and it shortened the distance considerably from the Trace route.

Springfield Manor glittered that evening with carefully prepared brilliance, as guests arrived from everywhere. Four fiddlers and a banjo played lively dance tunes, and the halls rang with merriment. All eyes were on the beautiful Rachel Robards. Her black hair and sparkling black eyes were set in a cameo face, expressive with warmth and humor. She was a lively dancer and threw herself into the reels and folk dances, her vivacious manner making her popular among the men. The evening was an unqualified success, and the guest of honor was accepted into the Natchez social circle.

Late that night Mary waltzed about their bedroom at the Matthews'. "I am still giddy from excitement. I'm too stimulated to sleep," Mary said. "Let's talk."

They talked as they undressed. Mary aired her impressions of the ball, of Jackson and beautiful Rachel Robards, of Governor Gayoso and his lady, Elizabeth Watts, whose courtship was no longer a secret.

Adam caught Mary in his arms and cradled her closely. The glamorous night away from home was a vacation from cares. They could shed the ominous thoughts which dwelt in their subconscious minds — the threat of invasion, and life in a rough and uncertain world. They took possession of the night as they took possession of each other, rapturously. At the height of ecstasy, in an intuitive instant, Adam felt they shared a spiritual identity. In the time of repose, he lay back replete with happiness, thinking in awe of that rare, profound experience. He sensed they had bonded both body and spirit with the new life now in Mary's womb. His eyes were moist with tears when he finally slept.

When Adam and Mary arrived home next day, the servants were in a turmoil.

"What is the matter?" Mary asked, alarmed. "Are the children all right?"

"Your children are safe," Maamba said. "Don' you worry about them little darlin's. It's the scary things that happen las' night to put the res' of the folks to wailin' and carryin' on likes it was the las' day before judgment."

"Scary things? Like what?" Adam asked.

Maamba and Dirk unfolded the events in a torrent of excited words. The previous night all the blacks had been in an uproar. Something disturbed the pig sty and frantic pig squeals had aroused Dirk, but he found nothing when he investigated.

"The nex' mornin' I went roun' the yard, and I foun' strange doin's," Dirk said.

"What sort of things? Come, let us have the details," Adam said.

"Well," he continued, "Yo' front doah was smeared wid dung. In the niggah yard I foun' a white-powder circle on the groun' with a raccoon in the middle. He was cut open and his insides all strung aroun' the circle. All the menfolks wuz so streaked dey wuz skeart to go to their bunks. Meg showed me dung smeared on her doah too."

Adam inspected the property and found the evil signs just as Dirk described them. None of the blacks would touch the unsightly entrails for fear of contact with the hex.

"Remove them, Dirk. They are only dead animal parts." Dirk hesitated. "Are you waiting for me to remove them? See, I have no fear." Adam grabbed a shovel and scooped up some of the mess. Dirk finished the job and cleaned the doors.

Adam then sent for Meg and Maamba.

"Meg, she use the *voudoun* magic aroun' heah and scare all the folks. We don' know what she up to," Maamba complained.

"'Taint my doin'," Meg said calmly. "De hex makes trouble fo' me an' Ramos. I string mistletoe aroun' our cabin and aroun' our necks. It's one of *dem*," Meg said emphatically. "Dey's one who after me. Dey after you, too, 'cause I yo' slave. Yo' house was cursed an' you gets bad trouble."

Adam understood Meg indicated someone from neighboring slave quarters had left a curse on them. He had arranged exchange work with slaves from other plantations recently, and one of the workers seemed a likely suspect.

"There's reg'lar ways to remove a hex," Maamba explained. "If de mistletoe don' work, we can nex' try de blue paint."

"What do you mean?" Adam asked.

"Well, suh, ya jes' paints the doah and window frames blue," Dirk said. "Cud do it if I had the paint."

"My doah," Meg demanded. "You paints my doah."

Adam cocked his eyebrow, suppressing a smile. He did not want to offend them. "Well, now, if that is a sure method, it is simple enough." He looked at Meg. "If you think the mistletoe has not worked, I will provide the indigo for the paint, if necessary. But I believe I have a better remedy for removing the hex. If you will help me, we can try it together."

Meg drew her mouth downward and scoffed in derision, but Dirk and Maamba were pleased that the master would join in removal of a hex. They tugged Meg's arm.

"Come on, Meg," Dirk pleaded. "The massah's a man of God. He knows magic ways to speak to Him."

"We'll help you, Massah Adam. Jes' you tell us how," Maamba said.

"Come to my door at dusk," Adam said. "Bring as many of the field hands who want to help."

Adam set up an elaborate altar in the parlor, using candles and the large silver cross. When Mary and Becky were assembled with all the blacks, he lit the candles and bade them kneel. He then chanted the Episcopal Evening Prayer Service in Latin, with the Short Lesson of Scripture in English. He ended the ceremony with a Latin metrical version of the hymn *"Phos hilaron."* The blacks were awed with the mysterious words and chants. The symbols and candles looked powerful enough to cast magic spells on any enemy. As the slaves left, Adam did not see Meg's sly, smug smile, but he thought Meg and Ramos looked less tense and more confident.

"That was a lovely service, even if they didn't understand it, Adam," Mary said. "The Latin was an inspiration and should reassure Meg that we have our witch doctors too."

"I'm ashamed that I haven't done more to convert the slaves," Adam said. "I'd like to keep our private morning prayers and vespers a family ritual, but I can hold a morning Sabbath prayer service for the blacks. The only attempt to enlighten them into Christianity has been your Bible stories for the women."

"Take heart, Adam. You'll win them over if you try," Mary reassured him.

The next morning Adam visited his bliss station in the woods. He agonized with guilt that he had done little to replace voodoo belief among his slaves. How long had it been since he was the spiritual leader on the journey to Natchez, when his companions looked to him for spiritual guidance and solace throughout their trials? It was not enough to visit the sick and read the prayer book and pray with neighbors on call, he told himself. There was a real need out there, and he knew he would have to start on his own plantation. He realized that all the high-minded discussion with Don Manuel on religious philosophy had a hollow ring unless he practiced what he fervently believed. *How easy it is to overlook the important needs within my reach while I dwell on the big picture of mankind and the universe,* he thought. He prayed for God's forgiveness, and gave thanks that the voodoo incident had reawakened him to his personal mission. In his contrite mood, Adam talked it over with Mary.

"The voodoo superstition still persists, Adam," Mary said. "I found something strange on my closet floor a while back, and forgot to find out what it was." She told him about the black stocking doll. "Your religious services for the blacks don't seem to be getting through to them, Adam. Do you suppose Meg is trying to work some kind of evil magic on us? Or does someone else have a grudge against us?"

Adam laughed. "Come, now, Mary, no such tokens can affect anyone unless they think they can. Whoever is responsible, just ignore the incidents as child's play. We know they have no significance."

Adam thought Mary's laugh sounded a bit nervous. "Just the same, I worry about Meg's state of mind."

"What would you think if I opened our home for Sunday services? People keep urging me to preach. Would it shock you if I broke the law?" he asked.

"Of course not, Adam," Mary replied. "The law is unjust, and many neighbors have expected you to preach. The Reverends Curtis and Swayze do, and everyone knows it. You have so much to give, and it would do us all good to have a regular Sunday church service."

Adam reasoned that the governor's lenience toward Protestants would protect him, and he sent out invitations for a Sunday service.

The following Sunday morning twenty families attended and overflowed the little house. Adam had the slaves set his altar under the front magnolia tree and arrange the chairs and benches outdoors. Dirk spread canvas on the ground. Mary looked about, pleased with this first church setting, the white families seated in front, the Negroes gathered in the rear. The day was sparkling with brilliant sunlight; birdsongs filled the air. The quiet majesty of the surrounding forest added a touch of holiness.

Adam modified the Anglican service, selecting liturgy from his *Book of Common Prayer* without responses, for no one present knew them. His sermon aimed directly at the present experience. Choosing texts from the Psalms, he opened with: *Thou hast brought a vine out of Egypt: Thou hast cast out the heathen and planted it.* His sermon progressed to lofty thoughts of God's purpose for mankind, and ended with a plea to read a different Gospel message each day. The departing guests left with handshakes and praise for Adam's message.

Mary sat and fanned herself after the last guest had departed. She was hot, and her pregnancy was suddenly uncomfortable. "The sermon was superb," she said, "but I am worried, Adam. You actually held a public service, right out where all could see that you broke the law."

"The Bowleses suggested appointing a sentry to watch for authorities. If he spotted intruders, I could hide the evidence in a hollow tree, and it would appear to be only a prayer session." He laughed at the thought. "I wouldn't relish punishment for preaching outdoors," he answered, "but I cannot see any difference in a quiet sermon indoors and one outside."

"Why not talk it over with Don Manuel for his approval?"

"No, Mary, that would only stir up a hornet's nest."

"If you let him know the service was requested by friends and neighbors . . ."

"Now, Mary, don't nag." Adam looked keenly at her disgruntled face. "You're just peevish because you don't feel well. You'll feel differently after the baby comes."

"I wouldn't count on it," she retorted.

After a few days of soul searching, Adam made up his mind. He would follow his conscience, one's ultimate responsibility in the long run. While he believed he owed his constituents to minister fully to their spiritual needs, he had too much affection for Don Manuel to put his feet to the fire in a test of friendship. He would not hold community services again, but would accept invitations to conduct private residential services upon request, which

Don Manuel had approved. He could straddle the fence and not disobey the law, as long as Don Manuel remained permissive.

Spring asserted itself in the mild Natchez climate. Two of Adam's newborn calves opened their eyes and wobbled to their feet. Newly hatched insects darted over wildflowers and streams, and fish jumped at their lure.

It was time to till the soil and plant for the season. Adam supervised the planting himself and spent many hours in the fields. He decided the tobacco future was so uncertain he would not take the chance on its further decline. Instead, his slaves cultivated new sections of his St. Catherine Creek farm for expanded crops of corn, flax and hemp, and sowed melons and pumpkins in the remaining space. The slaves replanted family vegetable gardens, and Cloudcrest took on the air of a growing enterprise.

17 Voodoo Baby

Early on the morning of the Fourth of July, Mary awakened Adam with signs of oncoming labor. Adam embraced her tenderly and helped her sit up in bed. He brought her dressing gown and propped the pillows. Then he alerted Maamba and the household and sent Dirk to the nearby Bowles plantation. Soon Jenny Bowles arrived with her Negro midwife, and news that John Bowles would fetch Dr. Todd in town.

Maamba and Meg bustled about supplying blankets, towels, and hot water. Adam stood by Mary and held her hand through her labor pains, but as her contractions quickened, Jenny ordered him out of the room.

Meg stood at the foot of Mary's bed wringing her hands, her eyes rolled up to the whites. She muttered softly to herself with Mary's every moan. Suddenly, Meg darted from the room and returned holding a brown, shriveled object which she twisted and pressed alternately to her forehead and chest. Her moans and chants, increasing to shrieks, intermingled with Mary's cries of discomfort. Between contractions, Mary felt growing anxiety over Meg's activity.

The midwife turned angrily to Meg. "Yo' token's no good heah. Dis lady in my hands. Now shut yo' mout' and git. We don't need yore goin's on."

Almost hysterical in her fervor, Meg stood her ground while Jenny tried to quiet her. The midwife suddenly threw back the covers of Mary's bed and felt around carefully at the foot. She drew out a soft cloth ball wrapped in strands of Mary's long hair. Mary looked at it, horrified, and Jenny shuddered.

The midwife screamed at Meg. "I jes knowed it. You conjure birth wid a haih-ball. You witch! You wants tie up baby so's not come. Now git out of heah," and she pushed Meg roughly out the door.

Maamba took Mary's hand and patted it soothingly. "Don' you worry, Miz Mary," she said. "De hex been took away, and yo' baby gonna come jes fine."

Mary gave the midwife a wan smile of thanks, and the birthing began in earnest. In no time it was over, much to her astonished attendants. Mary's heart leapt at the newborn's first cry. She looked tenderly at the little daughter placed in her arms, a sweet gift of love manifested in velvety pink flesh.

"Adam Cloud, you have a baby girl," Jenny Bowles called from the front door.

Adam flung Becky on his shoulder and bounded into the house. "Born on the Fourth of July!" he shouted with joy. "*Yankee Doodle went to town,*" he sang, and danced a jig to Mary's bedside, while Becky shrieked with glee. Mary held the swaddling bundle up to him.

"Our little Susannah," she said, her eyes shining.

Adam gathered the tiny new life tenderly in his arms and felt an emotional thrill unlike any he had ever experienced; he didn't know whether he wanted to laugh or cry. He swallowed hard and said, "Hello, Susannah. Meet your father," and sat down. His knees felt weak.

Dr. Todd arrived in the midst of the excitement. He examined mother and baby, and left to file the birth at Government House. Adam sat by Mary's bed, Susannah between them, and fondled the baby's tiny fingers. Both parents were wordless with joy, their eyes locked in a bond of silent communication.

The Formans arrived next day to greet the new baby. Sam announced that he and David would be leaving before the end of the month so that David could enter Princeton in the fall quarter. Mary knew it was inevitable that they should leave, but the shock left her saddened. David would return in several years, but perhaps she would never see Sam again. He had been so much a part of her life in Natchez, she would miss him. It was Sam who had urged her to come on the journey with her sister, and to return home with him. She could not imagine what her life would have been like if she hadn't married Adam and were going back with them now.

Sam suggested they make a list of items he could send from the States. He said that the governor had ordered a carriage from Philadelphia, and Mary and Adam began a wish list of things for their new home.

On departure day, they joined the Formans at the wharf. Everyone stood by in bustle and confusion while the luggage was put aboard a keelboat, and final farewells could no longer be postponed. Mary handed Sam a packet, her eyes glistening with tears.

"Here is a list of household items we need," she said, "and long letters to our families. Be sure to visit them as soon as you can." She embraced them both.

Adam ordered twenty copies of the *Book of Common Prayer,* which he needed for his services, and two sets of spoke wheels.

"When I replace our clumsy wooden wheels with a natty touch of civilization, we will be the envy of Natchez," he said with a laugh. He hugged Sam and held him at arms length. "Dear friend," he said, "I'm glad you came into my life. God bless you and keep you." He embraced David. "I expect you to have a great time exploring the legal world."

Meg lay awake beside the sleeping Ramos, nursing her wounded pride. She had not only been unable to complete the voodoo ritual at her mistress' bedside, but the other slaves had derided her when she was ejected from Mary's room. Meg believed the hair-ball token would have tied up the baby and strangled her before birth. And if that failed, she had felt the air full of spirits looking for an abode. She hoped the *vodun* dangling from her neck would arouse the *Tonton* to steal the baby's soul, making way for an evil spirit. The midwife had caught on too fast. Meg was angry at her failure.

She wondered why *Rada,* or *Wangol,* or any of the gods hadn't looked after her own safety in this strange land. Ramos was a poor substitute for the body ache. Only Kofi could arouse her passion enough to take care of the aching. And that planter-man, Vousdan, was too rough. She had to take over his clumsy coupling to prevent him from hurting her.

Meg arose quietly, without disturbing Ramos, and stole across the road to a delighted Kofi. They satisfied their passions in the barn until each was spent.

"I use a *vodun* on Massah Cloud's new baby, like your massah tole me," Meg finally spoke, "but de sneaky midwife catch on to de haih-ball and take it away. I need Massah Vousdan tell me what I do nex'."

"You're the *tsunga* witch, N'leeta," Kofi teased. "You should tell *him* what do nex' time. Clem say let him know when you come. He wake Massah to see you."

"Not befo' we has our happy time," N'leeta said. "I gets hongry — hongry for you."

"Me too," Kofi said, and they made love awhile until each was satisfied. Kofi finally left her in the barn while he went to awaken Clem.

Soon Meg heard footsteps enter the barn and she climbed down the ladder to face Vousdan. He held the lantern over her and glowered at her impudent manner.

"Well, Meg, what can you report?"

"I N'leeta!" she corrected him forcefully.

"All right, N'leeta, have you kept your promise to hex the Clouds? I want to hear they are properly frightened."

"Yassa, I hex Miz Mary when de baby come. She worry now what happen nex'." Meg told him about hiding the tokens at Mary's bedside, assuring him the *vodun* ritual had affected Mary.

"Good. Remember you have my permission to visit Kofi by using your magic talents on your master and mistress. And I expect more of you." Vousdan gloated inwardly at his successful ploy.

"Yassa. But when I gets to stay? You tole I cud be yo' slave."

"That will come in due time, girl. Now get up there in the hay and give me plenty of sparks. I expect a good ride."

When he had finished with her, he sent her off with instructions. "Next time I want you to bring real trouble to Cloudcrest.

Conjure with animals, to show that your master practices voodoo on his own property. You can have your revenge on them for separating you from Kofi."

Meg rolled her eyes with mischief. "Yassa, I fix 'em good. Kin I come back heah to Kofi?"

"You do your part, N'leeta, and you can visit Kofi. You will soon be here to stay."

Vousdan left with an uneasy feeling. N'leeta was cooperating all right, but he began to fear her dark power over him. He throbbed and ached when he thought of her, and her sexual prowess was ungovernable. He worried he was giving himself to her instead of retaining his power over her. Could she cast a spell over him?

Adam and Jeb Carter were working on the overseer's house at Cole's Creek when Lieutenant Garcia, one of the governor's guards, rode up and handed Adam a note. It was an invitation from Don Manuel for Adam to visit him that evening at Colonel Green's home, where he was spending the night. Colonel Green provided him a home-away-from-home when he came to Cole's Creek.

Adam settled down with the governor in the library that night, a carafe of port wine on the table between them. Don Manuel toasted him genially.

"I'm glad you came, Don Adam. I have need for a respite from my grueling defense building, and I like to get my mind off of impending war."

"How is the new fort progressing, Don Manuel? Have you had any further news of an impending invasion?"

Don Manuel explained that the fort was already framed, but the building had angered the Choctaws, who were acting aggressively. The threat of two enemies at the same time was unsettling.

"There is enough insecurity to go around, as it is," Adam said. "People are apprehensive over the constant invasion rumors . . . I have been wondering about Hannah Vousdan's troubles. I heard she has filed suit against her husband."

"Yes, it should come to trial soon. I have submitted to both Vousdans a list of citizen arbitrators from which to make their selection, but have not heard back from either of them. I have already received the report from the *alguaciles* who have investigated the case, and had hoped it could be settled at court this coming Saturday. Both Vousdans have been interviewed, and I must say it is an unpleasant affair. But why do you ask?"

"I have heard some ugly talk about my wife, which was reported to me by friends," Adam said.

"I hope *Doña* Mary is well. Congratulations on the birth of your new daughter. I trust nothing went wrong."

"All is well, thank you. We are both ecstatic over our Susannah. You should see her. She's beautiful." Adam then described the voodoo attempts at his daughter's birth. "Someone has twisted this event to look like Mary's superstition instead of the slave's," he said.

"I suspect that Vousdan might be behind this, in retaliation for you helping his wife. He must have been humiliated when she turned to you for help." Don Manuel paused, tapping his fingers together as he reflected. "Vousdan's behavior has annoyed me ever since I came, and if I had anyone else to recommend for local surveyor I would do so. But please do not worry. No one who knows you would suspect either you or *Doña* Mary of superstitious belief. Your many friends will defend you against such slander. If the rumor builds up, I will address the issue then. Just ignore it now."

"I will try," Adam said, "but the thought rankles nevertheless."

The governor reached for his cigar box and offered one to Adam, who shook his head. Don Manuel lit one and leaned back in his comfortable chair.

"As for the voodoo, the blacks are deeply influenced by their African culture," Don Manuel said. "Superstitions seem to fulfill those basic needs to allay human fears — protection from outside forces. By their reasoning, what else but evil spirits and supernatural beings could have caused these acts, and how would they overcome these forces except by a counter force of amulets, charms, or talismans? Seeking to turn the tide of events, they can feel a measure of protection."

"We have our own supernatural beliefs, also, such as the Holy Ghost," Adam said. "Jesus called the Holy Ghost 'The Comforter' who would teach his disciples 'all things' and help them remember what he taught them. Well, what is the Holy Ghost? No one really knows except what his own mind conceives."

"The Holy Ghost is a spirit, an enigma to people who struggle with the idea. Even the priests have trouble explaining it. Perhaps the Holy Ghost is the vast realm of silence that we all share."

"Yes, I like that concept — that inner silence which Plotinus tells us is the 'mystery that informs all things.' He directs us to enter this unseen, silent world of the inner self and be enabled to see the Divine Presence in illuminated moments." Adam paused, his eyes cast pensively into his wine glass. "I have experienced that instant. It was a moment of transcendence, a period of enlightenment which could only have come from another realm. Certainly I was not wise or holy enough to have produced it myself."

Don Manuel looked intently at Adam. "How extraordinary. I am deeply touched that you shared this with me. That, my friend, is the realm of our Catholic holy men, our monks and saints. They, too, find and eventually live in an inner world. But they reach it by the most severe abstinence and holy rituals which only they understand. It is a life of mysticism which few of us are given to explore."

Adam twirled the deep red wine gently in his glass. "My studies of the saints, and others dating back to pre-Christian centuries, revealed specific steps one must practice to be receptive of this moment of mystery. When rigorously practiced, the steps cleanse the mind and body of negative qualities, such as pride, prejudice, self-satisfactions. The regime is very difficult for an ordinary person, for it requires ability to reach a state of complete detachment."

"How many people would be able to discipline themselves to practice the rigorous routine?" Don Manuel mused. "As for detachment, that is a state of mind almost impossible for anyone but a saint to reach. How many can detach themselves enough to see the true value of things? Most people's daily lives are so filled with the urgent need to fulfill the basic necessities of existence that their attachments become the prime motivator of their actions."

"Yes," Adam answered. He leaned forward eagerly with his next thought. "But isn't that what Christianity should be all about? Learning that the one thing of value in life is the active soul?"

"Prayer encourages that indirectly, does it not?"

"Certainly," Adam continued. "To me there is an exquisite beauty in the idea of a potential mystical life in every man. I have always taught that if we would stop asking for things in our prayers, and would still our thoughts to a state of worship instead, God will enter and enlighten us. He will inform us in whatever degree we are ready to receive Him."

Don Manuel mulled over his thoughts as he replenished their wine glasses. "The mystical life is worrisome to many. The step between Dionysian frenzy and ecstatic vision is all too brief. The holy men of the ancient world were often thought touched with madness. Jesus penetrated the fundamental truths of life and brought them to light for His fellow man, and look how He upset His immediate world."

"He would surely be shocked to see what has happened to His deeper message," Adam said. "Christianity has been disfigured by priestly extravagances, and by the exhaustion of the profound ideas committed to their charge. The highest goal, spiritual growth, has been lost. Mystical Christianity has been displaced by institutional Christianity. Each religion has developed its own set of symbols and its moral code by which to live. In the process, the symbols, the moral codes, the ethical laws of society have become sufficient substitutes for the mystical message which informed the religion itself."

Adam's ability to strike at the heart of a matter was often disturbing to Don Manuel, and he responded carefully, trying not to show his inner protest. After all, Adam was only theorizing, and he must not take it personally.

"But symbols help the mind absorb the realities, the essence of Christ's messages, and the meaning of His life. Besides, how can the church teach the sluggish mind of the multitude to accept a life with such an elusive goal as you propose?"

"That's the challenge of Christianity," Adam answered with conviction, "making the spiritual connection that God surely must have intended when He created us. The esoteric elements of religion are guarded so secretly that man is not given a glimpse of his potential. I believe the mystical goal should be the bedrock of faith, and that it should be applied to the dirt, grime, and tragedy of life to work its way into people's lives, not just left on the shelf for a select few to keep for themselves."

"Ah, but Adam, remember Jesus' caveat, *Cast not thy pearls before swine.* Jesus knew too well that people will scorn ideas they do not understand," Don Manuel said. "Are you ready to teach this elusive goal to your followers, to abandon your orthodoxy?"

Adam caught Don Manuel's derision and grinned sheepishly. "No. I have too much to learn myself before teaching others. And you are right. We mustn't confuse people who have simple beliefs. It is up to each soul to seek its own level of wisdom, to increase its knowledge. A little knowledge leads to dogmatism, a little more brings questioning, and a little more opens the floodgates toward understanding that our souls are sustained through channels to God. Of course —"a small smile played at the corners of his mouth, "individual channels to God could weaken the church's hold, and what would we do without the rituals that provide so much pageantry in our lives?"

"I take exception to that," Don Manuel hotly retorted. "What you call 'elaborate ceremonies' of the church are important symbols. If we demystify our rituals we would take away the impact of church authority. Rituals represent the development in religious thought and practice, and serve as guidelines. I can experience some very profound moments through the rituals."

"As I do when I perform them," Adam agreed. It was time to close the discussion on an agreeable thought.

. . .

When Adam returned to Cloudcrest, Mary handed him a message from André Michaux, the French botanist who had traveled with them on their keelboat journey.

"You were so jealous of him, remember?" Mary's eyes twinkled with mischief. "He's at King's Tavern and hopes to see us before he leaves. Ask him to stay, Adam," Mary pleaded. "He is full of Nature's secrets, and he promised we could read his botany notes."

Adam was caught by surprise, but he consented to put up with the fellow for a short time. He grinned with the memories. "I suppose I really was jealous of André on the boat. He was so effusive and attentive of you when I selfishly needed your comfort."

Adam drove Mary's two-seater cart into town for André. The Frenchman was groomed and fashionably dressed, appearing far different from his frontier stint among the Indians. André's bright confidence seemed to disappear from his face when he learned Adam had married Mary, but his greeting to her was as ebullient as ever. He kissed her hand and gazed at her with the same adoration he showed on the boat. He presented her with a leather pouch decorated with colored pods and beads, gave Adam a pair of moccasins, and handed Becky an Indian doll.

At the dinner table, Mary sat enthralled while he described his life and research with the Indians. He said he had spent the last months with a Choctaw tribe, and a short time with the American colony at Walnut Hills. Besides recording regional plant life, he learned many new ways the Indians utilize plants for medicines and domestic needs.

Maamba cleared the table after supper, and Michaux opened a large case of notes and drawings, spreading them on the table. He explained the pages as they looked over his shoulder.

"I see you have drawn your maps in detail. What would the French want with such intricate maps of the American wilderness?" Adam asked.

"Ah, *mon ami,* everything I do is thorough. How can I describe where I found my information but through my maps?" He swept the maps back into the case and changed the subject.

André said he longed to speak his native tongue again and to be around his countrymen. He requested names of local Frenchmen, and Adam gave him a list of French settlers. Michaux rode into town the next two days. He then left for New Orleans with a profusion of thanks for their hospitality. After Michaux had departed, Adam described the Frenchman and his visit to Don Manuel.

"I am not pleased with this news, Don Adam," he said. "Most alarming is the fact that the man carries detailed maps with him, and that he made it a point to seek out local French families. Any native Frenchman is suspect in this territory. Governor Miró informs me that the French of New Orleans make poor citizens of the Spanish Crown. They show their disloyalty in various ways, and leave no doubt they would like for Louisiana to be French again. I shall dispatch this news to Governor Miró at once."

18 Nuptials and Nostrums

A dam was fastening the storage room joists for Evenstar when he heard a cheery shout from the road. He laid down his tools and went to the front verandah where he found Andrew Jackson astride his horse.

"Good morning, Mister Cloud. I'm in real luck to find you," Jackson said as he dismounted. "It was on a chance that I rode over from Springfield to see if you were here working on your house."

"Good morning, and welcome to my house. I'm putting on the finishing touches, at last," Adam replied. "To what do I owe this surprise visit?"

"I have a special favor to ask." The young man's eyes danced with excitement. "I guess in this instance I should address you as Reverend Cloud, for it is in your capacity as a clergyman that I seek you out."

"And what may I do for you as a minister that I can't do for you as a mister?" Adam teased. "You aren't ready for priestly advice, or a conversion, are you?"

"Not exactly," Jackson grinned, "but you may have to consider carefully what I have come to ask of you. Mrs. Robards and I wish to marry and, of the several Protestant clergyman in the district, we prefer that you marry us."

Adam was taken by surprise. His face became grave as he considered the request. "This is a serious matter, Mr. Jackson. It would require me to break the law. You must know that only a Catholic priest can marry you here. Nor would I want to bring down the governor's wrath on my head. He has become a cherished friend;

he trusts me and would be shocked if I did such a thing. And how could I live with myself?" he asked in an anguished voice.

"I realize it is a lot to ask of you, but we simply do not want to be married by a Roman Catholic priest. Mrs. Robards has been staying at Springfield Manor, and the Greens have concurred that we should sound you out. At first, Colonel Green volunteered to marry us, but his American title of magistrate was only a shadow one, and is not valid in Natchez." He hesitated when he saw Adam's brows creased with doubt. "No one need know," he added hastily. "You can be sure that neither the governor nor the Catholic church will ever hear of it."

"I understand your need for matrimony, and I rejoice with you in your decision. But for me to marry you . . ." Adam slowly shook his head. "I do not see how we could keep it a secret, and it is against my ingrained principles to act in devious ways."

"Perhaps if you talked with the Greens you might see how our wedding could be kept a secret. Would you be willing to ride over there with me? Please, sir, I beg of you to keep an open mind."

Adam agreed. After all, he reasoned, it would do no harm, and he respected the Greens' opinion.

At Springfield, Rachel greeted Adam warmly, and with pleading eyes, begged him to perform the ceremony.

"The thought of a Catholic marriage is abhorrent to me," she said.

"It is not as upsetting to be married by a Catholic priest as you might think," Adam assured her. "Mrs. Cloud and I had no choice, and we laid aside our reticence to the greater joy of matrimony."

"We understand their reluctance," Thomas Green said, "but they must be married before a scandal develops. We can assure you that in the privacy of our home there would be only our immediate families as witnesses. The children would be excluded."

Adam tapped his fingers together a few minutes in thought, and finally replied. "There is a small loophole we might use. Governor Gayoso told me of a Protestant marriage performed long before Natchez had a governor. The Catholics did not stand in the way because the couple was leaving to live elsewhere. If I do consent, I do so only under the promise that if you stay here you will ask Father William for a second ceremony."

Jackson looked tenderly at Rachel. "We don't intend to live in Natchez. Our home will be in Nashborough where I practice law, and where I have a place in the legislature." He took Rachel's hand. "We won't need a second ceremony."

"Under these conditions I will marry you," Adam said. "But you must all swear to secrecy."

On the appointed day, Mary and Adam rode in their carriage to Springfield Manor, their clothes for the wedding placed carefully beside them. They arrived in late afternoon in time to dress for the evening ceremony. Colonel Green and the Green couples were assembled, and the children were hustled upstairs out of sight.

Everything about the wedding titillated Mary's sense of romance. Fresh garlands of roses, day lilies, and Michaelmas daisies festooned the parlor. The couple stood in front of the huge corner fireplace. Adam faced them, attired in his vestments. Mary thought the bride enchanting in a soft pink voile gown, with a halo of pink rosebuds and blue daisies arranged in her black hair. The groom was handsomely attired in a cream linen suit and brown waistcoat, his luxurious sandy-red hair swept back in a queue with a velvet ribbon. Mary dabbed her eyes with her kerchief as Adam conducted the familiar marriage ritual from the *Book of Common Prayer.*

A lavish wedding feast followed in the dining hall. Everyone lingered at the table, telling jokes and teasing the newlyweds. Rachel finally arose and raised her wine goblet, her face radiant with joy.

"To our dear friends," she said. "Our heartfelt thanks for making our dreams come true. And to the Reverend Cloud for his uncommon act of trust and courage."

She kissed each one around the table, and the couple retired upstairs for the night in a secluded bedroom overlooking the flower garden.

The Jacksons had barely spent a month in Andrew's cabin at Bayou Pierre when Adam heard that a large contingent of travelers would take the Trace to Nashborough in September. He stopped to read the names of the travelers posted on the Government House notice board, and found the Jackson name among them. He rode on to Wooley's store, where he saw Jackson outside packing purchases on his burro.

"I am not surprised that you are leaving, but I'm glad I caught you to say goodbye," Adam said.

"Ah, my friend, I was going to ride by your plantation on the way home. I wouldn't leave without saying farewell. It's time to 'hop the twig,' as they say. My law practice can't be conducted from Natchez, and the legislature will meet next month."

"I regret you must leave, Andrew, but, in a way, it is best."

"Rachel and I are in your debt, and we will always be your friends, sir." Jackson drew Adam aside and lowered his voice. "We realized that gossip was bound to develop, and having been duly and honestly joined by the minister of our choice, we did not want to have to defend our life together. We had a glorious honeymoon."

"Your happiness shows," Adam gave him a broad smile. He felt relieved; it took the pressure off his own guilt. "Let's hope the secret never leaks out."

"It never will. You can count on it. Rachel sent you her farewell; she shares my grateful affection for you. If you ever come up our way, please be our guests in Nashborough." Jackson cinched the straps on his bulging luggage and turned to Adam. "Give our affectionate regards to the lovely Mrs. Cloud."

They clasped hands and Jackson mounted his horse.

"Farewell, my friend. God go with you on your journey." Adam's throat tightened as Jackson rode away.

To his dismay, Adam learned, through town gossip, that Hannah Vousdan had lost her suit against her husband, and he sought the governor for confirmation. Don Manuel told him that after hearing all the evidence, he had placed the matter in the hands of the vicar, Father Patricio Walsh, in Havana, who, in turn, had submitted it to higher authorities. Under the rules of Ecclesiastical

Law, the secular marriage was termed null and void. She was once again Hannah Lum.

Don Manuel was contrite. "There was nothing I could do," he said. "I was bound to uphold the Crown; my religious duties are dictated by church and king."

Adam was outraged. The decree was unbelievably cruel. The poor woman was an outcast, penniless and friendless.

He decided there was something *he* could do. He solicited the community for funds to help Hannah Lum purchase her return to relatives in Charleston. Don Manuel made the first donation, and, to Adam's delight, donations swelled. The injustice of the case rankled many Natchez citizens. Civil justice was so ingrained from former freedoms that they had little respect for an abhorrent religious law by a church they could not understand.

One morning Dirk reported that Meg and Ramos were missing. Adam was alarmed for their safety. He doubted they could survive an escape up the Trace. He galloped into town and reported the runaways to Governor Gayoso, who ordered a posse to hunt them down. Before nightfall Adam received a message that travelers had found the slaves on the Trace, and he could pick them up at the *calibozo*. He stopped at Government House to thank the governor for his help.

"There is a rumor spreading that your slaves ran off because of cruelty on your plantation," Don Manuel told him. "As ridiculous as that sounds, Don Adam, I have to ask if anyone has beat them?"

Adam was indignant. "Of course not, and I'm sorry you had to ask. But I suspect William Vousdan has had a hand in this. Mary thinks he wants revenge."

"The slaves were examined for bruises and lacerations, and none were found," Don Manuel said. "Take them home and I will have a talk with Vousdan."

Frustrating as Vousdan's slander and vilification were, Adam felt that bribing slaves to run away reached a new low in harassment. It had to be Vousdan, but how could he prove it?

. . .

The winter months of 1792 brought heavy storms and flooding, making travel to Cole's Creek impossible. Supplies at Cloudcrest began to dwindle, and the Clouds had their first experience of food shortages. Adam was unable to hunt regularly, and the larder ran out of fresh venison. Grain supply was low, and Maamba served dried venison in place of bread. Summer's bear grease supply dwindled, creating a shortage of tallow. Fresh produce was no longer available from the vegetable garden, and forays to the plaza stalls often rendered Adam more tidbits of news than of table fare. Small gatherings of settlers at the plaza between storms kept the news grapevine alive, and Adam came home with the latest rumors to share with Mary.

He learned that William Vousdan had married Colonel Hutchins' eldest daughter, Elizabeth Hutchins, sister of Lottie Green. As part of her dowry, Vousdan had acquired several tracts of land near the Cole's Creek settlement for his cattle spread.

"Too close for comfort," Adam commented to Mary. "I can't get rid of him as a neighbor."

There was news of Hannah Lum. She had reportedly left for Charleston, and the whole affair had left a bitter taste in everyone's mouth, Vousdan's most of all. Added to the lie that Adam beat his slaves, he was casting suspicion that the Clouds encouraged and used slave voodoo practices on their plantation.

The most alarming news was of Governor Miró's replacement by a new governor-general. The new appointment, Baron de Francisco Luis Carondelet, was formerly governor of San Salvador province, in Guatemala. Governor Gayoso had been summoned to meet with him in New Orleans. The news filled Adam with misgivings.

"The new governor might not be as sympathetic to the planter's tobacco problem," Adam said to Mary. "Let's hope he will not be critical of Don Manuel's lenient style of administration."

One morning Mary and Adam were enjoying a tranquil rainy day at home. Mary was now into the fourth month of another pregnancy, and Adam was filled with happiness. Mary sat with her mending basket beside her. Susannah, now seven months, played on a blanket at her feet. Becky, now three, toyed with a cloth doll. Adam sat on the blanket and joined his daughters as they each tugged at the doll.

"Where did you get this, Becky?" Adam asked. "Did you take one of Mama's stockings to play with?"

"I found it under your bed," Becky said. "See, the knots help Sue hang on."

Mary examined the cloth and discovered it was one of her camisoles. Adam examined it closely.

"The thing has nine knots, Mary. What do you make of that? I suspect this is some kind of voodoo token, and it has to do with your natal term."

"Well, evil or not, it can't harm me. I'm too healthy and sassy for a hex." Mary laughed. "If you can undo the knots I'll ask Maamba to try to salvage the camisole."

"That Meg! If I did whip my slaves, she would be the first to get it," Adam said.

Their dilemma was interrupted by the sound of a horse approaching the porch. Mary opened the door.

"Dusty!" she cried. "It's Dusty Rhodes, Adam."

Dusty dismounted, hitched his horse to the hitching-post, and announced he had come to stay.

His arrival during the slack winter season proved fortuitous. Adam laid out planting schedules with him, and Dusty became familiar with the slaves. He spent several weeks at the Forman plantation to learn how Benajah managed the Forman slaves and planting seasons. On returning Dusty to Cloudcrest, Adam stopped at a slave auction at the landing, where he bought two more male slaves.

"Here are two more boys for Tizzi to choose from," Adam joked to Mary. "They are named Sambo and Tom."

Tizzi liked them both, and it was some time before she made her choice. By the time of her wedding, she was pregnant, having slept with both of them for trial. Tizzi's wedding to Tom was a *cause célèbre* among the slaves. Adam hoped that the forbidden marriage rites for whites did not apply to slave marriages.

Arising early one morning, Adam dressed quietly so as not to arouse his sleeping wife and children. He stepped outside. The air was faintly fragrant with fresh spring blooms, and he noted the profusion of growth about the grounds. Flowering vines were creeping back into cleared areas, and their climbing tendrils mingled with new green tree leaves. He felt gloriously alive, vibrant, at one with the world.

Dusty and the slaves had almost finished planting the Cloudcrest fields. In a day or two they could begin planting indigo, flax, and rye at Evenstar. He suddenly remembered that James Moore had recently offered a Natchez town lot for a school. It would require the governor's approval, and he should sound him out on the future of their children's education. He had not seen the governor since his return from New Orleans.

After a quick breakfast, he rode to Government House and found that the governor was at home. He rode to Don Manuel's home, and Chico ushered him inside. "Wait here, *Señor.* I will tell His Excellency you have arrived. He has other visitors."

Don Manuel greeted Adam with genuine affection. "Ah, my friend, you are a sight for sore eyes. What a journey I have had. What frustrations I have endured, you cannot imagine. Sit down awhile. My guests are inspecting my stables, and will return here soon."

"How was your briefing with the new governor-general?" What did you think of him?" Adam asked.

"I came away with ambivalent opinions. I tried to assess him during our talks, and decided that at least he is decisive."

Don Manuel then described his meetings with Governor Carondelet. Carondelet agreed to holding a powwow with the Choctaw Nation to assuage their anxiety over the new fort and the Walnut Hills settlement. Gayoso said he had pled passionately for the Natchez settlers' financial plight over the diminishing tobacco purchases. After two days of deliberation, the governor approved extending the Tobacco Stay Law for a new moratorium on debts, with a cap on interest of no more than ten percent by the merchant creditors.

"That will make the merchants unhappy, but the planters will be overjoyed with your good news," Adam commented.

Just then the study door opened, and Chico led in two Indians. One was a tall chief in regal attire, his hair splendidly adorned with feathers, horsehair and beads, and a stunning breastplate across his black deerskin suit. Accompanying him was a young Indian wearing natural deerskin and a breastplate denoting high rank.

Don Manuel began an introduction, but stopped when he saw the look of recognition on their faces.

"Chief Payo-Mataha!" Adam exclaimed. The chief grasped Adam's hand, pumping it up and down. ". . . and Yellowtail!" Adam smiled and shook the young man's hand.

"This man my guest," the chief said, indicating Adam to the surprised governor. "How you do here?" he said to Adam.

"Very well, indeed sir." Adam turned to Don Manuel. "Chief Piomingo's valiant warriors rescued some of our fleet from disaster in fierce river winds on our way to Natchez. We were honored guests in his village at Chickasaw Bluffs."

"Chief Piomingo is visiting at my invitation," Don Manuel said. "He requests that his son stay with me and be educated in Natchez."

"Much to learn," Piomingo said. "The boy should know the ways of the white man and learn from your books."

Don Manuel smiled at the chief. "Of course, I have agreed to see that Yellowtail receives an education, and he will move with me into my new home. The inside work on Concord was almost completed while I was away, and it should be ready soon."

"That is good news. I only wish my new home could be finished as quickly," Adam said. "But it is a coincidence that I came to see you about education, also, Don Manuel," Adam said. "May I speak about it now? I will be brief and take my leave."

"Of course. The chief will be interested too."

Piomingo and Yellowtail sat on the floor and listened intently as Adam told of the residents' desire for an available, permanent tutor for everyone who could afford one. He explained James Moore's offer of the town lot, commended its desirable location, and handed the governor a scroll containing Moore's architectural drawing for a school.

Don Manuel scanned it briefly. He agreed that the educational situation was deplorable, and he would take up the matter with Governor Carondelet. He would hold his approval until he heard from New Orleans. Adam expressed his good wishes to Piomingo and Yellowtail, and left them to continue their private discussion. He felt encouraged. At least he had established a foothold toward building the first school in Natchez.

Adam dreamed he was on the river again. Indians were pulling a screaming Veralee into their canoe. He awoke with a start, the unpleasant scene vivid before him. The screams persisted, and he realized they came from the slave quarters. He crawled quietly out of bed, careful not to awaken Mary, and groped for the lantern.

By the time he reached the cabins, the screams had subsided to moans coming from the cabin of Meg and Remos. Other slaves were gathered outside their open door. He entered and saw Meg moaning and rocking herself on the bed, her head buried in her hands so none could see her sly pretense. Ramos turned to Adam, wide-eyed with fear.

"Massah, we's bein' hexed. They's thumps and bumps agin's the walls. The do' won't stay closed. We's scared."

Adam searched outside for signs of an intruder, but finding none in the dark, he persuaded them that it must have been the wind thumping tree branches on the roof and pushing against the door.

The next day was different. He found the front door of his house smeared with blood. One of the swine was missing from the pigpen, and he followed a bloody trail to the slave quarters. There he saw a disgusting sight. A circle of flour ringed the slaveyard brazier, and pig entrails scattered the ground.

Adam and Mary puzzled over the meaning of the ugly signs of a hex. They reasoned that Meg could not have perpetrated such an act on her own; it would have required great strength to carry a heavy pig. Mary wondered if anything unusual had happened at Tizzi's wedding feast that could precipitate a hex from an outside slave. Their suspicion focused on Vousdan because of his obvious hatred. They decided not to say a word to anyone about the event.

"Whoever is the perpetrator, and especially if it is Vousdan, we shouldn't give him the satisfaction of our discomfort," Adam said. "We will not have to suffer such incidents much longer. We'll soon be moving to Cole's Creek."

Nevertheless, news of the pig slaughter worked its way to other slaves, and from there to their masters. Adam's friends reported to him that Vousdan was spreading lies about him. Using the pig slaughter incident, he raised suspicion that Adam held secret sacrificial ceremonies on his plantation; that he let his slaves practice voodoo and celebrate primitive rituals at their harvest feasts.

"He is quite clever, Adam," Ezekiel told him. "He intimates that your ministry is a fraud, and that you lack the convictions of a Christian faith. This way he raises the question of what you believe or practice in private. Vousdan appeals to susceptible Catholic minds. I heard one fellow suggest that your slaves might have slaughtered your pig in retaliation for your mistreatment."

Adam felt vulnerable. The public proclivity for sensational news was easily satisfied. He suspected it would take an enormous campaign to counter the viscious rumors and juicy tales circulating about him.

To no one's surprise, Governor Gayoso's friends received invitations to his spring wedding with Elizabeth Watts. It would be the first wedding held in the new parish church, and the first social affair in the governor's new home.

Adam did not want Mary to go. He was concerned that her condition of *enciente* would cause comment, and the issue set up a storm between them. Mary pled her case and won over Adam's best judgment. They would ride in the Forman coach, and her cloak and a specially designed gown would conceal her figure.

The elaborate Catholic ceremony excluded Protestant participation, and they could only watch as Father Savage and Friar Brady performed the long rituals and mass. When Don Manuel and his radiant bride finally walked down the aisle and emerged outside, a band struck up lively Spanish music, and a cheering crowd waved as they entered the governor's handsome new carriage, recently received from Sam Forman.

The Forman coach followed the bride and groom to Concord. They entered the estate under a handsome arched gate and up a winding road through scattered oaks, old gnarled cedars, and weeping willows. The white two-story mansion greeted them in lofty grandeur. Glowing torches and lanterns lighted a broad gallery completely encircling the house on the ground floor. The most distinctive feature was a set of white marble staircases, one on each side of the entrance, winding up to the second gallery, where they met in a great marble landing.

The joyous couple awaited their guests on the upper floor. Mary puffed out the peplum on her bouffant skirt, confident that her expanded girth was well disguised in her gown of celadon green taffeta. Adam's approving smile further reassured her. They joined the other excited guests who were examining every inch of the ornate interior. Eliza said that most of the furnishings were imported from Spain and Santo Domingo.

Adam clasped Don Manuel's hand and kissed the sparkling young bride. "Your happiness shows, Don Manuel," he said. Their eyes exchanged genuine affection.

A sumptuous wedding feast followed. The scent of perfumes, wafted by ladies' fans, and trays of spiced food, offered by hovering servants, invaded the senses as the guests enjoyed the superb cuisine. Music and dancing followed into the night. The flickering of hundreds of candle flames lent a glamorous effect, as the ladies' gowns rustled over the floor.

During the evening the bride and groom slipped away unnoticed to honeymoon in their Cole's Creek hideaway. The elegant affair was unforgettable, and Mary's mind reminisced the event for a long time after.

Don Manuel's marriage added a buoyant lift to his outlook on life. Elizabeth proved to be a perfect governor's wife, and he experienced a new sense of calm and contentment. She took over the education of young Yellowtail, with daily lessons in Spanish, English, history, and mathematics.

The governor's connubial bliss in his new home made Adam eager to move to Evenstar, and he worked feverishly on the house as spring wore on. The farm began to take shape as planned. The slave cabins and overseer's house were ready for occupation. A herd of fifteen cattle, with several calves, now grazed the well-fenced fields, and Dusty had planted a small fruit orchard.

One day Adam stopped by Government House on his way home from Cole's Creek with a mission to see Don Manuel. Residents had voted to change the community's name to Villa Gayoso, and Adam was selected to ask the governor's permission. Don Manuel beamed with surprise at Adam's announcement, and he accepted the new name with pleasure.

Don Manuel had a request for Adam. It concerned the government liaison with Colonel Wilkinson. Wilkinson had informed the governors, in an October letter, that he had rejoined the United States Army to fight the Miami Indian tribes in Wabash County, under General Wayne. He had taken eight hundred volunteers with him from the Kentucky Militia, and had been appointed lieutenant colonel, commandant of the Second U. S. Infantry, assigned to Fort Washington.

Don Manuel glanced at the letter on his desk and chuckled. "He writes that his wife and sons are with him. For this, he says, he is especially thankful, and that he is a 'very uxorious and happy man'."

Adam laughed. "Whatever else the colonel may be, he is certainly a faithful family man. What else did he write?"

"Now, Don Adam, what follows must remain strictly confidential. The information I am about to divulge is very important to us, but its disclosure could be disastrous."

"You can trust me, Don Manuel. But what has this to do with me?"

"As you know, Wilkinson has been making efforts to separate the frontier settlements from the Union. Now this may startle you. Through his eyes, we have envisioned the breakup of the frontier into a new empire of three separate states — Kentucky, Tennessee, and Franklin-Bourbon. Colonel Wilkinson would head the new nation, something like a 'George Washington-of-the-West.' The whole plan is an agreeable one to us, and we would like to implement it."

Don Manuel stopped when he saw Adam's shocked face and the genuine alarm in his eyes.

"I doubt that the Kentucky legislators suspect him of his secret ambition, but I'm beginning to understand the controversy which always surrounds his name," Adam said. "What else is he hatching up?"

"He advises us that the United States is planning a new overland route from Kentucky to New Orleans. He suggests we could incite the Creeks to raid the road builders to prevent making the new road, which would add unwelcome access to our land."

Adam felt sickened by such tactics. Was there nothing this man would not stoop to do? Adam suspected that Wilkinson must be under the pay of the Spanish government, but if he was receiving a stipend, he dared not ask. He dragged his thoughts back to Don Manuel's disclosure, as the governor continued speaking.

"With his high rank in the United States Army, Wilkinson should be in a position to know the facts and the state of affairs, not only in Kentucky, but in the rest of the frontier territories, as well. He should also have prestigious stature among his followers and admirers. But the colonel's continuous assurances disturb me. I am not easily fooled, yet it is difficult to know how much he can accomplish in our behalf."

"It is beyond my ken how Wilkinson can play both sides against the middle," Adam responded. "It seems he is without loyalty to any country, and I fear that his double-dealing might bring harm to Spain."

"Exactly," Don Manuel said. "He expects us to believe he can accomplish this goal even though Kentucky is about to become a state of the Union. I have heard of no effort to repeal the petition for statehood. It is in this regard that I would ask a favor of you, Don Adam. If you decline I shall understand, and we will drop the matter."

"Try me," Adam said.

"I need reliable information from the frontier on how Wilkinson now stands with his countrymen. I need to know if his civilian leadership has been diminished or enhanced by his move to the army. I would like for you to inquire into these matters. You have friends in Louisville with whom you stayed on your journey . . ."

"Yes, Mason and Daisy Downs. They introduced us to Wilkinson. They should know his current reputation up there."

"Perhaps your families in the East would have some knowledge of the nation's regard toward Kentucky statehood. If you write to them, you can ask the right questions."

Within a week, Adam sent letters to the Downses, the Cloud and Grandin families, Sarah and John Wurts, and Sam Forman. He hoped Sam might somehow have stumbled onto inside secrets from the army. He filled the letters with news from Natchez, and disguised his inquiries as interest in news of what was going on elsewhere.

Governor Gayoso called a town meeting to announce the results of a recent meeting with the Choctaw and Chickasaw tribes, held on May 14.

"The powwow was a success," the governor said. "Two hundred Indians arrived with a contingent of chiefs and many warriors. We convened with them at Concord, where the chiefs assembled on the marble landing of the front staircase."

Adam wished he could have been there, as Don Manuel unfolded progress of the meeting.

"I told them that Spain had no territorial aims against the Indian nations," Don Manuel continued. "I explained that the

American government was powerless to prevent frontiersmen from encroaching upon Indian hunting grounds, even though the United States had pledged to forbid it. I explained that the new fort was intended to hold off any Americans who might try to take the territory by force, and that the fort would be a trading center for goods from the Spanish, Portuguese, and Italian nations. In addition, I emphasized that their continued alliance with Spain would protect the Indian nations as well as Spain against all aggressors."

Great diplomacy, Adam thought. No one could have matched Don Manuel's skill, in his opinion.

Don Manuel continued the account, looking pleased as he revealed the outcome. They finally agreed on a treaty which the Indians could sign. The land on which Fort Nogales was built would be ceded to Spain. The Indians would be assured of no further Spanish encroachment, or expansion, and the American settlers at Walnut Hills would be denied claims to any Spanish land. Indian hunting grounds would be secure, and they could live in peace and harmony from that day. Mutual protection clauses would be agreed upon and added to the treaty.

"In the end, all chiefs agreed to sign the treaty, which we named 'The Treaty of Natchez.' I gave King Tescahetuca, of the Chickasaw Nation, the key to the royal storehouse, and the Indians had a feast-orgy. I believe they went home very satisfied."

Adam left the meeting feeling relief. At least the Indians were pacified, and Don Manuel had accomplished a diplomatic triumph. His admiration and respect for Don Manuel deepened.

During the spring, Adam spent most of his time at Villa Gayoso finishing Evenstar. Current political news did not penetrate the remote settlement, and it was only on his brief visits to Cloudcrest that he learned anything of significance. Don Manuel kept him abreast of the latest O'Fallon filibuster threats, and complained of local unrest and crime within the province. Bandits were marauding riverboats. One bandit had killed an Indian, and the governor feared the Choctaws would blame the government and want to retaliate. He had decided to organize a provincial militia, and Adam agreed to sign on as a recruit. Colonel Wilkinson's letters informed them he had been promoted to brigadier general, and indicated he was still working toward their mutual goals.

July brought torpid heat and a deadly yellow fever epidemic. Residents collapsed everywhere, and Adam attended the sick and the dying. Even Cloudcrest was not spared. Tizzi had given birth to a baby boy, and the fever swept him away, his tiny body unable to ward off the deadly invasion.

Concord, too, had its tragedy when Elizabeth Gayoso was stricken. Don Manuel hovered over his new bride hourly, feeling her hands, her pulse, her brow. One by one the dreaded symptoms appeared and, with a sinking heart, Don Manuel recognized the telltale signs that had ravished the life of his first wife, Theresa. He stayed by Elizabeth day and night, rubbed her saffron skin and aching limbs, supplied hot bricks, camphor and peppermint, fed her nauseous brews of pepper and calomel. He wiped her lips, black with hemorrhaging, rocked her when she screamed with delirium. And he prayed — fervently — asking God for a miracle to spare her. His beloved Elizabeth died in his arms barely three months after their marriage.

Adam lent what support he could in frequent visits to his friend, and found Don Manuel's grief overwhelming. His anguish led to fits of melancholy, often rendering him speechless, his eyes dully staring inwardly in his battle with grief.

After a dispiriting visit one day, Adam described Don Manuel's condition to Mary.

"He is trying to pull himself together to return to his duties," he told her. "Yellowtail's presence brings painful reminders of Elizabeth's tutoring sessions."

To his surprise, Mary offered a solution. "Why not let Yellowtail live with us, and I will tutor him? It would be a welcome relief from boredom while waiting for our new baby to arrive next month."

At first Adam objected that Mary's health might be endangered. But she persuaded him that she was strong and healthy, and would be able to fit Yellowtail's teaching schedule into her regular motherly activities.

Don Manuel gratefully accepted Mary's offer, and they arranged for Yellowtail to sleep at Concord and spend his days with Mary.

Mary set aside a daily time-space for the lessons, and found Yellowtail an eager student. His keen, searching mind brought forth questions about the white man's ways, prompting Mary to examine the meaning and sense of her own culture. Yellowtail taught them Chickasaw words, spun them tribal tales and lore, and explained the Chickasaw cultural mores. The young Indian had a surprising sense of humor, and delighted the girls with native dances. Adam and Yellowtail hunted game in the forest and across the river in open prairieland, and Yellowtail taught him the skills of bow and arrow. Swiftly, he won a place in their hearts.

Mary's baby was born in August. The birthing came so suddenly there was no time for a doctor, and she was assisted by Jenny's midwife, Maamba, and Adam. Helping his first baby boy arrive was one of love's greatest experiences for Adam. He cradled the tiny newborn in his arms, and named him Samuel Grandin.

Soon after, letters from the Downses and Adam's family began to arrive. The Downses had little new information about Wilkinson since his army career began. Adam's brother Robert wrote that the Wilmington shipyard thrived, and their sea-trade had two barques plying Chesapeake Bay, trading produce between growers. His father imparted news that the Reverend William Hammett, the much-admired minister who first lured Adam to the Methodist church, was starting a Neo-Methodist movement in Savannah. News of Kentucky's admittance to the Union was welcomed in the States. His mother, Magdalene, wrote that younger brother Abner had graduated from college and was now practicing law in Lexington, Kentucky; his two sisters were engaged to be married and were planning a double wedding.

Sarah and John Wurts sent a large packet filled with long, affectionate letters to Mary and Adam. John enclosed newly printed copies of the Constitution, the Bill of Rights, and the *Federalist Papers*, a new title for the former *Publius Papers*. Sam Forman stated suspicions of Colonel Wilkinson still circulated. Adam gave his letters to Don Manuel, and loaned him the new books received from John Wurts to read at his pleasure.

September was the Clouds' moving month. Everyone was filled with excitement, and Mary most of all. The wagons were loaded with household goods, livestock, children, and slaves. Mary took one last look at Cloudcrest, where she had so many happy memories. Adam swung her aboard a wagon, climbed the seat, took the reins, and the Cloud family began their journey to a new life at Villa Gayoso.

BOOK III

19 Religious Freedom

Adam looked upon Evenstar with pride. Set back far from the road behind a giant spreading oak, the simple, graceful design of the cottage reflected culture and gracious living. The house was well-insulated with thick walls, high ceilings, and gib windows for cooler air in hot months. The inside work was his own, and he had paid careful attention to detail. The floors were of polished cypress, and the finished walls, faced with wainscoting, set off the new furnishings shipped from Philadelphia.

The outdoor vistas were more open than at Cloudcrest, and Mary enjoyed the view across the fields. Before harvest, they were ablaze with scarlet and gold, and later the acres of indigo flowers were a sea of blue. The governor's nearby Villa Gayoso compound was now in full use. The small military garrison provided space for a few guards, storage for arms and ammunition, and a quad for militia assembly. The new Catholic church was yet an empty shell, without equipment or furnishings, but Father Gregory White, newly assigned priest, had moved into the new presbytère. The Clouds became friends with village residents and began to feel very much at home in Villa Gayoso. Colonel Green had organized a study group called "Franklin Society for the Acquisition of Useful Knowledge," and Adam was invited to join.

News of a new slave shipment had brought Adam and Dirk to lower Natchez. The auction shed was packed with planters, always on the lookout for good labor. Adam joined his friend Job Corey in the crowd, and they surveyed the blacks brought forward by the auctioneer. Adam was struck by a female and her young son, offered together. On an impulse, he entered the bidding and won.

"Well, something good has come of the day," he said. "I could have used two strong males, but I believe that blacks are better workers if surrounded by their own kin."

Job smiled. "Not too many owners care about relationships. Leave it to you, Adam, to think of a slave's happiness."

Adam stepped over to the clerk to register their sale and manumission dates. While he was thus engaged, a bearded man approached him and leaned in his ear. In an Irish brogue, he whispered, "Sir, ef yer not mindin', there's someone's lookin' to speak with ye."

Adam shrank from the odor of a foul body and fetid breath. He turned and saw the man was a boatman.

"Where?" he asked, looking about.

The man nodded in the general direction of the street, and beckoned him to follow.

"Whatever it is, you'll have to wait until I find my slave. He will have to tend my two new blacks," Adam said.

He signed for the slaves' release, and turned them over to Dirk. He then followed the man to a tavern. The boatman jerked his head with a motion for Adam to go inside, and walked away. Adam stepped inside the open door. He was not sure what to expect. He was unfamiliar with the taverns Under-the-Hill, except for the cursory visit with his traveling companions on their first day in Natchez.

The tavern was fairly quiet with few patrons. The acrid smell of stale cigar smoke, liquor, sweating bodies, and rotting wood filled his nostrils. Several men stood at the bar, and two more played at a billiard table, watched by a bevy of "house girls" who were betting on the outcome. A few women clustered around a piano player, grinding out a popular ballad, and, at the far corner, a game of cards was in progress.

Adam stood, getting his eyes accustomed to the dimly lit room. A woman approached him from a stairway near the back wall. She moved with supple grace and an air of dignity. She was a light-skinned quadroon, her head swathed in a red and white tignon. He realized the place offered the doubtful nepenthe of an upper-floor whorehouse.

In a soft, mellow voice, she said, "Father Cloud, I am Consuela Ramirez. There is someone here who needs your help; she is very ill. She asked me to find you if you came to the auction today. Please follow me."

Consuela led him upstairs to a room at the end of a long hall and opened the door. Adam entered and saw Hannah Lum lying on a low, rumpled cot. He barely recognized her. Her skin was sallow, and her sunken eyes spoke misery in the shadowy caverns of her face. Consuela placed a chair beside the bed, and Adam sat speechless. Hannah Lum! How incredible to find her here, and in this deplorable condition.

Hannah spoke in a low, weak voice. "Dear Reverend Cloud, you are good to come. You must be surprised, but I am too ill to tell you my long story. Right now I need your blessing and absolution, for I am dying." Deep draughts of wheezing and coughing interrupted her speech.

Adam took her hand and held it between his own. Her flesh was cold, and her hand as feeble as her voice.

"*Shhh*," he said. "Dear lady, tell me what you believe is wrong with you. Perhaps you are not dying at all, but only need medication."

He leaned closely while Hannah described her symptoms. He pressed her hands and rose toward Consuela.

"Her condition is low," he said softly, "but surely not too low to revive. How long has she been this way?"

"I believe it is consumption," she answered. "Some months ago this lady was brought to my house by a pair of ruffians. They had found her moaning and lying in the rear of a storehouse where she had been attacked. I had her brought up here and tended her as best as I and my girls could manage. When she felt better, she finally told us her story. About how she had been denied her proper marriage, her money and her home, and cast out like a criminal when the church decided she had enough funds to leave Natchez. She came down here to arrange her passage, but was viciously attacked and raped, then robbed of her passage money, leaving her destitute and injured."

Consuela watched Adam slowly shake his head in dismay. She hurried on to end the sad story. "We nursed her until we got her on her feet, and she began to help with some of the chores to earn her keep. For a while her health seemed to improve, but her coughing increased until finally she took to her bed, too poorly to work and too depressed to want to help herself. I don't know what to do with her, and when she told me of your kindness during her troubles, I suggested that you might help her again. The slave auction was sure to bring almost every planter down here, and we were on the lookout for you."

Adam took a deep breath, exhaling slowly as he reflected. Hannah's condition was serious, but he knew others had recovered from the lung fever. He returned to Hannah's bedside and pressed her hand again as he spoke.

"The kind woman has told me your story, Hannah. Your misfortune need not be further compounded by your illness. I will get medical help for you. I feel certain you will get well. In the meantime, I shall leave instructions for your care."

He placed a coin pouch in Consuela's hand and said, "Please purchase whatever Hannah might need in nourishing food, clothing, or for warmth. I will send a physic at once, who can give her the professional care she needs."

Adam felt a boiling rage as he left Consuela's tavern.

He had left Hannah in the care of the Catholic church, which should have secured her safety until she left Natchez. What kind of church, or priest, would be so unthinking as not to secure her passage and see her off at the waterfront!

He found Dirk waiting in the wagon with the two new slaves. In garbled words, the woman tried to thank him for keeping her son with her. He smiled his understanding, and touched them both gently on the shoulder. He drove directly to Government House and, in fuming indignation, told Don Manuel the story of Hannah's plight.

"This tale is a nightmare," the shocked governor said. "It is incomprehensible that the lady should have been treated thus by the church, where sanctuary and protection is a sacred right. I am ashamed this has happened, for I am primarily responsible for church affairs. I should have been notified when she was ready to leave, and would have arranged for her passage. Thank you, Adam, for your help. I will send interns immediately to remove her to the hospital, where she will be under Dr. Faure's care."

Mary's eyes welled with tears when she listened to Adam's story of Hannah Lum that evening. "That poor, hapless woman. Think of the ignominy of living in a brothel! But the madam was inordinately kind to care for her, and I guess even her sort of women have good hearts. I hate to think of her so forlorn and alone in that dingy hospital, Adam. Can't we bring her here to help her recover? Maamba and I can tend her, and I am sure we can get her well again."

"My sweet Mary. Always willing to take the next step to make things better. Of course we can take Hannah, and I'll fetch her right away, if Dr. Faure will let her go."

Adam brought Hannah Lum home the next day with medicines and doctor's instructions for her care. Mary was shocked at Hannah's condition and began administering a dietary menu to overcome her emaciation and despondency. Hannah's health and happiness became a daily obsession, and her patient began to thrive in the loving atmosphere of Mary's household.

Adam stepped from the governor's marble porch to the exquisitely polished hall floor and waited. He tried to avoid coming to town now. Bad news was always waiting to spoil the peace and serenity of his Villa Gayoso paradise, but he had urgent business that could not wait. Chico led him to the dining room, where Don Manuel bade him sit and enjoy the meal with him. Chico poured him wine.

"Try this," Don Manuel said. "It has a fruity flavor. I just imported it from Italy. Not too rich for the midday meal, eh? Just right for the delicate trout."

Adam sipped and rolled the wine on his tongue. "*Umm* . . . it's indeed pleasant. Just right."

"What brings you to town, Don Adam, and what do you hear from the populace at Villa Gayoso?"

"I came to ask a favor of you. But to answer your second question, people are troubled by news from the States, especially now that you are spending so much time away building up defenses. We hear that the U.S. is rebuilding Fort Massac, on the Ohio River. Are we going to be under siege? Are U.S. troops stationed there a threat?"

"No, no. It is not a threat . . . Ah, here is your trout, Adam." Don Manuel waited until Adam was served, and they continued their conversation between bites. "Wilkinson writes that the fort is meant to fend off increasing attacks by hostile Miami Indian tribes. He also assures us that the army's presence will serve to protect Spanish territories from illegal attacks from the American frontier. He has been promoted to general, now, with full command of the Western Army."

"Yes, I heard. What a peculiar position he is in, now that he has to defend Spanish territories from attack. I saw newspaper advertisements for recruits for an 'expedition to Spanish territories.' That's a definite war maneuver."

"Yes, the recruitment has alarming aspects. As you know, LaCassagne serves as a keen eye and ear for General Wilkinson. From Wilkinson's spies he has scattered about, we have some very reliable information on increased independent army recruitment activities. Volunteers are being recruited as far away as Georgia and South Carolina."

"To join the Clark filibuster?"

"We do not know yet, but Adam," Don Manuel's face was grave, and Adam felt uneasy. "We have had some ominous news from Governor Carondelet, which you can share with the community. It will be posted in town. The French have declared war on Spain, extending their revolution into hegemony."

Adam listened to the governor with growing alarm. New Orleans Frenchmen were outwardly jubilant, he said, hoping the territory would be French again. All people of French extraction were considered potentially attracted to a French invasion, and were likely suspects to a conspiracy. The governor warned Adam to watch for suspicious strangers, and to spread the warning.

Adam shook his head in dismay. *War against Spain! Another plot, spies — conspiracies — now among the French,* he thought.

"Hold on to your seat, Adam, this will surprise you." The governor paused to let his words have maximum effect. "General Wilkinson is thinking of leaving the U.S. Army to give him better leverage on the Kentucky frontier goals. How much he can accomplish, either in or out of the army, is a key factor, but his words exude confidence, and we are willing to underwrite his efforts."

"Well, I hope all goes well for him, and for your sake too. His neck will be in a noose if he stays in the army. He risks exposure with every bribe he makes." *Ah — the insidious nature of men like Wilkinson, and Vousdan too. Where will it all end?* Adam wondered.

"One bonus in dealing with Wilkinson," Don Manuel said, "is that his advance news, obtained through his spies, has proven an asset we couldn't get any other way. Right now, I consider him an asset rather than a menace. Time will tell of his effectiveness."

"You can be thankful he is on your side. He might be able to swing a successful filibuster against Spain, if he so desired," Adam commented.

Don Manuel took a few bites, and sighed. "I only hope that people can be persuaded they are safe under our protection. I expect to be away much of the next few months, shoring up our defenses. No more fishing and hunting at Villa Gayoso for a while."

"We will miss you. I'll try to reassure residents that we will be prepared for an invasion." Adam hoped his own doubts did not show.

"By the way, Adam," Don Manuel said, "I am appointing a new priest to Cole's Creek Parish. Father Francis Lennan is coming from Nogales to replace Father Gregorio White, whom I have transferred to the Natchez Parish. It would be wise for you to make Father Francis's acquaintance. He is not overly fond of Protestants and has dealt with very few in his past service."

"I will call upon him as soon as I return." Adam finished his wine and dabbed his napkin to his lips. "Now, I have a proposal that might alleviate some of the tensions, and turn thoughts in other directions."

He told Don Manuel of Colonel Green's "Franklin Society for the Acquisition of Useful Knowledge," and reported that the group had decided to expand their activities to include the community.

"We plan to hold a series of soirees in various homes in the coming months. We will select interesting topics, with a different speaker each time. I have been named as discussion leader. I'll give some background information on the subject, and open the discussion to questions."

"What kind of topics, Adam?"

"Our sponsors suggested the first one be about Indian worship. George Matthews is a scholar of Indian lore and will present the subject in depth. We can't guarantee that the events will be popular, but you have often commented that intellectual discourse is rare in Natchez. The sponsors want a continuing dialogue that will increase knowledge and result in exploring ideas."

Don Manuel remained silent while they finished the last of the dinner, and Chico removed the plates. He raised his wine glass to the light and studied the amber fragments.

"If the meetings have no religious intent, Adam, I see no reason why you should not hold them. Our evenings of private discussion have been remarkably beneficial to me, sharpening my concepts, and, I hope, helping my judgment in the affairs of governance. Yes, by all means begin the soirees. They should help sweep the cobwebs from the collective brain. Let me know when you hold the first one, and I will try to attend."

"Good. Our Society will be pleased that you consent."

"Adam, I am reading your *Federalist Papers,* and have written down some thoughts for discussion. I must say the *Papers* are brilliantly written, and quite persuasive. Come to the library. My notes are on my desk. I would like to ask you some questions."

Adam followed him to the library, secretly pleased at the surprising turn of topics. He had been hoping for a chance to explain democracy to Don Manuel. The governor already employed some democratic principles in his fair-minded administration; he should be receptive to more if he understood them properly. He mulled over in his mind how he could introduce religious privileges into the topic of the Constitution. *I must be very careful,* he thought. *Our religious discussions have been only philosophical, and we have avoided government politics.* Adam knew that as open-minded as Don Manuel was, at times, the subject of Protestant rights was still so delicate that he would become defensive.

Don Manuel gathered his notes, and they settled in comfortable chairs. "My questions arose from reading the Bill of Rights. I must say, there is a lot in there to puzzle me. The ideas are so radical."

"In what way?" Here was the opening Adam needed, but he must tread lightly, he thought.

"It is an anathema to imagine the populace having so much to say about their rights. This would jeopardize government decisions and authority. I cannot conceive of the individual challenging the government in so many ways."

"On the contrary, the concept is genuinely benign because it is decreed by consent." Adam warmed to the subject; it was so ingrained in his consciousness. "The framers of the Constitution used the lessons of history, which is full of examples of the abrogation of rights of man to man, of government to men. They were determined that never again would citizens have to fight for those inalienable rights that were agreed to be inherent in man."

"If every man had the right to do as he pleased, we would have chaos, and eventually anarchy. Man's right to peace and contentment can be protected by government under the laws of nations, the laws of God and church."

Here we go again, Adam thought. *He is already defensive. Perhaps I should try another tack.* "But what constitutes man's ideal of peace and contentment?" he asked.

Don Manuel reached for his cigar box, offered one to Adam, and lit up both of their smokes before he answered.

"I would say . . . safety, freedom from savagery and crime, war, rape of the land and its people . . ." he paused in thought and continued, "also economic security, food, shelter, and noninterference with productivity."

254 The Righteous Rebel

"Would you not include in man's ideals of contentment his *consciousness* of freedom? Freedom from tyranny . . . right to pursue his interests without restraint?"

Don Manuel reached for a tray and tapped his cigar. He offered Adam an ashtray, as he mulled over the thought.

"Possibly," he answered, "but many restraints are necessary. Man cannot be allowed to do anything he desires. In barbaric times man could roam, pillage, confiscate what he wanted, and serve his own interests at everyone else's expense. A good government can prevent that."

"True," Adam said. "If men were angels, no government would be necessary. But tell me, Don Manuel, how are civil liberties defined under a monarchy?"

"*Mmm* — I would say civil liberty is man's freedom to do what state law does not prohibit, or to omit doing what the law does not command. It permits man to follow his own will in any matters not prescribed by state law."

"But can you agree that state law should be established by *consent?* There's a world of difference, and that is what the U. S. Constitution is all about, *government by consent,* representative government, with civil liberties protected without unjust government restraints."

"While government can, and often does, interfere with a man's action, it cannot coerce his will," Don Manuel said.

Adam pounced on the statement. He saw the opportunity he wanted. "Ah, but history is rife with the stories of punitive brutality reflecting the hubris of kings, and you know it. Freedom should assure that one need obey no law to which man has not given assent."

"Trouble with that is, men do not know what they want, and everyone wants something different. A good king can settle differences by rules that protect men for their own good." Don Manuel blew smoke and twirled his cigar. "Our form of monarchy protects man through church laws. I'm afraid I have no patience with the idea of representative government. The democratic process is very dangerous. It leaves decisions to people. In a collective society, people seldom act in unison, nor do they always understand issues which affect them."

Adam bit his tongue to suppress comment on this notion.

It would not do to antagonize Don Manuel now. Instead, he said, "Freedom also demands civil equality, the recognition that no one is superior in relation to himself, each man sharing equal obligation toward his citizenship."

"I don't go along with equality either," the governor countered. "Everyone is not equal to everyone else. You know it; I know it. Only the weak-minded have the audacity to proclaim equality for everyone."

"Well," Adam conceded, "we do need an elite for wise and high-minded leadership. Also, successful democracy needs to develop a strong public virtue — a common sense to deal with issues."

"Our state government based on church morals does just that," Don Manuel observed.

Adam waded carefully into his own case. "I haven't forgotten I live under a monarchy, but I believe that, no matter where I live, I am imbued with certain inalienable rights, and I hope you agree. Your personal style of governance reflects compassion for others, and your sense of justice reflects a belief in those rights."

"I do feel for others," Don Manuel said, pleased with the compliment.

Adam gathered momentum to make his point. "But the fact remains, Don Manuel, that governments often impose unjust laws, such as the British imposed on the colonies when they taxed them without representation, and when they kept free contracts among men under British yoke. Those acts constituted absolute, despotic power, depriving the colonies of a measure of self-government."

"So, what is the point of your illustration, Adam?"

"My conclusion is this. Freedom and law go hand in hand, but the important relationship between law and liberty depends upon whether the law is just, and whether a man is virtuous under the law, no matter if he believes it unjust. Personal liberty can be curtailed by law, and good men everywhere often live under unjust laws."

"And you believe the American Constitution can prevent this?" asked Gayoso.

"Of course. The Constitution provides for man to protect himself against unjust government laws. Government officials may not invade individual rights, and the will of the majority prevails." Adam took a deep breath, and plunged on. "Take the right to practice any religions, for instance. If such a democratic concept prevailed here, the religious practices of the Protestant population would outweigh, by sheer numbers, those of the Catholics, and would be in the majority. Simple justice would decree that the majority has prevailed and that religious rights should not be denied them. Under the Constitution, the same rights would not be denied the Catholic minority, either. Anyone is free to practice any religion he chooses, without interference from other persons, or from the government."

Don Manuel glowered. Adam had hit the sensitive core of Catholic law. He emphasized his words as he spoke. "But Adam, that does not apply here, and you know it cannot! You are on dangerous ground! Such utterances are punishable if spoken publicly."

"Don Manuel, I mean no harm." Adam was getting to his main thrust, and with this elaborate buildup he had to finish it out. "I signed the oath of allegiance to uphold laws of His Majesty, Carlos, king of Spain. But among them is a law which prohibits public preaching, the conduct of marriage, or baptism by any other than a priest of the Catholic church. I have long wanted to ask you if this law can be abridged to permit me to marry or baptize Protestants who request it."

"I do not make Spanish laws, I only enforce them," Don Manuel said tersely.

"Wait, Don Manuel. Hear me out. American justice is based on the premise that all men are created equal. I consider myself as equal here, as a Protestant deacon in the eyes of my church, as your Catholic priests are in the eyes of theirs; equal to marry and baptize people under the principles of Christianity. To deny me the same rights as your priests infers that I am unequal here to administer the same rites under God. We are all Christians, ministering in His name, are we not?"

Don Manuel's face was dark with displeasure. "I do not like where you are going, Adam."

Adam rushed on. "All I ask is equal justice. Don Manuel, can you see your way to circumvent these restrictions to allow me these rights? The Protestants feel sorely mistreated in this regard, and feel they are looked upon as inferior citizens."

"Adam, *stop right there!*" Gayoso almost shouted. "You try me with your logic. I cannot grant you this, even if I wanted to, for my authority over religious rights is limited. I must adhere to the edicts of the ecumenical council. The state and church are one in this country. My allegiance is to the king, who administers the laws of the Pope. There is no way I can grant you these privileges. I hope you realize this is my final answer."

"Forgive me, Don Manuel, if I try your patience. But for me, I have given up some of my freedom, and sometimes it tries my patience too."

Don Manuel looked keenly at Adam's flushed face. "You have not lost your freedom, Adam," he said affectionately. "You are free to do anything you want to, within the limits of the law. Man loses freedom in society only when he is mistreated, or misgoverned, and you have not experienced either."

"Man is mistreated and loses freedom when he is not treated as an equal of other men," Adam retorted. He realized he sounded petulant, but he could not resist the argument.

"You are a good man, Adam, and I respect and admire you for your qualities of goodness and decency. They are outstanding, and rare among men. That is why I have not constrained you when you have held services in your home. Yes, I gave you permission, and have received reports that your sermons are superb. One visitor praised them as 'inspiring messages of high concern and weighty truths.' Many families look to you for guidance and leadership, and I believe they have the right to turn to you for their special needs. Just remain discreet and go no further in your religious practices, and you will be safe with me."

Adam spoke testily. "Well, you could always have me ostracized, as Aristotle believed certain men should be when they seem to predominate too much. They were banished for a period in favor of the popular will. It was one way to promote equality in the Greek state. As you suggest, I'll try not to predominate too much."

Gayoso looked at Adam gravely and spoke as if he had not heard the sarcasm. "I hope you will constrain yourself, Adam, for you are far too valuable a subject of the state to subvert its laws. You have much to give in many ways, and I know you are a man of conscience. Put all of this behind you, and do not brood over what you cannot change."

The mood was tense between them, but Adam respected their friendship. He spoke lightly. "Well, at least I won't get myself run out of town. Isn't that what happens to recalcitrant preachers?"

"Yes, and several have been banished when they became a nuisance. I don't want to have to worry over you." Don Manuel rose and quashed his cigar stub in the ashtray. Adam followed suit, and they exchanged subdued farewells.

Adam rode home, smarting with defeat. Well, at least he had one concession. Don Manuel approved of the public soirees, and Adam set his mind to their first presentation.

Adam rode to the new priest's house one morning and found Father Francis Lennan in his garden digging a small plot.

"Good day, sir," he said. The priest looked up, and Adam dismounted. "Father Francis? I am Adam Cloud, one of your neighbors here at Villa Gayoso. My plantation is Evenstar, right around the bend. Welcome to the neighborhood." He extended his hand.

Father Francis wiped the soil from his hand on his black robe and reached out to shake Adam's outstretched hand. "Yes, Mister Cloud, I have heard about you. I know you are a friend of His Excellency, and that we have our theological differences. Nevertheless, I offer my services, and my parish as a sanctuary to you and your family."

Adam examined the priest as he spoke. The man looked priestly enough, and appeared of slight build under his robe. His manner seemed haughty, lacking in warmth, but his look was resolute, with tight lips and a firm jaw, in an otherwise undistinguished face.

"Thank you, Father. And may my home be your sanctuary for a pleasant meal or tea-time visit. What will you grow in your garden?"

"This is a vegetable garden. I have always grown my own food wherever the land has been available to me."

"Splendid. You must visit our gardens. Mrs. Cloud is a flower lover, and her garden is a sight to behold. You might enjoy seeing what she has wrought in only our first spring here, with Nature's help, of course. Should you plan to expand your garden we can furnish you with cuttings and seeds."

Adam bade "good day," tipped his hat, and rode thoughtfully home. He had hoped this new priest would prove as pleasant as Father Gregory had been, but he had misgivings. The man was cold and implacable, but perhaps he would warm up in time.

20 The Genet
Threat

Adam set out on the Trace to Selser Town. He needed to seek out an excellent craftsman recommended for his skills in building machinery, and had decided he would visit the Reverend Curtis while he was there. It was an easy ride down the Trace to the small settlement near the Indian mound, and he recalled stories he had heard about the Baptist preacher. Curtis resided with a group of families who had migrated together from South Carolina. Joe Perkins had described the clan as a close-knit group, praying and reading the Bible together day and night, and shunning the non-Baptists. He wanted to meet this man of extreme piety.

Concluding his business with the craftsman, Adam was directed to the Curtis home. There he rode into an extensive compound of houses and outbuildings and found the Curtis residence. A young girl ushered him to the parlor and left to find her uncle. In a few moments, the preacher entered and extended his hand.

"Reverend Cloud, thank you for this visit," Curtis said. His handshake felt limp and clammy. "I know much about you. Brother Joseph Perkins speaks well of you. Pray be seated, and we can get acquainted."

Adam inspected Curtis while he spoke. He was a tall, solemn man with intensely probing eyes set deep in a long, thin face. He wore sparse chin whiskers, which accentuated its length. At first he seemed in repose as he rested his long, bony hands in his lap. He spoke quietly of family and home, but soon their talk turned to current affairs, and Adam detected a fervor lurking beneath the exterior calm.

"The yeomen think they are keen farmers," Curtis said, his lips curled in derision, and his hands beginning to fidget, "but their lack of diligence and thrift has allowed them to sink into debt. And what has brought them to their low estate? Lack of reverence. Instead of letting the Lord guide them through their troubles, they let the devil plant slovenly habits in place of honest, hard work and love of God."

Curtis' adamant tone defied disagreement, and Adam murmured politely, "There is a lack of religious practice among most of the farmers, I must admit."

"And those high and mighty planters, with their hundreds of acres, and their swarms of black slaves to work the land . . ." Curtis spoke in a sneering tone. "They spend their time gambling and carousing together at immoral gatherings. They are even planning a racetrack Under-the-Hill. They fornicate down there, and their women say nothing. Condoning sin is a sin in itself. None of them are innocent."

"A few find pleasure in ways we do not condone," Adam answered, "but are you not making some sweeping generalities? The more affluent planters enjoy many pleasures, but most seek wholesome pleasure with their families and friends. I do not find them immoral at all."

Curtis scowled suspiciously. "Oh, yes, I suppose you would defend them. I hear you have friends among the high and mighty, and that includes the governor. He is among the sinners, encouraging all the sinful parties and fancy flings that take place in the district."

"If you include me in the category of affluent diligence," Adam said coldly, "I can assure you that I am a hard-working man of modest means, trying to make a place for myself and my family at Villa Gayoso."

"I know you are an Anglican preacher," Curtis said. "Why did you give it up? The wickedness of the world needs preachers to spread the Gospel. My father was a great preacher, and his father before him. It is my calling, and I feel I can never do enough to save others from perdition, no matter how hard I try."

"I was called to spread the Gospel also, at a very early age. I served six years as an itinerant minister for the Methodist-Episcopal Societies. I have spread the Gospel from Pennsylvania to North Carolina, so I know what it is to serve those in need of spiritual uplifting. After I was ordained a deacon, I served in the Episcopal church at Philadelphia."

"You gave that up to come *here*?" Adam saw Curtis' look of astonishment and decided he had earned the man's respect.

"Yes. When I came to Natchez I took my oath seriously not to preach in public. I have conducted services in some private homes, by request, and held several in my own home when I lived at St. Catherine Creek. But I feel nervous that I might be breaking the law. I have truly missed the opportunity to serve Protestants, especially when they marry, or have new babies to baptize. But the governor is adamant, and rules are rules. How do you manage to conduct your services here? They are open enough to be talked about. Do you not fear punishment?"

"I live with only one fear," Curtis replied somberly, "the fear of ending in hell for failing God's will. He chose me as a Gospel messenger. No one, not even those idol-worshipping priests, can interfere with my mission in life. Besides," his penetrating eyes widened and bulged as he drew himself up proudly, "we came here long before the governor and those nosy Catholic priests set any rules. We did not have to take an oath, nor would I now. I am not bound by the rules. I feel a certain justification in defiance of their rules, especially that decree just reissued by the governor."

"What decree is that?" Adam felt sudden alarm.

"I hear it warns of dire punishment to Protestant ministers for performing a resident marriage ceremony, either in or outside the Natchez District." He paused, then added defiantly, "I haven't performed any marriages up to now, but I've a mind to."

Adam left the Curtis home with a bad taste in his mouth. The man was a fanatic, he decided, typical of other preachers he had known who were intolerant and unforgiving.

Curtis' faults outweighed his virtues, and would probably be his undoing. But the news about enforcing the marriage ceremony decree was far more unsettling. *Could I have brought it upon the*

Protestants by taking issue with Don Manuel on rights to perform such ceremonies? he wondered. *Did Don Manuel learn the truth about the Jackson marriage?* He decided he would rather not know.

Riding up the Trace, toward home, Adam met a small group of well-dressed men riding toward Natchez. With a polite "Good day," he drew aside to let them pass. To his astonishment, he recognized André Michaux among the group, and called out his name. The Frenchman stopped and stared.

"Bon jour," Adam Cloud! What a surprise to meet you on this trail."

"What brings you here, André? Did you forget some of your plants and drawings?" Adam said lightly.

André beamed his infectious smile at the little joke. "Ah, no, Adam. I have been across the Western countree — gathering specimens and admiring your inland waterways. What great wilderness beauty, and what a wealth of data I 'ave collected for my science. How fortunate to meet you here. I hoped to find you in Natchez."

Adam explained that he had moved to Cole's Creek, only a few miles away near the river. Michaux explained that he had met his companions in Nashborough; they decided to travel together when they learned they were all going to New Orleans. He introduced them as M. Pisgignoux and M. Bonnevie, recently arrived from Paris. They would stop for a while in Natchez and look up the French friends whom he had met the previous year.

Adam's alarm system suddenly registered. He recalled Don Manuel's warning to be on the lookout for any French visitors, and he doubted that the three Frenchmen had met and joined by coincidence. He wanted to learn more, and explained there was a new road to Natchez that would save them time.

"Come home with me for supper," he said. "You can take the new rode from there. Mrs. Cloud would be happy to see you again."

André conferred with his companions, and they accepted.

Mary was delighted to see André Michaux again. She fed the visitors a light meal, and chatted animatedly in French, laughing at her mistakes and showing gracious consideration of their limited English. Adam purposely turned the conversation to current events.

"André, I must warn you that you might be uncomfortable among the Spanish just now. Rumors make us all tense here, and France's declaration of war against Spain leaves us wondering where we stand."

André's face betrayed his astonishment at this unexpected topic in their conversation. "How so, *mon ami*? What should you fear, safe and snug on your plantation?"

"My experience in American democracy often nags me. Our sympathy with the French Revolution arouses faint hopes that we might again experience freedoms that are denied us here." Adam hoped his statement would encourage André to reveal his intent.

André's look of incredulity was unmistakable. "*Monsieur!* Your appearance of contentment is deceptive."

"I must confess my inner discontent has been aroused by rumors of an American frontier army being recruited to overthrow the Spanish territories here. If they brought changes for new freedoms, I would welcome them. I am a student and admirer of your political philosophers, Rousseau and Montesquieu, and respect their contribution to political freedoms."

"You astound me, Adam. Nevair 'ave we discussed our political beliefs. Perhaps you might be interested in attending a small dinner among my friends in Natchez. We enjoy discussing the ideas of French philosophers, and you would find them stimulating. Besides, it would give me great pleasure to return the courtesies you have afforded me during our acquaintance. I will contact you."

Adam expressed his acceptance, and recalled his former suspicions of André's detailed maps among his botanical drawings. *Now,* he thought, *perhaps we shall see what you're really up to, M. Michaux.*

Soon after their meal, André rose to leave. "*Cher ami,*" he said, taking Mary's hand, "we must go before the day grows older. If you will see us to the new road you spoke of, Adam, we shall be on our way."

André gave Mary's hand a lingering kiss, and expressed his thanks for their hospitality. Adam led his guests to the Bluff Road and returned with his suspicions reinforced.

"There is something afoot with those three," he said to Mary. "I hope André invites me to meet his friends. Do you think he suspected I was fishing for information?"

"Oh, Adam, don't be so suspicious of everyone. André seems so innocent, and I am sure he would not willingly consort with spies," she scolded.

Nevertheless, Adam's alarm grew. He recalled Wilkinson's warning, back in Louisville, that Michaux's presence among the Indians warranted suspicion, and he had never really trusted the man during their river journey. He dispatched a letter to Governor Gayoso informing him of André's visit, and of his plans to host a dinner for the French residents whom he had met in 1791.

The next day Governor Gayoso read the dispatch from Adam. He handed it to Secretary Vidal, who scowled when he read it.

"What now, Don Manuel? Should we pursue this lead?"

"Most certainly, Don José, but how penetrate Michaux's circle of French friends? Where could he be entertaining?"

They decided first to contact King's Tavern, and Camus' Tavern, owned by a Frenchman Under-the-Hill.

"Find out if a room has been reserved for a meeting at either place," Don Manuel ordered. "If at Camus' Tavern, send Camus up here to me. Inform him that the miserable condition of his tavern and reports of unruly behavior there have reached my ears, and remind him he is up for his operating license renewal."

By noon Camus had arrived and confirmed plans for a meeting Michaux had arranged at his tavern. "Your Excellency, you can count on me to cooperate fully," the Frenchman said. "Just tell me what to do."

"I want you to plant someone in hiding where he can hear what is said at the meeting," Don Manuel said, "and I want a full report of the meeting in the morning."

. . .

That evening Camus observed as eight residents of French descent entered his tavern. One by one they strolled to the bar, ordered a drink, and drifted casually to the back room. William Vousdan was among them. Camus tapped lightly on the bar twice, and his eldest son slipped quietly through a connecting door and hid himself among the storage boxes. A tiny crack left in an opposite door allowed him to see and hear those in the next room.

Michaux greeted his guests and introduced his French companions, Pisgignoux and Bonnevie, as French artillery officers. The men settled themselves around the table. Michaux explained his mission in English, interspersed with French.

"The tidings, which I brought on my former visit, have now materialized into a beautiful . . . *umm* . . . project which will place this countree under French influence again, and possibly France will regain its possession. One of our *compatriots*, Citizen Edmund Genet, is a special emissary to the United States. As minister of affairs, he was commissioned to assist American frontiersmen, and French residents of the Spanish domain, to capture the Spanish territories of Florida and Louisiana. The land will be freed from tyranny under a monarchy, such as we have accomplished by our revolution in the homeland."

Michaux paused to appreciate the effect of this news on his listeners. Rapt faces, "oh's" and "ah's" expressed their approval.

"I am authorized by Citizen Genet to conclude alliances with the Creek Nation to join forces with Americans and Frenchmen to capture the Spanish forts below the American frontier. For the past year I have lived among Indian tribes and gained their friendship. As a botanist, interested in their indigenous plants and medicines, it was easy to gain their acceptance."

"That sort of alliance has been tried before," Benet, a lumber dealer, remarked. "A Captain Bowland came through here with Dr. O'Fallon last year, saying he was trying to form a similar alliance with the Indians. It came to nothing."

"Ah — *oui*," Michaux pounced on the statement. "We are capitalizing greatly on Dr. O'Fallon's efforts. We have now enlisted the same military genius, General Georges Clark, to expedite our Florida and Louisiana mission. It is far easier to recruit Americans under the French cause than under Dr. O'Fallon's limited goals. Americans are *sympathetique* to our French Republic, and 'ave tender memories of our help in the American War of Independence. Besides, *monsieurs*, is it not far better to be a friend of the free French, rather than of the Spanish monarchy?" He winked and smiled at his listeners. This infinite wisdom brought nods and grins of appreciation.

"Where do we fit into the plot?" one of the men inquired.

"Ah, that is my next point. I am authorized to induce all Frenchmen in Natchez and New Orleans to join our fight on the appointed hour of attack. Lieutenants Pisgignoux and Bonnevie are to help spread the word through New Orleans, and to enlist substantial support for our cause. If we can count upon you, and others whom you may persuade, to join forces with the Americans and French to overthrow the Spanish yoke, you will be richly rewarded with land and bounty."

"How can we be sure this venture will eventually take place?" Vousdan asked. "So many filibuster plans have evaporated over the years."

"This one has real power behind it," Michaux explained. "A French Executive Council, made up of Americans *sympathetique* to the cause, has enlisted prominent leaders, such as Senator John Brown, Judge Benjamin Sebastian, John Montgomery, and General Benjamin Logan, all in Kentucky. Leaders in Georgia, such as General Elisha Clarke and others in the Carolinas, are commissioned by the French to raise forces for an invasion of Louisiana."

Michaux paused and shuffled through papers spread before him. Behind the storage door the young Camus shifted his cramped position, and his elbow dislodged a small object from the top of a crate. Michaux looked about apprehensively. Hearing no further sound, he shrugged his shoulders, selected one of the papers, and read a list of supporters. The list was replete with titles of distinguished legislators and highly stationed leaders. Vousdan sat on the edge of his chair, his beady eyes crinkled in a smile of wicked pleasure. His blood tingled with excitement.

"What will be the nature of the Louisiana Territory after the capture?" he asked. "What will the French receive from it? Will we be Frenchmen again, or Americans?"

"It is the aim of the Council, and of Citizen Genet, of course, to claim Louisiana as an independent state, with the intent that it becomes a French colony. Use of the Mississippi and the port of New Orleans will provide unlimited commerce with the French and Americans, and great potential for wealth. To deter the British, Citizen Genet has outfitted privateer ship owners who now prey upon British merchant ships. It is France's aim to drive the British out of American coastal trade, and to have joint shipping control with the new Louisiana state."

"Whew!" one of the residents exclaimed. "How does this plan get past the American government?"

"Ah, I am glad you asked that question," Michaux replied. "Citizen Genet has met with President Washington and Secretary of State Jefferson, and has assured them that this venture will richly benefit America. There has been no effort to stop the French Executive Council activity, and, of course . . ." he paused for effect as he looked around the table, "French diplomacy would not allow any expedition against the wishes of the United States government."

Vousdan leaned forward, his curled fists on the table. "No objection by the American government? That is incredible. This will be the event of the century," he said. "I have just returned from New Orleans, where I attended numerous meetings and social events among my French friends. I heard much talk of independence, and I believe you can recruit every one among them who has felt the strain of the Spanish yoke."

While they dined, the group listed local and New Orleans residents whom they believed could be counted on to recruit other loyal Frenchmen to the cause. They discussed at length the tentative plans for invasion maneuvers against Spanish defenses.

Vousdan emerged from the meeting highly elated. He felt a newfound importance that he could have a role in such a monumental conspiracy — so monumental that a French naval squadron would be used to attack the Spanish at New Orleans!

The young eavesdropper crept from the storeroom and reported to his father at the bar, his head spinning with intrigue, and many names he must write down while he still remembered them.

A full report awaited Governor Gayoso on his desk in the morning. Camus' son had been both observant and literate, describing the conspiracy to Secretary Vidal almost to a word, and listing names of those attending.

"A sinister conspiracy in our midst! And so widespread!" Don Manuel said. "We can be thankful that Don Adam warned us of this extraordinary event. Let us see if Governor Carondelet has news of it."

The governor turned to the morning dispatches just arrived from New Orleans. The memoranda from Governor Carondelet were extensive, as usual, but there was no information on Genet. One informed him that new ships, provided to increase the light naval squadron, were now christened and ready for duty. Two galleys and a galiot, with a stateroom, would begin patrolling the river, with special expeditions upriver to the Ohio, and should be expected on short notice. He read on:

> "The well appointed stateroom is at your disposal. You will be using it often, as your presence is required to oversee the string of new forts and increase the military personnel within your province."

The letter went on to other things:

> "The enclosed letter from General Wilkinson is for your eyes only. I fear incitement of the Westerners, and if Wilkinson does not have full control, invasion without representation of Spanish interests can be disastrous . . . I have agreed to reimburse our confederate more handsomely if he actually breaks up the Clark expedition. One last item: I am in receipt of a letter (copy) sent to you by Viceroy Marquis de Branciforte. I trust your discretion in such matters."

Don Manuel opened Wilkinson's letter and read a lengthy report, covering most of what he had already gleaned from the Michaux conspiracy meeting. Reading on, he came to Wilkinson's appraisal. The important points were underlined.

"If Congress approved of the Spanish monopoly of river rights, it would result in the summary and infallible mode of accomplishing our wishes. Kentucky would immediately apply for protection of Spain, or England. To prevent an alliance with England, I would submit the following: The Spanish Minister, at Philadelphia, should provide $200,000 for bribe money. I have already selected the men to whom I will distribute it. Two are prominent judges, Harry Innes and Benjamin Sebastian . . . I need not remind you how important secrecy is in this venture. I trust you will keep faith with me, as I have with you. My life and future are in your hands, and I trust you to cover my tracks in our joint secret plans."

Intrigues, plots, bloody nefarious rogues, Don Manuel thought to himself. *Will we never have peace?* He riffled through the remaining dispatches until he found the one from the viceroy in Havana. Its contents astounded him. He read:

"I am apprised of your close friendship with one of your citizen residents, the Rev. Adam Cloud. While it is understandable that you should have a right to choose the company you keep, may we remind you that such a close relationship with a man of the Protestant religious order is unbecoming of Your Excellency, representing a province of His Catholic Majesty. It is our duty to remind you of your privilege as vice-patron of the Church, and of your responsibilities toward the development of a Roman Catholic population in Natchez Province. It is with the utmost respect for your distinguished administration that I send the above observations, and trust that you will take them under your serious consideration . . . Most respectfully yours,

H.M.S., Miguel de la Grua Talamance,
Marquis de Branciforte, 14 May, 1793."

Don Manuel was incensed. Who in the province — perhaps more than one "who" — was impugning his integrity and trying to make trouble for him, and for Adam? He suspected Vousdan's vile attitude toward Adam could be at the bottom of it. Information to the viceroy, however, would have to be from someone in authority. Could it be Father Savage, before his recent death, or Father White? Father Lennan was now in Villa Gayoso, and he distrusted all Protestants. The evenings with Adam in the privacy of his upcountry villa were generally undisturbed by outsiders, and it was no one's business how he spent his leisure hours, as long as he was not derelict in his duties. His mind roved over his friendships among the non-Catholic population. It was difficult to see why Adam was singled out among them.

The governor held back his rage as he answered the viceroy. His letter was delicately polite, stating the facts of his all-inclusive friendships, as he saw them. He decided to ignore the reprimand, refusing to accept it as a warning. He decided not to inform Adam. The poor man had enough troubles of his own, with Vousdan at his throat, and he would not want to tinge their friendship with any taints of gossip.

21 The Spy
Mission

The first soiree was held at Matthews' plantation, Cedar Grove, on an April Sunday evening. The topic, "Indian Lore and Worship," had aroused community curiosity and interest, and a crowd of forty settled down in the Matthewses' parlor for a serious evening. The governor made a surprise entrance, stirring a flurry of whispered comments.

George presented the Indian view of the relationship of all things in nature to one another and to the Great Spirit. He described Indian ceremonies and showed how their folklore reinforced religious worship. Adam touched briefly on how the white civilization could benefit from the Indians' deeply spiritual love of the land.

"The Indians recognize there is a world beyond the senses — a spiritual power that is revealed to us in and through the visible realm of nature," he ended. "A sense of the Great Spirit dwells within us, feeding our souls with beauty, with inner quiet, with sublime thoughts which pierce the sky like light from the stars. Through nature we can escape from our mundane lives, and be closer to the Higher Power which allows us to perceive that it exists. That knowledge nourishes our need to worship."

Lively discussion began over the obvious paradox of Indian love of a Great Spirit, and their slaughter of whites.

"What did you think of our first soiree, Don Manuel?" Adam asked, after most of the guests had departed.

"I thought the audience left with mixed feelings about Indians, but with a better feeling for nature and its Creator. It was thoughtful, but it did teeter on the brink of a religious topic. As long as it was about Indian worship, I will not fault you for slipping into human nature this time, but you were skirting on the fringes of a sermon. Father Francis is already incensed that this is taking place. He fears you will lure away his flock, and claims you are breaking the laws. I shall reassure him, since I have attended this session, but, Adam . . ." Don Manuel's eyes looked gravely into Adam's as he continued, "I cannot condone real sermons, nor can I protect you if you disregard the limits. You know that I have my master."

"You can count on me to keep the meetings on nonsectarian topics," Adam replied, "but surely no one would object to some inspiration. I believe no meeting is worth its time if listeners do not leave with uplifted thoughts."

"I leave discretion up to you, Adam." Lowering his voice, Don Manuel said, "I came up here not only to hear your discussion, but because something urgent required it. Please come to my villa when everyone has left. I need to talk with you. I have some serious problems at hand, and I believe you can help."

On the way home in their carriage, Mary added her comments. "For a while there, Adam, I thought you were going to render a full sermon on transcendental communion. That would have rocked the boat, and probably finished the soirees, but what you said was inspiring. What is this about visiting Don Manuel's villa? Can't it wait until morning?"

"No, my sweet, he said tonight. I don't know how long I will be, but don't wait up." He accompanied Mary inside and rode on to the villa.

Don Manuel conducted Adam to his study, and launched immediately into the problem.

"The reason for this visit must remain between us, Adam. Since our last talk about the impending invasion, Wilkinson writes that the western recruitment has reached 500 men from the Kentucky settlements. Tennessee, the Cumberland region, and Georgia have not yet been counted. We need to know much more. If the western army grows stronger by the day, we must know their exact plans in order to be ready to defend our territory." Don

Manuel paused and looked intently at Adam. "Now, bear with me, Adam, and don't be shocked at what I am about to propose."

Adam sat forward in his chair. This was serious, he realized, and he said, briskly, "Go ahead. Shock me."

"There may not be much time to gather more information from the scattered secondhand data we have gathered. We must have exact details of any planned invasion, and that means every little detail. We need to know the number of men, arms, ammunition, equipment, means of travel, conveyances, the rendezvous points, and the locations of where they will launch the attacks. I have just returned from a secret meeting in St. Louis with a Judge Benjamin Sebastian, one of the Kentucky leaders who has been influential in promoting a separation of that state from the Union —"

Adam interrupted. "How on earth did you manage a meeting up there with a Kentucky judge you did not know?"

"Michael LaCassagne arranged it. He returned from Philadelphia through Frankfort, and wrote to us. Judge Sebastian confirmed names of the men influenced by General Wilkinson's call for separation, and told me they have been making plans for a break with the U.S. for several years."

"What motivates Judge Sebastian to release this information to 'the enemy'?"

"He has had second thoughts since the invasion is now focused under French influence. He told me the breakaway leaders have organized a new movement called 'The Democratic Society of Kentucky.' Its purpose is to use *any means* of opening the river to navigation, and they have solicited funds for the cause. General Clark has donated $4,000, and the donation total grows every day. Sebastian said that the plans are more comprehensive than we realized. He has agreed to gather as much inside information as he can from the leaders of the society, for he has their confidence."

"Where does Wilkinson stand in all of this? Doesn't it upset his own aims?"

"Of course. He doesn't want the French intervening, nor does he encourage anything he cannot control. He has really laid some groundwork in Kentucky, and it restores my confidence in his genuine intentions. But his followers are getting out of hand, and that is why he has LaCassagne trying to stay on top of it all."

"You have to give him credit," Adam observed. "He keeps his eyes on the goal."

"He is very concerned, now, that he must continue to work in secret. I believe I told you he is considering leaving the U. S. Army and joining the Spanish government. Of course, he wants our complete protection."

What a crass double dealer he is, Adam thought to himself. Aloud he said, "What a coup that would be for you! Where do I come in on this intrigue?"

"We need a reliable man who can pick up the filibuster information firsthand from Judge Sebastian. He will accumulate all the invasion details and will convey them directly to a special courier I have agreed to send. I want you to be that man, Adam. You are ideal for the mission. You are one of the least suspected residents of Natchez, and no one would entertain a thought of your involvement in the affairs of Spanish defense. We can spread around a good story to cover a reason for the journey, and you would not be under suspicion, nor subject to any danger from suspecting persons."

Adam's blood tingled with excitement, and his mind whirled with prospects of the undertaking. He responded with as much sense as he could muster under the sudden shock. "What a mission, Don Manuel! It certainly would be a useful one, if I can accomplish it." He paused to consider his role. His brother, Abner, was now in Lexington, Kentucky. He longed to see him, and could make a visit there a credible purpose for the journey. Also, his desire to be ordained a priest might be worked into a plausible cause. He proposed the ideas to the governor, who thought them brilliant cover stories for the journey. With lingering doubts, Adam agreed to accept the role of spy-messenger.

"By the way, where would I *really* be going?" he asked.

"You will see Judge Sebastian in Frankfort, and from there you can go to Louisville. LaCassagne may have the latest news of any troop movements on the Ohio. Between the two of them, you should be able to gather as much valid information we could expect."

"I'm willing to go, Don Manuel, but I don't expect Mary to be enthusiastic. She'll be worried over the dangers of a horseback journey through the wilderness. She is with child again, and I would also worry about her condition."

"*Hmm* . . .When does she expect her *accouchement?*"

"In November."

Don Manuel reflected a moment on this news. "I realize it is a lot to ask, Adam — to leave your family, and especially *Doña* Mary, while she is expecting. But if you leave within the next two weeks, you should be back by mid-June, and November is still a long way off."

"It will take a lot of persuading to assuage her doubts, and I have my own to deal with."

Seeing Adam's hesitation, Don Manuel spoke quickly. "I will do everything I can to assure your safety, Adam. I will prearrange for your travel companions, and will have them carefully screened. I will ask Piomingo if Yellowtail can accompany you. His knowledge of the Natchez Trail and the wilderness is invaluable. That should assure you safe passage through Indian country. I will write Governor Carondelet and inform him of your reasons for leaving. He has to approve of the journey, anyway, but it is best that he not know your true mission."

Noting the surprised look on Adam's face, he added hastily, "The fewer who know of your mission, the safer it will be for you. The governor-general has his problems with secret leaks, also."

Don Manuel produced a map and they discussed the itinerary. Adam would journey with a party of boatmen up the Trace to Nashborough, thence across to Lexington for several days with Abner. If Abner could be persuaded to travel with him to Frankfort, it would help allay suspicion, they reasoned. From Frankfort he would go to Louisville, either down the Kentucky River to the Ohio, or overland by horseback. He could decide which would be faster. There he would confer with LaCassagne, and thence book passage down the Ohio and Mississippi.

"I will provide you with riding horses and a packhorse," Don Manuel said. "It is the least I can do to save your own fine horse from the rough journey up the Trace."

The next day, Mary was more shocked than Adam at the prospect of such a mission. "To be a spy! Oh, Adam, what a scary thought — of you out there on that wilderness trail for weeks and weeks, facing all the dangers of wild animals, Indians, bandits, thieves, and murderers. And there can be terrible storms and floods. I am not sure I could live through the suspense until you arrived safely home."

"Yes, you can. Don't think of such things, my pet. Many boatmen and others travel the Trace every year. Besides, Don Manuel has offered to screen the lot who leave with me. And don't forget, Yellowtail will be with me all the way. We'll be on the Trace only about twenty-one days. After Nashborough the trails between destinations will be more populated, with way-stations, forts, and settlements — therefore less hazardous. And to think! I will see Abner again. I will see the Downses again, and other friends in Louisville. By now it should be more civilized and built up."

Mary reluctantly approved, but only if Adam would agree to take Dirk with him. The slave's superior strength would provide safety, she reasoned, and his personal skills could care for Adam's comforts.

Adam told Dusty of the journey, but not the real mission.

"Lordy, boss, that's no kind of journey for a gentleman," he said. "I wish I could go with you."

Adam was touched. "No, Dusty. I will depend on you to look after Mary and the plantation," he said.

Dusty offered an idea. "Boss, I cud look over the Kaintucks who expect to make the journey with you. If the Gov will permit me, I can pick out the bad 'uns quicker'n a toad snaps a fly. I know so many of 'em — the scrappers, the mean ones — and can find out about others."

Adam informed Don Manuel that he believed Dusty's appraisal of the boatmen would be reliable. With the governor's approval, Dusty moved about among the boatmen in the next few days, arranging the composition of the travelers signed on for the journey. He returned to Evenstar with good news.

"Mister Adam, we had good luck. Five Kaintucks we already know have signed up. My two former partners, Mort and Jiggs, and the three who helped us clear your land that first year. Remember the brothers, Calvin and Drake, and that older fellow, Shorty? They consider it an honor to travel with you."

"Splendid, Dusty. Of course I remember them. They will be comfortable companions. Who else?"

"I screened the others careful as I could, askin' around about them. There are eight other boatmen signed on, and I didn't hear nothin' bad aginst any of 'em. I feel you'll be safe with 'em. That's as likely a bunch of Kaintucks as can be scrambled together in one hoecake. And you can be sure that Mort and Jiggs and the three that worked for ya will look after ya, personal. Oh, yes, the Gov gave me this note for you."

Adam opened the note and read that the governor was adding several men to the travel group: Turner Brashears, a trusted Indian agent who lived among the Choctaws and helped keep peace, and two young adventurous cousins named Pelletier, who were making the journey from New Orleans on their way back to the Seaboard. He had set the following Wednesday for departure date, and ended his message with: "God go with you, Adam! Your affectionate friend, Manuel Gayoso de Lemos."

Yellowtail arrived several days ahead of time, riding his fine Chickasaw prairie horse. He was seated on a colorful woven saddle blanket. His personal items were wrapped in leather saddlebags decorated with tufts of bright colored hair and feathers. Two strong hunting bows were fastened at his knee. As he dismounted, Mary noted he wore a newly made deerskin jacket and breeches. There were marked changes in him since he had left Evenstar. At eighteen, Yellowtail wore a stately mien and a manly look of pride in his high rank as son of a chieftain.

Mary held him at arm's length, viewing his splendor. "What a fine young warrior you are now," she said, "and how splendid you look. We have missed you."

Adam greeted Yellowtail warmly in Chickasaw. They clasped arms in the traditional Indian manner of cherished friends. In the parlor, Becky and Susannah clung to Yellowtail's knees with wild delight. He handed each a painted gourd rattle and lifted them to his shoulders. He pranced a short Indian dance, while the girls wildly shook their instruments and chanted song words together in rhythm. He then unrolled a woven Chickasaw rug and laid it on the floor. The girls immediately plopped down on the rug.

"For you," he said to Mary. "My mother sends greetings and many thanks from her heart for your care of her son."

Mary's eyes were moist as she murmured, "It is a splendid rug. Please convey my heartfelt gratitude to your honorable mother for this beautiful gift."

Yellowtail smiled at her pleasure, and handed Adam a package. "For you," he said.

To his amazement, Adam unrolled a newly made buckskin suit. He laid his hand on Yellowtail's shoulder and swallowed hard with emotion. "What a fine gift. Tell your honorable mother that I shall wear it with great pride. It is you who now will care for me, as a guide on my journey."

Yellowtail smiled, and his eyes spoke many words. Adam understood. Now he could repay the Cloud family for the months of care and education he had received from them. He was eager to show Adam his prowess and knowledge of his own world.

In early morning on departure day, Dusty readied the wagon for Mary, Maamba, Tizzi, and the children to accompany the men to the Trace junction, where they would join the contingent from Natchez.

Mary's emotions rose as she surveyed Adam riding alongside the wagon. He was mounted on a sturdy piebald mare, his travel blanket underneath, his rifle over the cantle, and a pair of bulging saddlebags dangled on each side. He wore his new buckskin suit, the gift from Piomingo's squaw, and on his head his old large-brimmed white fur hat. She remembered it from his early preaching days when he was riding the Methodist circuit. He kept it for memory's sake, he said, and still found it handy to keep off the sun and rain.

Yellowtail joked beside the wagon with Becky and Susannah, who were wild with excitement. Dirk rode close by Maamba's side on a wiry Opelousas, leading a pack horse. Mary was glad she had insisted on Dirk making the journey. His loyalty and devotion to Adam assured her he would be well tended. Dirk had helped pack the generous food provisions, and her mind reviewed the list. Had she left out anything important? There was plenty of jerky and hard biscuits to tide them over if their game catch failed. There was baked dry turkey, bacon, roasted Indian corn, powdered and ready for bread cakes, and plenty of conte, the powdered China-briar root, which made up into Adam's favorite fritters. She had added packets of honeycomb to spread over them, hoping it would survive the ants.

Adam held and kissed his children as they waited for the travel group. He took Mary in his arms and whispered in her ear. "My love, you will be in my thoughts night and day. Each day, as I awake, I will say 'Good morning, my love' in my thoughts, and receive your answer, sent on angel wings. Pray for my safe return, and I'll have no fear or doubts on my mission."

He turned to meet the travelers. He shook hands with the boatmen, and greeted those he knew. Two attractive young men stepped forward and introduced themselves. Adam judged them to be in their late teens. Their speech was nonstop, with bits of information jockeyed between them.

"I'm Jonathan Pelletier, and this is my cousin, Carlysle Pelletier. We call him Carl," one said.

In rapid fire, Carl followed with, "We've been seeing how the rest of the world lives."

Jonathan took over. "We had a wild time in New Orleans. It's another world, with plenty of action, whatever you have in mind to do."

Carl continued, "We have French ancestry, but have never lived among the French. Whew! What they won't do for a lively time!" He left the thought dangling for Adam to conjure the image for himself.

Adam turned to a man in the rear, sitting quietly on his horse. Behind him a train of pack burros, linked together by rope, were attached to a spare lead horse. Turner Brashears was as dark-skinned as the Choctaws among whom he lived, his face lined and gnarled from exposure to outdoor life. His thinning, pale-red hair and beard faded into gray.

Offering his hand, Adam said, "I have seen you on the water-front, Mr. Brashears, and Governor Gayoso has told me of your valuable services to the province. I consider it a privilege to have you accompany us."

"A journey on the Trace, prearranged by the governor, is most unusual," Brashears said. "He holds you in high esteem, and the privilege is mine."

"You have quite a pack train there, Mr. Brashears. How do you manage to keep them moving without handlers?"

"They carry goods the Indians will trade me for their wares. I have packed my burros back and forth to Natchez, and sometimes Nashborough, for so many years that the critters have the route practically memorized. Sometimes I bring a Choctaw or two with me. This time I arranged for two of the boatmen to help."

Adam introduced Dirk and Yellowtail and turned to Mary for a final farewell. Mary placed her hands on his shoulders and said, so all could hear, "God go with you, my dear. At last you should realize the dream of priesthood. I pray this dangerous journey will be justified when you return with new holy orders. And give my love to your brother, Abner."

"You're overdoing it a bit, my love," Adam whispered as they embraced, "but God bless you."

Adam, Yellowtail, and Dirk joined the group, and Mary and the children blew kisses as the men set forth on the Trace.

The boatmen took the lead, riding an assortment of scraggly horses, with several pack burros shared between them. The Pelletier boys, Adam, Dirk and Yellowtail followed, with Turner Brashears, his burro train and two boatmen in the rear. Brashears advised them that they should try to reach the lower branches of

Bayou Pierre for the night. In spite of their intentions, the pack burros set the pace, slowing the riders. Darkness set in by the time they reached the bayou, where stagnant water spread out into a marsh. The horses stumbled and sloshed in the swampy water a long distance before they could find a dry campsite.

The roars of bull alligators, stirred by the spring weather, occasionally shattered the forest quiet. Adam thanked heaven it was too early for frogs and mosquitoes, but there was enough discomfort to keep him awake during the night.

The swollen river at Grindstone Ford presented a precarious crossing, and the men were relieved they had waited until daylight. The animals had to be unloaded and the goods ferried across in a single canoe found near the shore, while the men and horses swam the stream. The trail followed ridges where possible, providing rain runoff, but the track was sunk low in places, sometimes as much as twenty feet, where the soft earth had been trampled by hooves and moccasins over centuries of time. Tall cane and brush on the sides and vine-covered trees overhead created a shadowy tunnel. The premonition of danger was close and real. Adam's apprehension increased in the eerie penumbras after the boatmen explained it was in such places that travelers were most vulnerable to attack from above by cowering bandits, or hostile Indians.

"A critter cud drap down quicker nor a alligator can chaw a puppy, and slit a feller's throat before he cud reach fer his shivvers," one boatman explained.

Within the first few days of travel, Adam recognized distinctive characteristics among the men. Calvin and Drake were simple, farm-bred, hard-working young men. Shorty had a similar background, but his longer years of experience on the rivers had made him wiser and more seasoned. He was good-natured, but cautious, and not prone to joke as often as the other men.

Mort and Jiggs were polite and respectful to Adam. Mort was a serious young man. Jiggs, nearing forty, was more jovial. He often expressed enthusiasm and emotional responses by performing a lively jig, prancing in a sprightly manner as though sparring for a fight, thus earning him his nickname.

Adam thought the remainder of the boatmen could be described as undistinguished Kaintucks, much alike in temperament, with varying degrees of crudeness and disarray. Their appearance was on the tattered side, their beards shaggy. They would not trim or shave again until they reached civilization, and each day their appearance grew more rugged. Their tanned faces were usually immobile, long inured to the boredom of river travel. Most chewed tobacco, and a daily rivalry took place as to who could spit farthest.

Adam found their colorful language and limited vocabulary entertaining. He marveled at their excruciating abuse of English grammar, filled with metaphors, similes, and punctuated with expletives. Everything was "liken" to something else, drawing humorous creative comparisons.

One man, named Pelky, tended to be quarrelsome, finding fault or picking fights over trivial matters. There were only four pack burros to carry the gear and supplies for thirteen men, which provided a constant irritant. Adam heard Pelky complain to one of the men. "You got bigger perporshun tied on this here burro. There's not enough room fer mine."

No one defended Pelky's claim, and his protests only heightened the argument, with curses and shouts.

"You durn'd ash cats," Pelky shouted. "You lazy dumblocks fast'n yer trappin's liken a tyke ties his shoes."

"Yer so dad-rotted mean an' ugly you scares folks, even while yer sleepin'," one man shot back.

Pelky faced up to him, fists ready. "One lick at you will knock yer heart, liver an' lights out uv ya!"

After observing several similar altercations, Adam spoke to Calvin. "Is Pelky always so contentious? Can he make trouble for us?"

"I'm not sure, sir," Calvin answered. "He's a legend on the rivers. Ya see that red feather he wears in his cap? That shows he's earned the Cock-o-the-Walk. He allus proves hisself the hardest man on the boat, like a fightin' cock kin lick the roosters every time. He wears that feather to prove it, and no one messes with him."

Pelky kept the others in a constant stew over their unforgivable peccadilloes, and it was clear they dared not "mess with him." Whether it was Pelky's garrulousness or their natural ways, the other Kaintucks were almost as contentious, and often in an uproar. Adam discovered that the slow pace of Brashears' burro pack train was becoming a thorn in their sides, and some grumbled daily.

"Why don't we jes' hightail on without 'em?" Adam overheard a Kaintuck say. "Them two dumblocks was hired to give that Indian-lover a hand with his load. Let 'em git there by theirselves."

"That would leave them two half-starved bastards on their own, after Brashears leaves in Choctaw country," Shorty answered. "We wouldn't want nobody to do that to us on this trail."

"Besides," reasoned another, "the governor 'spects Brashears to look after our Preacher Cloud. We wouldn't want to have the Gov after our tails when we git back to Natchez."

At least they were humane, Adam thought, *and more soft-hearted than they sounded.* They bragged and swore, were predatory and proud at will but, Adam discovered, often courageous when a companion needed help.

The two adventurous Pelletiers appeared to Adam well-bred, albeit a bit too impulsive. They were students at Harvard College, and Adam referred to them as "the Harvard Boys." Their well-equipped, expensive travel gear was strapped to Opelousas horses. They showed a particular fascination for Yellowtail, and made every effort to ride or sit beside him. Adam was amused with the way they hung on his every word, taking advantage of his Indian knowledge of the *flora* and *fauna* along the terrain. They showed a curious and academic interest in every plant and living creature. Jonathan kept a list of animals and birds, and Carl of plants and trees.

Dirk was the perfect attendant, and Adam thanked Mary silently, more than once, for insisting that he come along. The slave was not only seasoned by the overland journey across Pennsylvania, but his years of devoted service to the Clouds had developed an uncanny sense of what was needed on every occasion, and he took pride in serving Adam on this rugged trip. He handled their baggage, deftly unpacked it, pitched the tent, kindled the fires and cooked their meals, hobbled the horses at night, and swiftly repacked everything the next morning at dawn. Dirk's devotion to Adam, his high spirits and easy nature won him acceptance among the men.

The miles beyond Natchez became more gravelly, with poor soil and little timber. Open woods were interspersed with prairies, and the path grew steadily rougher, more broken, and brush covered. Swollen streams from late spring rains poured from muddy banks. Yellowtail rode ahead, skirting swamps, and searching for the easiest fording places across the streams.

"I can imagine the trials of making this journey on foot," Adam remarked to Turner Brashears one night at they camped. "What intrepid travelers they would have to be."

"You should see the walking boatmen try to get across the wider streams," Brashears answered. "They sometimes find rafts, or a canoe left waiting to ferry their packs across, but more often they have to wade or swim across. They scout for the easiest fording places, and hope to find a crossing with a fallen log."

At one swollen torrent fed by a waterfall, Yellowtail swam across with the horses while the men and goods crossed on a ferry provided by an accommodating Choctaw.

Brashears told the men they should give the Indian something of value, so that he would continue the service for others, in expectation of a reward. Most of the men gave him something, such as a coin, comb, buckle, or bandanna — whatever they could spare from their baggage. Adam noticed that the two men who tended Brashears' burros had nothing to give. He thought they looked emaciated, and surmised they had been living without proper food in order to make the journey.

One day the group reached a large section of open fields alive with bobwhite quail, rabbits, hawks, and a profusion of songbirds. Early spring wildflowers dotted the landscape with splashes of yellow and white.

"We are in Choctaw country," Yellowtail told them. "There are plants here that do not grow further north, but we gather them for our use when we pass through their lands." The Pelletiers gathered plant samples, and Yellowtail explained their medicinal uses.

The Harvard Boys soon discovered Turner Brashears also harbored a wealth of information. They absorbed his adventures as an Indian agent, and his tales of Indian wars, tribal bravery, and their reverence for the land.

"I learned from my squaw," he told them. "She is a good wife, and taught me the Indian ways. The Choctaws named me 'Indian Dog Running,' because of my red hair and beard. Survival in the wilderness can depend upon what we learn from the Indians. You better listen and learn from Yellowtail. He can teach you more than you could ever learn in books."

The young men took copious notes and discussed their information endlessly, lacing their talk with fantasies of becoming famous wilderness explorers. Adam wished they were not so brash. Their enthusiasm made him nervous. Yellowtail watched them closely, as though sensing their youthful inexperience and exuberance could eventually court disaster.

Climbing up over a ridge one day, the men looked down on a long valley of great beauty. A wide river ran through its center, myriad flowers covered the swales, and a spectacular buffalo herd grazed its sweeping grasslands.

Turner Brashears pointed below. "That is the Pearl River. My spread is just off that narrow trail, and I'll leave you down there."

"Look at the size of that buffalo herd!" Jonathan exclaimed. "There must be hundreds."

"Could be a thousand," Carl shouted. "Let's get down there fast for a buffalo hunt."

"You better stay away from them," Brashears warned. "You startle 'em, they get mean. And when they stampede, you better run for your life. They're stupid beasts, and get confused when they panic."

"And besides," Adam added, "we have no way to preserve or carry the meat. We could only enjoy it on the spot."

"We do not kill for sport," Yellowtail said gravely. "Our people take the buffalo only when hungry. Buffalo gives up his life to sustain us when we need him. When we abuse his gift, he brings us misfortune."

The men were disgruntled as they descended the trail, and the Pelletiers complained bitterly that they could not experience a buffalo hunt. Turner Brashears turned to Adam for farewells.

"The best of luck to you, Mister Cloud," he said genially. "I hope you can keep the lid on impulsive behavior. You have your hands full." The trader paid off his helpers and led his burro train on a northeast trail skirting the lake.

When Adam's group made camp that night, Yellowtail told them the tale of the "Buffaloes' Revenge," a story of greedy Indians who killed more buffalo than they could eat by driving the herd over a cliff. The buffaloes cast a spell on the Indian shaman, who was later killed, and the tribe lost its revered leader.

Adam hoped that the sulking Harvard Boys soaked up a little reverence and humility from the legend's meaning.

22 The Natchez Trace

T he travelers followed the Pearl River a few miles, skirting westward to avoid the swamps, and the country began to rise. Yellowtail said they were deep into Choctaw land.

"I hope the Creeks aren't on a warpath," Jonathan said. "Remember, Red Dog Running told us the Creeks sometimes crept into Choctaw country for unfriendly raids?"

"I wouldn't know a Creek from a Choctaw," Carl said, "and I hope we don't meet up with either."

"We mustn't live in fear," Adam said. "Yellowtail is with us, and the Choctaw and Chickasaw tribes are friendly. As for Creeks, have you heard news of any Creek hostility, Yellowtail?"

Yellowtail smiled at the Pelletier cousins. "None. We live in peace," he said.

Adam noticed that the Harvard Boys were apprehensive thereafter, startled at every sound — the hoot of an owl or a bird-call — suspicious they were Indian signals. The cousins took pains to carry their guns at all times, even into the bushes where they went as a pair to relieve themselves. On one such urgency, Adam saw the boys leave the trail, while the others went on. When they failed to catch up he became alarmed. He was about to speak of it to Yellowtail when a muffled shot rang out.

"The boys! They're in trouble," Adam cried out.

Yellowtail held up his hand for silence, and the group stood still to listen. Yellowtail immediately dismounted, and silently worked his way back through the trees and undergrowth toward the sound of the shot. Adam followed, carefully keeping a distance to cover Yellowtail's movements. Cautiously peering through the undergrowth, they came upon a chilling sight. A large band of Choctaw warriors, their faces fiercely painted for war, surrounded Jonathan and Carl, each held in a chokehold by a warrior. The Indians were in high spirits, noisily taunting their captives and joking with one another. Yellowtail and Adam silently crept back to the boatmen.

"The Indians are drunk," Yellowtail explained. "I have a plan. I will return on horseback. They are in good humor, and I can talk for the boys' freedom."

"I'll ride behind you and be ready to alarm our men here in case anything goes wrong," Adam said.

They remounted and Yellowtail led the way. Carl and Jonathan were still the center of excitement as the Choctaw warriors danced about them, poking them with sticks, celebrating their capture. Adam stayed a respectful distance behind, as Yellowtail approached the men. The noise abated when the Choctaws saw the intruder.

"Greetings. I am Yellowtail, son of Chief Payo-Mataha, Chickasaw Piomingo," he said in the Choctaw tongue. "I travel with a band of white traders who are on the trail ahead. These two men are part of the group, and are harmless visitors to our land. I have been appointed their protector by our friend, Chactimataha."

The name Chactimataha instantly impressed the warriors, and they sobered somewhat. Adam recognized the name, "King of the Choctaws," given affectionately by their tribe to Governor Gayoso during a former peace conference.

"Another of your brothers, Red Dog Running, traveled with us as far as the Pearl River," Yellowtail added.

The men restraining the Pelletiers loosened their chokeholds, but held on.

"Gawd! Are we glad to see you," Carl gasped through the grip on his throat. "Get these savages off us."

Yellowtail ignored the plea, and, noting the captors' reluctance, he repeated, "These men are from the north visiting our lands. Their mission is peaceful. They will join their families in north country. Release these two and let them join the others. They mean you no harm."

"Tell them I panicked," Jonathan cried. "My musket misfired, and there was no shot."

Yellowtail motioned to the young men to be quiet, and repeated Jonathan's explanation. The captors reluctantly released their holds, and the cousins glumly rubbed their necks. The Choctaws conferred among themselves, and their spokesman finally spoke to Yellowtail.

"Take your whimpering white jackals. We will go with you to see your band of palefaces whom you protect."

The tense moment was over, and Yellowtail motioned Adam to come forward. "This is White Cloud, friend of Chactimataha, and most honored leader of our group," Yellowtail said.

Adam swallowed hard, his heart still pounding from the crisis. "We invite you to join us," he said in halting Choctaw. In English he said to Yellowtail, "Did I say it right? Did I get us into more trouble?"

Yellowtail laughed and said in Choctaw, "My honored friend, White Cloud, graciously invites you to accompany us on the trail."

With the Pelletiers in front, they led the Choctaws back to the boatmen, the Indians meanwhile regaining momentum for their noisy celebration. Whooping wildly, they dangled objects tied on their belts. To Adam's horror, he recognized them as freshly dried scalps, and he tried not to look at them as the Indians recounted their war adventure. They explained they had just returned from a raiding party on the Caddo tribe, across the Great River; the scalps proved their fierce victory. The Choctaws were jubilant over their kill, and Adam realized that, in their present mood of drunken celebration, his companions had best celebrate with them. He knew their jubilant mood could turn like quicksilver from merriment to anger. He turned to the boatmen who were staring like frozen statues at the mob of prancing red men.

"Smile, laugh, grin," he said quietly. "They are celebrating a battle. Show them you appreciate their victory. They will remain friendly."

The boatmen began to grin and nod to the warriors.

"This man says they have just killed a deer," Yellowtail said to Adam. "They want to share the meal with us. It would be wise to accept."

"I agree," Adam answered, and he explained to the boatmen.

They followed the Choctaws to their campsite and spent the next several hours feasting on roasted chunks of venison, and sharing their *la tafia* rum. The Choctaws traveled with the group for another ten miles, gradually dispersing to their villages along the way. Adam blew a sigh of relief as they watched the last of the Indians disappear into the forest.

"To think, they asked nothing of us other than our company," he said. "Yellowtail, where did you get my new name, White Cloud? That was very clever."

Yellowtail grinned. "Name just right. You're white Cloud already."

"I don't know about you," Mort said, to no one in particular, "but I'm plain tuckered out from bein' aroun' them wild red men. They's too frien'ly to trust."

"Liken a lizard watchin' a coiled snake," Jiggs said.

"Liken a mouse in a cat's paw," said another.

Shorty summed it up best. "Liken walkin' a tight rope 'crost a b'ar's lair."

The travelers met other Choctaw bands coming and going to nearby villages. Adam noticed Jonathan and Carl were more somber after their near-death encounter, but Jonathan often retold the incident until the others grew tired of hearing about it

"You deserved what you got," Pelky said. "Yore sich a con-sarned nincompoop that ya don't know proper how to load a gun. Only a dim wit cud push in his ball before the powder's proper in, and get a flash-in-the-pan. That's what you are, a flash-in-the-pan. Ya shud thank Yellertail fer savin' yer life."

"He was too streaked to piss," Calvin said.

"Scared liken a jack rabbit under a eagle," said Drake, who often punctuated Calvin's remarks with one of his own.

Soon the trail brought the band to a creek that Yellowtail said was the border between the land of the Choctaw and Chickasaw tribes. It was called Nanih *Waiya*, he explained, The Hill of Origins. Adam noted a marked change in Yellowtail's spirits. He seemed less disturbed by the antics of the ruffians and the brash young cousins. He was more tolerant, and generous with his tales of Indian lore.

From the lower flat country, the land rose to rolling hills and they soon found themselves in dense forests budding into new spring foliage. The Pelletier collection lists lengthened, and passenger pigeons were added to the list of buffalo, black bears, elks, wolves, and cougars. The pigeons concentrated in an area the boatmen called "Pigeon's Roost." They filled the air in flocks of hundreds, soaring overhead from their roosts in early morning and returning at nightfall. Carolina parakeets and ivory-billed woodpeckers flashed their colors in the trees. Yellowtail and the men found plentiful game. The trail ran lengthwise beside the Yokanookany River, and they camped by waterfalls and deep pools created by beaver dams.

Yellowtail pointed out the paths leading to the many Chickasaw villages. At one sidepath Yellowtail stopped.

"This trail leads to Chief Tascahetuca, king of all the Chickasaws," he said. "His village is headquarters for our nation. He is greatly revered. With your permission, I would like to visit the Great Chief. It would add another feather to my headdress if the chief receives me as a chieftain's son."

Adam gathered the men together and explained Yellowtail's request. "It would add to his stature among his own people," he said. "Yellowtail has befriended and protected us and we must give him his due. We must be on our best behavior, for we will be guests of a powerful Indian chief. Do not stare at the maidens, or make personal advances to anyone. Indians often find our ways offensive."

With some trepidation, the travelers followed Yellowtail to the center of the village. He wore his distinctive breastplate of a chief's son over his deerskins, and sat proudly on his horse. The villagers came forward to greet him and escorted him to Tascahetuca's nearby dwelling, where he disappeared through a brightly woven flap that served as a door.

The travelers waited quietly in the open area, surrounded by curious villagers, who stared at them and chatted to each other. Adam picked up a few of their words, and found they were comparing skin colors. The younger Indians were greatly mystified over Dirk's dark complexion, and Adam surmised they had never seen a Negro before.

The village seemed to stretch out for miles, as far as the eye could see. Its structures and organization were similar to the Chickasaw Bluffs village, and Adam pointed out its features to the men while they waited.

"Land-o-Goshen," Jiggs said, "in all my trottin' years I hain't nivver been in a Indian village, and I sure nivver 'spected to be invited."

"Well, don't caper yet. We're not 'zactly invited," Mort reminded him. "What if the king has a grudge 'ginst Yellertail's pa?"

"That isn't very likely," Adam said, trying not to show his nervousness. He recalled seeing the mighty chief among the contingent of nations that rode into Villa Gayoso last year. Payo-Metaha and all the Chickasaw chiefs were subservient to Tescahetuca, as though they knew his displeasure could easily crush them.

Yellowtail emerged from the dwelling with the elderly chief beside him. "Greetings to the honored friend of my friend," Tascahetuca said in English, "and welcome to our village."

"Greetings to the honored Tascahetuca, king of the Chickasaw Nation," Adam answered in the Chickasaw tongue. The chief looked pleased. "These are my companions." Adam introduced them.

"I told the Great Chief that you visited our village at the invitation of my father, Payo-Mataha, and that I have been schooled in your home. He was very impressed," Yellowtail said.

"My squaw is a fine teacher, and she read him many books. This knowledge was taught over many moons. I helped when I was asked," Adam added.

"You have traveled many days, and have far to go," the old chief said to Adam. "Tascahetuca offers you a respite. Share the meat and cakes prepared by our good squaws and maidens. They will bring you water for bathing, then bring food."

Adam accepted the offer. It would be refreshing to be rid of the dirt and grime they had accumulated since the last river crossing. They were led to the longhouse where bathing vessels were set up outside. The Indian women brought scrubbing and drying cloths, and some men let the women scrub their backs. The travelers settled on the floor of the longhouse, and were joined by some fifty braves, along with Chief Tescahetuca and Yellowtail, who seated themselves among the guests. Soon, a train of women placed pottery vessels of food and drink before them. The men ate with their fingers chunks of roasted venison, bear meat, fish, and corn cakes.

After dinner the chief donned an elaborate headdress of hide, beads, and feathers and stood before Adam.

"Our white friend and his squaw have given a home and fine education to our Brother Yellowtail. I am sure that Yellowtaill will use his wisdom with great skill," he said. "Yellowtail tells us you are a holy man in your white man's world. We wish to honor you with a special ceremony."

To Adam's surprise, the chief held out another headdress and motioned him to stand. He placed it upon Adam's brow and addressed him in a solemn voice.

"From this day, Adam Cloud is a member of the Chickasaw Nation, and will be known as our brother, White Cloud."

"Great One, the honor is mine," Adam said gravely. "I shall treasure my Chickasaw name and walk with pride among my Chickasaw brothers."

The warriors formed a circle around Adam, and to the beat of drums and gourd rattles, they danced a solemn dance in his honor. Yellowtail interpreted the ceremony in English for the companions. They clapped and sent up a cheer as Adam and the dancers sat. Several braves brought ceremonial pipes which were lighted and passed among the gathering.

After an interval of smoking and conviviality, Tescahetuca said to Adam, "Dwell with us this night and rest upon beds of moss and pine. Let us serve you and show you a night of peace and comfort."

Adam did not want to delay the journey any further, but it was already late in the day and he saw it was impossible to decline the invitation. He turned to the travelers for their decision. The group accepted eagerly. The unexpected adventure was turning out to be a major event in their lives.

Yellowtail and the warrior chiefs bade good night and retired to the village. The women laid out pallets for the guests, then stood quietly in a group.

Yellowtail approached Adam and said, "The Great One has instructed me to offer you and your men each a woman for your beds tonight. He wishes to repay you for your kindness, and the men for their friendship today."

Surprised and amused by the gesture, Adam kept a straight face as he answered. "Tell the Great King Chief that White Cloud is touched by his generous offer. I am sure the maidens of your tribe can offer the most pleasing favors to their guests. Tell him, respectfully, that I cannot accept. Explain that it is considered a sin for me to lie with any woman but my own, and that tradition stands for the rest of the men, also. Please explain that I mean no offense. I would honor his traditions and laws the same way, if he were my guest."

Adam was glad the men could not hear the offer. He knew they would be furious that he had denied them the delights of sleeping with Indian maidens, but he wanted no trouble. The reputation of Kaintucks for brutality to women was legend. He could not risk any errant behavior.

Leaving the village next morning, they looked down on a vast valley nearly one thousand feet below, cut across by a wide river. Yellowtail made a sweeping gesture as he spoke.

"Down there, the Tombigbee Prairie. Many lakes and tributaries of water connecting with the great Tennessee River to the north," he said.

Adam was elated. They were nearing the Tennessee River, and soon would reach the Cumberland Plateau! The boatmen had warned him the Tennessee River would be the most difficult crossing of all. From there on they should move faster, he reasoned. They packed their saddlebags high on the horses and crossed the Tombigbee without any loss other than a packet of food. The trail climbed upward through spectacular scenery of high rims, water-falls, caves, and sinkholes to the Tennessee River Valley. At last they saw the Tennessee River below them. An awesome sight, Adam thought, a body of water to be respected. Its cane-lined shores were a half-mile or more apart.

"The surface looks quiet and smooth," Shorty explained, "but sure's water runs downhill, that there current underneath is so swift a man cud be carried down liken a ant in a torrent."

"I seen rafts carried downriver fastern' a hawk can snatch a mouse," Calvin said.

Drake added, "An' they like as not ended up in Indian country downstream."

Yellowtail sat quietly on his horse, gazing over the terrain. He then spoke to Adam. "The water is very high. A village of Our People is below and west of here. I will ride there. They can loan us a raft."

"It's worth a try," Adam said, "but be careful, Yellowtail. They might not want to aid the white men as gallantly as did your king."

Yellowtail rode off and the men waited anxiously on the shore. Hours went by while the Kaintucks rested and bragged of former adventures at this dangerous crossing. Several fights ensued among them and Adam broke them up. He began to fear that Yellowtail had met resistance.

Dirk suddenly cried out, "Heah he cum, Massah! They's lots of Injuns with 'im."

Yellowtail had indeed brought help. A contingent of twenty Chickasaw men rode with him, and on the river, Indians paddled canoes vigorously toward them towing two small rafts. The canoes beached on shore, and the horsemen dismounted in front of the travelers. The boatmen stared in disbelief. Their faith in Yellowtail soared even higher.

The crossing went swiftly and efficiently, like none had ever experienced before. The Chickasaws helped place the saddlebags, supplies, and equipment on the rafts, while Dirk and the boatmen laced the horses together for the swim across. The Indians bound the rafts together, the men climbed aboard, and the Indians launched the canoes and poled the rafts into the rushing river. Guided by sturdy Indian swimmers, the horses swam between rafts and canoes. The canoes angled downstream close to the swimming horses, preventing any horse in trouble from drifting and dragging the others with it. Adam's stomach dropped in the crossing, but he laughed at the men's jokes, which helped cover their anxieties.

The crossing landed them downstream only a quarter-mile below take-off point. Adam made the rounds of each Indian, pressing hands and expressing thanks in the Chickasaw tongue. The Pelletiers huddled the men together and raised up a cheer for the braves, who stood grinning on the shore.

Saddlebags and packs were again secured to the horses, and the travelers set off as quickly as they could, anxious to reach the Cumberland Plateau. Adam consulted his map; there was another hundred miles to go. The men moved along eagerly through sunken trails, glens, hollows and ridges, and forests rich with timber.

Many days later, at Swan Valley, the group stopped for a noon meal.

"Here I must leave you to return to my village," Yellowtail said. "The upper country has white men's ferries to assist you across the big rivers. I do not belong there."

Adam felt a poignant sadness as he said farewell. "I am forever indebted for your company on this journey. May the Great Spirit dwell with you and protect you."

The friends embraced, Yellowtail mounted his horse, and the travelers watched him turn back on the trail.

Shorty expressed their collective regrets. "I ain't nivver had a Indian friend before," he said wistfully, "and gol-durned if'n I ain't gonna miss him."

As they got closer to Nashborough, Adam's spirits began to soar. They were nearing civilization, and Mort told him they were about two days away from Nashborough. The men became restless and jubilant, and Jiggs cut a caper among the pine needles, whooping an Indian call.

Reaching the outpost of Nashborough, Adam saw a woman watching them from her cabin stoop. He rode up to her and removed his hat.

"Pardon me, Madam," he said, "but could you direct me to the home of Mister Andrew Jackson, the lawyer?"

She appraised him head to foot before answering. "Well, now, everyone knows where them two lives. They's over that way a few miles," she rolled her head toward the east, "down the next trail crosses here. The name's 'Poplar Grove' on the plantation gate."

At the crosstrail Adam bade farewell to his companions. He invited the boatmen to stop by Evenstar when they returned to Natchez. Then he turned to the Pelletier cousins. He had grown fond of them in spite of their youthful antics.

"I admire your fortitude in making this long, perilous journey from New Orleans. It took a special kind of courage, and I am sure you will have much to tell your family and friends about your adventures. Take care on the remainder of your journey, and go with God."

Adam and Dirk watched the men kick their horses to a gallop and race toward the settlement. *Probably to the nearest saloon,* Adam thought with amusement, and he and Dirk set off toward the Jacksons'.

They followed the road along the Cumberland River and turned into a private path marked "Poplar Grove." The path led directly through open tobacco fields to a framed log cabin nestled among the trees. The frontage site presented a spectacular view of a hairpin bend of the river, with a forest on the far side.

As Adam climbed the front steps, he wondered how much Jackson might have changed since leaving Natchez. He thought the setting unusually remote for Jackson's taste. Andrew's lively manner, his sense of fun, love of people, his penchant for the races, cockfighting, or any contest challenging his ingenuity had made him an outgoing personality, versatile and energetic.

A servant ushered Adam into the parlor and summoned her mistress. Rachel Jackson greeted him with genuine joy.

"Reverend Cloud!" she exclaimed. "What a surprise! Mr. Jackson has been summoned and should be here soon. He is somewhere on the grounds."

Adam studied Rachel as she spoke. He observed that her beauty was as vivid as before, but he detected a pensive look in her dark eyes. A bit too formal, not quite as fiery, he thought. He wondered if the Jacksons were happy.

Andrew's greeting was a warm embrace. "Welcome to our home, Adam. What brings you to Nashborough?"

Adam explained the suddenness of his journey. "I thought it well worth the effort to be ordained in Frankfort, for it has long been my desire to complete my holy orders in the Anglican church. I will also get to visit my brother in Lexington."

"Ah, yes, but your orders were certainly enough for us, were they not, my dear?" Jackson looked tenderly at Rachel. "Your kindness to us can never be repaid."

Adam noted a hesitancy and a look of anxiety before Rachel spoke. "Never in a thousand years. It was a lot to ask of you, and we hoped you did not get into trouble on our account."

Rachel led Adam upstairs to a guest room and ordered a hot bath prepared for him. A servant took Dirk to the slave quarters.

Dinner conversation dwelt on Natchez friends and events. In glowing terms, Adam told them about his family and his new home, feeling a surge of homesickness as he did so.

"Now, Andrew, I want to hear about you," Adam said. "By the looks of your fine property, you must have a good law practice."

"I'm fortunate in having established a strong base here," Andrew replied. "I still serve in the Tennessee Legislature. My work as district attorney of Mero District earned me the appointment of attorney general. Since we returned from Natchez, Governor Blount appointed me judge advocate for Davidson County, which added a new dimension to my life."

"Congratulations," Adam said. "Your new title is impressive, and I am sure you make a fine judge."

Jackson made a wry face. "I certainly don't miss those years of scraping together the merchandise of goods and slaves, or those weary, grinding journeys down the Trace, and on river boats to deliver my wares to Melling Wooley. I have realized a good tobacco business from my plantation."

"Our little borough is becoming more culturally advanced too," Rachel said. "We have established a new center of learning called the Davidson Academy, and Mr. Jackson has been appointed a trustee."

"We're also introducing some excitement with the layout of a new racetrack," Andrew added. "You know how I love the ponies, and I worked hard with my supporters to get the land and money allocated for it."

After dinner, they settled down in the parlor, where a servant brought wines. The conversation turned to current events. Adam opened the subject of a Natchez invasion.

"The governors are alarmed over the threat of a filibuster being organized by that Frenchman, Genet. I promised Governor Gayoso I would learn all I can on this journey, and he hoped you could give me some helpful information," he said.

"I'll tell you all I know, Adam, but I'm not a party to the expedition. General Clark sent an agent to solicit my support, but of course I declined," Jackson said. "Some of the Cumberland people are excited about General Clark's preparations, and will probably join him. If this attempt doesn't get off the ground, some zealots are even prepared to undertake a separate filibuster under a fresh start. While recruitment efforts here have aroused the settlers, very little funding has been raised."

Adam decided to be more direct. "Do you support the filibuster? Do you believe it can succeed?"

"No, Adam, I don't support the military invasion." Jackson sipped his brandy and reflected a moment. "I have a suggestion that might help you. You remember I told you about my friend Peyton Short, who was General Wilkinson's partner in his Frankfort store? The store went bankrupt, and Peyton lost a considerable sum of money. But that's beside the point. Peyton's brother, William, is a protégé of Mr. Jefferson, and now serves as his secretary. He sends Peyton the latest national news from Philadelphia. Perhaps Peyton can give you more accurate information of the Genet-Clark intrigues. If you are going to Frankfort, I can give you a letter of introduction to him."

Rachel had listened quietly, her face set in unhappy lines. She suddenly arose and took her leave, graciously excusing herself for the evening. Jackson kissed her tenderly, and they watched her move gracefully across the room. When she had closed the door, Andrew turned to Adam.

"Not to burden you with my troubles, Adam, but you have a caring nature, and you know Rachel well enough to see she is troubled. She has periods of depression, and since you may very well hear it from someone else, I might as well tell you why."

"Please do. I did notice her lack of spontaneity."

"Last December we were delivered a shock. We discovered that Rachel was still married to that scoundrel Robards. He had not actually filed for divorce, as we were told. It was only an enabling act, permitting him to bring suit against Rachel in the Kentucky Supreme Court. He waited to bring divorce action only last September, on the grounds that we were not married in Natchez, and were living in adultery. The scandal became the juiciest topic in the district, and Rachel suffered a damaged reputation."

Adam was stricken with sympathy. "This is incredible! What a terrible blow that must have been. It is enough to disturb her peace of mind. Now that I am here I can certify your marriage."

"No, Adam. Thank you, but no. I could not ask that of you, and place you in jeopardy with Governor Gayoso. There is no need now. Our lawyer advised us to remarry as soon as the divorce was made final, and we remarried in January of this year to appease the gossip-mongers. Rachel's humiliation was unbearable, but our friends came to our defense. We cling to our faith in each other, and Rachel is holding up as well as she can. She spends most of her time reading the Bible."

"That should be a solace to her. I wish I could help in some way. I feel so much a part of what has happened to you," Adam said. "May I speak of this to Rachel in the morning? I would like to comfort her, if I may."

"I hope you will. She needs comfort wherever she can find it. She holds you in high regard, and cherishes memories of your service when we made our vows in Natchez. Those were happy days."

. . .

That night Adam wrote a long letter to Mary, assuring her he was well and safe, and describing his journey on the Trace. He related the sad story of the Jacksons' troubles, and ended with ebullient messages of his love.

The next morning Adam held a simple prayer service with the Jacksons. He pressed Rachel's hands between his own.

"No matter what others want to believe, your conscience is clear," he said. "Your marriage was blessed in heaven. Remember that God is always present in our hearts to lift our heavy burdens. Abide in His love, and your indwelling spirit will bring you happiness and peace of mind."

Andrew promised to send Adam's letter to Mary by the next company of travelers headed for Natchez, and Adam tucked Andrew's letter to Peyton Short in his packet. He fondly embraced the couple, and left Poplar Grove with a heavy heart.

23 Kentucky

Lexington was a rough, bustling frontier town, and Adam learned that Abner Cloud's legal reputation was widespread. Adam was directed to a genteel boardinghouse in the center of town, where a polite landlady ushered him into the parlor to wait. He heard a wild shout from upstairs, and Abner clattered down to greet him. They embraced in a bear hug. "Just look at you!" Abner said, holding his brother at arm's length. "What has happened to the thin, wiry preacher that I remembered? You are husky, strong, tanned, and extremely smart looking. You look like a fashionable Southern planter."

Adam had dressed carefully, abandoning his travel buckskins for his best clothing. He wanted to look the part of the successful planter that he was; his pride mingled with longing for Abner's approval.

"You are much changed yourself, Abner. No longer the schoolboy that I left five years ago." He scanned with pleasure Abner's young, handsome face and figure. "I encouraged you to aim for the law, and I hear you are very good at it. You always were a quick thinker, and strong on disputation. I want to hear all about your practice. We have much to catch up on."

"Bring your things upstairs and we can talk in the privacy of my room. I'll see about a separate room for you. In the meantime, we mustn't waste a second now that we are together." Abner led the way to his room, and Adam threw his satchel on the floor.

"Dear God, how I have missed all of you," Adam said, with a searching look at his younger brother. "You must tell me about your personal life too. You are downright handsome, and still single, it seems. What a pity. My life with Mary is so perfect that my existence dwells in her and the children, and on the good future I'm building for my little family. Anne was a lovely creature, Abner, and my loss was devastating, at first. But Mary — dear Heaven what a woman! She pulled me out of my despair with a fire of determination that motivates all she does. She has a zest for life unmatched by any woman I have known. She never ceases to amaze me by her quick perception of truths, and in her unwavering devotion to my ideals. I hope you can be as fortunate in finding a perfect mate."

Abner watched his brother glow with pride and happiness as he spoke of Mary. "I envy you your married bliss, Adam. So far I have not found the love of my life. My time is spent mostly between my small law office, and this boardinghouse. My practice grows every day. Since Kentucky became a state, business activity is booming, and where there is business there is always litigation. I have recently gained entree into the inner sanctums of state legislative affairs. I'm meeting all the big-wigs connected with Frankfort and Lexington, and successful entrepreneurs who are making a place for themselves in the local and state economy. This new state is making history, Adam, and it's exciting to be a part of it."

The brothers talked long into the night. Adam was so exhausted that he finally collapsed on his bed in the neatly furnished room next to Abner's.

They spent the following day reminiscing, catching up on Adam's life in Natchez, and news of the Cloud family at Brandywine Hundred.

"Father's shipyard is overloaded with new orders, and Robert's venture into Chesapeake Bay trade has branched into coastal trade between Delaware, Cuba and the West Indies, even to New Orleans. Don't be surprised if you see one of our ships in New Orleans one day," Abner told him.

"I have yet to visit New Orleans," Adam said. "I have a reliable overseer who acts as my factor, and who takes my produce to New Orleans. Dusty strikes a better deal than I ever could. He is an experienced river trader."

"How could you not go to New Orleans, just for the experience?"

"A journey to New Orleans doesn't tempt me. It's easy to make the three hundred miles by canoe or flatboat, but getting back is a real test of endurance. One can only return by horseback — a one-hundred-fifty-mile ride up a trail that sometimes disappears after floods. Yes, Natchez is a truly isolated place, but we love it. I wouldn't trade it for the same sixteen hundred acres in the States."

"Sixteen hundred acres!" Abner was impressed. "How did you acquire so much land, and what do you do with it all?"

Adam explained about his first-year allotments from the governor, and added that he would receive five hundred arpents more for his services in coming to Frankfort. "The governor is generous with land grants to those who serve his causes. The rest of my land I purchased." Adam described his plantations, his crops, livestock and slaves. "It takes special organizing to plant and work two plantations in one season," he added. "I am learning methods of economy and efficiency. Don't laugh, Abner. I have changed a great deal in this new life."

"I'm not laughing, Adam, I'm simply overwhelmed."

Adam then told Abner of the governor's concerns for defending the Genet invasion. "My mission is highly secret; I travel under subterfuge. While I can't tell you all, I can tell you I act for the governor alone. I am to bring him vital information from local resources, but my mission must appear innocent. *Voila!* How lucky I can use you as the main object of my journey. I have also planted the rumor that I may be ordained as a priest by a bishop who *might* be visiting Frankfort this month, and that I have applied for ordination. I only wish that were true, but you must support my story, if need be." Adam paused to let the information sink in. "It's a lot to throw at you at once, Abner, but thank God you are here to support me. Do you know a Judge Benjamin Sebastian in Frankfort?"

"Of course," Abner replied. "I have appeared before him in two cases already this year. His wife invites me to dine with them when I am in Frankfort." He chuckled, and added, "She's trying to match me up with the 'right' local girl. She thinks it deplorable to be unmarried at my age. I can give you a note of introduction, if that's what you want."

"Better still," Adam, said, "can you go with me to Frankfort? It would help explain my inquiries in town. You can act as the host, showing me the sights. Besides, another bonus in this journey is the chance to purchase a good Kentucky stallion. I have long dreamed of owning one. Andrew Jackson was going to bring me one when he returned to Natchez, but he brought his future bride instead."

"You know *Andrew Jackson?*" Abner was further impressed. "He has made waves in the Tennessee Legislature. I hear about him from Peyton Short, who knew him when he was single."

"I met Mr. Jackson by chance when he entered Natchez with a contingent of slaves. I bought several from him and our friendship grew. I just visited Andrew and Rachel, in Nashborough. He gave me a letter of introduction to Peyton Short."

The following day, Abner, Adam, and Dirk set out for Frankfort, trailing the pack horse.

"I have long wanted to see Frankfort," Adam said. "General Wilkinson has told us so much about it. He said his wife enjoyed their early years here, and I gather they lived the good life, as good as the frontier had to offer."

"You know *General Wilkinson* too?" Abner exclaimed. "You say you live in an isolated Spanish province, yet you know some of the most important people on the frontier. Not to mention the fact you represent the Natchez governor."

"Merely my good fortune to meet Wilkinson in Louisville on my journey to Natchez. He was kind enough to give us firsthand information about Natchez and an introduction to the governor. We met again when he came through Natchez on a trade mission to New Orleans. He was my houseguest."

The mention of General Wilkinson gave Abner pause for thought. The extreme secrecy of Adam's mission was so unusual that he felt uneasy.

"Adam, what is this all about? Does it have anything to do with Wilkinson's efforts to prevent Kentucky statehood? I admired Wilkinson's efforts, motivated by the need for river rights, but now that we have statehood we rejoice at our good fortune."

"No, Abner. It has nothing to do with Kentucky statehood. Why do you ask?"

"If it has to do with river rights, I must confess something that you will not like," Abner said. "I stand behind the efforts for a filibuster, and some of us are counting on the men behind the new French efforts to succeed."

Adam did not want to believe what he was hearing. "Abner, you would approve a violent takeover of the Spanish government? How could we who live there be assured of our land grants if Americans took over the territory? Besides, most rabble groups bring destruction and pillage, and we would be at their mercy."

"Well, I would expect the U. S. government to claim the land grabbed in a filibuster, and our laws would be fair to Americans living there."

"I can't believe President Washington would stand behind an independent takeover, even after the fact. It would mean war with Spain. Are you ready for that?"

Abner ignored the question. "While I feel for your position, I believe you would benefit in the long run." He hesitated and his eyes probed his brother's face. "Adam, what has happened to you? You left all of your democratic rights behind when you became a Spanish citizen. Don't you want them back again?"

Adam exploded with anger, and reined his horse to face his brother. His eyes blazed, his composure gone. "Of course I do, but not at the price of losing all I came for," he retorted. He could no longer suppress his indignation. Abner was too perceptive; he had struck at his most vulnerable spot, pitting his sacred political convictions against the glaring inconsistencies of his untenable position under a monarchy.

Abner reined to a stop as he replied, "You can't have it both ways, Adam, and your future may be at risk under either government."

The brothers glared at each other, and Adam gritted his teeth to suppress his resentment. He would not admit Abner was right, even though he had opened a long-festering wound of frustration.

Instead he gave his horse a lusty kick, and the brothers rode on in cool silence, each brooding over their differences. Suddenly, Wilkinson's Spanish conspiracy looked brighter to Adam in the light of Abner's attitude toward an invasion. Diplomatic ties for river rights were preferable to violence any time. But he could not share the Wilkinson-Spanish conspiracy with Abner; he would not demean a man so highly regarded in his home territory. *Let them keep their hero*, he thought. *If Wilkinson rides to a fall, it will be through his own actions, not mine.*

By the time they reached a wayside station for the night, Adam regretted his outburst and hoped he could make it up to Abner in the morning.

The next day the brothers put their rift behind them while Abner showed Adam the town. Frankfort was everything he expected, and more. Signs of General Wilkinson's fame and influence were everywhere. Streets, buildings, and trading establishments bore his name, or names he had chosen in the early days when he had first laid out the town.

Abner arranged a meeting in Judge Sebastian's office, and the brothers arrived at the appointed hour. Adam was favorably impressed with the elderly judge's courtly manners and tall, distinguished looks. His shoulder-length hair and trimmed beard were tinged with gray; his blue eyes were alert with interest.

After introductions and the usual social amenities, the judge inquired of Adam's life and prosperity in the Spanish territory. Abner took his leave, and Adam got right down to business with the judge. He assured him that whatever information he learned would be delivered to Governor Gayoso in strict confidence.

"Governor Gayoso told me he would send his most trusted representative. He must think highly of you, and you of him, to have made this journey in his behalf," the judge replied.

"I am privileged to be his friend," Adam said. "There could be no finer example of a gentleman, and superb administrator, than Governor Gayoso. But I know you have met him and made your own assessment."

"The finest of gentlemen, assuredly," the judge replied, "and decidedly on his mark to maintain the territory for which he is responsible. Since meeting him, I have tried to imagine what it would be like to live under a monarchy again. But we can save that until later. I hope that you and your brother will be our guests overnight while you are in town, and that you will join us for supper this evening. We can have a lively discussion. If you accept, I'll send a message to Mrs. Sebastian."

"I accept with pleasure, and believe I can speak for my brother, who regards you highly." Adam knew Abner would appreciate the invitation to stay with such a prominent family.

Judge Sebastian dispatched a message to his wife through an aide, and turned to the business at hand. "I have been gathering all the information available to me, and believe I have the most recent facts, down to the least detail. Of course, some of it is subject to change, but I do not expect the basic plans will be altered." He paused to consider how to begin. "I assume you are familiar with the Kentucky frenzy to gain free trade use of the Mississippi River. If so, I needn't go into that."

Adam nodded. "I am well acquainted with those facts. General Wilkinson told me of his early efforts to convince Kentucky leaders to break away from the Union in order to accomplish that goal."

"Ah, you know General Wilkinson too? You are well up in the ranks of influential persons, sir, and you probably know more than I do about his affairs, since Wilkinson has been away from Frankfort these years. But, suffice to say, there are some very prominent and well-meaning gentlemen of this state, especially in Frankfort, who earnestly desire that Kentucky's trading future includes use of the river. As we have dreamed our dreams, over the years, it has been frustrating that our own government will not raise a hand to reach an agreement with the Spanish for our use of the river. It is little wonder, then, that anxious planters on the frontier are willing for the French to help them get what their own government will not. It is ironic that the men who enlist feel grateful to the French because they helped us win the War of

Independence. Yet the French do not offer any financial support to the military plans, even though they promote the invasion efforts."

"Is that the reason for your disenchantment with the filibuster efforts, sir?" Adam asked.

"That, and the fact that I have come to believe our nation's future lies in our Union. I was a strong supporter of separation, but since Kentucky attained statehood we have prospered. Our influence in Congress is still young, but not unnoticed, as previously. I believe fervently that we should support our state and federal governments. I have come to believe anything else is treason, especially when armed invasion is encouraged by a foreign government. Our fragile nation has had enough turmoil, and it is time to lend our collective strength to its development. We cannot do that by breaking away and fragmenting the Union. I believe America's future lies in its frontier."

"I'm glad to hear that, sir." Adam's admiration for the judge soared.

Judge Sebastian then disclosed complete plans for the invasion, while Adam took notes. The invasion was planned on three fronts, the judge said. Col. Samuel Hammond, a prominent gentleman of Georgia, and leader of the valiant Georgia Militia in the War of Independence, had been commissioned to raise an army of 2,000 men from the backwoods of his state and South Carolina. Their mission was to attack St. Augustine and secure Spanish Florida. He had already recruited 1,500 men, who were assembled and ready for war.

Commander-in-Chief William Tate was to take New Orleans with 2,000 men recruited from the Carolinas, descending the Tennessee and Mississippi rivers to join forces with a third unit. His agents were attempting to influence the Creek Nation to fight in support of the frontier army.

The third front would be led by George Rogers Clark, named major general of the invasion forces, with 2,000 men from the Kentucky and Cumberland frontiers. They would take the Spanish fort at New Madrid and forts downriver to Natchez, joining forces with Tate along the way, at a point not yet determined, and finally would capture New Orleans. The French fleet would block the mouth of the Mississippi, and New Orleans was expected to fall easily with support from resident Frenchmen and Americans. Simultaneously, a small force would capture and reduce St. Louis, which would become the principal place of independence for the Upper Country.

"So far, Clark has not met his enlistment goal," Judge Sebastian said. "He has no more than two hundred recruits, I hear, but he has laid in stores of powder, lead and beef at Clarksville, Tennessee, for the two thousand expected recruits. He has stored more than eleven hundred weight of bear meat, seventy-four cured venison, and many hams. Flatboats and pirogues are assembled for the trip, and the take-off point is the mouth of the Cumberland River. The original date for attack was set for mid-February, but now it's nearly May, and a new date has yet to be announced. It is imperative that the invaders embark from territory outside the U.S., in order to avoid government intervention."

"Do you believe the government will intervene?"

"Of course it will. President Washington has proclaimed that to embark upon the enterprise will be considered a criminal act, subject to condign punishment for those involved in the activities."

"That should be enough to make people think twice before enlisting or providing funds," Adam said.

"Of course, that doesn't mean the invasion will necessarily be aborted. There are too many determined leaders committed to the cause to stop them without more drastic means than persuasion. There are always the glory seekers, you know."

"We heard of an advertisement offering recruits cash inducements. It would require considerable cash to pay more than five thousand men. Won't finances be a key factor in their success?"

"Certainly. So far, General Clark has raised only four hundred dollars from his recruits. He has put up considerable cash of his own, and a few wealthy zealots have contributed. The whole operation could be suspended for lack of funds." Judge Sebastian leaned back in his chair and paused, as he gazed into space. "Now, Mr. Cloud, that is the gist of the affair, plans to this date, and the status of the mission. I would advise your governor that the whole operation looks doubtful. While he should be prepared, the Spanish need not fear an imminent invasion unless, of course, the U. S. government becomes a party to the cause, which is unlikely. Now, sir, do you have any further questions?"

"No, sir. You have made everything abundantly clear. In behalf of our governors, may I express my deep appreciation for your information, and for your candid assessment of the situation. I shall report everything from my notes, exactly as you have told it to me."

"Well, then," said the judge, "let us put all of this behind us and leave as soon as your brother returns. I am looking forward to a pleasant evening of conversation."

Adam's face did not reveal his inner turmoil. After his argument with Abner, he saw it was still possible that the United States might join the invasion, even though the judge believed otherwise. The government could still decide to support the French cause in repayment for the deep indebtedness for their help in the War of Independence. His life of the past four years, his prosperity in Natchez, and his hopes for the future flashed before him. He had been so confident that the American government would never collaborate with the French that the possibility was unsettling.

The following day the brothers visited the office of Peyton Short. The two lawyers were acquainted in the courts, and Adam's letter from Andrew Jackson resulted in a cordial welcome. Adam decided to include Abner as a listener, for he realized he could no longer hide from his brother the nature of his mission. They found Peyton quite open and willing to talk about what he knew.

"My brother William writes that the foment this Frenchman, Citizen Genet, has stirred is of considerable embarrassment to President Washington, and to the French representatives," Short told them. "Mr. Jefferson believes the French are trying to force an alliance for purposes of their war with Spain. William learned that De Fourges, the Jacobin Minister of Foreign Affairs, advised Genet to try to gain the confidence of the president, rather than influence segments of the population, in order to accomplish his mission. Thus far, Genet has not only failed to win U. S. approval, but the French Embassy now disavows his conduct. This has had little effect on changing his *modus operandi*."

"*Hmm. . .*" Adam mused, "and still the recruitment continues." Yet he felt encouraged from what he had heard. "If filibuster enlistment is considered a crime, then Citizen Genet will be guilty of stirring up treason among the populace, and the threat of a noose about one's neck should deter further enlistment."

"Of course. The next step, which brother William expects, will be a public rebuke, and a request for France to recall Genet. This may have already occurred, but it will be some time before we know for sure."

The men dined in warm camaraderie at a local buttery, and the evening lasted into late night over a bottle of port wine and cigars. The next morning Peyton introduced Adam at a horse farm, where he examined the stock and selected his cherished Kentucky thoroughbred. Abner watched with amusement as his brother lovingly stroked his new roan stallion, Capuchin II, and led him gently around the ring. He had never seen Adam so excited.

"It's a dream come true," Adam said, his face beaming. "I feel like a small boy again. I thank you, Peyton, for your assistance in making this deal." The stallion's price was dear, but Adam had traded the horse Don Manuel had given him as partial payment.

"My pleasure," Peyton Short said. "And may you realize many fine offspring from your new stock."

Adam was ready to leave the Sebastian home before noon. As he embraced his brother, his throat tensed with emotion. "Farewell, dear Abner. May you prosper here. When you are ready to marry I would be honored to perform the ceremony — just let me know in time."

Abner laughed to hold back his tears. "When I'm as lucky as you have been, you'll hear about it. Go with God, dear brother."

Abner and the Sebastians watched Adam ride away on his smart new stallion, with Dirk and the pack horse trailing him on the road to Louisville.

. . .

Adam found the Downses, his friends in Louisville, as warm and hospitable as ever. Their surprise and delight to see him was heartwarming, and Mason Downs insisted that he be their guest during his stay. Daisy praised Adam's changed appearance, in her soft Southern drawl.

"My, how you have filled out, and it becomes you. How long has it been? Four years? Oh, we have so much to catch up on!"

They talked into the night, exchanging news of Natchez, and of their mutual Louisville friends. Adam was again seized with a fit of homesickness when he spoke of Mary and the children. He felt the hopeless frustration of time and distance between them.

The next day Adam called upon Michael LaCassagne at his plantation on the Ohio River. LaCassagne's delicate airs and fastidious demeanor belied his rugged life as a planter, trader, extensive traveler, and agent-informer for Gen. James Wilkinson. He shared willingly with Adam the latest information of the Genet affair, recently gathered from a visit to General Wilkinson at Fort Washington. Most of his news was a repeat of what Adam had learned in Frankfort, but with several additions. The French Embassy had proclaimed the expedition a violation of French–United States neutrality, and had revoked the commissions of the illegal army generals Clark, Tate, and Hammond. Also, General Wilkinson had received orders for the army to prevent any expedition movements in the territories.

Adam felt that the information clearly outlined the U. S. position. He felt a weight lifted from his recent burden of worries.

"You can count on General Wilkinson to do everything he can to abort the plans," LaCassagne continued, "but he worries over where all of this commotion is leading Kentucky. If the expedition under French sponsorship had not been so appealing, the general believes the frontiersmen would have relied on him to secure the navigation rights in a more diplomatic way."

Adam noted LaCassagne did not reveal any hint of a Wilkinson–Spanish conspiracy. *When one stirs up a hornet's nest, one risks getting badly stung*, Adam thought. He almost felt sorry for Wilkinson.

"The situation in Kentucky is very confused now," La Cassagne concluded, "but Clark's fortified camp is four hundred miles below here, well within the Spanish border. Heavy persuasion continues for recruits, and there may be no stopping the forces once they assemble."

Adam sold the two remaining horses the next morning, and with Dirk and Capuchin II he boarded a small keelboat. The float downriver was less formidable than Adam's first journey had been; the keelboat had a sail, and the crew were experienced boatmen.

As they approached New Madrid, the sight of the Spanish squadron in port raised Adam's hopes that Governor Gayoso might be there, and his spirits soared when he saw the governor's small galleon. He requested the boatmen to draw alongside the vessel, and Adam hailed a sailor on board.

"Ahoy, sir. Is Governor Gayoso aboard?"

"Who inquires?" came the reply.

"Tell him Adam Cloud, of Natchez, with an important message, at his request."

A beaming Don Manuel appeared on deck. He waved to Adam and ordered a ladder lowered for him. On board, his greeting was jubilant. "My dear friend! I have worried about you. My relief at your safe return is boundless! Come to my stateroom and we can talk in privacy." He commanded an officer to inform the boat's patroon, waiting below, that their passenger would be returned shortly. In the meantime, they could visit the trading post.

Adam surveyed the sumptuous stateroom. "I am indeed impressed, Don Manuel. Your quarters are fit for the king!"

"Nonsense, Adam. It is only appropriate that I sail in comfort. But forget all that. Tell me what you have learned. I assume your mission was successful?"

For the next hour, over a bottle of port, Adam laid out for the governor the invasion plot, and other information he had recently received. He pointed out Judge Sebastian's assessment, the improbability of the filibuster, and LaCassagne's conflicting information of the frantic recruitment and Clark's fortified camp deep into Spanish lands. Don Manuel listened quietly, and when Adam finished he paced the floor in sober thought.

"You bring a wealth of information, Adam, but I do not like the discrepancy between the two major informers. I am bothered that there is no final conclusion from which to draw. There is no assurance that these plotters can be stopped. What are we to think?" He tapped his fingers together nervously as he considered the options. He then turned to Adam with a bright smile. "But your mission, Adam, was not in vain. We are better off knowing what you bring us. Now it is up to us to be ready for any contingencies that may arise."

"LaCassagne told me that he and Wilkinson now own the trading center here at New Madrid. He wants you to know he will continue to relay any messages and news of impending invasion to you through Captain Portell."

"Yes, the new arrangement has been fortuitous. I relay messages to Wilkinson in half the time, and receive news more quickly, direct from LaCassagne here."

Adam left the ship in a reflective mood. He sympathized with Don Manuel's dilemma, believing the threat to Spain was still embryonic. He had great respect for the governor, and trusted his judgment.

It was the last week in June when Adam disembarked at Cole's Creek landing. Dirk took the travel gear upstream in the freight canoe Adam maintained at the mouth of the creek. Adam galloped his stallion all the way home. Evenstar never looked more beautiful. The lush green of Junetime blanketed the countryside; the pungent odor of lofty, green cypresses and pines mingled with the intoxicating scents of magnolia blossoms, and a profusion of blooms surrounded the plantation in their summer glory.

Adam's happiness spilled over unashamedly into sentimental tears when he embraced his wife and his little family. The children shrieked with delight and covered him with kisses. Mary had never appeared more desirable to him than during the moment of greeting after this, their longest separation. He held her before him, searching her familiar face and form as though he could probe her very soul with his eyes.

"Never again must we be parted for so long," he said. "Oh, how I missed you!"

"And I you," she murmured, overwhelmed with happiness as she felt him close once more.

24 Father
Lennan

The next morning Mary told Adam a chilling tale that had happened at Evenstar during his absence. They had been terrified in the night by the nearby howling of wolves. Next morning they discovered a ghoulish voodoo hex with blood circles, and a snake hung from a branch of the front oak tree. On the following day, Mary had encountered William Vousdan in the village. In a loud and ugly manner, he had accused her of living in sin; that Adam had gone north to finalize his divorce from his wife, and that he frequented a brothel Under-the-Hill. She retorted that he should be ashamed of spreading lies about the Cloud family, and that he was guilty of cruelty to his wife.

"All of this took place with a group of spectators, right in front of the shoemaker's shop," Mary said. "Maamba said I really gave him a verbal punch, but I don't know. It was humiliating and demeaning, whatever the outcome."

Adam seethed with indignation, picturing her ordeal.

"You poor darling," he said. "What a terrible experience for you. But you showed amazing courage to stand up to him on his evil lies. He probably wasted no time spreading more malicious calumny, and some people will undoubtedly believe him."

He decided to bring suit against Vousdan, but first he must have absolute proof of his guilt. He thought he might obtain help from his former St. Catherine District neighbors. As soon as he could, he rode into town to John Bowles' plantation, where John and Jenny greeted him with surprised pleasure. They exchanged family news, and Adam described some details of his adventures on the Trace. Adam then explained his mission.

"Vousdan must be stopped," John said. "Joe Perkins has endured Vousdan's machinations longer than anybody. Perhaps together we can hatch a plot to catch the bastard as the source of the voodoo tricks and rumors."

The two men rode to the Perkins' farm. Joseph Perkins was equally sympathetic and amenable to any means that might prove Vousdan had perpetrated the tricks.

"I've an idea," he said. "The voodoo is obviously aimed at scaring slaves as well as your family. Let's engage them in our plan. One of my blacks is a trusted fellow who, I think, is skilled enough to tap some of Vousdan's blacks for information. I'm told he fancies one of the female slaves among the lot. I'll ask him to pry."

"That gives me an idea," John Bowles said. "Vousdan's overseer is a tight-lipped fellow, but I have long suspected he is terrified of Vousdan's temper, and probably suffers abuse. Under some pretext, I'll send my overseer there, and perhaps he can get him to talk. The men are somewhat friendly, but the atmosphere over there is so tense most of the time he doesn't stay around long. He says everyone on the Vousdan plantation is too nervous around outsiders."

Adam knew he could count on his friends, and he rode on to Government House to seek the governor's help. He found himself in luck; the governor had just returned from his upcountry forts.

"Welcome, Adam. I was about to send for you," Don Manuel said. "I wanted to thank you properly for your recent mission. What you did was above and beyond the call of duty. It was a very patriotic and courageous effort, and we are using the information you brought to further our defenses. Now, I promised you some land, and have set aside for you a plot of five hundred arpents on Bayou Sara. Here, let me show you." He produced a map and pointed out the acreage. "I hope it will be to your liking."

"It looks like great bottom land near the creek," Adam said. "I'm sure I will like it, Don Manuel, and thank you."

"Well, that settles it, then. Now, come with me." Don Manuel lighted a lantern. "I have something to show you."

Adam followed him to a small storeroom. The governor held the lantern high over a black leather saddle mounted on a rack.

Hand-tooled in intricate Moorish design, and exquisitely inlaid with silver, it was the most dazzling saddle Adam had ever seen. He examined it, touched it, turned it, and felt the smooth, sleek leather, tracing its pattern and the finely wrought silver with his finger.

"*Mmmm* . . . elegant," he purred, almost wordless in appreciation of its sheer beauty.

"It is yours, Adam. I had it made for you in appreciation of your valiant service. I could not think of a more appropriate personal gift. And now that you have brought back a Kentucky stallion, it is fitting that he wear a saddle to suit his image."

"What can I say, Don Manuel? I am overwhelmed with such gifts. I'll cherish this magnificent saddle to my dying day."

They returned to the governor's headquarters and Adam told Don Manuel about the lurid events at Evenstar, of the false rumors about him, and Mary's staunch defense.

"I am seething with anger, Don Manuel." Adam's face was grim and, as he spoke, his exasperation mounted and his voice crackled with wrath. "I have decided to bring suit against Vousdan as soon as I can prove he was the perpetrator of the viscious events. Can you imagine the cad using the fact I was seen coming out of a brothel, when the only time I was ever in one was the day I was summoned to see his dying wife? And you, of all people, know that I came to Natchez grieving over the loss of my wife, Anne."

Don Manuel shook his head in dismay as he listened. He had never seen Adam so filled with anger. "These depraved events are not trivial, Adam; they go far beyond pranks, and it is plain that Vousdan is out to destroy you with his poisonous tongue. I will do everything in my power to bring justice to you and Mary for defamation, and for pain of your ordeal. Proof is essential. Let me know when you have reliable evidence, and I will schedule a civil court with a jury of your peers to try the case."

Adam decided to take advantage of the governor's sympathetic mood. "One more thing, Don Manuel. May I have your final blessing to use James Moore's town lot for the school? We talked about it before my journey."

"Yes, we need that school. I have received tentative approval from the governor-general. It will be refreshing to undertake something less formidable than dangerous journeys and preparations for war. I will record permission for the lot clearance. Be sure to confer with me before any construction begins. I will need to see the structural design before we plan further.

"By the way," he added, "royal visitors are coming this month. General Wilkinson informs us that Prince Edward, Duke of Kent, will visit us in August. General Wilkinson will show him Fort Washington, and will bring him and his entourage downriver after he has seen enough of the United States. The general needs to see Governor Carondelet, and this provides him an opportunity to come without suspicion."

Don Manuel sighed. "He wants to entertain the duke here with a formal banquet, but that poses a dilemma. I am not sure we can afford the duke just now. Such an event will be a strain on the budget." His face crinkled with amusement. "I'm thinking of letting General Wilkinson share the honors — and the cost. You will receive an invitation when the banquet is scheduled."

Adam laughed. "I've never dined with a duke, and the experience should be unique. By the way, I have an invitation for you. Our next soirée is scheduled for July tenth, at John Girault's plantation, Richmond Hill. It is a series titled, 'What is Man?' Our first sub-topic is 'Life and Imagination.' Do come, if you can."

Interest, fanned by curiosity, brought a large group to Richmond Hill for the soirée. John Girault opened with a scholarly overview. He traced the forms of life from the simplest organisms to the more intelligent creatures, and compared them to man. He showed man's distinction above all other forms of life through his ability to reason, to enable him to use knowledge in an infinite variety of ways. Writing, science, philosophy, logic and mathematics, art were all products of imagination, enriching man's life without limits. "Like Ariadne's Thread," he concluded, "we can follow our line of imagination out of the cave of ignorance into infinite realms of beauty, of astonishing facts, of elegant analyses."

Adam had planned his conclusion in secular terms, but hoped it was inspirational enough to create a lively discussion.

"Primitive man found that there is a world beyond the one which greets the senses," he told them, ". . . a fleeting perception of a Higher Power revealed in and through the visible and palpable realm of nature. Man drew upon this dim perception, and discovered his soul. Lo! he has created a veritable Eden from the mind's realm. Man's independence to think and create, to imagine unknown possibilities, have brought great discoveries to the world."

He spoke of Joseph Priestley's recent contribution to chemistry, from its elegantly simple first components to the profound and complex chemical compounds which scientists were still trying to comprehend.

"We need to wipe the cobwebs from our minds, and let our imaginations discover new mysteries. Think of the glorious thoughts we can receive, if we open our minds to a universal river of wisdom! Such is the mind of the poet, who brings us concealed truths, and feeds us sublime thoughts couched in mysteries. Such is the mind of the holy men who opened their minds to revelation, and instilled a sense of worship in every civilization. The ancient Hebrews, who listened to Yaveh, the Oriental mystic, Buddha, the Hindu, Krishna, our Lord Jesus Christ, and later, the Muslim, Mohammed — all brought a spiritual truth, a revelation which pervaded religious thought in their lands. Through their apostles, they established a covenant with God throughout the world.

"Civilization is continually renewed by the discovery of new mysteries through the inner eye of the soul. It is only through creative thought that every truth has found its certainty. But we must be ever mindful of Pascal's observation: *Truth on one man's side of the mountain may be false on the other.*"

The meeting ended with thoughtful discussion, and some guests lingered to pursue their ideas. Adam announced that the next soirée would be held in the St. Catherine Creek District, with John Bowles as the host. The topic would be "Free Will: The Choice Within."

"How did we sound, Mary?" Adam asked anxiously when they returned home. "Did I overstep any bounds?"

"I hung on every word, Adam, appraising your point of view. Even though you touched on how imagination spawned religious thought, I hardly see how anyone could accuse you of promoting any particular religion. Your point of view was so broad, and covered so many elements of creative thought, it was enlightening. I liked it."

Adam's spirits soared at her praise. He hoped he had inspired a few minds.

Father Francis Lennan was a waspish man, quick to criticize any statement not in conformity with the Roman Catholic church. He accepted the Pope's every word as gospel, and strictly adhered to laws of the Ecclesiastical Council. He rejected any thought which deviated in the slightest degree from his strict interpretation of official dogma, and placed it in the category of cardinal sin. Toward those who disagreed, he was harsh and unbending, sometimes officious and tyrannical. In his vainglorious image of himself, he had created a mantle of superiority, reinforced by his cherished friendship with Father Patrick Walsh, vicar of the Spanish Province. He could communicate directly with the vicar, bypassing the established pecking order.

He now sat in the tiny cubicle which served as the church office, his face grim with disapproval as he listened to his visitor's tirade. William Harrison had attended the community soirée and was greatly disturbed by the content of the presentations and the discussion that followed.

"Father, those people were using quotations not only from philosophers and scientists who are controversial, in my opinion, but the Reverend Cloud also dared to suggest Bible prophets as examples of man's vivid use of imagination. He even defended the Jews' concept of a covenant with God, as though it was equal to the Christian covenant, and that the same applied to any inspired religion of the world! I thought the meetings were to be strictly secular. I'm a good Catholic, Father, and I found his references heretical."

William Harrison's report strengthened the priest's opinion of sinful Protestant theology, and that of Adam Cloud, in particular.

"I might attend these meetings myself, if I felt welcome," he said, "but, on second thought, I believe I could not sit through one without creating a scene. His Excellency has permitted the meetings, and I cannot protest. But I would like to be advised of their content, for I believe the governor has been misled, and we may all regret they are allowed. I want you to attend the series and report back to me."

"I will be your eyes and ears, Father, and tell you what I hear."

Left to himself, Father Francis mused on the problems of Protestant aggravation. He regretted his slim record of Protestant conversions to Catholicism. But his mission to build the church, under Gayoso's supervision, was circumvented by the governor's lenient attitude toward the heretics. He believed that Adam Cloud was using the soirées as a subterfuge to reach non-Catholics through philosophical and controversial ideas. This devious assault on the One True Faith must be curtailed, he decided.

The Baptist Reverend Richard Curtis, Jr., came to mind. As bold and brash as Curtis' zealous ravings were, at least he was honest and open, in his obnoxious way. The priest recalled his recent skirmish with Curtis. Unfortunately, it had occurred in public, near the entry to the Curtis compound, when Father Francis had been visiting a parish member in Selser Town. Curtis had stood at the gate bidding farewell to his congregation. As Lennan rode by, Curtis had called out to him.

"Ah, the Holy Priest! Father Francis, are you ready for redemption for the sins of idolatry? 'Worship of the Golden Calf,' Moses called it. Are not your statues made of gold? Your church-folk worship them as fervidly as the heathen worshipped the Golden Images at Mount Sinai."

Father Francis regretted now that he had let his temper get the best of him. He had reined his horse and retorted, "That, sir, is blasphemy and slander. It is you who are the heathen in your ignorance of the Holy Church. Would that you could take the time to visit my services and develop the true worshipful reverence that Christ intended when he appointed Saint Peter, His Chosen One, to perpetuate teachings of the church."

Curtis had retorted in loud derision. "True believers would burn in hell before they could be persuaded to worship amidst the lavish pomp and ceremony you flaunt in Saint Peter's name. It was from ignorance and false interpretation, not from Peter, that such rituals were devised to pervert true Christian worship."

The Baptist onlookers had applauded the Reverend Curtis. The whole episode had been demeaning, and Father Francis wished he could erase it from his mind. It was painful to lose face among the villagers. He would have to find a way to permanently discredit Curtis, and while he was at it, expose the duplicity of Adam Cloud. They were both dangerous to the church.

His indignation was further fanned by Father Gregory's news that, with the governor's permission, Adam Cloud's blacks were clearing a lot in town for a school near the parish church. It was humiliating that neither Father Gregory nor he had been asked to participate in this important plan. *Is the school another subterfuge for Protestant proselytizing, a way to spread their dogma?* The thought was insufferable and infuriating to Father Francis.

Mary pulled the gowns from her wardrobe and piled them on the bed. She held each one to her figure in front of the mirror. With a gesture of disgust, she threw one after another aside.

"Oh, Maamba, what shall I do?" she wailed. "Here I am in confinement again, and the biggest event of a lifetime is happening. I simply have to attend the banquet for the Duke of Kent, but I certainly can't get into any of these gowns. I'll have to order a new gown to cover my shape." She turned sideways and surveyed her swollen abdomen. "Ugh! I can't parade this figure in public and disgrace the Cloud name."

"Now, Miz Mary, don't you fret so," Maamba said. "You nevah show much anyway, an' you ain' so big yet as you can't go out in public. You gonna look jes' fine. Why don't you let me fetch Miz Mazie here? She one fine dressmaker, an' I jes' know she can make one of your gowns to cover you right. Maybe she kin fine enough of the extra material she save on this one." She held up the gray gown that was Adam's favorite. "Ain' nobody goin' see anything but a pretty lady when you strut in the doah."

"Maamba, you are a perennial optimist, and always encouraging. You are right. Please see that Mazie Carter gets a message that I need her."

"Yes, ma'am." Maamba left to dispatch a messenger to the Carters', and returned to put away the gowns.

Seated in front of her mirror, Mary surveyed herself as Maamba took the bristle brush and began to stroke her long, dark hair. Her twenty-five years were becoming to her, Mary decided. Face not too thin, no double chin, no little lines. The humid weather here was kind to the skin, keeping it moist and soft. She had been tempted to pluck her eyebrows once, but now they seemed attractive because Adam thought them so. She closed her eyes. Maamba could make her feel so relaxed . . .

Dear Adam. He was not yet thirty-five, and was an absolute perfection of manhood. So caring, so handsome, and so ardent a lover. She felt the arousal through her body that always came when she thought of his lovemaking. *Dear God*, she thought, *what a life you have given us. Everything seems to fall into place for Adam. He is doing well as a planter; he is so admired, and has so many friends, except for that dreadful William Vousdan. What more could any woman ask from life?*

If only she could continue to control her pregnancies. There would be twenty-seven months between Samuel and the baby she was expecting. Something had worked for her, and it must have been the rhythm cycle that Eliza had taught her. She would like to hold off another one now for two years, but never, never would she keep Adam at arm's length, as Anne had done. She wouldn't let his amorous flame die as long as her own blood ran hot with passion.

The Clouds joined the Formans in their coach, and set out for the banquet at Concord.

"You never looked lovelier, my sweet," Adam said, as he helped Mary into the carriage. Mary glowed with the compliment, confident that the redesigned gossamer gray gown, with flowing pink scarves, concealed her figure in becoming style. Now she could concentrate on the grand event itself.

"It seems beyond belief that Natchez could be entertaining royalty," Eliza said. "I can hardly wait to meet the future king of England. I wonder how many are in his entourage? Do you suppose they are all royalty?"

"I believe His Highness travels only with his officers," Adam answered. "He is on the way to take command of the British Brigade of Grenadiers, at Martinique."

"Didn't you tell me the governor is sharing the cost with General Wilkinson?" Ezekiel asked.

"Not only the cost, but it required him to share the honors too," Adam explained. He added, with a chuckle, "That means equal time for speeches and toasting the royal visitors."

"It's hard to imagine either man sharing anything equally with anyone. General Wilkinson is as grandiloquent a figure as Governor Gayoso," Mary remarked.

Concord was elegantly resplendent when Adam and Ezekiel escorted the ladies into the banquet hall. They joined the receiving line with other guests who represented the wealth and gentility of Natchez families. Mary thought Prince Edward, in full uniform, wore a mien of stately indifference and, as she curtsied, she thought him a rather ordinary-looking man for his royal blood and his lofty military title of major general. She reached General Wilkinson in the line, whose imposing stature distinguished him among men. Mary felt the magnetism of this handsome man, so full of vigor; his large face, which always exuded confidence, and his huge brown eyes were responsive with intelligence and attention.

Wilkinson greeted them with his famous smile and gracious air, very much at home as co-host of this gala event. He kissed Mary's hand. His eyes sparkled with genuine pleasure. "My army life now precludes travel to foreign territories, but who would ever expect British royalty to bring me here to see friends again? I trust we may visit together before I leave. I want to hear about your life together." He turned to introduce an officer of the Royal Grenadiers next to him.

And so it went, down the receiving line of officers to Colonel and *Señora* Grand-Pré, and the Stephen Minors, who graced the end of the line. Katherine Minor, dressed in her habitual yellow, made a splendid *finis* in a gold brocade gown.

"The Yellow Duchess must be suffocating in that heavy cloth," Mary whispered to Eliza. The August temperature was in the nineties, and the room was stifling hot.

"Any sacrifice for effect, my dear," Eliza answered. "At least we can be grateful for the artificial breezes." She indicated the dozen punkahs hanging from the ceiling, swung slowly back and forth by black youths dressed as Nubian slaves.

Adam found himself seated at table between Mary and Sir William Dunbar. The venerable gentleman's mind was a vast compendium of knowledge, and Adam enjoyed their stimulating conversation. The time arrived for speeches and toasts, and Don Manuel led off with a polished welcoming speech. Sparkling wit laced his stories and remarks, arousing laughter and applause in special tributes, and an elegant toast to His Royal Highness and his officers.

"Please remain standing," he added. "No welcome would be complete without an Invocation in the name of His Majesty, King Carlos of Spain, and of His Most Holy Catholic Highness, who blesses these shores of New Iberia. I call upon our good Father Gregorio White, of our parish *Iglesia Parroquial del Salvador del Mundo de Natchez.*"

Father Gregory rose, bowed to Prince Edward, and gave a Catholic invocation. As he concluded, Adam heard whispered remarks from Protestants seated around him, expressing their disapproval of a Catholic prayer before the royal adherent of the Church of England.

General Wilkinson arose and, with wit and polish equal to the governor's, charmed the guests with a tribute to King George III of Great Britain. Adam thought it unfortunate his speech then turned to the sensitive political issue of Continental control. He

congratulated the British for opening the North American continent to settlement, the Spanish for their far-sighted conquest by
treaty, and the Americans for their vigorous exploration and
expansion.

"The only losers are the Indians, who are being gradually dis-
possessed, and the French, who are now knocking at the door to
be let in again." Adam heard more gasps at this boldness. "We must
all admit that the tempting beauty and vast emptiness of this continent is hard to resist. In one way or another, we dream our dreams
of the land and what it means to us, either individually, or as patri-
ots of our own nations. Sharing its abundance and beauty is the
outcome of our peaceful intent, and for that I raise a toast to
Spain, and to the United States. May we share and prosper without
the pain of bloodshed and the despair of war."

Everyone applauded and toasted, and the meal progressed
with lively conversation and more tributes from the hosts.

As the meal and ceremonies were ending, Wilkinson rose and
raised his hands for silence.

"Our gracious Spanish governor has drawn upon the traditions of his Catholic nation for an invocation to this historic occasion." Wilkinson bowed slightly toward the governor and Father
Gregory. "Now, in honor of our illustrious guest, His Highness,
Prince Edward, and of His Majesty, King George, defenders of the
faith and the Church of England, may I call upon the Anglican
minister of this illustrious assembly, the Reverend Adam Cloud,
for a fitting benediction."

Adam was stunned. The blood rushed to his head, and he felt
his heart pounding wildly. He sat immobilized, trying to control
his breathing, while his mind raced through his predicament. An
Anglican prayer could be seen as an affront to the governor's well-
planned rites. Did he dare join Wilkinson's defiance of them? On
the other hand, the general had a right to half of the agenda. If he
declined it would only emphasize the religious controversy. Was
Wilkinson's invitation a mockery, or was it justified? He felt the
comforting pressure of Mary's hand in his.

Wilkinson saw his hesitation. "Ah, this has come as a total surprise to our Reverend Mister Cloud. My pardon, sir, for not giving

you advance notice. The occasion is so momentous that one cannot anticipate the unexpected. Please, sir, your benediction. Everyone rise."

Adam slowly rose, his heart still pounding. He dared not look at Don Manuel or Father Gregory, but he was conscious of many triumphant faces looking at him. The Duke of Kent inclined his head slightly, as though in encouragement. Adam bowed to the prince while his mind rapidly riffled through prayers and thanksgivings for special occasions from the *Book of Common Prayer.* Some were too long, others too Anglican in a mixed society. In a lightning-like decision, he chose one called "Peace Among Nations." In a confident voice, he prayed:

> "Almighty God, our heavenly Father, guide the nations of the world into the way of justice and truth, and establish among them that peace which is the fruit of righteousness, that they may become the kingdom of our Lord and Savior, Jesus Christ.   Amen."

He sank into his chair, and for the rest of the banquet heard hardly a word that was spoken. His mind was in turmoil. Had he chosen the right prayer? Should he have declined the request? Blast the general, anyway. And blast the governor. It was unfair to be caught in the midst of a subtle religious controversy while they jockeyed for position.

News of the banquet controversy spread rapidly next day when people turned out en masse for a dress parade of the Spanish troops. They escorted the British Grenadiers to the Landing, where the British and Colonel Wilkinson embarked for New Orleans.

The residents of Natchez were curious, not only to see the duke in person but to hear about the splendor of the banquet. Among the Protestant majority, gossip weighed heavily in Adam's favor. They considered it an insult for a Catholic priest to lead the Anglican prince in a strictly Catholic prayer. The loyal Catholics, meanwhile, criticized Adam for intruding into the religious prerogatives of their honored Catholic governor and priest. William Vousdan was busy among the crowd maligning Adam for one more offense. Oddly, General Wilkinson received no blame for requesting the prayer; only Adam suffered damage from the critics. The controversy spread, and the more Adam heard of it the more worried he became. He spoke of it to his most trusted critic.

"Does it seem curious, Mary, that Don Manuel has not once mentioned my banquet prayer in our conversations since then? I find it very odd, and am not sure where I stand."

"Whatever the reasons for his reticence," Mary answered, "I have never been more proud of you than at that very moment. Had you declined the request you could have created more controversy than actually occurred. And your choice of prayer was a stroke of genius."

Don Manuel's silence nagged him, however, and Adam finally broached the subject on a visit to Government House. The governor seemed cordial enough, but he did not ask Adam to be seated, as he usually did in their informal discussions.

"Don Manuel, since the banquet," he said, "I have heard many disparaging remarks, as well as encouraging ones, about my being asked to give the banquet benediction. I hope you are not among those who hold me accountable for the incident. It was extremely embarrassing for me, and I see no cause for my blame."

"Do you not, now?" Adam winced at Don Manuel's bitter sarcasm.

"You must surely know that I was caught off guard, totally unprepared for such a request by General Wilkinson. There was nothing I could do but find a message so neutral that it could not further arouse religious controversy."

A long, anguishing moment ensued before Don Manuel answered. He looked steadily into Adam's eyes. "You could have declined," he said flatly.

Adam was shocked. He had not expected rebuke; possibly a questioning, but not outright criticism from the governor.

"Would you not agree that my prayer was appropriate?"

"The prayer was all right, but you need not have accepted the invitation. After all, it was not a command."

Adam felt the sting of his words and retorted hotly, "Has it not occurred to you that you brought on the controversy yourself by ignoring the sensitive history of the Anglican and Catholic churches?"

Don Manuel's indignation mounted to fury. "Sir, you insult my judgment!"

"I am sorry you feel this way, Don Manuel. Please accept my pardon, if my act offended you."

With an exchange of stiff goodbyes, Adam left the governor with a heavy heart.

25 The Boiling Pot

The last days of the hot summer of 1794 had faded away, and the forests blazed with deep shades of bronze, crimson, and gold. Chimney smoke curled in the crisp autumn air, a welcome relief to slaves and settlers alike as they harvested the last of the crops. Adam's two plantations rendered bumper crops, and he held a combined harvest celebration for the slaves at the Bowles plantation at St. Catherine Creek. Mary stayed at Villa Gayoso, expecting to give birth any day.

Adam sat with Jenny and John Bowles on their porch, listening to the shouts of fun and confusion among the blacks as they roasted pigs, chickens, and ears of corn in the slaveyard.

"Have you wormed any information out of Vousdan's overseer about his villainous behavior?" Adam asked of his host.

"Yes, Adam, as a matter of fact, Clem will be here soon to pick up his blacks. He was scared to talk, but he hinted at a dastardly plot between Vousdan and your slave, Meg, to rattle your household with voodoo tricks."

"A collaboration between Meg and Vousdan!" Adam was incredulous. "How did they manage *that*?"

"A talk with Clem will clear it up when he arrives to collect his slaves, Adam. We might try some hot buttered rum to loosen his tongue."

When Clem arrived, the rum took its effect, and he gradually shed his inhibitions. "Meg was bribed," Clem said. "She was allowed to visit Kofi, her African husband, if she helped him."

"Her *African husband*!" Adam exclaimed. The story was getting more preposterous.

"Yeah," Clem's eyes crinkled with sly pleasure as he revealed this privileged information. "They wuz separated at auction. Master Vousdan offered to let Meg steal over at night and be with Kofi if she would agree to use her voodoo skills on you. He promised she would eventually be his slave if she helped run you out of Natchez. He also bribed her to run away. It wasn't only Meg who stole around your grounds with her voodoo at night, but Kofi and some of the blacks on our plantation helped. I wuz ordered to fetch a raccoon and strip his guts. Lordy but our niggers wuz put on over that trick. I didn't like doin' it, at first, but when I seen the ruckus it made, I got the laughs over it." Clem paused and snickered, his eyes darting back and forth between Adam and John. "Now don't 'spect me to say out loud that I done it. I ain't givin' out no testimony, even if you paid me."

They could get no more out of him, and he soon left with his slaves.

Adam stayed the night, and the following morning he rode to Joseph Perkins' farm. Perkins had good news. Vousdan's female slave turned out to be Binah, Hannah's personal servant. She might be able to substantiate some of the episodes.

"Now we are getting somewhere," Adam said, "but how do we get her to testify?"

"It will be a problem, Adam, but I'll offer to buy the female from Vousdan. I can then give her protection. It would be a good investment for expected progeny."

Adam gathered Jenny's midwife and his wagonful of slaves to return to Villa Gayoso, feeling confident he would have enough evidence to win a suit against Vousdan. But it was unlikely Vousdan's slaves and overseer would bear witness against their master for fear of a brutal beating.

As he drove through town, Adam stopped by Government House to update the governor on his Vousdan information. It was time to heal the breach between them, if any remained. To his relief, Don Manuel greeted him cordially, as though the banquet incident was forgotten.

"I believe I have enough proof of Vousdan's complicity in harassing us to take him to trial, Don Manuel —" Adam started to explain but was interrupted.

"Don't tell me the details, Don Adam. I must try the case as impartially as I can. Perhaps I already know too much." Don Manuel conferred with Secretary Vidal for an open trial date and turned back to Adam. "Saturday, December sixth is open. If that date is suitable, I will post the public notice on the government notice board, and send you a list of arbitrators you can choose from."

"That date is satisfactory, Don Manuel. I shall prepare to defend myself. Ezekiel Forman wants to represent me, but I would rather he be a witness in my own behalf."

That night Adam slept fitfully, in dread of the coming trial. Suddenly, he bolted wide awake as he felt Mary shake him. She cried out, "Adam, wake up! Our baby wants to greet the world!"

Adam took one look at Mary's tense face and aroused Maamba and Jenny's midwife to make ready. In another of Mary's miraculously easy births, and to their ultimate joy, the Clouds' second son, Robert Devereaux, was born.

The court case of *Cloud vs. Vousdan* proved to be a sensation for Natchez residents. The unusual accusations of malicious prosecution had been widely discussed, and the session drew a large crowd. Don Manuel presided, as magistrate. He marveled at Adam's thorough refutation of each act and lie against him, and at the credibility of his witnesses. But the Vousdan lawyer found many loopholes in unsubstantiated evidence and produced witnesses who could attest to Vousdan's innocence, including Father Francis Lennan. The four arbitrators rendered the verdict in a tie, and the case rested on Don Manuel's shoulders. He realized the case called for a display of impartiality.

"The case against the defendant, William Vousdan, as the perpetrator of the villainous acts and calumny against the plaintiff, Adam Cloud and his family, is placed in doubt by a split verdict. On the basis of this inconclusive vote, I hereby render the following judgment: The record will show that Adam Cloud, his family and heirs, have been unjustly harmed by the perpetration of malicious acts against his household by a slave and by numerous

336 The Righteous Rebel

accomplices. Great harm has also been suffered by the plaintiff
from unfounded rumors and lies repeated throughout the
province.

"It is the decree of this court that such acts, herein described,
and such rumors, as detailed in this hearing, be immediately ceased
by the unknown perpetrator, or perpetrators. Be it further understood that any future proof of such villainy will bring criminal
punishment on the head of anyone involved. May I remind you
that this is a Christian community, and that we must live together
under the precepts of our Christian faith, defended by his Catholic
Majesty and the Holy Roman Church. This case is hereby concluded."

Adam stopped by Government House on his next visit to
town to thank Don Manuel for his efforts in his behalf.

"How do you feel about the verdict, Don Adam? Are you as
disappointed as you appeared after the trial?" Don Manuel asked.
"I tried to be as fair, in your favor, as I dared to be."

Adam laughed at this oxymoron. "Disappointed, yes, but not
discouraged. It should put a stop to any further harassment and
wild tales from Vousdan. The indecisive conclusion still leaves
doubts in people's minds, and should deter him from further
aggression. From now on, people will take note of what he says
about others, and proof of slander will be verifiable from the
public."

"That's just what I meant by the decree. Vousdan is forewarned. He will always be suspect . . . And now for the most
recent news. I am glad you came, Adam. Because of your personal
involvement in matters of our defense, I thought you might want
to know what is happening. After our illustrious banquet, General
Wilkinson's visit with Governor Carondelet in New Orleans rendered astonishing results." He gave a wry smile. "His Excellency
reported, in a lengthy dispatch, that Wilkinson is deadly serious
about resigning from the United States Army. They discussed tentative plans for Spanish land grants, and other concessions to him,
subject to the Crown's approval." Don Manuel paused.

"Now get a good grip on your chair, Adam. This was the shocker. General Wilkinson made a stirring plea to His Excellency to *persuade the Crown that it lay in the best interests of Spain to open Mississippi navigation for Americans.*" Don Manuel paused again for effect and grinned when he saw Adam's astonishment. He pulled the dispatch from his desk. "Here, let me read Wilkinson's statement, which the governor copied for me:

'The impending French threats hang over our heads like hornets ready to strike. Not only have they openly declared war on Spain, but the hornet's nest in the States stirs unrest across the land almost assuring a frontier invasion. Think seriously about your position. If Spain were to make this official grand gesture, you would gain Kentucky and Tennessee as allies, thereby avoiding any eventual clash with the United States Government.' "

"Amen!" Adam was overjoyed. "A final solution! It would solve all your problems, Don Manuel."

"I sent the governor my approval, and he has taken up the matter of American navigation rights with Captain General Luis de las Casas, in Cuba. The general's pension will continue after his retirement. It is well worth the cost. His commercial and political ties are still valuable to us."

There, it was out at last! Adam thought. His lingering suspicions of Wilkinson's pension were true. Somehow, the pension seemed less dishonorable, now that the general had proposed the best solution to the Mississippi River problem, and even without guarantee of his new "nation." He had to hand it to the general; he was a skillful negotiator.

But Don Manuel added more. Exploratory discussions were under way. His Majesty's land possessions had to be protected if river rights were granted. The outcome might also include Missouri River rights. The possibility of a drastic Spanish turnabout had been beyond Adam's wildest dreams, and the subject preyed on his mind.

. . .

Mary sensed Adam was more disturbed than he showed. He spent more time in his chapel, and rode the countryside by himself. One day she found him in his study, writing rapidly. She approached his desk and placed her arms around his shoulders.

"Are you preparing for the next soirée, Adam? You seem so preoccupied lately. Are you ready to share your thoughts?"

"Of course, Mary. I have no secrets from you. This is a letter to General Wilkinson. Ever since Don Manuel told me of the possibility of the Spanish granting navigational rights to the United States, new vistas have opened for me.

"Since Wilkinson recommended that Governor Carondelet urge the king to grant free river rights, I believe I can call upon his geniality toward me to extract further information. The outcome will affect our lives immeasurably, and I will not rest until I know the results of official discussions on the matter. I have many questions to ask him."

"Such as?" Mary sat to consider this important matter.

"Such as, how would this new right affect the status of the Clark filibuster plans, and the French threat? Would it preclude all further aggression by frontier leaders? If so, and this is the key reason for my inquiry, does Wilkinson think the unthinkable — that an eventual treaty might be concluded which would soften the Spanish attitudes toward American culture and religious rights?"

"Oh, Adam, you still dwell on overturning the system, one way or another. You only court disaster!" The thought was ominous, and Mary's rising voice reflected her dismay.

"Not necessarily, Mary, but the subject cannot be left dangling now that such important changes might take place. I have described for Wilkinson the recent Natchez events, Curtis' defiant religious practices, and the danger of persecution in a revolt against unjust laws. I related what I said at the recent soirée. Here, you read it and see if you think I am being too bold."

Mary read the letter carefully. "That's a very diplomatic letter, Adam," she said. "Perhaps his reply will bring us hopes of peace and contentment."

Adam placed the letter in the hands of a gentleman traveling the Trace to Nashborough, thence to Louisville, care of Michael LaCassagne, Esq. He hoped for a reply by early spring.

Far from the Clouds' hopes for peace and tranquility, a series of tumultuous incidents rocked the district residents. Following his verbal vanquishment of Father Francis, the Reverend Curtis boldly opened his compound to the public to hear him preach. Not content with expanding the community audience, he preached in homes nearer to Natchez. Encouraged by greater audiences, he next preached in the town plaza. As the reverend's Natchez audiences grew, Father Gregory attempted to prevent any further blatant disobedience the next time Curtis preached in the plaza. The episode ended in a shouting match between priest and preacher. The spectators took sides, and news of the controversy spread, dividing the district into two factions.

News leaked out that Don Manuel had reprimanded Reverend Curtis and threatened him with expulsion if he did not cease the public sermons. Curtis was reportedly very defiant and stated that he had equal rights with anyone else. Adam worried over the dangerous direction Curtis had taken. Perhaps he could persuade him to tone down. He would invite the Reverend and Mrs. Curtis for a visit to Evenstar. Mary agreed to his plan.

"I would be happy to entertain them, but 'entertain' may be a misnomer." Mary laughed. "From your description, the man has no sense of humor."

The noonday dinner went well. Mary liked Mrs. Curtis; she had a shy, sweet quality that made her endearing. She revealed that she was related to the Reverend Samuel Swayze, Jr., and that they once attended his Congregational service at the Jersey Settlement.

"Samuel holds church services at his home, and outdoors in good weather," Mrs. Curtis said. "His son scouts the roads and entrances to his property on Sunday morning, and if there are no signs of Catholic intruders, he blows a loud horn, summoning his members to church. He sits in the hollow of an oak tree and reads from his Bible. The service I attended was very simple, in a beautiful setting."

"That is an astounding story," Adam exclaimed. "How does he get away with an open ceremony every Sunday?"

"He is fortunate to be free of spies," the reverend explained. "There is no separate Catholic parish down there, and the priests go only on a limited schedule, or when summoned for a marriage or a baptism."

After dinner, the ladies' talk soon turned to children and the home. Adam tried to converse with Richard Curtis on subjects of local interest, but the reverend's mind inevitably returned to religious topics. Adam invited his guest to see his chapel, where he displayed his cherished sacraments used in formal Episcopal services. Curtis showed little interest in them, and told him a chilling tale of religious repression.

"Did you know that Spain appointed a commissioner of the Holy Inquisition for the Louisiana Territory in 1787?" Curtis asked. "He was priest of a local New Orleans church. He instituted religious courts that led to the arrest, jail, and burning at the stake of those accused of heresy. His mission was so repugnant to Governor Miró that he petitioned the church to abolish the institution on these shores. The commissioner was removed and the Inquisition never gained a foothold here." He paused and looked at Adam. "Just think of our fate if any of us had spoken our minds then, even unintentionally!"

"That presents horrible images, does it not?" Adam shuddered at the thought. He decided that this tale was just the right opening for a discussion of Curtis' safety.

"Since your encounter with Father Gregory at the plaza," Adam began, "I have learned that people are shocked at your boldness, and I cannot help but worry that you will be arrested."

"God will protect me," Curtis retorted.

"If I may say so, you are not doing yourself, or your family, any good by openly defying the laws against public preaching," Adam went on. "You can play a strong role in religious life by bringing succor to those in trouble, caring for the sick, or the dying, and without preaching in public. I have found it difficult to live under the religious constraints. Perhaps I have stepped a mite over the line sometimes, but I try to abide by the law."

Curtis curled his lip as he spoke. "Yes, I have heard about your soirées, Reverend Cloud," he scoffed. "Do you think that you are fooling the governor or the idol-worshippers with your spurious title, 'Adventures of the Mind'?"

"The governor has given permission for them, and even attended one himself. He found no fault with the topics. 'A little stretching of the intellect,' he says. We are careful to stay away from sermonizing. We don't want to bring down the wrath of the Catholic church on our heads. I wish you would attend one of our soirées. You might find them stimulating."

Curtis responded with biting sarcasm. "I get all the stimulation I need from daily scripture reading." He paused a moment, looked keenly at Adam and continued in carefully measured words. "I refuse to be repressed any longer from performing my duties to God and to man. I shall marry any couple at their request, and baptize friends who are beseeching me to take them into communion with the Holy Spirit."

"That is shocking news, Reverend," Adam shook his head. "I regret that you seek trouble with so defiant an attitude. You are far too valuable to cause distress among your constituents."

"Be that as it may," Curtis said resignedly. "I defy anyone who tries to stop me. The Lord chides me for my timidity. I am bound to honor my covenant with Him to save souls. It is my destiny." He turned abruptly toward the chapel door. "Thank you, sir, for your hospitality. It is time Mrs. Curtis and I return home before the Trace becomes dark."

Adam saw the Curtises off with an unease he had not known since his arrival in Natchez.

The next day Adam rode to Canterbridge. There he found the Forman family in joyous turmoil over David Forman's arrival. After warmly greeting David, Adam announced news of his new-born son. With two arrivals to celebrate, the Formans embraced Adam into the festivities.

342 The Righteous Rebel

"David's years at Princeton have produced a mature mind, tempered with a sound store of legal knowledge. He is anxious to make use of it," Ezekiel said, with a wink at his son. "I am willing to turn over to David any of my clients who could use his sharply honed legal mind. Adam, perhaps you might welcome David's more up-to-date services."

"I would never discard your wisdom and advice, Ezekiel. But David, I will include you in discussion of my affairs. Right now I need you both on a matter of grave importance. Eliza as well."

Adam looked so serious that Eliza was summoned to hear his problem, and the three listened in rapt attention as Adam poured out his concerns.

"I came today to consider the implications of the Reverend Richard Curtis' religious activities," Adam told them. "I believe the present direction of events casts a shadow on my own activities, and on the Reverend Samuel Swayze's also."

Adam recounted his effort to persuade Curtis to desist from his unlawful activities, and of Curtis' decision to marry and baptize anyone who requested it. "I am concerned for my own religious rights, and fear great public upheaval if Curtis stirs the populace further."

"Your predicament is indeed precarious, Adam. Something curious happened recently that seemed also offensive," Ezekiel said. "It took place at the Natchez church, where we attended a multiple wedding of three Protestant couples. All the guests were seated in the church. The altar boys lit the candles, and everyone anticipated the appearance of Father Gregory and Friar Brady in the sanctuary. Suddenly, Joseph Vidal appeared instead. He said, 'Please accept Father Gregory's apologies. It was necessary to make a sudden change of plans, and we must postpone this event'."

"Everyone buzzed, curious and excited," Eliza added. "This was most unusual, to say the least."

"Secretary Vidal held up his hand with a plea for quiet," Ezekiel went on. "He said, 'Please, I beg of you, take no offense. Just rise and leave the church quietly. We will be in touch with the families of the brides and grooms later.' Well, you can imagine the uproar from the guests. Everyone felt insulted. I have a standing appointment to see Don Manuel about this event as soon as he returns."

"The governor was away when it happened?" Adam asked, alarmed over this peculiar affair. "Could it mean that, in his absence, a change of policy has taken place toward Protestants?"

"That's exactly what I intend to find out from the governor," Ezekiel said. "Several others will go with me for the interview. They are outraged over the whole affair, which hasn't yet been explained."

Don Manuel groaned at the load of dispatches on his desk. "There must be an end to frustration short of jumping in the river," he said to Joseph Vidal. "I am exhausted, and have not caught up on my sleep."

He had just returned from a grueling trip. Traveling by horseback on backwoods trails, he had inspected inland fortifications and, at the same time, tried to placate the Indian tribes who always misunderstood the Spanish goals. All the while, he had received continuing reports of the pending American invasion which he could not disregard. Governor Caronedlet made repeated demands to tighten the defenses and increase the manpower in the Northern territory. Now, as if there were not enough worries, Reverend Curtis was acting beyond reason. Curtis had to be curbed, but Don Manuel was reluctant to make an example of him lest it stir up the Protestant community. His present concern was how to deal with enraged families over another matter.

Vidal had forewarned Don Manuel of the indignation felt by the families whose weddings had been postponed, so he was prepared when a deputy announced the arrival of Colonel Forman and two other settlers for their appointment. The governor made an effort to subdue his inner turmoil before he asked Vidal to show them in. He greeted them by name, and asked that they be seated.

"What may I do for you, gentlemen?" he asked graciously.

"Your Excellency," Ezekiel began as cordially as he could, "your presence has been sorely missed in this town. Too many important things happen while you are away. I am sure you are

344 *The Righteous Rebel*

aware of the wedding postponement at the church. We three were present with our wives and children, and I can assure you the incident was an unpleasant shock to everyone. On behalf of the aggrieved families and guests, we have come to inquire if there has been a change in the policy that offers Protestants a church wedding by a Catholic priest. The restrictions on Protestants make it impossible to have our own churches and weddings, and now people do not know what to expect."

"Please, Don Ezekiel, let me explain," Don Manuel said with a weary look. "It was an occasion we regret immensely, but, at the time, it seemed right to protect Father Gregory White. Only several people knew that he has suffered epileptic seizures since childhood. Just prior to entering the church for the marriage ceremony, he had a particularly violent seizure. Friar Brady sent a messenger to Government House, and, in my absence, Colonel Grand-Pré decided to cancel the ceremony to protect Father Gregory's long held secret."

The three men were silent; the explanation was totally unexpected. But the governor was not speechless. The confrontation suddenly got the better of his natural poise, and all his frustration over uncontrollable events suddenly surfaced in anger.

"Now, *Señors*, I would like to have my say," he began. "Your suspicious attitude toward government intentions gives me cause to doubt your own intentions. My administration does not change laws without official announcement. In light of your demand for explanation of our intent, I have every right to demand the same of you. I want a reaffirmation of your loyalty oath, which you took as subjects of the Crown. These are perilous times for our country, and it is incumbent upon every subject to show his and her loyalty to His Majesty, and to uphold the laws and edicts promulgated through his sovereign rule."

To their astonishment, the governor ordered Vidal to bring a copy of the Loyalty Oath which they had taken years earlier. He directed them to stand. With the document in hand, and with a grim face, he stood before them and read the oath. When he finished he added, "Now, do you faithfully reaffirm this oath and swear allegiance to the king and country? If so, raise your right hand and say after me, 'I do swear allegiance to His Majesty, King Carlos, and the dominion of Spain'."

After they swore allegiance, Don Manuel dismissed his visitors with a brief "Thank you." He could see they were chagrined and hurt that he felt the ceremony was necessary. After all, he thought, they were his friends, and it was difficult to imagine disloyalty from them. Nevertheless, the church could not be threatened, he decided, and he could not be too careful. Questioning their loyalty was a good way to spread the message to behave among those who had disloyal tendencies.

Father Francis Lennan now enjoyed the distinction of serving the principal parish, comprising most of the Catholic families in and around Natchez district. After his transfer from Villa Gayoso to replace Father Gregory, he soon learned that the parish was a center for Natchez information. The priest's role carried more responsibilities and added burdens not experienced in outlying communities. Residents from both parishes turned to him for guidance, increasing his importance to the faithful. He hoped that his influence among the Catholics would extend to the Protestants.

Father Francis looked at the pile of memoranda Friar Brady had placed on his desk the previous evening. One letter bore the governor's seal, and he opened it eagerly. He thought it would be a reply to the request he had made of the governor last week for use of the empty lot next door to his house. His face fell as he read. The governor denied his request for his frivolous use of the lot, pointing out that town lots were designated strictly for tradesmen and business headquarters.

He found it to be an infuriating answer. He wondered about the lot Adam Cloud was clearing for a school. The governor had been very lenient when it came to favoring his friends.

The more Father Francis thought about it, the angrier he grew. Now that he was the principal parish priest he would have to assert himself more forcefully, especially in the matter of education. Was the governor considering a school without the proper church curricula? Was the curricula to be chosen by Adam Cloud too? Surely this matter should be handled by higher church authorities, he believed. He would write to Vicar Walsh for his thoughts on establishing a school in Natchez.

26 Religious Rebellion

Mary held baby Robert to her breast, rubbing her hand over his downy head as he nursed. Now back to normal activities, she felt vibrant, exuberant, happy when she considered her little family. Everything in the Cloud world seemed right and wonderful . . . if only Adam were not so upset.

Ever since that day of Reverend Curtis' visit, Adam had been different. He pored continuously over his books, and the subjects centered on freedom of speech. He wrote copious notes from Jefferson's *Ordinance of Religious Freedom*. Mary recalled it was written at a time when the established Church of England had a stranglehold on Virginia's government, and religious intolerance of other sects was rampant. Jefferson struggled to get his ordinance adopted by the legislature, but his perseverance had finally won out with result of a clean separation of church and state. Religious persecution gradually subsided in Virginia, and Jefferson's treatise became the basis of the American constitutional right to worship freely without government interference.

She noted that Adam was also reading Montesquieu, Calvin, and other proponents of human rights, among them a recently acquired folio of ringing speeches made by defenders of the French Revolution. Mary broached the subject that evening as they retired for bed. She looked at Adam in the mirror as she swept her brush through her hair.

"You appear to be deep in the study of freedom of speech. Isn't your next soirée topic on 'Free Will'?"

Adam was struggling with his boots. "Of course," he replied, " but how can you separate free will from freedom of speech? Free

347

will becomes a matter of conscience, no matter how we address the subject, and one cannot avoid the direction in which it leads. The more I study for my presentation, the more I am impressed with the significance of man's conscience as he uses his will, as he makes his choices."

"I can guess what you may be trying to do. Adam, don't rock the boat for religious freedom. You fear that Curtis will be in real trouble if he continues to abuse the government religious privileges."

Adam slipped into his nightshirt and a warm robe. "You uncannily read my mind, sweet one." He grinned, and took over the brushing of her hair. "If we do not stand up for the right of freedom of expression, whether it be on religious thought, or any other opinions, the Protestants will never gain any ground here in this rigid Catholic country. I now realize we Protestants have been very timid. We have obediently cowered under the restraints upon us. My own conscience nags me for repressing my convictions."

Mary turned to face him. "My dearest, the politics of religion can be very dangerous, as we know from the American experience. Here I fear it is even more dangerous than we can imagine under the awesome power of church and state. Please, please, Adam, do not assume the burden of trying to overturn the system by yourself."

"There is no way I can overturn it, my sweet." He posed a wicked grin. "I will not try to overturn anything but you. And that I can do." Adam pulled her to bed, flung himself beside her, and wrapped her in a tight body hug.

Mary's advice was sobering, and Adam decided to confer with John Bowles before he completed his part of the "Free Will" lecture. John's overview would open the subject.

"I see this as an opportunity to speak out for religious freedom, even civil disobedience," Adam told him. "Mary scolds me for being too rambunctious, but if we don't speak out for the Reverend Curtis' rights, where will our own religious future lie?"

"Mary is right, Adam. That's very radical thinking, and is dangerous in such a controversy. Perhaps we should just let Curtis boil in his own juice."

"No, John. If we sidestep this issue, we will be less than honorable men. I would like to face it head on, and try to vindicate Reverend Curtis, no matter how much I disagree with the way he expounds."

"We might lose our right to hold our soirées if we go too far," John cautioned.

"Not if we are careful about what we say. I wouldn't want to get our associates in trouble, nor myself. But I believe I can inject some subtle ideas into our subject that will put the bite on the present laws, which are an infringement of free speech. Curtis is right to speak out. There is a religious vacuum among the Protestant majority, and they need community churches where they can turn for solace."

"You are very convincing, Adam. I'll go along with you, provided you use a subtle touch in your presentation of 'The Voice Within.' It can be a small step toward a long-term goal."

Guests attending the soirée at the Bowles plantation were a mixture of Cloud friends in the St. Catherine Creek District, some who had attended Adam's several services, and others they had tended during illness. Some came out of loyalty and admiration for the Clouds; others were attracted by the topic.

Adam had written his speech carefully to avoid controversy, but hoped it would challenge his audience to think and act through informed reason. He warmed to the subject as he spoke, and his convictions began to seep through the prepared speech. His sense of self-preservation cautioned him not to go too far, but his sense of justice prevailed. He finally threw caution to the winds and spoke his final words fervently, without a text.

"How we choose, and what we choose to act upon, is ultimately dictated by our own conscience. But conscience cannot act under suppression. Conscience must be free to choose, and to voice its convictions wherever they lead the individual, whether in matters of human relations, justice, government, or religion. And having chosen, we must be free to act, provided the action does not harm others. Just as we have the right to choose our religious beliefs, we have the right to express them openly.

"The jewel of Christianity is many-faceted, and can be viewed from various points. But Protestant views are not tolerated here, and Protestants struggle to uphold their faith and preserve their traditions under very trying circumstances. Every church needs to defend the faith, to preserve its traditions, Catholic or Protestant. Every Christian church should have the right to open its doors, spread the Word, welcome any believers and defend its tenets and property. That, my friends, is the ultimate voice of Free Will — action from choice — the Voice Within."

The listeners had been stunned into silence. When discussion finally began, the Protestants were stirred as never before, and the Catholics shocked beyond recall. Difficult questions were posed and left unanswered, many comments bounced off the wall, and the audience left frustrated but stimulated by the arguments. The Clouds spent the night with the Bowleses, and they discussed audience reactions far into the night.

As Adam prepared to extinguish the bedside candles, Mary remarked, "You really opened Pandora's box, and nothing will be settled unless the community keeps the subject of free speech alive. I only hope you will not be in trouble for your outspoken views."

The letter in Father Francis' hand exactly suited his purposes, and he perused it a second time. He shared it with Friar Brady, who read it with astonishment. The letter read:

Dear Sir, I was to hear Mr. Cloud the other Sunday and was very much suppris'd to hear him speak as he did. he made mention to his hearers that he did not know how soon it might be that there might be a stop put to their injoying their Religion in Publick and I thought his conversation was rather inflameing the minds of the People and he allso took his text agreable to it, he urged them to hold out at the risk of lives and property. It appeared to me that in case government thought it proper to silence them, he wanted the people to inforce it. I never was moore surpris'd in my life to hear such language from any man who was so favor'd as to be permitted to speak in publick. I can prove all I say, if you desire it. I am rally afraid both him and Curtis will currupt the minds of the people if there is not a stop put to them. It is not only once or twice but he always is upon this same subject moor or less. I first thought to of mentioned this matter to His Excellency, But again I concluded to you would be sufficient. If required I can be moore full upon the subject.

I am, Dear Sir with the Greatest Respect,
y.r Affectionate Humble Servant.
Joseph Harrison

Father Francis spoke triumphantly to his assistant. "Now, at last, this letter is something irrefutable that I can report to our superiors."

Friar Brady looked up from the letter with bewilderment. "Mr. Harrison's report does not sound like the Adam Cloud I have come to know," he said. "I assisted in his marriage, attended his celebration, and learned to know his character since then. He is a kind, personable man, and I understand he does good works among his Protestant following. Why did Mr. Harrison bypass the governor and send his letter directly to you? Was not that an affront to His Excellency?"

"It is well that I received the note," Father Francis answered, "and it was entirely proper in the governor's absence. His leniency with Protestants is a matter of concern, not only for the church, but now you can see the faithful are alerted to this danger. I shall write to Governor Carondelet and enclose the letter. Eventually it will reach Father Walsh. It is advisable to have the letter on file with the church hierarchy, especially the vicar for the Spanish Province; that way any reports of Cloud's future activities will be better understood."

Father Francis felt an inner triumph. At the rate the Protestants were defying the church, he judged they would hang themselves before long.

. . .

Adam felt peevish and frustrated. He couldn't sleep at night. Important issues hung in the balance, incomplete. The last soirée had ended in confusion. Adam had tried to get the committee together, but members made excuses for not meeting. He was convinced that the soirées were the best method to continue the dialogue on free speech, and he spoke to Mary of his concerns.

"Adam, your heart is in the right place, but the message from your friends is clear," she said. "Your performance at the last session has been called into question. You turned the meeting into one of dissention, and many people do not enjoy such discourse."

"What do they expect?" Adam retorted. "No venture up the mountain of knowledge can skirt the paths of controversy, for the mountain looks different from every side. That's what the meetings are all about."

Mary was filled with apprehension. "Adam, you are out of step with the social order. I worry that you are obsessed with freedom of speech. I urge you to go no further."

In his heart Adam knew Mary was right, but his indignation continued to mount over Reverend Curtis' position. He realized he had been too compliant. His compulsion to preach and his mission to serve others was too strong to ignore.

He met separately with the committee members and found them reluctant to continue the soirées, unwilling to be identified as dissenters. He suggested topics of Tolerance, Prejudice, Justice, and Fear. No subject was deemed acceptable, and he realized his friends had lost interest in presenting the soirées. Adam decided to proceed without them. He had Don Manuel's permission for the soirées, and for private home religious services; he reasoned either event would receive the governor's approval.

Mary cautioned him. "Your favorite topics are explosive, Adam. Just be careful how you present them."

To Mary's surprise, the following Sunday meeting drew a crowd, with standing offers from residents to hold more in their homes. The soirées continued into the spring, with Adam expounding his themes as Mary's fears grew.

A cascade of events began to fall upon the Natchez province, adding meaning to Adam's sermons and speeches, and greater resolve to his mission to lift restrictions for Protestant preachers. The Reverend Curtis increased his indiscretions, precipitating the first event. Father Francis received a letter from a Catholic named Paul Skinner that prompted immediate action. Scribbled on rough paper in a childish, laborious scrawl, the letter described the marriage of Phoebe Jones and John Greenleaf by the Reverend Curtis, and the public baptism of Willard Chamberlin and Steven DeAlvo.

Father Francis glowed with satisfaction. This letter held the proof he needed, and now Curtis would have to account for his misdeeds. He selected official church paper from his desk and wrote two letters, one to his mentor, Father Walsh, in Cuba, and the other to *Commandante* Grand-Pré, who was acting in the absence of Governor Gayoso. He delivered the letters to a deputy at Government House. Within minutes he was summoned into Grand-Pré's office.

The *commandante* got right to the point. He thanked him for the information, and assured him that the report would be thoroughly investigated and corroborated. The government would act upon the matter, and he would forward Father Francis' letter to the vicar at once.

Father Francis returned to his church doubly gratified. This turn of events was more favorable. In the absence of Governor Gayoso, Colonel Grand-Pré could be counted on for stricter compliance with the law.

A few days later, parishioners informed Father Francis of a warrant for Curtis' arrest posted on the government notice board. The priest hurried over to read the news for himself. Not only was the Reverend Curtis named in the warrant, but those who had received baptism were included.

News of subsequent events hit Natchez like a prairie fire. Soldiers sent to arrest the men at the Baptist compound found the preacher and his friends had fled. Posses searched for them in vain. Speculation was rampant that they had been forewarned by sentinels posted at the compound and had escaped into the woods. Some residents were elated at their escape; others seethed with condemnation. The religious controversy revived anew, and the debate over Curtis' activities raged throughout the district.

Adam felt genuine alarm. He slept poorly and awakened mornings with a feeling of emptiness, as though something incomplete nagged at his subconscious. He could not get Richard Curtis' plight off his mind.

"You need a calming down period, Adam," Mary advised him. "You mustn't try to carry Reverend Curtis' burden. He acted deliberately, not innocently. It does not reflect on you."

But the more he thought of it, Adam rationalized his own position. He had been so careful, so law abiding, except for the Jackson wedding, for which he felt exonerated. Any preaching he had done was with Don Manuel's knowledge, and sometimes his permission. Staying within restrictions was commendable, but he did not feel good about it. He was convinced he had failed in his mission. To what use is any clergyman, he reasoned, if he has to subdue his very purpose in life, his calling to minister and spread the Gospel, the love of God? His life had become a contradiction. The Reverend Curtis had led the way for Protestant resistance to the repressive laws against them.

Father Francis strode briskly to Government House, answering a summons from Colonel Grand-Pré. The acting-governor greeted him gravely.

"Father, I believe your personal assistance in the Curtis case entitles you to know of its progress," he said. "I am sure that this confidential official correspondence will interest you."

The priest unfolded the letter and saw it was from Governor Carondelet, addressed to Governor Gayoso in care of the *commandante*. The letter read:

> . . The Curtis case proves that if disputes and quarrels over religious matters are not cut off at their roots or checked, they will have the most perverse and evil results. I leave the matter to you and to the district priests to keep watch over this dangerous trend, monitoring the activities of the Ecclesiastical Ministers, and taking what action is necessary under the circumstances that might occur.

Father Francis returned the letter to Colonel Grand-Pré, clasping his hands together to hide their trembling. His emotional jubilance was almost overwhelming, and he chose his words carefully as he spoke.

"You can count on me, Your Excellency, and on the church faithful, to monitor the situation carefully. The two Protestants who bear watching now are the Reverend Swayze and especially the Reverend Adam Cloud. If he oversteps his bounds you shall be informed."

Reports to Governor Carondelet of mounting Protestant activities became more distorted with every dispatch. Father Francis made sure his letters about Adam Cloud joined the pile of evidence which the *commandante* sent to New Orleans and Cuba. Even Ezekiel Forman's meeting with Governor Gayoso, questioning the intent of the Catholic church, became part of the record in a growing list of indictments for unlawful religious activity.

Another local event aroused bitter controversy. During one of his brief returns to Natchez, Governor Gayoso granted the planters a hearing to discuss the expiration of the three-year Tobacco Stay Law. The public hall in Government House was filled with a crowd of angry gentleman planters, yeomen, and merchant creditors. Adam attended out of sympathy for the planters, anxious to see justice prevail for those who were still heavily indebted. One by one the farmers rose to illustrate the problem and to demand another extension on their debts.

As he listened to the animosity unfolding, Adam's indignation mounted toward the unknown Spanish officials who had created this long-standing tobacco problem, causing bitterness and dissension. His mind crowded with thoughts, and he felt compelled to speak out on the injustice. He swept away his reluctance to make accusation, and stood to speak. His heart pounded fiercely. He hardly recognized his own voice as he spoke.

"This is a shocking experience and a sad day for Natchez, with its residents displaying vituperation and insults. Debtors and creditors, good farmers and honest merchants are at each other's throats; and all because of a gross act of injustice by Crown officials. From my purview, I see disloyalty generated by an insensitive government decision, and consequent mistrust of government by its subjects." He cleared his throat.

"There are other insensitive government decrees which also create a gaping hole in our social fabric. Such injustices create a devisive society, and when the state acts against its loyal subjects they cannot know what to expect. What *can* we expect next? The greatest loyalty is engendered by governance designed to *protect* the king's subjects, not to *persecute* them or bring them to financial ruin."

The listeners applauded. Adam sat, his heart still pounding. He was short of breath, and his legs felt weak. He thought he had made an honest protest, but was unsure of how he should feel about it. He looked at the governor. *What does Don Manuel think?* he asked himself. *None of this should fall upon his head.* He determined that he would make amends with Don Manuel as soon as possible.

Don Manuel did not respond to Adam's heated soliloquy. Instead, he waited for order, and calmly assured the angry planters that he would submit their request for relief to New Orleans. He then adjourned the meeting. The crowd filed noisily outside, and Adam felt his shoulder tapped from several sides.

"What did you really mean in there?"

"You were just getting started when you sat down. Why don't you finish it off and tell us what you had in mind?"

Adam stopped, and a crowd gathered around him. "Not here," he said, dreading that Don Manuel might overhear. "We can walk to the plaza and I will lay it out for you as I see it."

By the time Adam reached the public square, the crowd around him had multiplied, drawing curious shoppers and merchants from their booths and tables. Adam recognized the need for caution, but he decided to amplify his thoughts on justice and free speech. A hush fell over the crowd as he stood on a bench and cleared his throat. He began with the text he had chosen for his next sermon.

"People have demanded justice from their government since ancient times, and the Lord demands that judgment be just. The

Bible tells us, in Isaiah 59.14: *And judgment has turned away backward and justice standeth afar off, and the Lord saw it and it displeased him that there was no judgment.*"

Adam quoted stirring speeches from French Revolution leaders on the inalienable right to freedom. As an extreme example of repression, he described an ancient Roman law which specified the crimes of *lese-majeste,* four crimes of treason which impaired the majesty of the Roman people, and which carried with them the punishment of death.

"There came a time, under Emperor Augustus, when he extended the *lese-majeste* crimes to indict those whom he wanted to punish. Subsequent emperors kept adding more clauses in order that they might place citizens under proscription, until none was exempt. The slightest action became a state offense. A simple look, a careless word, or even silence became *lese-majeste,* an act of disloyalty.

"This is our fate if religious forces are politicized to the point of declaring treason for innocent acts." Adam paused and looked around him. The crowd was transfixed, poised in thought. He felt encouraged and continued.

"That is what I meant when I asked, 'What can we expect next?' Justice is served only when government is equally just to all of its subjects. Under our governance, justice is served with two separate court systems, the system of *fueros,* for the Catholics, with special protection under the shield of the church, and another less protective system for Protestants. Some subjects here are more free than others, and we must speak out or we may lose more freedoms than we have now."

Adam took a deep breath and stepped down from the bench. The crowd murmured quietly among themselves. He hoped his words, spoken from the heart, touched a raw nerve in those who recognized their own thoughts. He felt a tap on his shoulder and turned to see an orderly.

"You are to come," the soldier said. "His Excellency waits for you."

. . .

As he faced Don Manuel, Adam could see his displeasure. His grim, unsmiling face searched Adam's without his usual look of compassion and understanding. Adam felt his throat tighten, and spoke first.

"I must speak what is in my heart, Don Manuel."

"No need, Don Adam. I know you well enough to read your mind, and I have seen this crisis building up in you ever since your return from the north. Where do you think this attitude will get you? Speaking out is one thing, but to insult the government that protects you borders on treason. From your very nature I know you are not capable of that, but how can I defend you?" He did not wait for an answer.

"I have been meaning to summon you ever since I received an ominous letter from Governor Carondelet. He was shocked over the Curtis affair, and someone has been writing him about your sermons, and about the soirées you and your friends presented. His information is undoubtedly cluttered with exaggerated and misinterpreted reports of your statements. But he demanded that I explain my lenience in allowing you to preach openly, when it is forbidden.

"I want you to know how I explained my decisions to him. I defended your soirées as public events requested by others of intellectual pursuits, and I described them as nonreligious. I attested to hearing one of them myself, and explained that it was thought-provoking, but harmless. I sent him a list of proposed future topics drawn up by the group. I praised your own intellect and prodigious scope of knowledge as an asset to the community. I cited your unceasing efforts to serve others, and your well-deserved popularity. I then reminded him of your selfless and dangerous journey up the Trace to bring back information vital to our defenses. I cited your contribution as one far beyond average acts of loyalty and devotion to the Crown."

Don Manuel paused and looked for Adam's reaction. Adam sat perfectly still, chin in hand. Don Manuel continued.

"I defended you as honestly as I could, Don Adam, and I ask you, what more could I do? Please do not destroy the crown of mercy that I have tried to place upon your head. Chances are slight that you will be regarded by other officials with such tender favor as I have for you, but my words may have helped a little. You have enemies who have joined the clergy in maligning you. It is my deepest wish that you not be hurt, or suffer in any way from the indiscretions of the Reverend Curtis. Stop defending him. Let your anger subside, for your fate is no longer safe in my hands alone."

Adam gave a deep sigh. He noted the governor had added the formal prefix "Don" to his name when he addressed him. He felt thoroughly chastised, but he was not cowed. He was emotionally touched by the defense and friendship of this gentle, noble friend, but he would not argue his case with him. He cherished their friendship too much to defend his position.

Both men stood and Adam affectionately placed a hand on Don Manuel's shoulder. He spoke tersely. "I understand, my good friend, and I am deeply grateful for your support." He left the chamber without further words.

In late January Adam was surprised to receive a letter from General Wilkinson. It was posted from New Madrid, and explained the early response. Wilkinson's letter was cordial, and he spared no words to express events and his vision of the future. He wrote:

> I have resigned from the Army, and have turned over Fort Washington command to Capt. Henry Harrison. I am in New Madrid where I have a trading center in partnership with Michael LaCassagne, and maintain close relationships with both Spanish governors. My presence here is closely related to the cause of which you enquire.
>
> Capt. Thomas Portell, commandant of the fort, has been commissioned to work with me and several distinguished advisors. Mr. William Short represents Mr. Jefferson. We are to draft negotiation for free navigation of the Mississippi and Missouri Rivers by U. S. citizens. Our suggestions indicate a treaty of greater magnitude than the limited conditions of our original assignment. We are proposing a treaty which could change the course of Spanish-American history on these shores. Of course, final results will be in the hands of the two

governments after higher authorities have received our recommendations.

What did this mean? Adam saw that these negotiations could range from a Spanish treaty on river rights to one of land rights, which would surely be involved in the outcome. Would the Spanish give up land rights too? Could it mean the United States might carve out new territory by these Spanish concessions? The possibilities were mind-boggling, and he found it frustrating not to be able to discuss the information with anyone, for Wilkinson did not grant him leave to reveal it.

27 Adam's Choice

A dam knew that Mary was right, that he had truly opened Pandora's box. The plaza became a battleground of angry, shouting residents — Protestants, troubled for years by restricted worship, and Catholic detractors incensed by Adam's offensive plaza attack on their system of justice. At times, the rhetoric became so vitriolic that violence erupted, and unruly groups had to be dispersed by a squadron of Richard King's mounted citizen police.

John Bowles was among Adam's staunchest supporters. In dismay over the trend of public demonstrations, he called together a group of Adam's friends.

"What can we do to take Adam's feet from the fire, and at the same time support Adam's stand on religious rights?" he asked.

To Bowles' surprise, the question brought out conflicting views of Adam's right to defend all of the Protestants. Some were fearful of stirring up more trouble, and preferred keeping the *status quo* to preserve the peace. Others were eager to show open support for Adam's views. Eventually the group narrowed down to those willing to take a stand in Adam's favor. They recommended enlisting Colonel Forman to speak for their case.

John Bowles rode to Canterbridge Manor, where Colonel Forman greeted him in the parlor. One look at John's troubled face and the colonel sensed impending disaster. They wasted no time with amenities.

"I am here, sir, in defense of Adam Cloud's stand for justice and free speech," John Bowles said hurriedly.

"I, too, am troubled by the turn of events," the colonel said gravely.

John spoke of Adam's friends' loyalty, and their fear that Adam might become the scapegoat from the aftermath of Curtis' escape from arrest. The escape was an embarrassment to the government, he said, and Adam's activities might now be placed under Catholic scrutiny, which could escalate into unpleasant consequences for him.

Colonel Forman's face was hollow with anxiety as he spoke. "I am worried sick over this affair. If you are here about litigation, John, I would like to have my son David present. He handles much of my legal business these days, and takes the load off my shoulders. Getting old, you know." Ezekiel managed a slow wink, which softened his grave expression. He summoned David and Eliza, and the three settled down to hear what Adam's friend had to say.

"On the basis of your personal relationship with the Clouds, we hoped you might suggest an appropriate way to unite community support for Adam," John said. "A public tribute would be appropriate, in recognition of his mark of courage, and of his unmatched qualities of love and consideration for everyone."

Ezekiel sat quietly for a moment, and John searched his face, awaiting a reaction. He thought the colonel looked old and very tired. Finally, Ezekiel spoke.

"If the governor would speak out for Adam, we might then focus the controversy on the Catholics, thus relieving the burden on Adam."

"That would be splendid!" John Bowles exclaimed. "Exactly what we were hoping. Perhaps you can learn if there is a possible sentence hanging over him for defending Curtis. If so, we can all intercede in his behalf and organize a public tribute."

"I'll do what I can, but I heard the governor will not return for about a month. I will arrange a meeting for the first day of his return," Ezekiel promised.

"In the meantime, I'll gather a contingent of Adam's supporters to accompany you to the meeting, if you so desire," John Bowles offered.

"I would like that. I may need heavy support." The colonel sighed, and John Bowles noted the sag in his face.

On the appointed day of his meeting with the governor, Ezekiel and David Forman set out in the coach for Government House. Ezekiel felt uncomfortable, and his ears were ringing. He assured himself that it was just an attack of indigestion. He knew he must sway Don Manuel to speak out for Adam. Adam's future was in the balance.

When the carriage pulled up in front of Government House, he noted that a large group of men had assembled.

"John Bowles has rallied quite a support group," Ezekiel said approvingly, as he and David dismounted from the carriage. Suddenly, he felt an agonizing pain and pressure in his chest. He clutched his coat over his breast and stumbled forward, as darkness enveloped him. David tried unsuccessfully to break his fall, and knelt beside him as Ezekiel lay prostrate on the ground.

"Get a physic!" David shouted, gazing in panic at the many faces above him.

The crowd hovered helplessly about; there was nothing they could do without a doctor. In a few short minutes Ezekiel's heart had failed him, and he died in David's arms before he could speak another word.

The next few days were traumatic for the Formans and the Clouds. The families and slaves mourned in shock and disbelief, while friends rallied at Canterbridge Manor with comfort and support. Adam conducted a private "Service for the Dead," attended by Ezekiel's closest friends. On burial day, hundreds gathered at the plaza for the funeral procession. In tribute to the man who had won their hearts and respect, they followed the bier uphill to the cemetery.

At the graveside, Ezekiel's one hundred slaves sang their beloved master's favorite hymn, "Amazing Grace." As Adam listened to their mellow, heart-rending chorus, he mourned for his dear and beloved friend, Ezekiel, who had brought him to Natchez. He felt as though the ground had opened under him, swallowing his life and its meaning in a single cruel stroke. Ezekiel's support and friendship had been a mainstay in his life.

After friends eulogized the colonel's long and successful career, and his brave war record, the mourners disbanded. Adam escorted Eliza and Mary to the carriage waiting at the cemetery. He looked up to see Philip Nolan, Colonel Wilkinson's protégé and occasional messenger.

"Mr. Cloud, I have a message for you from the general," Nolan said. "I would not bother you now, but I am leaving town today and will not have another chance to deliver it." He turned to Eliza. "My deepest sympathies, Madam. I admired your husband." He kissed her hand while she murmured her thanks. He turned back to Adam. "May I, sir?"

"If it is that important, I suppose so." Adam waited until Mary and Eliza were seated inside and excused himself for Nolan's message.

Nolan drew him aside and spoke softly so as not to be over-heard. "General Wilkinson has instructed me to inform you of recent developments pertaining to your inquiries of negotiations taking place over river navigation rights." Adam nodded his head, and Nolan continued. "He trusts you will welcome news that the Spanish have agreed to surrender land to the United States above the 31st parallel. This includes Natchez, and portends drastic changes. He further instructed me to give you leave to discuss the matter with whomever you believe can enlighten you more fully."

Adam gave Nolan a grateful look. "The news is overwhelm-ing, sir. When you see General Wilkinson, please thank him and give him my kind regards."

He returned to the carriage in mild shock. He assumed Nolan meant that Don Manuel could enlighten him, but the governor was in New Orleans. He would have to ponder this news further, but now his attention must remain on Eliza and her family.

Adam was named executor in Ezekiel's will, and the following weeks were filled with helping David fulfill the formal legal requirements following a death. David proved indispensable as a lawyer and advisor, and together they completed and filed the complicated papers at Government House. In the carriage, on the return to Canterbridge, David's youthful face showed its strain as he settled back in his seat and looked at Adam.

"I thank God, Adam, you are our closest friend and advisor. We all appreciate your help and concern. I know how worried Father was for you, and if I can be of any help to you, please call on me for anything I can do."

"David, you are now my lawyer. I want you to acquaint your-self with my financial affairs and property holdings, and handle any legal matters that may arise in my lifetime."

David managed a brave smile. "That I can do, and with plea-sure, Adam. You are my first personal client, and I'll study your files tomorrow."

The impact of General Wilkinson's news nagged at Adam, and he pondered what to do with the vital information. It was too important to keep to himself, yet was it his prerogative to disclose it publicly? The outcome of negotiations would affect the lives of every person in Spanish territory, and it was only fair that people be forewarned.

Mary agreed. "But Adam," she looked long and earnestly into his eyes, "I do wish someone else could break the news. You are already treading on thin ice. Think about it further before you fall through the cracks into the abyss."

Adam took her gently in his arms. "Oh, my precious, you do so worry about me. I have thought about this news day and night, carefully turning over the consequences of speaking out. I have made my choice. I have already rocked the community out of its complacency, and have created a forum through which people can be informed."

Adam knew he must plan next Sunday's soirée very carefully. His speech must not be seditious, but it should be prophetic enough to start new community dialogue. He would include in his text the news of Spanish-American land negotiations now taking place. The outcome would not only make Natchez an American colony, but would help preserve traditions of Protestant faith. In the interim, there were months of negotiations ahead. The Spanish could change their minds, and positions could be reversed. If the dominion remained Spanish, he reasoned, war could become a reality over territorial rights, and Protestant faith might only be preserved through acts of civil disobedience.

He sent out a message that his topic would be "Tolerance," and that the service would have special relevance to Natchez concerns. He prepared for a large crowd and was not disappointed. People attended from every corner of the province. They seated themselves below Evenstar's steps, and out beyond the spreading oak tree.

Adam addressed them from the verandah. He chose a text from Psalms 79:4: *We are become a reproach to our neighbors, a scorn and derision to them that are round about us.* His sermon substituted the Biblical heathen persecutors of early Christians for the Spanish Roman Catholics, and spared no words in the analogy. He focused on a contrast of religious faiths, and a plea for tolerance among them.

"The Catholic church," he explained, "provides the authority by which people's lives can revolve around a secure and benevolent paternalism. It thus brings comfort to believers, and helps the devout through their daily crises. But the church also assumes that men and women are powerless, that they need the intercession of saints and the Virgin Mary, as though God cannot be reached, or does not hear. The church assumes that it is the nature of men and women to fail. It provides the rituals, confessionals, and artifacts to seek salvation from purgatory, or a hell without hope.

"Well, the saints protect Protestants as well as Catholics. But Protestants teach that the central experience of faith is that of the individual standing alone before God, needing no intercession. He alone is responsible for his acts and must face God privately, with humility and repentant prayer. It is a daily healing process. We believe that Christ enriches the spirit and provides a sense of victory over sins and sorrow.

"The Catholic church fears the intrusion of Protestantism because, by its very nature, it has the conviction to defy authority.

Must we be forced to preserve our faith only by acts of civil disobedience? Is it really a sin for Protestants to preach Christianity, or for any other faith to preach its gospel?

"Individuals choose diverse paths in discovering their own profound relationship to the Creator, and we must learn to respect the integrity of other faiths and traditions. When religion becomes politicized, we are divided; but the force of spirituality can remind us of our oneness . . . I declare it is time for an ecumenical debate on the subject of Tolerance." Adam paused for the dynamic effect of his next statements.

"There are secret negotiations now in progress by Spanish and United States government representatives. The time is drawing near when we may look to a freedom here that we have not known, and we must handle that freedom with tolerance and compassion. If we fail, we may have to fight for that freedom in a more critical time — a time in which we would have to defend our faith in the loss of our possessions, and possibly even our lives. God forbid! Let us gain our freedom of speech and worship through peaceful means, through tolerance, through acts of integrity by men of good will, sanctified by their love through Jesus Christ." He paused, and felt the awesome silence charged with emotion. "God be with you."

"And with Thy Spirit," those present answered in a body — all except Joseph Harrison and several other listeners. They had much to relate to Father Francis.

Every household in Natchez, from the Homochitto River and Bayou Sara to Bayou Pierre, from the lowliest and least informed to the privileged and erudite, rang with the debates Adam had opened. Arguments for free speech rights and religious expression intermingled with the divided concern of farmers and merchants for the right to an extended debt moratorium, which remained unsettled. Concern and alarm were further engendered by fear of foreign invasion, fostered by the feverish Spanish efforts to fortify defenses. Furor over these issues was intensified by news of the mysterious land treaty being negotiated in secret. Worried settlers discussed these troubling events they could not control.

Soon after Adam's Sunday service, his soirée committee and friends called him to a meeting at Colonel Green's.

"You seem privy to more information than any of us," Colonel Green said. "We need you to clarify your hints of the impending land treaty. You owe us that much."

Adam smiled to himself. Who owed what to whom in the name of loyalty was now a matter of question. But he answered willingly and told them what he had learned.

"The current direction of treaty negotiations indicate that Spain will surrender land above the 31st parallel to the United States. If there is no reversal, Natchez will be an American colony," he said. He waited until their reactions subsided before he continued. "We should have no fear of invasion. I know to a certainty that the United States is trying to maintain its neutrality. Orders from President Washington have gone out to abort the invasion of American frontiersmen. Why the governors still expect a possible invasion I cannot understand. Citizen Genet has been repudiated and recalled. I have this news from General Wilkinson, and confirmed by Peyton Short, whose brother is secretary to Thomas Jefferson."

More questions arose, and Adam could see there was great doubt and speculation among those present. Nevertheless, his disclosures spread through Natchez like bees from the hive. American settlers began to look forward to being Americans again, while the Spanish natives began to feel afraid. Nerves were at the breaking point, including Adam's.

Father Francis reflected in his study. News dispatches, following Adam's speeches on persecution, free speech and tolerance, flew from Natchez to New Orleans to Cuba and back. He had initiated some himself, creating a chain of letters from Colonel Grand-Pré, as acting governor, to Governor-General Carondelet, to Vicar Patrick Walsh, and back again. In the absence of Governor Gayoso's benign control, the priest felt infinitely superior, and thoroughly masterful in his newly found powers. He would see to it that justice was meted out to the Reverend Cloud, especially since he now had powerful allies in the matter of Cloud's seditious acts.

Father Walsh communicated frequently, and had sent him a copy of a long dispatch to Governor Carondelet in New Orleans. Father Francis slowly read the letter, relishing every word. It was from the vicar in Havana, Cuba, dated February 28, 1795.

> In answer to your request of the 23rd instant: After scrupulously reflecting maturely on each paragraph which it contains: I have found nothing whatsoever that can clarify the maxims which D. Adam Cloud has dared in the public preaching in his house, and in others, in the said plaza, congregating families in them and those neighboring them to hear teaching of his Protestant sect: exhorting them to follow them, observe them, and defend them, even if it were necessary to shed the last drop of blood in said effort: thus, in one of his preachings he has said the following: 'As for me, and for my people, we will serve the Lord, and I warn you not to listen to false preachers or persons who adore crosses made of silver or of gold, and that a critical time is coming in which you will have to defend your faith with the loss of your possessions and even your own life.'
>
> These acts, in place of stimulating those inhabitants to the exercise of moral virtue, and encouraging them to execute the designs of our Catholic Monarch . . . are sowing in their spirits systems opposed to the true Religion and Government: From what can be deduced, that far from supporting said designs, he cooperates in weakening them which will result in the Protestant religion dominating, and the Catholic and its ministers in the District of Natchez being dispised.
>
> The errors of said Cloud being, as they are, diametrically contrary to the principles of sound morality and therefore to the thought of His Majesty, it is impossible to tolerate them, or silently ignore them, (even given the case of their being observed in secret) they cannot and should not be permitted in any way with the publicity with which the said Cloud has conducted them: evidently the Governor protects said Cloud, as has been stated in his own letters.

I feel that, omitting all judicial formality, and to extirpate similar abuses, the said Protestant Rev. Cloud be expelled from the Province without ever being allowed to return to it: and in this manner our holy Religion being preserved, the children of the family will come to the true ministers to embrace it, and the latter's work will bear fruit, without that obstacle . . ."

Father Francis leaned back and savored his feeling of justification. He was jubilant the vicar shared his views, confirming all his efforts to bring about this lofty condemnation. But he read on. The next subject concerned the mystery of Adam's journey up the Trace.

That which has not been verified over many years, either by current officials or even in the time of D. Guillermo Savage, is the part in which the cited Sr. Gayoso claims in said paragraphs, that Cloud, when he went to the American states, went believing he was to be ordained: From what can be inferred, he certainly would have had knowledge of his intent in this matter from the antecedents with which he is familiar . . .

Father Francis reflected. The vicar did not clarify the purpose of the journey, or confirm the fact that Cloud was ordained. The priest realized there were some dangers involved here. He must warn Governor Carondelet of the smoldering situation in Natchez. Adam's popularity was so widespread, and his support among the Protestant majority so strong, that it would be hard to convince people any crimes had been committed. He drew out a sheet of notepaper and wrote a letter to Governor Carondelet, warning him to move against Adam Cloud silently, lest his apprehension create an uprising over the religious situation. He pointed out that the public mood was very dangerous, with the tide of opinion riding in favor of Reverend Cloud's stand on greater religious freedom. He dated the letter, March 30, 1795, carefully blotted and sealed it, and dispatched it to New Orleans. He was confident he had acted in the best interests of the church and His Catholic Majesty.

. . .

No further news of the land exchange came Adam's way during the following months, but he noted great unrest and anxiety among the populace. Fear of invasion lessened, but other worries remained. He couldn't put the troubles back in Pandora's box, but he could help mitigate the general anxiety through more moderate speeches. He focused his soirées and sermons on less controversial topics, hoping to provide some measure of encouragement for a peaceful future.

28 Resolution

Twilight was fading and darkness closing in as Mary left the slave cabin and took the path that led toward the house. She had just looked in on Sanga, their youngest slave, who had a fever.

Mary felt weary. Her mood all day had been one of worry and concern for Adam. She was cross with him too. While his sermons had become less controversial, the brunt of his forceful stand on religious freedom had fallen also on her shoulders. Every time she left the plantation, people wanted to engage her in talk, some praising Adam, others giving cautious advice. What could she do about it, anyway? Her advice to her husband had fallen on deaf ears.

She reached the porch steps and was startled to hear a horse entering the far gate. She saw it was Yellowtail, and she waited for him on the verandah.

"Greetings, Lady Mary." Using his affectionate name for her, Yellowtail dismounted and signed his Indian greeting. "I am on my way to see the factor at Natchez. We have troubles at the Trading Post. There is dissension among my brothers who sell items at the store. I would be pleased to stay the night here and continue my journey early tomorrow."

"You are always welcome as one of the family, Yellowtail." Mary led the way inside. "Come in and see the children, but brace yourself! They will pounce on you, for sure! Adam should be back from the fields soon."

Mary's spirits felt restored as joyous routines of fun and frolic with Yellowtail filled the house with the children's laughter and chatter.

Maamba and Tizzi finally fed and tucked the children in for the night, and the adults sat in the keeping-room for a light meal. When the meal ended, Mary was glad to turn over the kitchen to the servants and call it a day.

They retired early and the house was finally quiet. Yellowtail stretched out on a pallet in the guest room. Adam was already asleep as Mary climbed into the big four-poster. She was too tired for her mind to recapture the day's events, and she joined him quickly in slumber.

A commotion of horses awakened her and she lay still, listening intently to make sure they were riding into the entry road. As they drew nearer, Mary sat up, alarmed. A loud knocking sounded on the front door, and she shook Adam's shoulder vigorously.

"Adam, wake up! Someone's pounding on the door. I think there is more than one of them. It could be bandits! Do you think it's safe to open it?"

Adam sprang swiftly out of bed, lit a lamp, and by the time he reached the front vestibule, Yellowtail was standing at the front door. Adam threw him a quick glance for support, and called out: "Who's there? What do you want?"

The answer was terse and clipped. "Captain Juan Garcia, in command, from His Majesty's Infantry Regiment, Natchez Garrison. We have come for Adam Cloud."

Mary placed a lighted candelabra on the desk and stood by Adam as he opened the door. Yellowtail stood by their side as they peered into the night. Garcia stepped briskly inside, and Adam spoke to him in a friendly tone.

"What is it, Captain? What brings you here in the middle of the night? Is the governor ill? Is there trouble?"

"*Señor*," Garcia's voice maintained an impersonal tone, "I have a warrant for your arrest which I shall read." He drew a paper from inside his jacket, and under Adam's lamplight, read the terse message:

"New Orleans, 1 August, 1795

By order of the Crown, the Rev. Adam Cloud is hereby served notice of his arrest for crimes perpetrated against His Majesty's government, and shall be remanded to the custody of the Commandante, Post of New Orleans, Louisiana.

Baron de Francisco de Carondelet,
Governor-General, Louisiana Province"

Adam felt weak in his legs, as his solar plexus absorbed the shock. He looked at Mary. Her face reflected his own horror and disbelief. *Arrest? It was impossible. In the middle of the night? Inconceivable!*

Adam responded quickly. "Captain Garcia, surely you could have chosen a better time to come with this order. What are the charges? Of what crimes have I been accused?"

"I do not know, *Señor*. I was instructed to come at this time. I am sorry, *Señor*, but I have orders to bind you."

Garcia motioned to two men on the porch, who began to unwind heavy chains.

Mary shrieked, *"No, no! You cannot do that!"* She threw herself in front of Adam.

Adam set the lamplight down, gently placed his arms around her shoulders, and drew her aside. "Now, my dear, there is nothing you can do. It is their orders." He stroked her face soothingly and turned to Garcia. "Surely, Captain, you can let me get dressed. As you see, I have been asleep and am unprepared to go out."

Garcia hesitated. He had strict orders not to let the Reverend Cloud get away into the night as the other preacher had done. He was still smarting over the blunder that had allowed Reverend Curtis and his friends to elude their arrest. He looked at Mary. It was hardly likely she could abet her husband to escape. He agreed that Adam could dress, and left one of the soldiers to guard him.

Mary went into the bedroom with Adam and the guard. Her legs felt hollow, but this was no time to show weakness. Adam needed her. She began to sort out warm underclothing for him, while he looked into the armoire for clothes.

"Where are you taking me?" he asked. It made a difference what he might wear.

"You will be taken directly to New Orleans, *Señor*. You will need enough to last a few days."

Adam chose casual planter's attire, and as he dressed his mind raced. The situation looked bad. Who could help Mary through this ordeal? And the children?

Mary placed the bundle of spare clothes in a satchel. She was rigid, stiff with fear. Her shoulders shook, her hands trembled. She followed Adam and the guard to the front door and watched with horror as the men shackled Adam's wrists with the heavy chains, then his ankles. He said nothing during the ordeal. His lips were white with suppressed emotion. Whether it was anger, mortification, or distress, Mary did not know. She threw her arms around him, breathing gently into his ear.

"Have heart, my darling. I will do all I can to get you back here soon." She squeezed his weighted hand, and filled him with her tender look.

Adam's throat felt dry and he swallowed hard. Through compressed lips he answered her as best he could. "It might not be too bad for me," he lied. They both knew the worst was possible. "I will do what I can. I trust my friends to help. Kiss the babes for me." The words came from deep inside his heart, and brought stinging moisture to his eyes.

Yellowtail stepped forward, his face gripped in distress. He grasped Adam's shoulders. "You can depend on me, Brother White Cloud. I will watch for Lady Mary."

"I know you will, my friend." Adam gave him a look of loving appreciation, and then he was gone through the door. Held between two soldiers, he hobbled awkwardly down the steps, his ankle chains clanking.

Mary stood frozen on the verandah as she watched the soldiers place Adam sidesaddle on a horse, mount after him, and draw the horse away with a lead rope. She stood there in the dark, her soft gown and robe hugging her figure, as the warm night breezes stirred the fabric in motion.

. . .

Before dawn Mary arose and dragged herself to her wardrobe. She caught a glimpse in the mirror of her shadowed eyes, her pale drawn face, evidence of her sleepless night. Rest had been impossible. She had reviewed every scene, over and over: Adam's arrest, his look of anxiety as he was led away, and the horrible sound of the clanking chains as he was led down the steps. Her support from the household servants had been strong and caring, and George Matthews and John Smith had arrived quickly after Dusty's summons.

Mary laved her face repeatedly with cold water, hoping to erase some of the shadows and anxiety lines. When she had dressed, she entered the chapel and knelt to pray, but she was so filled with apprehension that she found it difficult to pray calmly. Appealing to God for Adam's safety made her feel more helpless, and brought her close to tears. Instead she prayed for her own strength and perseverance to be able to help him, for she knew that any assistance depended on her. The prayer was stabilizing, and Mary began to feel her fortitude return. As she rose, she felt a sharp, hollow pain in her shoulders. Fear still gripped her. She straightened her shoulders and breathed deeply to throw off the weakness. Finally, erect and resolute, she felt ready to begin a plan of rescue for Adam.

She considered the situation. It was especially ominous that the arrest warrant was signed by Governor Carondelet. Her best hope would have been Governor Gayoso, but George Matthews had told her last night he was away. If only Ezekiel were here! His influence was so needed now. Mary's heart sank with a feeling of helplessness, and the little pain in her shoulders was there again when she breathed. David Forman might think of something, and there were many other good friends with influence who would join her in a plea for Adam's release. George had offered to help this morning, and she decided they should ride to the Formans' at once.

Mary tried not to think of what was happening to Adam as she rode toward town with George and Yellowtail. Surely he would get decent treatment under the protection of Juan Garcia.

By the time they reached the Canterbridge plantation gate, she was shaking again. George Matthews supported her firmly as they mounted the steps.

"What in heavens name has happened?" Eliza asked, as she examined Mary's ashen face. She looked at George and Yellowtail for answers.

"Adam has been arrested," George said tersely, and guided Mary inside to a seat. "You had best tell them yourself, Mary. It will help to talk about it."

David and the girls were summoned and looked on helplessly as they watched Mary's violent trembling. Mary squared her shoulders to curb the shaking. "Yes, it is true, Adam has been arrested," she said, and she blurted out the dreadful story, her body racked with sobs. She described the scenes of the terrible midnight arrest, her eyes hollow with disbelief as she came to the frightful chains clanking down the steps after Adam. The Formans remained in shocked silence, looking at one another and back to Mary, as though unable to absorb the truth.

"What a rotten, stupid thing for the government to do to a man so loved and revered," David finally said, his voice raging with indignation.

"The poor, dear soul. How horrible for him," Eliza said, her face wet with tears.

"I think Mary and I should go immediately to see Colonel Grand-Pré." David suddenly began issuing orders in his father's resolute style. "George, you spread the news to Adam's friends in the St. Catherine District. Tell them to meet here at Canterbridge at five o'clock for a strategy conference." He turned to Mary. "I doubt if the commandant will appreciate our visit on a Sunday, but we should see him as soon as possible."

"What can I do, Lady Mary?" Yellowtail asked.

"Oh, Yellowtail," Mary said, "we simply aren't thinking straight. Why don't you conduct your business with the factor, and when you are finished, join us here again? We can ride home together. When we receive news of Adam, there might be something special you can do."

Mary's hopes rose as she and David rode the several miles to Hope Farm, but the meeting with Colonel Grand-Pré got off to a bad start. A servant left them standing on the porch as he summoned his master. The *commandante* peered at them from a crack in the door.

"You arrive at my home on a Sunday, *Señora*." His voice was reproving. "What is your mission?"

"Please forgive us, *Commandante*, sir, for intruding on your privacy. But it is urgent I see you about what has happened to my husband."

The colonel opened the door a few inches wider. Mary clenched her fists and resolved to force Grand-Pré to deal with her. She pushed her way inside and confronted him, her anger mounting as she spoke.

"Of course you know what has happened to him. Surely Mr. Cloud has not offended the Crown in such a way as to merit the indignity of his arrest. He was hauled off in the middle of the night, shackled in heavy chains." Mary's voice rose with the memory of Adam's humiliation. "It was a dreadful experience for any man to suffer." She realized her stridency and paused to recover her poise. She chose a conciliatory tone. "Can you declare a period of leniency for him, at least until some kind of charges are brought in a normal manner?"

David intervened before Grand-Pré could answer Mary. "He should be released on his own recognizance until such time as he is brought to trial. Adam Cloud is an honorable man, sir, and would not try to escape."

"That is out of the question," Grand-Pré answered hotly. "The whole matter is in the hands of the governor-general. His Excellency issued the order to me from New Orleans, and I have no jurisdiction over *Señor* Cloud's arrest. Those were my orders, and he will be brought to justice in New Orleans."

Nothing they could say would sway the *commandante*, and Mary felt near tears again as she realized further pleas were useless. He spoke frankly to her.

"You had best get your affairs in order, *Doña* Mary, and be prepared to leave Natchez. Your husband's fate is in the hands of a very disturbed governor. The Reverend Cloud's actions have been carefully documented, and if he is found guilty of crimes against the state, you may find it necessary to leave the country."

Mary's face was so stricken that Grand-Pré paused. He saw her lips quiver with dispair, and he softened a bit. "It is a pity that the innocent have to suffer the consequences of misdeeds by another in their family. Your husband has made a good name for himself here, in many ways. Perhaps his standing may benefit him in the long run. I hope so, for your sake."

Sixteen residents of the St. Catherine Creek and Natchez communities gathered with Mary that afternoon at the Forman plantation. A feeling of helplessness pervaded the group, but they finally decided to draw up petitions from the various districts asking for leniency, and for Adam's release before a trial. Mary, George, and Yellowtail spent the evening discussing with the Formans necessary strategy for finalizing Adam's business affairs and for Mary's departure.

"We must take care of any of Adam's indebtedness in case the government should hold you hostage in lieu of payment, Mary," David advised. "You will need ready funds for travel to New Orleans."

"I have thought of something else, Mary," Eliza said. "Sad as it may sound, you might lose all your possessions if Adam is found guilty. We all know that is often the punishment for government crimes. If you agree, I will buy your slave family of Dirk, Maamba, Tizzi and her husband, providing the cash you need now. We can draw up the papers tomorrow. Should everything turn out for the best, and you can keep your possessions, we can cancel the sale."

"Dear friends, how can I thank you! Your kindness overwhelms me. If only Adam could hear you now." Mary kissed them all. "I would just die if Maamba, Dirk, Tizzi, or any of our slaves were abused by strangers." She paused in thought. "Now I have to think of how I am going to join Adam in New Orleans. I must go at once. I want to take the children with me and be there when he is tried."

"David can book your passage on a keelboat when we receive word from New Orleans," George said.

Yellowtail listened with a sinking heart. His beloved adopted family was in deep trouble. He spoke up. "I can take Lady Mary and the children to New Orleans."

They all stared at him. "You? How can you do this, Yellowtail?" David asked in disbelief.

"Let him finish," Mary said. "Tell us what you have in mind, Yellowtail."

"I am known as a great warrior among my tribe," he began, "but it is nothing compared to my skill on the water. I have paddled canoes on the great river all my life, and outrivaled all my brothers in skimming great distance in the shortest time. I can get Mary and the children to New Orleans in half the time of the white men's keelboats." He looked gravely at Mary. "If you will let Dirk go with us, Lady Mary, we can skim the water night and day. He is a good man, and I know how hard he can work for his master. He showed that on the trail."

Everyone thought a few moments. "Yellowtail's plan makes sense," David said. "I only wish you could get more of your warriors to take the extra paddles, Yellowtail, but they are hopelessly too far away. Mary, you and Adam have that freight canoe moored at Cole's Creek. You're good enough with a canoe paddle to fill in as a relief for Dirk and Yellowtail. You could rest in shifts."

"Of course I can help," Mary said, her voice filled with excitement. "Oh, Yellowtail, I would trust my family's life to you any time, and, as for Dirk, he has always proven himself in our causes."

Several weeks went by while Mary prepared for her journey. She walked through her household and maternal duties almost unconsciously, as she anxiously awaited for word from New Orleans. The community petitions in Adam's behalf had been dispatched to New Orleans, and still no word from Adam. Then Yellowtail materialized upon her doorstep.

"We should leave tonight, Lady Mary." Yellowtail spoke soberly. "I have received an omen that we must go quickly. White Cloud is in grave danger."

"Tonight!" Mary was unprepared for the sudden announcement, but she took Yellowtail's omen seriously. The young Indian was Adam's soulmate, sensitive to mysterious inner messages. "You are probably right, Yellowtail. My nerves are on the breaking point, but I, too, have had my own inner messages that Adam is in peril."

Mary and Yellowtail quickly planned for the journey. Maamba, Dirk, and Tizzi sat with them, glum with consternation and despair at the outcome of events, but ready to help in any way they could. Mary did not tell them of their ownership transfer to the Formans. No use adding to their fear, she decided. She planned to go quietly that night. The servants would help her pack and get the children ready.

Mary flew to the bedrooms, gathering clothing and snatching small ornamental and household objects which could be well hidden. Maamba and Tizzi rounded up packing boxes. Mary wrapped her silver, some of her cherished bric-a-brac from Virginia, and as many of Adam's favorite books as she could put into leather boxes. Maamba and Tizzi packed food. They would need enough to last the trip, for there would be little hunting time while they traveled. Yellowtail and Dirk readied the canoe at Cole's Creek, and loaded it with the satchels, boxes, and wrapped goods. It was time to get the children ready, and Mary woke the older three.

"Shhh," she said, as she shook them gently. "Yellowtail is going to take us to see Papa. We will be on the river for a few days and nights, and you must be very brave. Don't cry, or make a sound. Maamba and Tizzi are here to help you dress. We will tiptoe outside and down to the creek before anyone knows we are gone."

"Like hide-and-seek?" Samuel said, rubbing his eyes.

"Yes, my darling. It's like hide-and-seek."

Mary selected clothing for them, layering the garments so they could shed or add them in any weather. Tizzi dressed Robert without fully waking him, and Mary gathered him in her arms. Maamba assembled the children at the front door, where Yellowtail and Dirk waited. Mary looked about her at the familiar parlor that had recently rung with laughter and joy. Now it had seen the terror and despair of a disrupted family, and it seemed uninviting. She knew she might never see it again, nor Maamba and Tizzi, who were weeping. She hugged the women and wiped away her own tears. Dirk embraced his family and picked up a lighted lantern.

"Take good care of everything until I get back," Mary said. "Master Adam will thank you himself." Maamba and Tizzi followed them out the door. "Don't come to the creek with us, Maamba. Tell Dusty tomorrow that I will join Master Adam, and that the plantation is in his care until we return."

Holding the lantern high, Dirk led Mary and the children to the creek. They settled into the canoe, and Yellowtail shoved off. They silently glided downstream to the mouth of Cole's Creek. Mary saw the children's apprehension as they turned into the river.

"Where are we going?" Becky asked.

"Don't worry, children. We are going on a wonderful adventure," Mary told them. "Yellowtail and Dirk will row us down the river to New Orleans, where Papa waits for us. We might even get to sail on the deep blue ocean in a great ship to a faraway place, to a land of sunshine and honey."

"Will there be dragons to slay, and giants guarding the shores, like in the storybooks?" asked Becky.

"Will there be fairies and goblins, and a great mountain?" asked Susannah.

"We will not have to slay dragons or giants," Mary said reassuringly, "but it will be a beautiful place, and perhaps it will even have a mountain."

The next days and nights were a desperate race for time. Yellowtail lived up to his prowess with paddles; his excellent health and lithe physique stood him in good stead. Mary marveled at his smooth, rapid strokes that never wasted motion. The canoe skimmed swiftly and smoothly over the water. Dirk's prodigious strength seemed inexhaustible, and his broad shoulders and corded back muscles rippled like silk as he paddled half-naked beside Yellowtail. Their strokes seemed almost effortless on the river's placid, even course as it deepened in its descent toward the delta.

The canoe raced through the night as Mary and the children slept. Mary took over Dirk's paddle at sunup, giving him a chance for a quick nap, and Yellowtail snatched intermittent sleep when she relieved him. The children remained manageable, and the girls proved helpful, taking turns holding Robert. Mary was thankful she was still nursing him at ten months, which solved his feeding problems. Samuel kept occupied with river sights, spotting animals and birds, and pretending they were being pursued by imaginary pirates.

Mary feigned enthusiasm for the children's interests, but she felt tired and depressed. They passed bayous and an occasional plantation, relieving the monotony of forest and muddy banks, but the sight of other peaceful families living undisturbed on their river plantations only increased her melancholy. She was thankful for the children's chatter, and for the brief stops made to relieve themselves, to rearrange positions, or to cook a fish dinner. It had become readily apparent that the journey would be exhausting, and she prayed for the strength to endure it. They were all in God's hands, and she would not capitulate to weakness.

One day they caught up with two flatboats loaded with goods for New Orleans. The noisy Kaintuck boatmen hailed them with good cheer, and Mary felt comforted in their company after the miles of silent river. *If only we could join forces for safety*, she thought. But the flatboats were slow and the boatmen were in no hurry, and Dirk and Yellowtail skimmed the canoe easily past them.

Mary decided to spend the next night ashore, and they pulled into the lee of a bayou to escape the rising wind. The men were exhausted and the children quarrelsome from strain and boredom.

"Sky looks bad," Yellowtail said. His face was grave, and Mary had a premonition that this night would be different. Yellowtail and Dirk beached the canoe and secured it fast to several trees. After supper a harsh wind rose, and rain began to fall. Dirk and Yellowtail had pitched canvas tents among the trees, but soon the rain came down in torrents, blowing horizontally in the force of the wind. The canvas flapped against the ground stakes and both tents tore loose in the gale. The driving rain stung Mary's face, and she wiped her eyes so she could see. The ground was soaked, their clothing was saturated, and she felt the sting of tears mingle with the rain in her eyes. She transferred the children under canvas in the canoe, but soon the canoe was filled with water. There was no place for shelter.

Shivering, numb with cold, and near collapse, Mary was dimly aware of the Kaintucks' flatboats pulling into the bay. She felt rough hands gently carry her inside and place her in a cubicle beside her children. Mary slowly revived enough to undress the children. She rubbed them vigorously and placed them in dry blankets piled on the bunks. Not until the children were asleep did Mary tend to herself. Somehow, the activity of caring for the children restored her own warmth. She strung out their wet garments in the cabin to dry, undressed, and gratefully pulled a blanket around herself and fell into a fitful sleep. Throughout the night the ungainly craft pitched and rolled, and Mary was half-conscious of the boatmen shouting and cursing as they struggled to secure the tossing boat.

"Gol-durned storm liken drowned us."

Mary bolted upright as she heard the rough voice outside. It was daylight, and the storm had passed. She looked about her in the cabin. The children were still asleep, and as she bent over each one, she found them warm and dry, their pink cheeks restored. She breastfed little Robert and replaced him on the bunk. Donning her still damp garments and tucking her hair up as best she could, she joined the boatmen on deck. The men were shouting back and forth, repairing the damage to their craft. They were unkempt in their ragged clothes and shaggy beards, rough and harsh with words. But they are heroes, she decided, ready to help unstintingly in her despair. She thanked them one by one, clasping their hands and smiling gratefully into their eyes. They grinned with embarrassment at her warm praise.

Mary looked about at the landscape. The storm's toll had left the forest devastated — trees lay on the ground, and the tall canebreaks were bent double. Yellowtail and Dirk had unloaded the canoe, bailed out the water, and were drying out the contents on the soggy ground. The Kaintucks fed them a warm breakfast, and they made ready to leave. A hazy sun and slight wind helped dry out the canoe and their goods, and by midday the canoe was reloaded. They were on their way, with cheery thanks and good-byes to the boatmen.

Two days downriver, Mary felt the need to spread out ashore for a while. She selected a large island surrounded by a mangrove inlet where they could find shelter from the rising wind. Yellowtail and Dirk turned the canoe shoreward, and Mary looked for high ground. Suddenly, around the bend, a band of rough men appeared on the island. Shouting and gesturing, they launched a canoe and headed straight for Mary's boat. Mary's heart sank.

"Bandits, Yellowtail!" she gasped. "Children, keep down. Hurry, hurry! Do you think we can outpace them?" She groped in the canoe for her musket while the boat turned swiftly toward midriver.

"Our load is too heavy to stay ahead," Yellowtail called out. "Lighten the boat or they will be at our throats." He plunged his oar frantically, as he measured the distance between them and the advancing canoe.

"Are they real pirates?" Samuel's little voice shrilled and trembled as he look back wide-eyed at the men.

"I'm afraid so. Keep down, Sam. Don't look outside. Grab Robert, and hold him tight. Becky, you stay down and find the musket. Hand it to me quickly."

Mary was near panic. Where was the gun? Was the powder wet from the storm? The canoe was gaining on them, and she saw the fierce pirate faces — cruel, determined and relentless faces, high-lighted with evil expressions. She bent forward and grabbed the first thing she felt in the canoe, pulled it up, and threw it overboard.

"Quickly, girls, throw out anything you can lift."

Mary and the girls threw well-packed articles overboard as fast as they could. Her mind raced; the heaviest were Adam's books, and Mary hauled a leather book box up and overboard with a splash.

Suddenly, the boat rocked violently, and Mary looked into leering, jubilant faces as the pirates reached their canoe and grasped the side. Several brightly garbed pirates rose up from their boat, and Mary caught the flash of knives and scimitars at their belts. The canoe rocked dangerously and the children shrieked with terror as the pirates tried to fight their way aboard. Yellowtail and Dirk, their paddles high, bashed them against the intruding bandanna-covered heads. One pirate gained a foothold and shouted in triumph. Mary could smell his hot, fetid breath on her face as he lunged toward her. She raised her paddle and delivered a sounding *thwack* to his skull. From the corner of her eye she saw Dirk and Yellowtail each struggling with a pirate. *We are lost*, she thought. *How can I save the children?*

"*Mama, a galley! Mama, mama, a galley! Downriver!*" Becky shrieked.

Mary looked up and saw not one but two galleys rounding a bend, sails billowing and oars plying the water. The pirates suddenly drew back into their boat in noisy confusion, and the man astride Mary's canoe tumbled into the water as his boat pulled away. He was hastily hauled aboard, and the pirates paddled toward the inlet as if the devil were after them.

Mary looked at her companions. Dirk's nose was bleeding, and he rubbed his shoulder. Yellowtail had a fierce red welt on his cheek. They grinned back at her. Samuel and Susannah rose sobbing from the canoe floor, and a shrieking Robert was still tightly clutched in Samuel's arms.

"Thank you, God, oh thank you." Mary's voice trembled, and her shoulders sagged with relief. "And thank you, Spanish Navy, for coming to our rescue in the nick of time." She never thought she could be grateful to the Spanish for anything again.

29
Retribution

Adam awoke in darkness. He lay still, disoriented. Where was he? It was not home. He lay on something hard, and as he reached out, his hand felt a cold brick floor. He groped and encountered a slimy substance. Quickly withdrawing his fingers, he wiped them on his breeches. He moved his legs. They were bound in cold iron, and shackles clanked as he moved.

He tried to assemble his thoughts, groping to sort out where he was. He could barely make out the corner of a brick wall. This had to be a dungeon. Or was it the pit of hell? He had never believed in such a place, but a sudden terror swept over him. No! He was alive. He could attest to that by the ankle pains from the fetters that chained him to the floor.

Then he remembered being pushed violently into a dark opening. His head must have hit the bricks. But he was conscious now; he could think and feel. Gradually, mental images paraded before him. It was like a nightmare. He remembered . . .The sudden midnight intrusion in his home. Mary awakening him. Soldiers. Captain Garcia, whom he had known for five years. Vague thoughts intruded, but he shut them out. *Concentrate,* he commanded himself. *Think about why you are here. Oh, yes. Mary stood by my side when Garcia read the warrant for my arrest.* The words double-echoed in his brain . . . *for crimes perpetrated against His Majesty's government. Mary had shrieked. Why was Yellowtail there?* He recalled the awful humiliation of being shackled, and the stricken look of horror on Mary's face. *God bless her. Mary! Dear God how I love her! Concentrate . . .*

He recalled hazy nightmare hours in a pirogue, when soldiers rowed him downriver. It was a different set of soldiers. Juan Garcia was not among them. They docked the boat in daylight, and he was led roughly across an open square into a dark corridor. He knew now. This was New Orleans, and he was in the *calabozo.*

His head throbbed with sharp pain and he found a large swelling on his forehead. He felt dizzy, sick, his stomach heaved, and he tried to sit up. Finally, he turned on his side and vomited as far away from his body as he could manage. He lay back in weakness, closed his eyes, and drifted into oblivion.

When he awoke, he was conscious of the accumulated stench of the poor wretches who had preceded him in this miserable cell. It was almost more than he could bear. He retched again, but nothing came. Water dripped monotonously somewhere. He heard squeaking rats nearby.

In the ensuing hours Adam relived his "crimes." His arrest was not unexpected. He knew he was asking for trouble when he delivered that last speech on "Tolerance." It was too much to expect the Catholics to accept such blasphemy of their religious practices. Perhaps he went a bit too far, but he had intended only to show the contrasts of Protestant and Catholic faiths, each sacred to its Christian adherents, and that tolerance could support them both. There was nothing subtle about his message; it was intended to disturb the *status quo.* He had kept within the law in the months afterward, but perhaps that did not atone for his blasphemy.

After what seemed an eternity, deep in thought, and sick at intervals, Adam heard hollow, measured steps click on the brick floor.

"*Socorro! Alguien! Señor!*" he called out.

The steps approached his door and he saw light through a small flap being lifted near the floor. He called out again, in English. "Help! Somebody. *Guarde, Señor,* I am bound too tightly. I need water. *Agua, agua, Señor.* "

There was no answer. He squirmed and inched his body forward, finding the limits of his tether just barely allowed him to reach the opening. He lifted the flap, let in a slit of light, and saw a plate of bread and a cup of water on the floor. His mouth was dry and he emptied the cup in large gulps. He ate the bread slowly. Whatever was to come, he knew he must keep up his strength in order to stand up to any further ordeal.

Would he be beaten? He tried to dismiss the thought. Only dangerous prisoners were beaten. He shuddered, recalling stories he had heard about the tortures of Inquisition prisoners . . . the rack, the whiplashes. Didn't the Reverend Curtis tell him New Orleans had a Grand Inquisitor only a few years ago? That was recent enough; the practices could still exist. He wondered how he would hold up under such torture. He recalled another form of punishment. When Richard Curtis had escaped arrest, a rumor circulated that "he was better off facing the wilderness than being sentenced to work in the Mexican mines." He must think of something constructive. He was being irrational.

Adam drifted from periods of sleep to wakefulness. He could not tell when it was night or day, but he assumed his body responded to the natural rhythm of sleep. He scratched a deep mark near the flap to mark the passage of each day, tracking his periods of sleep and meals.

Despair crept over him. He had committed a terrible wrong. He had jeopardized Mary and his little family for another cause chosen before their needs. Remorse overcame him, and he found himself sobbing — great, deep sobs. He began fervent prayers for forgiveness of his sins, for betrayal of his family.

The black, empty dungeon, mortally still, contributed to his concentration, and his worship increased in intensity. Adam now realized he had the perfect bliss station. He would discard despair; he must meditate, practice the presence of spiritual consciousness. His years of study and practice had advanced his ability to empty his mind, leaving it open to inner perception. The realm of unseen consciousness hovered ever closer. He sat erect, his abdomen taut, and began each step, breathing in and out slowly, in rhythm. There was no movement in his lungs, and the air seemed to filter from his abdomen. With his will he blocked out all incoming thoughts until his mind lay in a void, in the blackest of black. A tremendous peace enveloped him. His body seemed weightless, drawn into the blackness. There was only his soul, reaching out into the incomprehensible, infinite realm.

Adam followed his soul into his second transcendental journey, into the Light, the beautiful, awesome Light in which his spirit mingled with forces so wondrous that he was engulfed in a sea of ecstasy. Transcending all sense and all feeling, his spirit broke through a cloud of unknowing, and penetrated a higher wisdom. He perceived divine truths through the mind's eye, discerning no one particular wisdom yet rising above all that may be known or understood. How long the transcendence lasted he could not tell; time and space were suspended. But when he descended he felt transformed. He was at peace.

It was truly a mystery, and Adam lay enraptured in ecstasy long after the light and vision disappeared. A profound perception flashed before him. He saw that man must reach deep into the cavern of himself, wrestle with his own shadows, and eventually discover what lies in the human heart and mind. He saw that each man is the epitome of life's experience, linked to the infinite wisdom of the universe. With the awesome wisdom came affirmation of belief in his own values. He had followed his own light, and the reward was pure rapture. He had entered the mystical world again, experienced so long ago when he was a youth, and now, at last, he had learned its meaning. He understood that the mystical communication revealed truths upon which the spirit rests. It was a pathway to a Higher Stream of Knowledge. A revelation. He thanked God for the experience, and his eyes swam with grateful tears.

Now he could think rationally. He knew he had been right to rise to Curtis' defense, to speak out for Protestant rights to worship freely, openly, without restrictions. He knew that to act in behalf of a greater cause brought peace. Renunciation of his own self-interests brought triumph of principle over politics. He lay quietly for hours in a cocoon of pleasant aftershock.

The canoe rounded a riverbend, and the full sight of New Orleans lay before them. Mary uttered a small cry, and the children squealed with delight at the sight of the many tall ships in the harbor. Exhausted and relieved, Mary disembarked with the hope she would see Adam soon.

"Where is Papa?" Samuel cried out.

"Wait here, children, with Yellowtail and Dirk," Mary said. "We will find Papa." She stepped ashore and looked about her on the dock, bewildered at the noise and bustle of the commercial activity. White men and blacks worked feverishly between warehouses, docks, and ships, shouting in loud confusion as they transferred cargo. She approached a gentleman dismounting from a carriage.

"Is this carriage for hire?" she asked. "Are you dismissing it?"

The man looked at Mary's distraught face and her rumpled condition. "The carriage is mine, *Señora*. Are you in trouble?" he asked.

"No, I need a carriage. I have just arrived with my children from Natchez," she explained. "My husband expects us."

The gentleman smiled. "Then we should get you there quickly," he said. "I am Don Enuncio Hernandez, at your service, *Señora*. Where do you want to go?"

"I am not sure." She looked ruefully at the gentleman. She could not bear to reveal that Adam was in prison. "Perhaps I should inquire at the *Cabildo*."

"The *Cabildo* burned down and the government is spread about in different locations. If you do not know which one, you should inquire of his whereabouts at the governor's headquarters. Everyone has to register there, you know, in order to stay," he said. "Where are your children?"

Mary told him, and they walked to the boat where her companions waited.

"Wait for us here, Yellowtail, Dirk. I will send for you when I know where to go," she said.

Señor Hernandez helped Mary and the children into the carriage and ordered his driver to the *calabozo*.

"Do not be alarmed, *Señora*. The governor's headquarters is on the upper floor. The *gaol* is in the cellar."

Good, she thought. She could see Adam at the *calabozo* without having to reveal his identity to *Señor* Hernandez.

When they arrived at the building he assisted Mary and the children to alight, and surveyed the little family huddled together on the brick pavement. The gentleman was not to be shaken easily.

"*Señora*, I cannot leave you here alone. If you will permit, I will accompany you inside. I am well known here and can help you find your husband. We will inquire at the proper office and it will save you much wandering about with your children."

Mary looked at her children, clinging to her gown, their tired, questioning faces, and the little one in her arms. For their sake, she decided, she would trust this gentleman, for she could use help. She told him of Adam's arrest, and of her need to see him before he was tried.

The gentleman's face showed his concern. "*Señora*, your story is heart-rending. I will do all I can to help. Let us go inside and start with the prison authorities."

It seemed an eternity to Mary before a clerk returned from the prison records. "The prisoner is here, but you will not be allowed to see him," he said.

"That cannot be! I must see him. Whom do I see to get permission?" Mary asked.

Señor Hernandez intervened. "Please, *Señora*, do not despair. I can take you to the governor's aide. I know him well." He gently took her arm, and placed Samuel's small hand in his. They walked down a long, broad hall and stopped before a richly carved door guarded by a sentry.

"Sit here, dear lady. I will return with the aide," *Señor* Hernandez said.

Mary barely felt the kind pat on her arm; she was numb with exhaustion. She sat in a high-backed, tapestry-cushioned chair. The girls clung to the chair, silent and wide-eyed at the mysterious surroundings. Samuel darted to a nearby console and examined each article upon it. On her lap, Robert whimpered from hunger. Mary's mind was whirling with unanswered questions. As the minutes ticked by, her anxiety grew. Had the trial taken place yet? How would Adam deal with the verdict if it were expulsion? It could be even worse — punishment, perhaps. She shivered. She felt cold and terribly alone. *Señor* Hernandez emerged from the door and motioned her to step inside.

"The sentry will look after the little ones," he said.

Mary knelt down to the three children. "Children," she said, "Mama must be gone a few minutes. Becky, you hold Robert and guard him carefully. Do not stray from this chair."

Inside the room *Señor* Hernandez introduced her to the governor's aide. "This is *Señora* Cloud. She will tell you her story, in hopes you might grant her an audience with His Excellency."

Wasting no words, Mary pled her case. "*Señor*, I am Mary Cloud, wife of Adam Cloud, one of your prisoners." She told him the story of his arrest and of her long journey down the river. "It was a race against time, *Señor*. I suffered with fear that I would not arrive in time to attend my husband's trial. Has he been tried? Am I too late?" Mary felt near to tears, but she held a steady voice. Weakness would not become her now.

The governor's aide studied her for a few moments. Mary's air of confidence had its effect. He recognized a lady when he saw one, in spite of her disheveled appearance. The lady had indeed endured great danger and sacrifice on her perilous journey in a canoe, and he pitied her predicament. But there were rules.

"I am well aware of *Señor* Cloud's incarceration," he said. "He has not been tried, and I doubt if you can attend his trial when it is held. I admire your courage, and I wish I could help you. But your husband has committed high crimes against the state, and such prisoners are not allowed visitors."

Mary's heart sank. She looked at *Señor* Hernandez and saw only pity in his eyes. She summoned her courage. "May I have an audience with Governor Carondelet?" Mary asked. "Perhaps he will understand. I must see my husband, and I must attend his trial." Mary saw the aide and *Señor* Hernandez exchange glances. "Please, I implore you. Let me see the governor-general."

"I will ask, *Señora*. Please wait." The aide knocked discreetly on a door at the end of the room and disappeared into the room beyond.

It was frustrating for Mary to know that Adam was somewhere in the building. The thought was agonizing, and Mary began a prayer of supplication. Somehow God would make Carondelet compassionate. But her hope vanished when the aide returned.

"No, *Señora*. His Excellency cannot see you. He does not grant audiences in behalf of serious offenders."

The aide saw her despair and added, "But the prisoner will be tried within a few days. If you let me know where to reach you, I will notify you of the date and time. You can plead then for the right to attend the hearing."

Mary walked in a daze to the building entrance, hardly conscious that she carried Robert, or of the children by her side. What should she do next?

Señor Hernandez saw her confusion. "*Señora* Cloud, have you any other plans? Where did you plan to stay? I will take you there," he said.

Mary shook her head. "I had no plans. I only thought to see my husband, and nothing beyond that."

"I do not like to think of you alone here. Most of the inns are no place for small children. I have a large home nearby," he said, "and several older children of my own. We have plenty of room and you can be our guests, if that pleases you."

It took a few moments for Mary to absorb the invitation. "You mean, *Señor*, that I, we, can stay with you? How very kind you are, sir, and I hardly know what to say."

"Say no more. I will take you there at once, and I will fetch your servants and luggage from the boat."

Casa Hernandez was indeed large, and Mary found herself and the children surrounded with household help and two thoughtful Hernandez daughters, who took charge of Mary and the children at once, with food, baths, and beds. After nursing Robert, Mary sank gratefully into a feather bed and into sound sleep before dark.

The following day Mary felt refreshed enough to begin her plans. Adam's hearing was days away, but she had to consider the worst contingency. If the outcome was favorable, she and Adam could plan together. She learned from her host that banishment meant dispossession of all property — land, residences, all goods and slaves. The slaves would be sold at auction. Eliza had been wise to purchase Maamba and her family, but Mary thought sadly of the other slaves who would be sold, even Meg. She hoped Meg would get to join her Kofi. She knew firsthand now of the wrenching experience of life without one's beloved.

Señor Hernandez advised that Mary look into ship passage. He drove her to the wharf, where Mary inquired of the harbormaster of any ship bound for the American Seaboard. "Wilmington, Delaware, especially," she told him, "but New Jersey or New York would do fine."

"You must be sure the ship is sound, and has a good sailing record," *Señor* Hernandez told her. "If you will permit me, I would like to examine any ship on which you decide to book passage."

Mary agreed, and they went to the harbor each day, hoping that if she found the right vessel it would not sail before Adam's hearing, or best of all, not be needed at all. Most of the ships were not acceptable. They plied between New Orleans and Spain, and even the American traders charted a stopover in Cuba before sailing up the coast. Mary would not allow Adam near another Spanish town once he was safe.

They inquired daily at the *calabozo* of Adam's hearing date, and finally learned it was scheduled for two days hence. Mary prayed fervently that night for the Almighty to end Adam's ordeal with his release from further reprisal.

The next morning she and *Señor* Hernandez left early for the wharf, and to Mary's delight, the harbormaster informed them an American trading vessel had arrived the night before, and would be sailing directly up the Seaboard.

"She's *The Magdalene*, out of Wilmington," he said. "Do you know her?"

Mary felt her heart beat fast. Wilmington! That was Adam's father's shipyard. *Could it be? Oh, thank you, God. You heard my prayers*, she said to herself. They walked down the wharf to the newest arrival, and Mary stared into the name painted on the prow: *The Magdalene*.

"Oh, *Señor*, that is one of Adam's family ships! It is named for his mother. Adam is even a part owner." *Oh, dear God, thank you,* she repeated as they climbed the gangplank.

Captain Merriweather received her warmly when she explained who she was. He did not know Adam, but he would be honored to have the Cloud family for passengers.

"Of course," he added, "there will be no charge for passage, but you may cover food expenses, if possible. Your husband will understand. I will earn a percentage bonus if my profits exceed expenses. Our cargo will be traded for Spanish and European goods from the continent, and my every expense will be calculated on my return."

Adam counted as many as twenty periods of sleeping and waking before he heard the sound of another human voice. He ate and drank the meager victuals placed through the slot, but were there one or two meals a day? He could not determine the length of time periods. He began stretching exercises to restore the use of his legs. He prayed, and thanked God for his peace of mind.

Finally, one day, the approaching footsteps were different. A broken pattern of heavy boots made an ominous sound as the hollow echo of their tread bounced against the stone corridor walls. *There's more than one of them,* he thought. A cold frisson of fear tingled down his spine as the footsteps stopped at his door. When it creaked open, he shielded his eyes from the bright lantern held before him. He made out two men, one a soldier, the other probably the jailer.

"Adam Cloud, you are to come with me," the soldier said in halting English. "I am to take you for a hearing. Are you well? Can you stand? Here!" he commanded the jailer, in Spanish, "unlock his fetters and let him try his legs."

Adam struggled to his feet and found his legs fairly strong. The exercises had helped keep them supple. He noted the officer's insignia.

"Lieutenant, I have been confined here for I don't know how many days and nights. The stench of the dungeon floor is upon me, and I would ask if I may have a change of clothing. My wife placed clothes in a satchel, in keep of my captors, but I do not know what became of it. I would like to cleanse myself before appearing at any kind of tribunal."

The officer hesitated, then said, "It is only fitting that you be allowed to go like a gentleman, which I presume you are. A good wash and clean clothes is the least I can provide to return you to your status."

He ordered the jailer to find Adam's clothing, and took him to a small room on the floor above to wash and clothe himself. They then walked down a long, broad hall to a vestibule filled with people. Adam stopped in his tracks and stared. There, sitting in an oversized, tapestry-cushioned chair, was *Mary!* She rose and went to him with arms outstretched.

"Mary! Oh, dear God . . . my darling, my precious Mary!" He engulfed her in his arms.

"They wouldn't let me see you in the dungeon, Adam. I have died a thousand deaths until this moment." Mary held him at arm's length. "Let me look at you. You are pale. How do you feel?"

"A bit nervous about what's ahead, but they treated me all right. I didn't starve, but probably lost a few pounds."

He noticed a man standing by watching them. Mary turned to him and introduced *Señor* Hernandez. She explained his kindness and that they had been staying at his home. The children were being cared for by his family.

"The children! They are all right? Mary I can't imagine how you got here. *Señor* Hernandez, my heartfelt thanks for all you have done for my family." Adam clasped his hand warmly and glanced nervously at the lieutenant, patiently waiting for their reunion to end.

"*Señor* Cloud, it was my pleasure to serve your charming wife and children in what small measure I could." He glanced toward the lieutenant. "We cannot linger. I have obtained a favor from the governor's aide. *Señora* Cloud will be allowed to witness your hearing, but without prejudice or plea in your behalf. She may go inside when you are called, and will sit at the back of the room."

"It was wonderful news, Adam. I am forever indebted to this generous man for using his influence in our behalf." Adam's eyes feasted hungrily on Mary as she spoke. "Oh, my darling, you know I will pray for you during your ordeal."

Soon the heavy, carved door in the vestibule opened and an aide called out, "Hear ye, hear ye! I summon prisoner Adam Cloud."

Adam entered and Mary followed. She was motioned to a chair near the door. Adam found himself in a large room, richly carpeted and furnished. Behind a massive polished table sat a row of men. Adam examined them as he stood. In the center a man with a long, narrow face and a white wig was undoubtedly Governor-General Carondelet. He was richly dressed and spoke with an air of authority. He was flanked by four black-robed clergymen, and a fifth who wore a bishop's cap and vestments. A seventh man, at one end, was a gentleman official, probably the *alguacil-mayor*, Adam surmised.

"Come forward," the governor commanded in English. Adam did so. "*Señor* Adam Cloud, you are brought before this tribunal to answer for the crimes you are accused of committing against His Majesty's government, and against the Roman Catholic church. So that you may understand the crimes of which you are accused, the clerk will read them aloud."

He motioned to a clerk, who stepped forward and, in a Spanish monotone, read a long list of activities Adam had supposedly committed. Some of them he recognized, but others were wildly false.

"Do you understand them in Spanish, or shall I have them translated?" Carondelet asked.

"I understand Spanish, sir. May I answer to them now?"

"Not yet," and the governor bade the clerk read the laws governing religious rights and exceptions for non-Catholics. Adam found them thoroughly familiar.

"You must know that yours are crimes committed against the state, for which there is no tolerance in this court. What have you to say in your behalf?" Carondelet glared at Adam, his head thrust forward in a belligerent posture.

Adam's body ached from standing upright, but he squared his shoulders before he answered. He would not speak without dignity, nor let them think he spoke in defeat. He began slowly, in English.

"Your Excellency, and Venerable Clergy. Some of these activities I have carried out, but others are clearly not of my doing." Adam looked directly at his listeners. "It is not surprising that many of my words have been misinterpreted and exaggerated in the reports, for there are many, no doubt, who disapproved of my messages and did not understand them. The public meetings were held with Governor Gayoso's approval, for they were not of religious content. The Sunday services in private homes were also approved. I conformed to the normal policies of the province, which were within the law. My public speeches at the plaza, and at the soirées, were not sermons. They expressed purely a political point of view, and I would expect that freedom to express one's views is not a crime. If there are complaining witnesses to my acts, I should be allowed to confront them and defend my position. Am I not to have a trial and an opportunity to face my accusers? I can defend myself, Your Excellency, but I have a right to rely on witnesses who might help me mitigate my cause."

"There will be no public trial. You may speak on your own behalf, here and now, before the highest representatives of the Crown and the Holy Catholic Church. We will then determine disposition of your case," Carondelet said.

This was unbelievable. The governor-general was a tyrant, a *Grand Inquisitor,* and he was at the mercy of the unbending clergy. Adam gathered his thoughts and began his defense.

"Your Excellency, Venerable Clergy," he inclined his head in a slight bow, "I have acted innocently in the name of Christianity. His Majesty has encouraged a Natchez colony made up of a preponderance of Protestant Christians who have been accustomed to practicing their religious beliefs without interference. Coming to this Spanish Catholic territory has created a clash of cultures, and the settlers are expected to mold themselves into the culture entirely dominated by the church. Most of us try to conform to these restrictive laws, but many believe them unfair.

"I was willing to give up my ministry, and did so for some years, until it became obvious that the Catholic church was not reaching out to the needs of non-Catholics, who could not accept the Catholic tenets. I stepped in to fill the breach wherever I was called, in sickness, in death, in consultation and prayer. I did not preach openly, but I was called upon by my neighbors to provide services in private homes, or in my own. I was even married in a Catholic ceremony to satisfy the laws.

"The turning point in my adherence to the law came when I saw another minister persecuted for practicing religious rites that I myself was taught and ordained to hold. No Christian should look upon religious rites, or on preaching, as a crime. It was then I realized how grossly unfair was the whole set of restrictions placed upon Protestant Christians. They were no longer tolerable. The Reverend Curtis had a right to do what he did, and I was willing to say so in order to get the attention of the church, that all was not well within the Protestant community. We do not inculcate our children with inflammatory religious views, but rather explain to them that while a free society must be willing to accept differing views, it is the duty of responsible citizens to work to change the laws if they believe them morally wrong and harmful to others.

"Protestants do not have full religious freedom here, and I believe that is morally and ethically wrong. I stand before you today to plead from my heart, and in the name of Christianity, that you lift these unfair restrictions from Protestant ministers. I could not feel myself a whole man, or face my Maker, and not make this earnest plea in behalf of the many Christians who are denied their churches and their familiar rituals."

Adam stood silent while the governor conferred among the others. The stony faces at the table glowered with displeasure, and the bishop looked horrified. Adam knew they were shocked. Nevertheless, he felt good about what he had said. *So be it*, he decided. *I can take whatever comes; I gave the subject my best argument and I am ready for the consequences.* He hoped Mary would concur. He felt strangely at peace with himself, without fear.

The judges concluded their conference and Carondelet turned to Adam with a stern face. "*Señor* Cloud, it is the decision of this august body, representing His Majesty and the Holy Mother Church, that your actions have been reprehensible, and that you should stand trial for heresy. The trial will be conducted by higher authorities in Cuba, or Spain, where you will be taken as a common prisoner of the Crown."

Adam was stunned. His blood pounded in his ears, and his stomach felt at though it had dropped a few feet. It never occurred to him that he might be sent away for trial in Spain or Cuba. And for *heresy!* There was to be an Inquisition after all, and he was helpless. What more could they do to him? What would this do to Mary?

The governor was speaking. He had missed a few words, but he caught the rest.

". . . to say that you may make a choice. In order to avoid the long delay of a voyage, and the necessity of a trial, you may choose either to have your day in court, or you may choose banishment from Spanish territory, with no hope of return. If you choose the latter, your lands, and all possessions you have acquired here, will be confiscated. What, *Señor*, is your choice?"

Adam did not hesitate. "I choose banishment, Your Excellency, if that is the final word. I have a wife and four children here, and will need to make arrangements for our departure."

The governor conferred with the others again and replied, "As long as your family is here, you will arrange to depart immediately, within the week."

Carondelet dictated a message to the clerk who wrote carefully on official paper. Dismal thoughts raced through Adam's mind. How could he be expected to find a ship going up the American Seaboard within the week? Perhaps the governor might give him an extension. Expulsion itself was not unbearable, but harm must not come to his family. Adam wanted to speak again, but when the message was completed the governor read it, added his seal, and ordered the clerk to call the sentry at the door.

"You may summon *Señor* Hernandez," he said, without a glance at Adam. Hernandez entered the room. "Take the prisoner to the administration offices and see that he is appointed a syndicate procurator-general to assist him with his legal matters. Further orders are in the document."

Mary rose to meet him when Adam crossed the room, and they locked hands while they walked out to the vestibule. They looked deep into one another's eyes, reading the messages of resignation, of hope and abiding love.

"Follow me," *Señor* Hernandez said. Still holding hands, they quietly followed him down the hall to an office, where Adam was seated before an officious little man who began an interrogation. He twirled his mustache nervously as he scribbled answers to his questions. Was he married? Children? Land holdings? Cattle and livestock? Crops? Slaves? When he got to slaves, Adam interposed.

"Three of my slaves came with me to Natchez from the United States," he said. "They should not be included in the dispossessions."

"It will not be possible to keep any possessions," the syndic said without glancing up from his writing.

"But if you look at the order for my exile, you will see that the governor-general has written 'confiscation of all goods acquired as a resident *of Natchez*.'" Adam hadn't read the edict, but he guessed on a longshot that what he heard was in the document. The syndic read the passage again. His face showed it was there, but he ignored it.

"That is still a matter to be determined," he said, and continued his inquiry and recording. When he finished the questions he bade Adam follow him. With Mary and Hernandez trailing, they entered another room where the clerk handed over two documents, the governor's edict and his own assessment paper. Adam saw the official scribe write his banishment orders in a huge Spanish record book. The detestable little syndic with the mustache then left without a word.

"How in the world can we depart this week, Mary?" Adam looked at Mary and *Señor* Hernandez with despair.

"Cheer up, Adam. We can leave this very day if we want to." She laughed at his look of astonishment. "Yes, I have found us a trading vessel, fortuitously named *The Magdelene*, sailing for Savannah and up the coast to Wilmington."

"The Mag . . ?" Adam caught the smiles on their faces. He shouted for joy. "My mother's — my father's ship! Our ship. Abner told me it would come here. Mary, we'll go tomorrow! Where are the children? Come on. I must see them before I burst."

That night, in their room at Casa Hernandez, Adam and Mary related their experiences since Adam's arrest. Mary told him of the petitions circulated by the community, pleading for his release or leniency. When she described the frantic efforts of his steadfast friends, Eliza's purchase of their slaves, and David's strong support in making financial arrangements, Adam was almost overcome with love and gratitude. Mary described their nightmare journey down the river, and her companions' undaunted courage.

Adam took her in his arms. "That's all over now, Mary. The Lord gave you strength. And may He bless Yellowtail and Dirk for their courage and loyalty. If Dirk wants to go with us, I will offer him freedom and send for his family when we get settled."

"Now tell me about your ordeal, Adam. What happened in prison?"

"Mary, my incarceration brought me a wonderful gift. I am at peace with myself. I experienced that other dimension, a transcendental event like the one I had in my youth, and it culminated a lifetime search for truth within myself. I'll try to describe it.

"I was chained to the prison floor. I had reached a state of despair, Mary, despair and agony from my guilt at harming you and the children. I felt death would be better than life. I prayed for forgiveness, and suddenly found myself transfixed in a flood of inner light and wisdom. What I perceived enlightened me beyond description. I can face up to anything, to anyone. Not only did I shed my guilt, but I learned that being true to myself, to my own values, rewarded me with the sweetest knowledge of all: that renunciation of self to a higher cause brings inner peace; that principles come first over political advantage. I acted by my own inner light, and no one else's. I have paid the price, but life ahead looks brighter to me, though I do not know what it holds."

Mary lay in Adam's arms, her tears running onto his chest. "Adam, I was never prouder of you than when I heard your words at the hearing. I saw then that the greater sin would be not to have acted at all," she said. Adam felt there could be no finer tribute than hers.

Adam and his family stood at the gangplank, their meager possessions stored aboard *The Magdalene.* Adam and Mary had agreed to stop in Savannah, where Adam hoped to find his cherished friend, the Reverend William Hammett. The esteemed preacher had played an important role in his earlier life, and Adam had the feeling he would again.

They concluded embraces and tearful goodbyes to Yellowtail and Dirk, and to *Señor* Hernandez and his family.

"I cannot bear to leave them," Mary bravely blinked back her tears.

Dirk hesitated on the quay and suddenly stepped beside them. Adam swallowed hard. He took Mary's arm and guided his children up the gangplank. Dirk followed, never looking back. As the ship weighed anchor and sailed toward the open sea, Adam watched Yellowtail until he was only a distant speck on the shore.

"Come on, Becky and Sue," Samuel shouted. "Let's explore the ship. I want to find the captain!"

Letter from Adam Cloud to John Bowles sent from Newport, Liberty County, Georgia, ca. 1798 (three years after Adam was expelled from Natchez Territory)

Mr. John Bowles. St. Catherine's, Natchez.
Kindness of Mr. Walker

Dear Sir:

Mr. Walker, the gentleman who hands you this, is from the State of Georgia. My particular acquaintance with his brother induced me to recommend him to your notice. Any favors shown him will be a favor to myself.

I have been unfortunate in my family since I came hither. In the three years I have lost three children, my two eldest and the youngest I had when I left Natchez. The country is very sickly. I have in contemplation to move to Natchez as soon as the time may appear settled. I intended to have set out next summer but the news of a French party at Natchez caused me to hesitate. I fear the settlement may be injured if the people should oppose the government of the United States. Our Executive is now determined upon defensive measures. The people are unanimous for the defense of government, one that is at sea . . . [illegible] *. . . Take my advice: Let it be. Be true to the government that protects you.*

I have been anxious to hear from you and have not had a line from any person in Natchez since I came to the States, nor ever received a six-pence of my property. I will thank you to send me the best account in your power how my business has been conducted, and who you may have reason to think has it in possession. I expect Col. Forman's executors the persons. If so, try to find out what measures they have taken and by what authority, whether by an order of government or only by Col. Forman's executors. At the same time, keep the matter a secret. You can find out the affair without their knowing, and give me an answer by Mr. Walker, direct to Newport,

Liberty County, Georgia. My respects to all your family and neigh-bors. Expect me as soon as the time will admit. Your humble ser-vant,

(signed) ADAM CLOUD

Notation of outside of the above: "The handwriting of Adam Cloud to the within letter proven by J. Bowles, 3/27/1805."

[From "Unrecovered Land Claims," in Mary Wilson McBee's first volume of *Mississippi County Court Records* (Greenwood Press, 1953). Claimant was George Matthews, March 22, 1804. Claim denied, as land had been adjudged to Richard King. Matthews claimed 130 of Adam's acreage by purchase and deed of conveyance, dated February 3, 1803, from Adam Cloud, who held it by an instrument of transfer on the letters patent of J. Cory, and dated January 24, 1794, which letters patent from the Spanish Government to the said Job Cory were dated June 8, 1792.]

Rev. Adam Cloud: The Effects and Outcomes of His Life

"Adam Cloud was a free lance Episcopal clergyman whom the slow moving Episcopal organization of the time never quite caught up with."

> Bishop William Stevens Perry
> *History of the American Episcopal Church*
> (Boston, 1885) Vol II, p. 212

"The Reverend Cloud spoke mysterious secrets of a high concern and weighty truths, explained by unaffected eloquence."

> The Rev. Joseph Holt Ingraham
> *"The Southwest by a Yankee, 1800-1835"*
> in *"Dots and Lines,"* Natchez — *Sketches*
> *of the West* (Harper & Bros., 1837)

The Rev. Benjamin Abbott, elder preacher of the Methodist Church of America, noted that young Adam Cloud did not seem to approve of "these tactics" [listeners falling and crying out at sermons]. He described a Cloud sermon as "a smart exhortation."

> John Firth (Ed.)
> *Experiences and Gospel Labors of the Rev. Benjamin Abbott* (New York, 1833) p. 90ff
> *also*   John Lednum

A History of the Rise of Methodism in America (Philadelphia, 1862) p. xviii & p. 286ff

These quotes, and many others, were clues to Adam Cloud's character and unusual approach to his religious convictions. He was a religious maverick of his time, with an open mind.

After a seven-year stint as a Methodist circuit rider, he became an ordained deacon of the Episcopal church, serving at St. Thomas Church, Kingwood (now Alexandria) New Jersey, and in his early Natchez years. In Savannah, Georgia, his church was Methodist, reportedly affiliated with the Hammettites, a Neo-Methodist movement of the Rev. William Hammett. When he returned to Natchez in 1815, he built the first Episcopal church in Mississippi, where he served as rector.

Historical and Bibliographical Notes

The facts of Adam Cloud's story, his journey to Natchez, his property, religious life, friendship with Governor Gayoso, the spy mission, his civil disobedience, his arrest and expulsion after five years of residency, are true. Most of the characters are real. The political and social history is woven into Adam's life as it might have affected his activities. Letters concerning Adam's speeches and final expulsion are authentic records translated from the Spanish archives. The letter from Adam Cloud, written to John Bowles in 1798, was recorded in *Natchez County Court Records, 1767-1895*, Vol. I of *Mississippi County Court Records*, compiled by Mary Wilson McBee (Greenwood Press, 1953), p. 520 in "Unrecorded Land Claims."

Adam Cloud spent twenty years in Savannah as a minister and as a successful cotton grower. Adam and Mary lost five of their seven children. Samuel Grandin Cloud was educated in medicine at the University of Lexington, and John Wurts Cloud graduated from Yale University, attended Theological seminary, and was ordained an Episcopal priest. Adam Cloud returned with his family to Greenville, Mississippi, in 1815 and built the first Episcopal church, a log cabin, at Church Hill. He was a founder of the Episcopal Diocese of Mississippi. Adam Cloud died in Brazoria, Texas, in 1834 on the pioneer plantation of his son, John Wurts Cloud.

Adam Cloud was mentioned or recorded in many publications and research resources. The most complete records were found in:

1. Burger, Nash K. "Adam Cloud, Mississippi's First Episcopal Clergyman." *Historical Magazine of the Protestant Episcopal Church*, June 1948, Special Missionary No. II, pp. 164-173.

2. Muir, Andrew Forest. "New Light on Adam Cloud." *Historical Magazine of the Protestant Episcopal Church,* June 1956, pp. 201-207.

3. *Archives General De Indies (Sevilla): Papeles procedents de la Isla de Cuba.* (Letters, references about Adam Cloud.) Spanish archives, pp. 22, 43, 102, 2353.

4. *Narrative of a Journey Down the Ohio and Mississippi in 1789-1790,* by Major Samuel S. Forman. Edited by Lyman C. Draper. Clarke & Co., Cincinnati, 1888. (Out of print.) By courtesy of Mrs. Eualalie Bull, of Natchez, MS.

5. Claiborne, John Francis H. *Mississippi as a Province, Territory and State.* Jackson, MS, 1880, p. 528 (Appendix No. 1).

6. Claiborne, W.C.C. *Official Letters and Books of W.C.C. Claiborne, 1801-1816.* 6 vol. 1917. Governor of Territory, New Orleans, U.S.A.

7. Holmes, Jack D.L. *Gayoso: The Life of a Spanish Governor in the Mississippi Valley, 1789-1799.* Peter Smith, Gloucester, MA, 1968, pp. 80-83.

8. *Mississippi Provincial Archives,* "Spanish Dominion," 1781-1796, Vol. IV, p. 786; Vol. V, pp.772-775 op. cit. (Department of Archives and History, Jackson, MS).